Praise for Clay Reynolds's
Franklin's Crossing

"EXCITING, GRITTY."
—This Week in Texas

"Unforgettable."
—Kirkus Reviews

"Gritty realism on the 1870's Texas frontier . . . expertly crafted, very moving . . . this is the way it must have been . . . lingers in memory long after the last page is turned."
—The Dallas Morning News

"A superb tale of the American West . . . remarkable characters and knowledge of time and place."
—Dee Brown

"A big novel . . . packed with fast-moving action, romance, historical detail . . . it's got everything."
—The Houston Post

"Vivid . . . spellbinding . . . you can't stop reading."
—South Bend Tribune

"A novel about the *real* west . . . about fighting and dying for the future . . . anyone who loves true western action will thrill at this book."
—Ocala (FL) Star-Banner

"Exciting . . . wonderful . . . full of adventures, courage, and convincing characters."
—The Anniston Star

"Forceful, brutal, gritty . . . complex characters and unyielding tension."
—Elmer Kelton

THE TENTMAKER

Clay Reynolds

BERKLEY BOOKS, NEW YORK

A Berkley Book
Published by The Berkley Publishing Group
A division of Penguin Putnam Inc.
375 Hudson Street
New York, New York 10014

Copyright © 2002 by Clay Reynolds
Book design by Kristin del Rosario
Cover design by Jill Boltin
Cover illustration by Bruce Emmett

PRINTING HISTORY
Berkley trade paperback edition / December 2002

Visit our website at
www.penguinputnam.com

Library of Congress Cataloging-in-Publication Data

Reynolds, Clay, 1949–
The tentmaker / by Clay Reynolds.
p.   cm.
ISBN 0-425-18270-3
1. Texas, West—Fiction.   I. Title.

PS3568.E8874 T46 2002
813'.54—dc21
2002016432

PRINTED IN THE UNITED STATES OF AMERICA

10 9 8 7 6 5 4 3 2 1

For Tim, my brother

For a whore is a deep ditch,
And a strange woman a narrow pit.

—PROVERBS 23:27

Under an oak, in stormy weather,
I joined this rogue and whore together;
And none but he who rules the thunder
Can put this rogue and whore asunder.

—JONATHAN SWIFT

REGULATOR

———◆◆◆———

J EFFERSON O'HALLORAN TAY, known as "Ol' Jeff" to his friends, of which he had none, sat casually on top of a huge brindle stallion—a horse he had stolen because its size and color caught his eye—with one fat leg looped over the saddle horn. In Texas, men prized good horses above most anything else, and they would hang a horse thief more quickly than a murderer. Jefferson Tay was both, and he had no regrets.

Tay's stubby fingers were gripping a pan of freshly made cornbread, a piece of which he occasionally dipped into the buttermilk-filled tin pail that rested in the crook of his fat knee. Coming directly from the cold cellar as it did, the buttermilk was tasty and refreshing. He lifted a sopping hunk to his mustache-covered lips and stuffed it into his huge mouth.

"Ambrosia," he muttered around the mass. "Pure ambrosia."

In spite of the pleasure he derived from this impromptu breakfast, Tay felt melancholy as he watched the horrific depredations in front of him. His four men—Ty Manypenny, Zeke Bastrop, Alvin Coolege, and a man he called simply Mr. Blasingame—were in the process of utterly destroying a nester's homestead. The quartet was far from the quality of individuals with whom Tay had associated in the past. Those had been brave men with a sense of integrity about them, a sense of purpose. Rough-edged and generally unlettered, they were no less adept at destruction of human endeavor, but they were somehow nobler in their efforts. These four, Tay admitted with a deep sigh, were mere prairie trash. Any one of them would happily put a knife in a man merely because the idea occurred to him. Such an eventuality wasn't likely, in Tay's opinion. He estimated that they probably would have to sit and think for half a day to come up with an idea as original as murder.

Tay spent half his energy trying to find mischief for them to make to keep their homicidal tendencies directed somewhere that would be profitable to them all. It was almost like the war, he thought. Only then, at least, when he committed mayhem, it didn't earn him a price on his head.

Tay's long wavy hair was golden, his eyes a murky brown—the color, his mother had told him, of the Sargasso Sea, across which she and her horse trader husband had sailed on their route away from the famine and poverty of Ireland. Fergus O'Halloran Tay, Jefferson's sire—an illegitimate descendent of ancient Irish royalty, he claimed—had always worshiped the third president of the United States, had indeed read and practically memorized all of Thomas Jefferson's writings. Naming his firstborn after him was as natural as leaving behind the horrible conditions in County Cork.

Tay shifted his mass slightly and fingered the last hunk of cornbread into his mouth, then washed it down with the dregs of the buttermilk. Around his capacious waist were buckled two Colt's .45 pistols, and an old cap-and-ball Navy .36 was comfortably installed beneath his left arm. A long, finely honed cavalry saber hung from his belt. He was well qualified to kill with any of the weapons, and had done so often.

Before him, among the smoldering ruins of what only an hour before had been a promising family farm, his "associates," Coolege and Bastrop, were busying themselves with a girl-child they had discovered hiding in a haymow. She was about spent, Tay judged with a quick glance at his gold pocket watch, a gift from John Bell Hood himself. They had been at her for the better part of an hour. Tay wondered idly how old she was. He was guessing about twelve or thirteen—truly too young, but that wouldn't matter to the two vermin who now had her pinned down behind a blazing corncrib while each took repeated turns with her.

To Tay's relief, she had stopped screaming, and he hoped they would do no permanent harm to her, no damage that couldn't be easily healed or repaired. He briefly chastised himself for allowing the men to have their way with her and wondered how much higher a price she would have brought had he protected her virginity. But then, he dismissed the thought. The sacrifice of her maidenhead, even to those animals, was necessary for their continued obedience.

Manypenny, typically, had nothing to do with the girl. As was his wont, he was wandering around with a blazing torch, helpfully adding more fire to any structure that wasn't burning well. The problem with these dugout houses, Tay reflected, was that they were dampish in the early morning and refused to catch and burn efficiently. He had experienced the same problem with soddies on the high plains, but there, the settlers usually had ample supplies of coal oil or kerosene to get things properly started. These Texas clodhoppers relied too much on candles and rendered animal fat for fuel. Still, old furniture and dry grass would eventually catch and burn with enthusiasm. It merely took perseverance.

Manypenny had piled the scalped and mutilated bodies of the farmer and his two sons inside the looted house. Tay personally found such personal depredations against the dead to be repugnant, but he bowed to Blasingame's claim that it was a necessary ruse. All around the area, the men had placed a number of Apache arrows to make it appear that their handiwork had been the result of hostile marauders. Tay wasn't certain if there had been any Apache in the area recently, and if there had been, he was less certain that there might have been even a suggestion that they were on a rampage. But the hope was that the discovery of any arrow— Apache or otherwise—would keep such agencies as the Texas Rangers off guard and misdirected.

Tay's eyes drifted to the small, rodentlike outlaw, who continued his arson on anything combustible that crossed his sight. They'd first became associated a year or so before when Manypenny inadvertently distracted a town constable from discovering Tay's theft of the same lawman's horse by setting fire to the lawman's office and the jail—and to the lawman himself, although Tay didn't learn of that until later. Tay at first thought he had discovered a steady and trustworthy companion. Soon, though, he discovered that the diminutive man would rather burn something than steal it, rather watch flames than count money. He sometimes lit an entire box of lucifers one at a time and watched each burn down to his gnawed fingertips. Manypenny's dark eyes followed the dancing flames as he fed them with anything flammable that came to hand. Tay rarely slept well after witnessing these scenes.

Flames now licked out of the crude door and windows at the front of the dugout. The grass roof was also burning. The morning's dew had retreated, and Tay felt the sun's warmth on his shoulders and the fire's heat on his face. He consulted his watch again. It was nearing time to leave. One never knew when some meddling sheriff would be riding nearby and see smoke. The frontier's vastness was no longer the safe haven it once was.

Bastrop and Coolege were whooping obscenities at one another, egging each other on in their work on the girl. Tay sighed once more. They were barbarous, he thought, with no morality whatsoever, no sense of conscience. Shabby in their dress and indifferent in their personal care, the pair were constantly filthy, and wore their hair in long, greasy knots bound with rotting sinew. Ignorant, illiterate, and brutal, they reminded him now of a couple of half-grown wolves, snarling and snapping around a fresh kill, each howling his supremacy over the other, when it would have been apparent to the born blind that neither was truly worth the cost of a bullet to join him permanently to the soil he so enjoyed wearing on his person. At times, Tay found himself surprised that they understood simple English and didn't require a whip to be motivated into obedience or discouraged from insubordination.

Blasingame was different from the others, though. In their short association, he had proved to be one of the few reliable men Tay had met recently. A big man, though not nearly as large as Tay, he wore a blood-stained linsey-woolsey shirt and similarly ruined canvas trousers. He preferred flat-soled, squared-off walking boots. He also enjoyed a wide palm hat that bore a greater resemblance to a planter's headgear than to the more stylish broad-brimmed plainsman's covering. To Tay's practiced eye, he looked like a dandy, a sport, possibly a gambler or a pimp. But the way he wore his large, unusual weapon in a custom-crafted holster belied that impression, as did his frequent demonstrations of expertise with a large butcher knife when he deftly took their victims' scalps.

The practice appalled Tay, but he had learned the necessity of tolerating each man's particular eccentricities in order to maintain his loyalty. He regarded such toleration of abhorrent habits as the price of leadership. And Blasingame was proving to be a difficult man to lead.

Now, the big man was prowling through the trampled remains of a vegetable garden, pushing aside the dying plants with his knife. "Mr. Blasingame," Tay called over the flames' roar. "I somehow doubt that anyone is lurking among the squash and bean plants."

Blasingame looked up. His mouth parted. His teeth were gapped in front, and a half-grown beard scraped along his jowls. He was very nearly handsome, in a brutish sort of way.

"Ain't so sure, Tay," he said. "Folks have a way of hiding where you're not looking."

Jefferson Tay winced. He didn't like being addressed by his naked surname by a subordinate. Again, though, he swallowed his pride and focused on the matter at hand. He gathered his patience as he lit a short, stubby pipe, then urged his horse forward. He held the reins loosely and guided the brindle mostly with his knees as he surveyed the ruined farmyard.

"Gentlemen," he called out at last. "We need to be away, and promptly. Mr. Manypenny, would you be good enough to harness those mules?" He gestured with his pipe's stem toward a crude corral where the four animals in question milled around, made nervous by the odor of burning flesh in the air. Manypenny touched the brim of his derby in acknowledgment, adjusted his long rifle on the sling across his back, then reluctantly gave up his work and flung the torch into the house. "I'm certain Mr. Blasingame will provide whatever assistance you need," Tay added, then shouted, "Mr. Coolege!"

Coolege appeared, fastening his trousers, which were streaked with blood and filth, and stepped up to Tay, nearly breathless. "You sure you don't want some of that?" A broken-toothed grin scarred his bearded mouth. "She's young, but she's sweet. And she's got a lot of fight left in her."

Tay shook his head, with no effort to conceal a shudder of disgust. "Collect Mr. Bastrop, if you please, and load whatever provisions you find in the wagon. Then gather your mounts."

"What about her?" Bastrop stumbled up. He was in his stocking feet and carried his boots and trousers in his hands. His underwear was stained and torn. His toes stuck out of the ends of his rotting socks. Tay idly noticed that two digits were missing from one dirt-blackened foot.

At that moment, the girl, naked, her stomach and legs streaked with blood, came running around the flaming crib. Her arms, bent over the top of her head, carried a short-handled hatchet in a double-fisted grip. Her mouth was open, as if in a silent scream of rage. In the instant it took for her to cover the ground between the crib and the two men, Tay assessed her age to be even younger than he first thought. Small fleshy mounds jiggled slightly beneath tiny, burgundy-colored nipples. A fine patch of hair wove itself across her pubic mound. But apart from that, she looked more like a boy than a girl. Her eyes were huge in rage and terror. Tay was momentarily stunned by the speed with which she closed the distance.

Neither man on the ground saw or heard her approach. There was no time to say anything. Tay instinctively reined his horse to the right and drew one of his heavy revolvers. He should have pulled his mount to the left, so now he had to try to shoot across his body. Coolege, still ignorant of the girl's approach and apparently thinking the horse had shied and that Tay had lost control, stepped forward and reached for the bridle, but the animal, unused to such rude handling, balked and reared, throwing the big Irishman off balance even more. It was too late to stop her. The girl was there just as Bastrop sensed her presence and turned to face her.

The single blade of the small axe buried itself in Bastrop's right shoulder, high on his neck, immediately bringing forth a crimson fountain spraying over the girl's blonde head and covering her with gore. With a shocked, almost helplessly amused look on his face, the outlaw collapsed to his knees and brought up his left hand to finger the hammerhead side of the tool.

"I'll be damned," he said in a clear, almost boyish voice, and pitched forward into the blood-muddied dust.

Coolege, also sprayed with Bastrop's blood, danced away and flung his trousers at the girl. The flying cloth caused Tay's mount to shy again, spoiling his aim, and he fired into the dirt. The girl reached for the hatchet's handle, put a bare foot on Bastrop's head, and pulled with both hands. When the blade came suddenly loose, she stumbled backward, then regained her footing, raised the gore-sopped tool high over her head, and charged Tay's horse.

She took only a single step before, almost comically, she was jerked to one side and flung violently to the ground, as if by an invisible hand. A large, ragged hole appeared in her left side, and blood flooded out of her into the dust. Only then did Tay's ears register the weapon's report.

Tay steadied his mount and looked around. Blasingame walked up slowly, his gun still smoking in his hand. It was the first good look Tay had of the unique firearm. It appeared to be a shotgun with the barrels sawed off and fitted with a thick wooden pistol grip. Tay looked at the girl's body and marveled at the weapon's effectiveness.

Bastrop was still alive. Blood jetted out of his neck where his fingers dug into the wound. He made gurgling sounds, mewing like a blind kitten as he tried to sit up.

"You going to let him bleed to death?" Coolege demanded. "Damn near took his head off."

Tay looked down at the dying outlaw, then pointed his Colt's revolver at him and put a .45-caliber bullet directly into his forehead. Bastrop jumped backward and flopped down into a bloody puddle of his own brains.

For a moment, the only sound was the crackle of the fire. Coolege's mouth hung open, and he stepped toward the Irishman, but Tay cocked the pistol once more, held it easily across his pommel, and chewed his pipe's stem while he shook his head in disapproval.

"You kilt him!"

"Damned foolishness," Tay said.

"You see that?" Coolege demanded of Blasingame, who had reached the girl's body.

The larger man holstered his weapon, drew his large razor-sharp knife, and reached down and neatly scalped her.

Coolege turned and stepped toward Manypenny. "He just kilt him! Just like that," he railed. "Like he wasn't nothing but a gut-shot dog. Just kilt him."

Manypenny only nodded and returned his gaze to the conflagration he had set. Blasingame carried the bloody scalp over to a stained carpetbag that contained the others he had taken, and dropped it in.

"I mean, we just going to stand here and let him kill us all off, one by one?" Coolege stamped around and waved his arms. "Crazy goddamn mick," he yelled.

"I'd aver, Mr. Coolege," Tay responded calmly, "that you both were wandering around without sidearms, half-naked. Mr. Bastrop paid the price for his lack of watchfulness. Now, I suggest you collect your breeches and other belongings and be about your business. Otherwise, I shall be forced to call you to account as well, and double the burden on these two gentlemen."

"What?" Coolege asked, his mouth hanging open, dumbfounded by Tay's speech.

"Get to work, Mr. Coolege," Tay ordered quietly, and reined his horse away.

In a half hour, the wagon was loaded with everything of value the settlers might have had. What remained of the nesters' settlement was crackling and popping in the flames, and Bastrop's body, along with the girl's, had been put inside the burning dugout. A large cloud of black smoke rose to obscure the azure perfection of the sky.

In a month's time, it would be hard to recognize that this had been anything but a temporary stopover for some luckless family. Some sympathetic citizen would come along and bury the whole house, along with the bodies inside, and put up a marker indicating that they had been killed by marauding Apache, and some officious schoolmarm would doubtlessly make a note of it for the county history.

They pulled out. Coolege sulked in his saddle, and Manypenny, his derby pulled low on his forehead, broke his customary silence. "Where to now?" he asked.

Tay pulled a folded oilskin map from his tunic and consulted it. "I believe the next homestead is over to the northwest, about thirty or forty miles, I should say. We must be more careful in our handling of women," he added. "That is raw profit and not to be discounted."

"I'm always careful with women," Blasingame muttered, glancing at Coolege, who kept his head down. "But I leave the young'uns alone."

Tay shifted his bulk again, seeking a comfortable position, and Manypenny lit a match on a brass stud on his saddle. Tay watched him hold up the lucifer and contemplate the flame with a maniacal stare. Blasingame looked over at him and chuckled. Coolege cleared his throat, spat, and shook his head. Tay took a deep cleansing breath. No, he thought, times were just not what they used to be.

BOOK ONE

Gil Hooley

THE TENTMAKER

—◆◆◆—

1

ONE BRIGHT SPRING morning, Gilbert Dartmouth Hooley's cumbersome Studebaker wagon rolled across a depression in the grassy West Texas prairie. A poorly matched two-mule team drew the wagon, and Hooley was nearly asleep when he felt the balance of the vehicle abruptly shift, then crash down with a metallic crunch. The jolt almost threw Hooley from the seat, and only a fierce grip and a viciously shouted "Son of a bitch!" prevented him from being pitched onto his head into the waist-high grass. The mules heard the oath and came to an automatic halt, then hung their heads as if it was their fault. From Hooley's point of view, it was.

Hooley climbed down and looked curiously at the splintered wheel and broken rear axle. After a few moments' contemplation of this bewildering development, he lit his pipe and squatted down in the vehicle's meager shade and thought the situation over. "This is one hell of a note," he said to the morose-looking mules.

Hooley's wagon was overflowing with quality canvas and muslin, miles of thread, kegs of oakum, cakes of hard clear wax, boxes of brass grommets, and stout steel needles. He was a tent-and-awning maker by trade, the occupation Hooley's father, Simon, and grandfather, Dartmouth I, followed. In spite of the wishes of his mother, Bertha Hooley, that he read law or study medicine, Gil began learning the family trade as soon as he was old enough to thread a needle.

"It's your destiny," Simon Hooley told his young son. "I put a lot of stock in a man's destiny."

Though he had yet to own his first pair of long trousers, Gil knew a load of horseshit when he heard one. He also knew his father was less interested in destiny than he was in obtaining what free labor he could from his son.

Bertha Hooley agreed with her son. "It's the dumbest thing I ever heard of," she said to her husband. "Waste of time and energy. If I'd have known what you were going to do, I'd have made a girl child instead." Bertha's greatest lament in life was that when she married Simon Hooley, she thought he was in the building trade. She had no idea he was a tentmaker. She thought tentmakers all lived somewhere in Africa. Or that they should.

Even so, the occupation turned out to be suitable to Gil's nature. It could be quietly performed, required a minimum of physical exertion, and permitted a good deal of contemplative remuneration for anyone who possessed digital dexterity. It had also provided his father with political influence, owing to the fame Hooley tents enjoyed among heads of state and military leaders. They had been used in every American war, as well as in a variety of campaigns against savage Indians. From George Washington to Andrew Jackson to Winfield Scott, some of the greatest generals in the country had slept snug and dry under the taut canvas roofs of Hooley tents.

Each Hooley tent was made by hand, one at a time, sewn with care and built to last. Hooley tents were preferred among the officer corps of the United States military services, and the military soon provided young Gil with his own opportunity to spend some time under a Hooley tent. But when the War Between the States broke out, he expressed no desire to enlist.

His mother however, nagged him for nearly a year, complaining that she was the only "mother of a coward" in the St. Louis Social Register. Gil protested his mother's urgings that he enlist right away by pointing out that any injury to his arms or hands could result in an end to his career as a tentmaker. "Why should I care if you're a tentmaker or not?" she scoffed. "Now, if you could play the violin or the pianoforte, we might have something to worry over."

Her attacks on his character became fiercer, and Simon finally suggested that, to keep peace, Gil should join the army. It took him another month to get around to it, but the youngest Hooley finally volunteered and entered the Union Army of the Ohio. Gil's natural ability to avoid any strenuous duty quickly caught the eye of his officers. They promoted him to the rank of sergeant. In the meantime, Gil served in a number of battles, which his commanders invariably lost. Also lost were several thousands of Gil's comrades-in-arms. Most of them, he observed, died badly. He wrote to his father that he was certain that he would also soon be dead if he remained much longer in the service of the infantry.

"It appears to me," he wrote, "that they have found the dumbest sons of bitches in the country, made them officers, allowed them to drink themselves into insensibility, then sent them here to consort with prostitutes and imbibe opium while people like me lead men to grisly death and dismemberment." After every battle, he wrote, the piles of severed limbs outside the hospital tents were higher than the ridgepoles. The resulting stacks of corpses were higher still.

"These are *not* Hooley tents," he noted. "They are Sibley tents. They tend to leak prodigiously when it rains. And it rains all the time." He concluded with his observation that excessive cannon fire seemed apt to produce violent thunderstorms.

Alarmed by his son's report and fearful for the boy's life, Simon Hooley evoked his political influence to have Gil transferred to the Quartermaster Corps. There, Gil quickly understood, the mission of the officers and men was to do as little as possible, except in the matter of keeping themselves as far as they could away from the danger of battle and remaining as comfortable as possible for the duration of hostilities. Gil proved most capable for this assignment. He discovered that the government was far more interested in saving money than in spending it, so the fewer supplies actually issued to the troops, the better off the entire country.

His career highlight occurred when he filed a requisition order for one hundred stout Hooley tents to accommodate General William Tecumseh Sherman and staff at Pittsburgh Landing. After the Battle of Shiloh and its huge cannonade, Hooley's prediction of heavy rains came to fruition and threatened to wash every man, living and dead, into the Tennessee River. Sherman and his officers and assorted female friends, though, remained snug and dry beneath the stout seams of Hooley tents, and the general was properly grateful.

"Only good night's sleep I've had since this goddamned circus started was after those goddamned tents arrived," the feisty little general said to Hooley after he summoned him to thank him personally. He also insisted that Hooley tents be sent to Ulysses S. Grant and Phil Sheridan. "Don't send any to that goddamn imbecile Burnside, though," Sherman ordered. "The man sleeps too goddamned much as it is." After determining that Hooley was neither an immigrant nor a Roman Catholic, Sherman promoted him to the rank of captain.

As the war started to wind down, though, handmade tents became almost obsolete, thanks to newfangled inventions such as the automatic sewing machine and newfangled ideas such as mass production. Fewer and fewer people were interested in spending the premium required for a fine-quality, hand-sewn Hooley tent, but Hooley's father still refused to mechanize his business. "It's the way my father and grandfather did it," he said in response to Bertha's demands that he purchase machinery, hire more laborers, and expand. "It's the way I'll do it."

"Thank God *my* father left me a pension," Bertha replied. "He must have known what a damned fool I was marrying."

Simon Hooley had not been previously aware that his wife had a legacy, but she assured him that it made no difference, as she did not plan "to subsidize the old age of a common tentmaker." Therefore, he steadfastly struggled along until the war's end with a handful of temporary laborers, most of whom were as poorly paid as they were overworked. The enterprise took its toll. Gilbert Hooley returned from his service to find the family business facing leaner times and his father ailing, ready to retire and leave the fate of the Hooley Tent Company totally in Gil's hands.

Still flush with whatever disciplinary enthusiasm the military had taught him, and cautioned by his mother that neither he nor his father would ever see one dime of her family's money, Gil determined to save the business. He added awnings and wagon covers to his inventory and advertised heavily all over Missouri and western Illinois. He also provided tents for small circuses, traveling sideshows, and itinerant preachers and photographers. But, to his mother's unconcealed glee, the business continued to fail.

"Whoever heard of a tentmaker in a modern society?" she demanded. "The only place people live in tents is in Africa and Arabia. You need to find an honest trade or profession before it's too late for a white man to get ahead in this country."

Hard times are inevitable, and in the early 1880s they came to St. Louis. Hooley saw his fate as clearly as a whipstitch in raw canvas. Economic panics and depressions seemed to arrive in waves from the East, each chasing before it wagonloads of pioneers heading west to make a new start. Most arrived in the city already equipped for their frontier journeys, complete with wagons covered with stiff, machine-sewn canvas. Merchants stopped ordering new awnings. Traveling shows and revivalists were the first to cease operations when money became tight.

For a time, Hooley thought of changing tactics and opening a full-scale factory of his own, but the amount of ambition required for such an undertaking discouraged him. Also, there were alarming reports of workers organizing into trade unions. He had no desire to deal with a bunch of angry employees he couldn't afford to hire in the first place. But his business was steadily growing worse, so Gilbert Hooley decided that he had to do something to avoid starvation.

Thus, one bright autumn afternoon, Hooley loaded spools of thread, papers of needles, and bolts of canvas and cloth onto a Studebaker wagon covered by a huge white canvas and left St. Louis. He had no practical knowledge of the West, but heard that in the mountains there were all kinds of new towns, places that relied completely on sturdy canvas for shelter. Many of these were mining communities, he learned, and the temporary nature of their settlements required housing that was both reliable and portable. In short, they needed tents.

Hooley felt a kinship with the pioneers who were leaving their failed hopes behind them and moving "out yonder," as they called it, to discover a better future. It might be a foolish dream, he told himself, but at least it didn't require much effort. Apart from securing the wagon and team, loading his materials into it, and spending what available cash he had for supplies, a stock of good whiskey, and two baleful mules to pull it all, there was nothing to it. West he went.

2

NEVER A MAN to face a challenge when he could avoid it, Hooley detoured down through Arkansas and passed through Shreveport, Louisiana, and into Texas rather than venturing into Kansas and Nebraska, where he heard that outlaw bands and hostile savage Indians liked to prey on single wagons traveling out on the trackless wasteland. Texas, he was told, was now free of savage Indians, their having been forcibly removed to Oklahoma Territory, and except for pesky Mexican bandits who refused to stay south of the border where they belonged, the state was by and large peaceful. Moreover, it was regularly patrolled by a famous fierce force of ruthless lawmen known as the Texas Rangers, in whom Hooley invested high confidence, based on his extensive reading of their adventures in dime novels.

He'd often stop along the way and earn a few dollars making tent roofs and awnings for new buildings in shantytowns and small settlements. Even in early winter, East Texas proved to be a warm place, and he found that even a penny-wise merchant might pay well for a handsome piece of striped fabric to shelter the porch of his concern, or a traveling family might trade a pound or two of bacon and cornmeal for a repair on a wagon cover.

The farther west he went, the less abundant grew the trees, and he realized that he was offering one of the most valuable commodities in Texas: shade. It stood to geographic reason, Hooley decided, that in time he would reach a place where there was no natural shade at all.

"Hell," one grizzly plainsman ripe with the odors of travel on the frontier assured him through a mouth jammed with tobacco juice, "they's places out yonder where the onliest shade there is under your horse. And if you're not careful, you're apt to get pissed on that away."

When summer came to treeless West Texas, Hooley decided, manufactured shade might be worth its weight in gold, and he carried bolts and reams of shade in his Studebaker. But the farther west he went and the greater the demand for his talents, the less hard money there was to be made. Towns became hamlets and then rough encampments, and even these grew smaller and more rustic as the ground grew drier and the climate harsher. Many potential customers had nothing more to offer him in exchange for his talents but a dog or a pig.

So, he decided to push ahead with speed. He set Colorado as a goal, from where he planned to enter mining communities of the high Rocky Mountains. There, he believed, whole cities made of canvas were common, and there would be a huge demand for his work. Every night when he settled into his camp, he set a stick on the ground to point toward the spot where the sun set. Then next morning, he whipped up his mules in that direction, confident that eventually he would arrive somewhere he could settle down and stitch his way into a sedate prosperity.

After several weeks of such determined travel, he crossed the bed of the Pease River, which he found boggy and salty, and entered the empty rolling prairie of North Central Texas, heading northwest. The gentle undulations of the prairie pleased him, and he took a childlike delight in the sharp descents into depressions as well as the titillating thrill of reaching the apex of one of the grassy dells. He was dreamily remarking how completely desolate the country was when he ran over the half-buried granite boulder and busted the rear axle on his wagon.

Now he was stuck. He knew that he would run out of civilization, but couldn't believe the caprice of fortune that caused such an eventuality to coincide with a broken-down wagon.

After he smoked and brooded for a space of time, Hooley determined that the vehicle was beyond any repair he could effect. Rousing himself when the mules began to stomp and bray, he lucked upon a small, spring-fed creek about a hundred yards from where he broke down. The creek ran into a gully filled with scrubby cedar trees and clogged with tumbleweeds. An ancient beaver dam was also present. Hooley saw no alternative, so he spent what part of the day he had left fetching water for his mules. He could have led them down to the creek, but the walk back and forth would involve less trouble than to unhitch and stake out the whole team.

"Besides," he told the thirsty animals as they sucked the water from his bucket, "if I unharness you, you might run off. Where would I be then?"

Where, indeed? The question assaulted Hooley all at once and made him wonder for the first time about his particular location. He finished his chore with the mules, then climbed up onto his listing wagon seat and looked around. He could see for miles in every direction, but there was nothing in sight. He had finally arrived on the utterly treeless prairie he had heard about, and everywhere he cast his eyes looked the same as where he was. Only scraggly thicket along the creek bed provided respite from the vast monotony of waving grass surrounding his wagon, only the blank blue of the sky provided a canopy for the dancing sea of waist-high vegetation.

"This could be a matter of some seriousness," he mused aloud, surprised by how small and insignificant his voice sounded in the wind.

Among his goods, he located a map acquired from another rustic frontiersman who claimed to know the region. It was a crudely drawn chart, and the land he presently inhabited was mostly blank, except for a few tentative squiggly lines suggesting waterways and wavy circles he took to be mountains or mesas. To his eye, the creek that was his main beneficiary was not marked, though there was a large elevation labeled, "Medicine Mountain." He recalled a giant hump of granite he had spotted to his north just before he crossed the Pease River. He also noticed that a freight and stage route was marked, but far south of his present position, which was, as near as he could figure, thirty miles from the Prairie Dog Town Fork of the Red River and forty miles to the west of a small X on the map, labeled "Pease City," which he had inadvertently bypassed along the way.

Forty miles was a formidable walk. He could unhitch the mules, ride one, and lead the other, but the prospect of covering such a distance bareback was daunting. Hooley was not an experienced equestrian, and he had no idea whether or not the mules were even broken to ride.

Hooley stowed the map. It was early in the season, and he was confident that someone would eventually come along. His further hope was that whoever it was had tools and expertise to repair his wagon. There was nowhere to go and nothing to do for the time being but sit and wait and maybe read a bit, so he did just that for several days. He interrupted his pastime only to make himself something to eat, feed and water the mules, gather a bit of firewood from deadfalls down by the breaks, or to relieve himself behind a small, thorny bush. At night, he went to sleep listening to the howl of coyotes and the singing of crickets and frogs down by the water, and concentrated on finding a solution to his dilemma. None presented itself, so the next day he again waited patiently for fortune to take another turn.

3

AFTER FIVE DAYS of inactivity, Hooley rigged an awning on his wagon to provide relief from the blistering sun. He found it annoying to constantly shift his position to stay in the relative cool of the wagon's shadow, which at high noon utterly disappeared. If he had an abundance of shade at his disposal, he argued, it was foolish not to use it. Besides, his hands and fingers wanted something to do other than stoke his pipe and turn pages of a book. He had never before been so afflicted by a lack of work that he actually itched to do it.

The awning was brightly striped in green and white, supported by cypress poles he'd hired a man in East Texas to cut and whittle, and anchored by stout line used by boatmen on the Mississippi to secure cargo aboard their vessels. After he completed the erection, he also gave in to the mules' obvious needs and turned the animals out onto a nearby flat of land to graze. He neglected to hobble them properly, so, true to his earlier prediction, they wandered off. When he discovered they were gone, he searched for them, but soon he tired of tramping around uselessly in the high grass. He was astonished that such large animals could disappear so completely in a country where everything was so visible, but they somehow eluded his notice, and he came back for a drink and a smoke. He figured they would return on their own, or they wouldn't. Without a workable wagon to pull, they were more trouble than they were worth anyway.

Another worry soon arose. He now became concerned about his food supply, which was diminishing daily. He was not prepared for a long stay out on the prairie.

Hooley had never been a hunter, though he prided himself on being a crackerjack shot with rifle or pistol. During training for the Army of the Ohio he had learned to use weapons, and had surprised himself by mastering them easily. He had the sharp eyes and deft touch of a tentmaker, so his ability to sight a target and then strike with a careful shot seemed natural. But the only weapon he possessed was a rusty Winchester rifle with a cracked stock, taken as exchange for an awning over a gunsmith shop's front door. As he anticipated meeting no savage Indians or outlaws, it had never occurred to Hooley that he would need weapons on his journey.

Nevertheless, he was determined to secure something besides coffee, cornmeal, and beans to eat—which, by this time, was all he had left except for a decent supply of bourbon whiskey packed in straw-cushioned crates. He walked down to the creek and considered trying to fish—certainly he had sufficient needles and thread to rig up tackle—but the shallow run didn't seem to offer a promising prospect. He understood that the large bullfrogs that lined the banks were edible, as were the considerable number of turtles that basked on flat rocks near the creek, but much as he adored turtle soup, he couldn't bring himself to kill and then eat a wild reptile.

He finally decided to shoot something. Accordingly, he set out the next morning armed with his rifle, freshly oiled, and confidence that he would run across an edible creature. By noon he had seen nothing alive, save grasshoppers, dragonflies, horseflies, and a rattlesnake that slithered away. When he moved through the grass, it seemed to be alive with movement, but he saw no rabbits or other small game. No large animals such as deer or antelope presented themselves, which was fine with Hooley, as he had no idea how to prepare such a beast for eating anyway. Some distance from the wagon, he stumbled over a prairie dog village, but none of the chattering rodents offered itself as a potential target or meal. Hawks and other large birds soared overhead, also hunting, Hooley imagined as he watched them swoop to the ground, but he never could find what they might have spotted as prey.

Finally, hot, thirsty, and out of patience, he started back toward his wagon. Suddenly, a covey of quail shuttered to wing in front of him. Startled, he raised his rifle and squeezed off a shot, delighted when one of the shadowy fowl exploded in a blast of feathers and fell to earth. When Hooley reached it, he discovered that there was precious little left of the small bird, only a cocky head and a mass of bloody feathers. He was glad now that he hadn't tried to shoot a rabbit or prairie dog. There would be little left but sinews and bone had he hit one.

"It doesn't pay to be stupid, you son of a bitch," Hooley swore aloud, noting that his hearing was numb, a result of the rifle's blast. Though the rest of the flock was nowhere to be seen, he marked the spot and resolved to figure out how to rig up a snare of some sort.

Later that night, after several dismal failures at creating a trap, Hooley cursed his lack of frontier knowledge. In the dark distance, he heard the by now familiar yelping howl of coyotes. Frightening at first, he now welcomed their nocturnal companionship. He fancied he could identify a particular animal's moan apart from another's, and he considered naming them until he decided this might be a signal that he was losing his mind.

Staring off into the inky jet surrounding his camp, he felt the rocky truth of his situation weighing on him and contemplated the unique voices of the frontier animals. It was entirely possible that he was about to die, alone and forgotten, in an unknown place where no one would discover his bones before they were reduced to dust. The coyotes' howl also reminded him that even that probably wouldn't happen. Scavengers would find him and carry parts of him to the dark recesses of this wilderness place, and there would be nothing left to indicate that he had ever passed this way, ever made a mark of any kind on the world.

THE CARPENTER

———◆———

1

GILBERT HOOLEY WAS never before aware that he was a lonely man, although he had never had or sought friendship or society. His single attempt to achieve marital bliss had been less than rewarding. He married when he was twenty-two, just after he returned from the war. His lethargic nature yielded an inclination to sit without talking for hours, content to smoke his pipe, read, and yawn or nod now and then when a thought struck him. He believed that sexual congress, pleasant as it could be and desirable as it was, often entailed too much work to be sought with frequency. His experience with romance, therefore, was limited.

Such attitudes distracted his bride to no end. Her name was Ruthie Milligan, and she was four years younger than he. She worked in a milliner's shop, where Hooley met her one afternoon when—at his father's insistence, curiously enough—he stopped by to pick up a new hat ordered for his mother. As it turned out, there was no hat on order, but Ruthie was most definitely a part of the shop's available inventory. Flaxen-haired and dark-eyed, Ruthie was the daughter of an alderman and fashioned herself to be a beauty and a prize catch. She had a trim figure and a lively manner, and Hooley found her appealing enough, although her high-pitched voice made his teeth hurt when she laughed, something she seemed to do more than was necessary. No one was more surprised than Hooley when she agreed to marry him. He had only known her a few weeks, and he had only asked her—again, at his father's insistence—to step out with him three times.

Hooley was no more fooled by this obvious ploy than he had ever been by any of his father's manipulative shenanigans. He knew Simon was sickly and was eager to have a male heir born to continue the family trade, which he knew Bertha Hooley would demand sold unless Gil could show some gumption, or find a woman who could. The prospect of marriage was neither desirable nor repugnant to Gilbert Hooley. It was just one more thing life put in front of him to deal with.

Hence, Gil once again followed his father's continuing instructions and, with no expectation that she would do anything more than politely refuse, invited the sprightly young woman to be his wife. She enthusiastically accepted, then laughed so hard she cried and made Hooley's teeth hurt all the more. Typically, Hooley's mother seemed less pleased than his father, who all at once announced that he had discovered the wherewithal to pay off many of his long-standing debts. Bertha's principal observation was that "Ruthie Hooley" was a silly name.

The wedding was a quiet affair. Hooley's father was too ill to attend. His mother decided to visit her cousins in the country that month and was also absent. Having no close friends, Hooley was reduced to asking the publican at his favorite tavern to stand up for him. Ruthie's parents appeared entirely too grateful to see their only daughter wed to a tent-maker's son. They took boat for New Orleans the same afternoon of the wedding. From there, they sailed to Italy, where they intended to remain for a few years.

Ruthie was delivered of a child six months later. It strangled on the cord and the midwife told Hooley that it was premature. He glanced one time at the stone-dead but fully formed, eight-pound infant, with its large tuft of curly black hair, and agreed, but not for the same reason.

The couple then settled into a thoroughly dissatisfying routine of life. Since the war, Hooley had developed a tendency toward chronic dyspepsia. His mother said he was just naturally cranky, while Ruthie averred that his condition was caused by his expressed disinterest in her. It was true enough that he harbored a growing resentment of her interference in his life and of her continuing dalliance with a former beau, a curly-haired riverboat captain who often sought her company while Hooley was at work. In any event, Hooley was easily provoked to outbursts of anger marked by loud swearing whenever Ruthie annoyed him. After each display, his stomach remained in an uproar for days.

A year later Smion Hooley died. Bertha Hooley claimed her family legacy and moved to the country to join her cousins for good. Hooley and the failing business were left to their individual fates. He asked Bertha for help, but she refused. "I'd give you some money," she told him, "but you'd only waste it on that silly tent business. If I cut you off, perhaps you'll take up some respectable profession. I wouldn't mind if you became a policeman or a whiskey peddler. They're not much more acceptable, as vocations go, but at least you'd have to show some ambition."

To economize, Hooley and Ruthie moved into a small inexpensive flat, comfortably near the business district but uncomfortably near a noisy street. Hooley learned to ignore the bustle going on outside and to find solace in his reading and his pipe. Some evenings, he would sit for hours without saying a word, just reading and smoking, nursing his upset stomach by occasionally taking a sip of bourbon whiskey to remove the edge from Ruthie's caustic comments and withering looks.

Ruthie hated their home, but she loved the theater and the music hall. Both bored Hooley. She planned long carriage rides down along the river for picnics, which Hooley believed involved too much work merely to fight flies and mosquitoes. She also liked the attention of other men, something Hooley pretended to ignore. They never could find compromise, so she fussed and complained while he took refuge in his pipe and his books when he wasn't sewing canvas and trying to make a living. Basically, he wished she would go away. One day, she did.

After two years of whining complaint, she took up with a dry-goods drummer out of Cleveland, and they ran off to try their luck in the gold-fields of the Dakotas, or so her good-bye note informed him. A few months later, Hooley heard that they both wound up killed and scalped by savage Indians, but he doubted it. It would have been more likely, he thought, that she sent the story back to vex him.

Although his mother had never cared for Ruthie at all, she regarded Hooley's abandoned state to be an outrage. She openly called him a failure and a disappointment. She told everyone that she thought he was "a waste of breath and pain." Every time he visited her, she accused him of disgracing her, called him "the shame of my bosom," so he soon stopped visiting her altogether.

Eventually, the only people he saw were a handful of saloonkeepers and a duet of mulatto prostitutes at a disorderly house who were more interested in the ring of his coins on their bedside tables than the art of conversation. He was delighted that they didn't mind doing most of the work involved in satisfying his carnal needs, and they were pleased by his habit of making a rapid departure after completing his business. He made a visit to their establishment a regular part of his fortnight calendar and noticed a corresponding reduction in his dyspeptic fits.

A few years later, when he left for the West, he said good-bye to no one. In living there more than thirty years, he had never made a friend. He worried, though, that he would miss the whores. Sure enough, he did.

2

ANOTHER FEW DAYS went by with no change in Hooley's situation except for a steady diminishing of his food stock. He had just begun wondering in what posture he might want to die of starvation when he spied a large wagon on the eastern horizon.

The vehicle was an oversized prairie schooner drawn noisily through the grass by six oxen. Aboard were two oddly dressed men and a poorly covered load of fresh-milled lumber and heavy tools. There were also fat nail kegs lashed to the wagon's sides along with a variety of sawyer's and carpenter's implements arranged in a cunning and efficient display.

"Welcome, strangers!" Hooley called out. He tried to make his voice sound earnest and hospitable. They paid him no attention, though, and continued to rail at each other in a foreign tongue that sounded like raw gibberish. Their weary oxen apparently accepted his greeting as a command, however, and halted next to Hooley's listing Studebaker, although neither man noticed.

"Slide down and rest," Hooley offered. They continued their argument and Hooley deduced that they were ignorant of the native tongue of the country surrounding them. They were now bouncing up and down on their wagon and berating each other in increasingly belligerent tones.

"Quit that, now," Hooley admonished them. "You gentlemen step down and have some refreshment. I have coffee and a drop of good bourbon whiskey, if you're so inclined." They just continued their fight, dancing from the wagon seat up to the neat pile of lumber and making threatening gestures. Finally, one of them climbed down to tend the oxen and the other came to the ground and chocked the wagon's wheels. Their yelling did not abate.

Hooley spat in disgust. It was just his luck that the only two people to happen upon him were ignorant immigrants with no word of English or scrap of social amenity between them. Once they were on the ground, their argument escalated in rancorous excitement, and the men began kicking dirt on one another and slapping each other on the shoulders and head.

Hooley sat down under his awning, lit his pipe, stoked up his fire, and tried to remember if the coffeepot had fresh water in it. He was about to check when one of the men pulled down a three-foot length of two-by-four from the load of lumber and knocked the brains out of the other.

It was a quick, spontaneous kind of action, and it left the perpetrator standing over his companion's dusty, bloody corpse, stunned speechless by what he had done. Hooley had seen more than his fair share of mayhem in the War, but this sudden violent act amazed him. He examined the thoroughly pulped head of the man on the ground and swallowed hard. "You sure killed the hell out of him," he said.

The man started at the sound of another voice and looked as if he just discovered that he wasn't alone. This irked Hooley, since he had been talking to them from the moment they arrived, and he was suddenly in no mood to strike up a conversation now that he had been ignored for so long. He also was somewhat afraid of this large killer. He reminded himself that his Winchester rifle was in easy reach and warily eyed the bloody length of wood in the man's hand.

The man, though, seemed empty of fight. He looked around Hooley's camp in blinking wonder. He observed the bright green-striped awning-shaded rig, tilted wagon, well-established campfire and cooking utensils, and Hooley himself. Then he glanced down at the body and commenced wailing. His cries echoed off the wind, and huge tears ran down his bearded face.

Hooley watched him warily, but he had a flickering hope that maybe all the noise would summon back the mules. Finally, the man dropped his milled cudgel and thrust his hands out in front of him. He walked over toward Hooley, who quickly reached for his Winchester. The man noted this with his tearstained eyes, and when he reached Hooley's campfire, he stopped, cried and jabbered some more, then pushed his hands out, palms down, toward the confused tentmaker. It took a few minutes of wild gesturing and a great deal more wailing, but at last Hooley gathered that the man expected to be put into chains for the murderer he was.

"Are you crazy?" Hooley asked. "This has nothing to do with me."

The man pointed at his companion's body, gestured at his own chest. "Mino," he said. He then thrust his hands out again toward Hooley.

"No," Hooley said. "No, no, no." It was ridiculous. He had no shackles and no right to arrest the man. So far as he was concerned, the crime was as much an accident as a homicide, and he was moved by the killer's remorse.

The man kept repeating "Mino" and showing Hooley his hairy wrists, but Hooley kept shaking his head and saying, "No, no, no." He finally started adding "Mino" to the phrase and decided that that must be the man's name, although the rhyme nettled him.

After a while, Mino ceased trying to convince Hooley to arrest him. He paced around a bit, kicking up dust and muttering in his strange tongue. He was several inches shy of six feet tall, Hooley calculated, and his huge

chest and arms pushed his weight well over ten or eleven stone. He wore
a curly dark beard, and his black hair cranked out from a sweat-stained
leather cap. His eyes were bright blue, which meant he was not a Negro,
though his skin was the color of many mulattos Hooley had known—
walnut-grained and rippled with thick muscle when he moved. He wore
heavy denim overalls and a plaid shirt, with thick-soled high-laced work
boots.

Mino continued to pace and talk to himself in his foreign tongue. Finally, with one more pleading glance at Hooley, he heaved his victim's
body across his big shoulders, pulled a shovel off the wagon, and took him
up onto the nearby flats, apparently to bury him. Hooley let him go.

The task occupied the rest of the afternoon, and as Hooley was frying
up the last of his beans for supper, Mino returned, intoned some strange
chant, then crossed himself in a dramatic fashion. He then sat by the fire,
a dirty, tired grin on his face. He obviously expected to be fed.

Hooley dished him out a portion of beans. He pointed at his own chest.
"Gil Hooley," he said. Mino stared mutely at him. "Mino?" Hooley asked.
Mino continued to stare. "You Mino?" Hooley repeated. Mino nodded.
That, Hooley decided, would have to do.

After they ate, Hooley allowed Mino to take the tin dishes down to the
creek and wash them. When the man returned, he unhitched the oxen and
led them down for watering. To Hooley's surprise, Mino returned with
the mules and tethered them to a rope rigged between the wagons. The
oxen were placed alongside them.

"That won't do," Hooley noted. "Not for long. We'll be up to our ears
in ox shit. The mules draw enough flies."

Mino nodded, then bowed slightly, said something soft in his strange
language, and climbed into his wagon. Before Hooley finished his final
pipe of the evening, he could hear him snoring.

"The sleep of the just," Hooley grumbled. But as the coyotes' familiar
wail lit up the darkness, he had to admit that odd though it might be, he
was glad for the human company.

3

MINO PROVED TO be a paraclete for progressive development. Within a few
days and without uttering a single intelligible word, he used his lumber and lengths of stout rope to fashion a corral for the animals, then
added sturdier bracing for Hooley's awning. He also dug a sluice from the
creek, forming a surface well to use as a trough. He then constructed a
crude frame between the two vehicles, creating a shed.

Hooley was so moved by Mino's display of labor that he stirred himself from his customary lethargy and set to work fabricating a canvas roof for the shed. For a time, Hooley entertained the notion that Mino would get around to repairing Hooley's broken axle. But even though Mino expressed some visible curiosity about it, he made no motion to fix it.

They rarely spoke, only communicated through gestures and actions. But Hooley counted himself most fortunate to have been nearby when Mino decided to usher his companion from the world. The man had an industrious nature large enough for both of them. He also had food.

Mino's supplies included stores of salted pork, bacon, hominy, beans, cornmeal, coffee, and flour, which Hooley supplemented with his own cargo of coffee, tobacco, and bonded bourbon. For the time being, at least, it appeared that the men would have a comfortable, if quiet, while. Hooley was even moved to take his rifle and go out once more hunting for something fresh to eat, but all he came back with was a skunk—which Mino skinned, dressed, and cooked up with wild asparagus and onions. The result, Hooley admitted, was delicious. He pronounced it the best meal he'd had in months. Mino didn't understand a word of the compliment, but he apparently gathered the tone correctly and thanked Hooley by producing a cunning little concertina and entertaining him with a splendid array of tunes he coaxed from the squeezebox. He added a thick, baritone voice and words from his strange, unintelligible language.

The men got along well and communicated without conversation. Mino jabbered continuously in his personal tongue, which Hooley refused to make sense of, although Mino exhibited uncommon patience in pointing at various things and slowly naming them, then peering at Hooley as if he expected the syllables to magically transform themselves into understanding. For his part, Hooley merely gestured when he wanted something and said very little out loud. Once in a while he would take a stick and draw a design in the dirt, then act out the purpose of the idea. Mino would study the drawing for a moment, nod vigorously, and set to work.

Hooley also pitched in, much to his own surprise. He was marvelously content to be sewing canvas again. He fashioned a tent to cover a privy Mino was pleased to dig, as well as two small shelters behind the wagons in which the men could sleep with individual privacy.

Mino made a cross for his victim's grave and devised a front for their wagon shelter, covered by a canvas wall Hooley sewed. Mino then set to work building a small boardwalk down to the privy and creek so that they could make it there and back without having to put on their shoes for fear of scorpions, snakes, or red ants, stinging and biting vermin that were uncommonly plentiful in the area.

They continued in this way throughout the spring and into the summer. Hooley's hunting abilities improved, although he was still reluctant to go out tramping around for too long in the heat and could rarely find anything to shoot with the rifle. He did discover that prairie chickens often appeared in the tall grass. The birds didn't fly well and were dumb enough to stand still while he approached and knocked them down with a stick. They made remarkably good eating, but sometimes they were hard to find, and as the weeks went by, they became more wary of him.

He finally gave in and rigged lines and hooks out of needles and thread, and set Mino to fishing. He also made a frog gig with a large needle and a cypress pole. Their diet was soon supplemented with fat catfish and perch, frog legs, and several edible water plants and tubers that Mino found growing by the creek and boiled up with whatever meat they had. Mino also proved adept at mixing utterly delicious soup from the turtles and mussels near the creek.

The morning the boardwalk was finished, Hooley was astonished to see a rider casually stroll up on a piebald mare. He sat quietly for a moment and studied the scene, then made his howdies to both men as if he visited every day. As Hooley stood gape-mouthed, the young man finally broke the awkward silence by announcing that he was a cowhand.

Hooley vaguely surveyed the horizon. "What cows?" he asked. "Where?"

The youngster's mouth turned up in a grin. "Oh, there's plenty of cows around here," he said. "Though we call them 'cattle.' Cows are usually milkers."

"I've been here nearly six months," Hooley said firmly, "and I've not seen any kind of cow." Suspicions gathered in his mind like clouds as he recalled his dime novel reading. "Are you sure you're a cowboy, not a road agent? We don't have one damn thing worth stealing."

"We prefer the term 'cowhand,' " the youngster said, "or 'cowpuncher.' But 'cowboy' ain't offensive. Now, 'road agent' is a whole different thing. That might be mistook for an insult."

Mino came rushing up with wide-armed gestures, clearly delighted to have an unexpected guest. He jabbered and gesticulated and tried to entice the youngster down from his pony.

The cowboy remained firmly in the saddle and studied the camp while ignoring Mino's gestures. "Y'all from around here?" he asked at last.

Hooley let his eyes sweep the featureless horizon. "No," he said. "Are you?"

The youth shrugged and grinned. "I am now."

He looked to be about eighteen. But he had a large pistol holstered on his hip and a sharp knife in his belt, and the lines around his eyes suggested that he'd seen more of life than most his age. Beneath the thin growth of beard, however, the face of a mere boy could be seen. Hooley's manner softened slightly, and he invited the youngster to step down and take a seat by their campfire.

"Name's Henry Mitchell," the cowboy offered when he squatted on his hams by the fire and accepted a cup of coffee. "But my pards call me 'Hank.' Reckon you can, too."

"You have 'pards'?" Hooley still wasn't convinced that this young man was a bona fide worker of cattle.

"Sure," Hank replied with a boyish grin. "There's a whole bunch of us. We been working round here for near onto a year now."

Hooley could barely find words to speak, so astonished was he that apparently people such as this young horseman had been regularly riding back and forth the whole while he'd been stranded here and that none had previously thought to stop by and offer help. He held his tongue, though. Hank's youthful grin and bright eyes were welcome company.

They shared a noon meal of prairie chicken and wild onions. The cowboy listened intently to Mino's gibberish, nodding wisely, and Hooley briefly wondered if perhaps the big man had been speaking sense all along. At last, though, Hank gave Hooley a serious look.

"He don't speak a whole lot of English, does he?"

"None at all, from what I can tell."

"Well, he ain't stupid," Hank said. And Hooley agreed. He decided that he liked young Hank just fine.

Mino seemed to share the sentiment. He stood, and while waving his arms and dancing back and forth in the dust, made a long, impassioned speech. And Hank nodded politely. "Beats hell out of me, pard," he said to Mino, who grinned and nodded and looked extremely satisfied with himself as he sat down and wiped his face with a piece of scrap canvas, took a long pull from a bottle, then sighed deeply and made a final, melancholy-sounding comment.

"No shit," Hank said, nodding. Mino nodded back in philosophical agreement.

"That's a mighty fine-looking shed you've rigged up there," Hank said, casting a wistful eye on the wagon shelter. "Wonder what it'd take for a man to catch a little shut-eye inside it?"

Hooley stared at him. "You want to sleep in the tent? When?"

"Why, right now! I got a bellyful of grub and I'm hankering for a short nap, if one's available." It was a hot day and he had been up all night chasing mavericks down in the breaks. "Mavericks is the only business there is this time of year. Ain't a hell of a lot of that. There ain't one hell of a lot of anything around here, if you know what I mean."

Mino nodded wisely at this statement and replied in his personal language.

"No shit," Hank drawled as if he understood.

"No shit," Mino imitated in his thick accent. Hooley was momentarily stunned. It was the first time the large dark man had attempted to imitate English sounds. His unwillingness to do so had been a constant source of irritation to Hooley. He stared at Mino, who winked back. Hooley was furious with frustration, but he said nothing.

"So how 'bout it, pard?" Hank asked, oblivious to Hooley's sulk. "All right if I take a little siesta under the shade for a bit?"

Hooley collected himself. He was reluctant. He now began worrying once more that Hank might be an outlaw sizing them up for robbery. But Mino somehow deduced what the youngster wanted and bunched up some unused canvas and made a pallet behind the false front between the wagons. To Hooley's shock, Mino went through a series of gestures and mimes that resulted in the extraction of a ten-cent piece from Hank's pocket. Hooley was so amazed that he lit up an uncharacteristic second after-dinner pipe and contemplated this new development over an equally uncharacteristic afternoon cup of whiskey.

Hank had his nap, then rode off, promising to be back. Hooley, who was on his third pipe and fourth bourbon of the afternoon, was mulling over the idea that they might charge more for the privilege extended the cowboy if their accommodations were to seem more formally presentable.

He explained his idea to Mino, with no other result than a bobbing, grinning lack of understanding, but then he aroused himself and drew a series of designs in the dirt. Mino studied them intently for a few moments, then got busy. Hooley set himself to work as well. By noon the next day, with Hooley's fingers busily adapting the heavy canvas from his wagon and Mino's big hands fashioning frames, they had constructed a sizable tent and four comfortable cots.

Hooley made a sign advertising a bed and a meal for twenty-five cents a night, one of the most ambitious things he had done in his entire life. "Looks like I'm in business again," he said.

Mino traced the lettering on the sign with a grimy finger, grinned, and nodded with enthusiasm. "No shit," he replied, as if he were reading the printed words.

"Oh, shut up," Hooley said. For the first time in a while, he felt a surge of dyspepsia.

Hank returned two days later, driving three skinny, unbranded calves in front of him. He saw the sign, asked what it said, and, after Hooley read it and pointed out the new tent and cots, eagerly took advantage of the offer. "That's still cheaper than Pease City," he said. "All you need now is a whirlago gal and a faro table."

But there was a problem. He had no cash on him and nothing of value to offer in exchange. So, Hooley offered to trade one week's free lodging and supper for one of the maverick calves, butchered—provided Hank stayed around to stretch the hide.

"That's a hell of a deal," Hank said, "if you'll throw in a little drink of whiskey. Say one shot per quarter of beef?" Hooley reluctantly agreed, and Hank immediately killed one of the calves and set about rendering it.

Hooley watched him, his mouth watering over the meal he knew would soon be cooking on the fire. He also noted the stinking pile of offal that resulted from the work and reminded himself to ask Hank to conduct such business farther from the camp in future.

4

WITHIN A MONTH, Hank and a dozen of his cowboy pards were making regular stops at Hooley and Mino's camp, and a small herd of cattle, including two fine milkers—"cows," as Hooley remembered to call them—were now penned in a newly enlarged corral. Hooley used the last of his canvas fabric to cover an annex Mino built onto their onetime shed, which now boasted a new sign that proclaimed it to be a hotel and saloon. Cash prices were raised to fifty cents for a cot and a meal. The bourbon, which Hooley personally poured into one of a half-dozen tin cups he located among Mino's belongings, was going for two bits a gulp. Mino also demonstrated a willingness to go down to the creek and wash out shirts and trousers for a nickel a garment.

Although there was now a ready supply of beef, supplemented by fish and reptilian produce from the creek and small prairie fowl and varmints Hooley found, supplies of staples and necessities were still a problem. Hooley was completely out of canvas and low on thread and other items. The saloon was little more than a covered shed held up by two stripped cedar posts, with stumps arranged for seating, and he noted that Mino's lumber supply was growing short, too.

The whiskey was nearly gone also, and this was a more serious threat. "I don't know how much longer we can go on," Hooley said one morning as they ate a fresh breakfast of catfish eggs and calf fries brought in by the boys. "I used up the last of the cornmeal making this. Fact is we're nearly out of everything. Soon as this wagon's fixed, I think it'll be time to move on." Hooley had no idea how a repair could be accomplished, or who might do it. No cowboy had shown more than the most casual interest in the listing wagon.

"I'd sure hate to see you do that," Hank said sadly. "This is the only place round here we can get a good meal and a decent place to flop down for the night out of the wind and rain."

Hooley studied the bright blue sky. Although the wind seemed to blow all the time, it had not rained a drop. It appeared that it had never rained in this country at all. He observed to himself that what was wanted was a good half hour's cannonade to summon some thunderclouds.

"These afternoon siestas are about all keeps me going some days. Some days," a short, skinny boy named Underwood, who tended to dither, said. The other cowboys agreed. "I'd like to see you stay," Underwood went on. "Reckon what it'd take? Take?"

"Well, a wagonload of supplies would answer nicely," Hooley muttered more or less to himself. Then he asked, "But where would that come from? And how could we pay for it? You boys never have any ready money. All I have is that bunch of scrawny cattle."

"Well, actually, them cattle's probably worth something," Tidmore, a fat cowboy with buck teeth, offered. "Rancher McPherson'd think so."

"Who's that?" Hooley inquired.

"Fellow we work for," Hank allowed.

Hooley returned to the problem. "What about that Pease City? Probably a store there."

"Ain't nothing but a trading post. Post," Underwood said. "Rancher McPherson owns that, too. Lets a guy named Cherokee Charlie run it. But he's crooked as a dog's hind leg. Gets three prices for everything. Everything. Anything we buy there goes down on a piece of paper. Then, at the end of the month, Rancher McPherson makes deducements in our pay. We never can tell if we're getting a fair shake or not. Or not. Cherokee Charlie keeps all the records in Indian. Indian. All I know is that 'fore you showed up, I was in the hole every month. Month."

"I'm near even now," Tidmore said. "Thanks to you taking a few of Rancher McPherson's cattle in trade."

"Those are Rancher McPherson's cattle?" Hooley stood, alarmed. What Hank was telling him now sank in. This was a ranch and somebody named McPherson was the owner. He was trespassing. For a moment, he had dime novel visions of a well-armed cattle baron riding over the horizon, guns blazing, hanging rope dangling.

"Well, not exactly," Hank explained. "Not till they're branded they ain't. They're just mavericks till they're branded." He studied the fear in Hooley's eyes. "Simmer down, Hooley. Way we look at it, if you found them, they're just as much yours as anybody's."

"How's the law going to look at it?" Hooley asked, not completely assured.

"What law?" Underwood asked, glancing around to the empty prairie stretching away from the encampment. "Onliest law around here is Rancher McPherson. McPherson. And he's way off at his ranch house, diddling his missus and counting his money."

"I've seen his missus," Tidmore offered. "And she ain't worth much of a diddle."

"You could cut yourself on that woman. Woman." Underwood agreed. "Got more sharp edges than a busted out window light."

This brought a burst of hearty laughter and a call for drinks all around.

Hooley was still worried, but pushed it aside and poured out whiskey, noting how little was left. "That doesn't solve the problem. Where can I find supplies in this wilderness?"

5

THE COWBOYS RETURNED the afternoon of the following day leading a stagecoach they had commandeered at gunpoint. The driver, whose name was Gabriel Heinz, was not in a good mood.

"I wish you'd tell me what in the name of the blue-eyed Jesus this is all about!" he yelled when the boys led his team up to the camp. "Who's the boss of this outfit?" Heinz demanded. Hooley could only stare, but Heinz took that as an affirmation of his part in the hijacking. "I done told these yahoos that I ain't carrying no gold, no cash dollars, no nothing," he explained in a roaring rage. "Alls I got is a bunch of citified sons of bitches who are more than righteously put out by this detour. I got me a schedule to keep!"

From the coach lettering, Hooley observed that it was part of the Fort Worth and Santa Fe Deluxe Excursion Line. He recalled from his map that its regular road was some distance to the south.

"Got him barrels and crates and such strapped onto the back," Hank noted. "Probably food and stuff in them you might could use."

Hooley was as alarmed at the notion of being a receiver of stolen goods as he had been at being a receiver of stolen cattle. He started to point out that this might not be the best method of acquiring supplies, but before he could do so, the coach's door creaked open and five passengers stumbled out and began knocking the dust off their clothing.

"Damndest thing I've ever seen in my life!" a fat man in a black serge suit complained.

"Watch your goddamn language," a slighter man with a gambler's mustache and a brocade vest shot back. "There's ladies present, you son of a bitch."

The ladies, Hooley saw, consisted of two older women and a young girl, all of whom were covered with dust. Their hats were askew, and their hair was in ravens' nests of tatters from the rough ride across the trackless prairie. Their vexation was obvious, and Hooley suddenly feared that he was about to be in more trouble than he had ever imagined.

"Why don't you all come in and freshen up," he offered. "Mino!" he yelled in too loud a voice. "Put some coffee on to boil."

Mino, who was standing no farther away than Hooley's elbow, merely stared at the scene in front of him. He didn't move until Hooley fetched the coffeepot, put it into his hands, and shoved him toward the creek. Hooley then escorted the ladies down the boardwalk toward the privy, proud of himself for having thought to cover it with sturdy canvas.

Heinz was stamping around in the dust and spitting tobacco juice. The cowboys were warily watching him, but none had a pistol drawn. The youngsters' sheepish grins testified that they were more amused than wary of him. The short, rotund, and bandy-legged driver was so angry, he sprayed when he talked. The front of his shirt was crusted with expectorated tobacco juice from an apple-sized plug rooted inside his jaw. His salt-and-pepper beard was similarly stained, but his face was crimson with rage, and he spat deliberately at Hooley as he tried to explain that this was none of his doing, that the cowboys had just been trying to fetch in supplies from the nearest possible source.

Finally, Heinz spent his anger. The ladies returned and began sniffing the aroma of boiling coffee while they joined the men in looking around the camp. They were delighted to find that a few coins would bring them hot beans, fresh meat, and cool creek water.

Hooley stepped over and offered them each a dram of bourbon "on the house" in exchange for their trouble, and the male passengers took him up on it right away. For his part, Heinz accepted his drinks with very little prodding and no charge for seconds, or thirds. Hooley thought it was the least he could do to pacify the discommoded driver.

As Hooley hoped, Heinz was soon placated by such hospitality. He listened at last to his host's expression of regret for the inconvenience. "We were in need of supplies," Hooley repeated. "I doubt, though, that what you're carrying will make much difference."

Heinz's dark teeth now centered a clever smile, and his pale blue eyes twinkled. "I reckon I *could* forget what these boys look like. Keep them from hanging too quick," he said with a tilt of his empty cup toward Hooley, who rapidly refilled it. A few more drinks from Hooley's nearly exhausted supply prompted Heinz to announce that he could alert his company to send regular freighting trips to the camp, delivering new shipments of canvas and lumber, food, and other necessities, provided, of course, that Hooley was willing to pay cash for such shipments.

"Fact is," he said with an appreciative study of a fresh dollop of amber liquid in his cup, "I reckon I could bring the run my own self, now that I know the way and all." He drank deeply. "Fact is, I been thinking about quitting the stage line and starting to freight for good. Work closer to home." He looked narrowly at the cowboys, who stood off to one side and watched the passengers. "I'm getting too old for this hoorahing, and," he noted, "I'm always obliged for the pleasing warmth of male hospitality." Hooley poured him another drink.

"Alls I'm carrying on this trip is white flour, pickles, and potted beef," Heinz apologized. "There might be a sack or two of cornmeal squirreled away someplace, but don't count on it."

Hooley offered him five dollars for the lot, and after two more dollops of liquor, Heinz agreed that it was quite likely that the commodities could have "fallen off" the back of the stage. "Considering that we was held up and had to make a run for it and all," he said with another twinkling wink as he accepted the money Hooley counted out.

Hooley decided to offer Heinz a proposition: a ten-percent cut of all profits, provided their orders were filled in good time. Heinz considered the offer over the time it took him to down two more cups of liquor, then accepted. Hooley did not consult Mino in this matter—not that such a consultation would have mattered or been understood—but he did think to extract a ledger book from his Gladstone bag and to start keeping records.

The passengers were by now alert to the idea that this side trip was endangering their schedules and might compel them to spend the night in this crude camp. "I, for one, do not intend to sleep on that," one of the women announced, pointing her parasol at one of the rough cots beneath the tent. "It looks licey, and this entire place reeks of manure." That was true, Hooley acknowledged, making a note to move the corral even farther from the camp as soon as they had the materials to do so.

Eventually, Heinz pronounced himself sufficiently drunk to continue. Hank and Underwood tied him to the driver's seat, knotted the reins around his fists, and gave the team a swat to get them rolling. With Hank leading the horses, the stagecoach made its way toward its regular route. Heinz was already snoring loudly over the jangles of harness and creaks of leather springs when they pulled away, while the passengers waved handkerchiefs from the windows.

"There goes the possibility of sustained prosperity," Hooley said to Mino with satisfaction.

"No shit," the large, dark man said happily.

As promised, Heinz showed up ten days later with a freight wagon overflowing with provisions to fill the small camp's needs. Hooley noted each commodity and placed an order for nails, more tools, and, to Heinz's enthusiastic expression of agreement, several cases of gin and bonded bourbon.

"If I was you, I'd order rye," Heinz suggested after a moment's thought. "It's cheaper, and these boys are used to it. A steady diet of high dollar sour mash might give them a notion of theirselves."

"Seems we're here to stay a bit," Hooley commented to the already half-drunk teamster.

"Fine by me," Heinz said. "Always did like a place where I was welcome."

The Deputy Marshal

1

After weeks of steady toil, the camp took on a more permanent look. Shipments from the cooperative Heinz brought canvas and specially ordered oakum-soaked twine and thread, as well as a load of milled lumber for Mino's talented hands. The happy giant also restored the ancient beaver dam, then worked the oxen with improvised dredge to deepen the surface well into a genuine pond. Gradually, he dismantled the wagons, converting boards to doorjambs, shinboards, and window frames for Hooley's canvas covers. Soon there were four tent-buildings—one residential structure for each of the two men, a large one for the hotel, and the whiskey shed, which remained more or less open on three sides.

With his two-word vocabulary, Mino had apparently reached the limit of his aptitude for English. Hooley spent hours every day directing the tireless carpenter through mimes and gestures regarding any number of necessary chores. Afterward, Hooley sat in the open door of his canvas house, smoking his pipe, sipping his whiskey, and stitching canvas. He was, in a word, content. He had the advantages of society and solitude at once, and no one placed any demands on him. As a bonus, he mused, he was now actively about the only vocation he was ever good at, and somehow, incredibly, he was making a half-decent living out of it.

Wouldn't his mother be surprised? he thought. Then he remembered

her last words to him and decided that she wouldn't be, and that she
wouldn't approve, either.

More of Rancher McPherson's employees availed themselves of a night's
rest on two dozen canvas cots, all snugly positioned under the large tent.
Although Hooley was weary of working so hard to establish what he considered an overlarge campsite, Heinz was pleased to bring more material
for Hooley's nimble fingers to stitch, and he also provided a cargo of sturdy
hickory saplings for ridgepoles, center braces, and cross beams for larger
tented structures.

The cowboys were always a rowdy and loquacious lot when they arrived,
but after sharing what little news they might have, they seemed content
to sit by the fire and listen to Mino play his squeezebox. Sometimes, one
would add a mouth organ or a Jew's harp to the tunes, and Mino proved
adept at picking up the melodies of numerous songs the pards liked to
sing. From sober hymns to harmonious expressions of patriotism to bawdy
songs of lively adventure on the frontier, evenings were filled with group
renditions that would, Hooley sometimes thought, overmatch the chorus
of any music hall Ruthie ever dragged him to.

Even though the boys talked wistfully of sweethearts, Hooley put aside
the occasional longings he felt for the pleasures of women and averred that
he now preferred stouthearted camaraderie. Females, he sometimes opined,
were the cause of most all male misfortune. The men laughed and agreed,
and Hooley warmed with their acceptance. Out here, far from the annoyance of his mother and memories of Ruthie, his old dyspepsia was utterly
gone, and except for his oath-laden histrionics when dealing with Mino,
he hadn't even sworn aloud in months. He was happier than he had ever
been in his life.

But sometimes during the long, lonely nights when the coyotes' calls
echoed off the moonlit sky, he idly wondered if such contentment could
last, and, if it couldn't, what its end would be.

2

AS AUTUMN APPROACHED, the wind finally blew up a heavy rain. The first
norther of the season—albeit a mild one—forecast the possibility of
cooler weather to come. Even so, the rapidly chilled atmosphere and
raging thunderstorms of the predawn hours gave way to a warm, sticky
afternoon. Hooley and Mino were alone because the cowboys recognized
the problems with cattle that accompanied a weather change and had ridden out as soon as the storm passed.

Hooley was contentedly smoking his pipe, pleased that Mino and his handiwork had sustained the overnight blow. Not a drop of water had dripped through the finely stitched, wax-sealed seams. The pitch of the peaked canvas roofs forbade any dangerous bulges overhead, and although the shrieking wind tore fiercely at every structure, Mino's stout carpentry held up well.

So, in spite of the heavy damp air that smothered all activity with sweat, Hooley was thinking what a good day it was when he saw a lone horseman riding toward their camp.

Unlike the cowboys' ponies, which fairly pranced, this animal plodded wearily through the grass. As the horse and its corpulent rider drew closer, Hooley noticed a remarkable dark fog hovering around them. In the yellow humid light, the hazy cloud swirled ferociously as the man pushed his tortured horse forward. When he reached the camp perimeters, Hooley observed that rather than a phenomenon of weather, the fog was actually alive. It was made up of fat, ugly blue-black flies that the rider was continually swatting away from his face and hands. His dun mare's tail worked like a fierce windmill as she plodded forward in the midst of the swarming pests.

The rider was grotesquely fat, with rotten teeth and a sour disposition. He might still have been reasonably presentable, Hooley thought, if he ever bathed or had happened upon an oculist at some point in his life. He had a stubble of beard on his face, and his small, dark eyes were deep-set and looked slightly away from one another. These defects gave him a stupid but menacing countenance. It was an appropriate natural disguise, for, as Hooley soon determined, the stranger was a no-nonsense lawman.

"Craggy Phillips," he announced loudly after he reined his suffering animal up at the outside perimeter of the campsite. "Deputy United States Marshal." He waited for Hooley's reaction, but the tentmaker only relit his pipe, unsure of what response was required. "You wasn't here when I come through last winter."

"We've been here a few months. I broke down, and decided to see what developed."

Phillips scanned the horizon dubiously. "Onliest thing likely to develop around here is a bad case of the dumbass. You a dumbass?"

"I'd say no to that, Marshal." Hooley decided he didn't like Marshal Craggy Phillips.

After working a plug of tobacco around in his mouth and swatting flies on every exposed part of his body as his horse danced to escape airborne torture, Phillips climbed down.

"What's the freight for a hot and a cot?" Hooley mentioned that he had just upped his rate to six bits, owing to the rain-proof housing now available. "That's pricey." Phillips gave Hooley a slanted glance. "You cut rate for federal employees?"

Hooley shook his head. "No, it's the same for everyone. White or colored."

Phillips scowled and dug a cartwheel out of his vest, flipped it to the tentmaker. "I'll need change and a receipt for that," he said. "Who takes care of the horses?"

Hooley was confounded. His only customers had been the cowboys and Heinz, and they attended their own animals. "You can board her for free," he said at last, nodding toward the flats. "There's a new corral and fresh grass up there, and there's a creek down there a ways."

"Looks buggy," Phillips said, scowling toward the creek.

Hooley studied the swarm of flies angrily buzzing around Phillips and his horse and wondered what difference a few mosquitoes might make. "It's what we have," he said.

"Hell of a note," Phillips grumbled, and he set about tending to his mare. The animal was gaunt, covered with open sores. Bloody wounds from fly bites pockmarked her nose and mouth, and one eye was swollen nearly shut. Hooley disliked seeing a beast in such bad state.

Phillips noted Hooley's inspection of his mount. He explained gruffly that her poor condition was indebted to the circumstance that every time she was turned out to graze or tried to take water at a stream or river, the flies lit all over her and drove her to distraction.

"All I can do to make her hold still long enough to take off her saddle. Hadn't run into that spate of rain, she might have gone completely loco." He looped the dark, stained bag around the horse's neck. "Can't lose that. Can't get no found pay if I don't bring back the evidence."

"What evidence?"

Phillips clearly wanted to explain, but before he could, Mino wandered up, soaked from the waist down. He had been dredging out a pool on one end of the pond to deepen the fishing possibilities in the creek. He smiled at Phillips as if he were an old acquaintance.

"It's been a damned miserable trip," Phillips complained, one made more uncomfortable by a case of piles. "It's them damn chilipeppers the Mescans put into everything. Even the coffee. Makes a man shit his innards out."

"No shit," Mino offered, and squatted down by Hooley.

Phillips gave him a studious look, then continued. He said he'd been in South Texas chasing three outlaws from Oklahoma Territory. He ran them all the way to Mexico, where two of them beat him to the river and made good their escape. He caught the third when his horse pulled up lame, but before Phillips could shoot him, the young scofflaw pulled out a pistol, shoved it into his mouth, and took his own life. Phillips didn't approve. "Violates the principalities of sound law enforcement," he said solemnly, "to say nothing of the vestitudinal underminings of justice."

"Such as?" Hooley asked.

"If he got hisself caught, then he ought to let hisself be hung. Don't show nothing but irresponsibility and disrespect for law and order to shoot hisself like that. How's he supposed to learn a lesson that away? It's smart-alecky, and I don't like it. I don't know what to make of this new bunch of outlaws we got today."

He explained that he was required to return some identification of the outlaw to his headquarters at Fort Sill. "It's too far to tote a corpse, so all I could think to do was to cut off his head and stuff it into that gunnysack."

Hooley observed the bloodstained bag hanging from his horse's neck. After nearly a week, it was emitting a sickening odor and was obviously what was chiefly attracting the huge flies.

"Fouls me up," he said about the suicide. "This was to be my fiftieth arrest. Never lost one like this before."

The pungent stench of rotting flesh and the swarm of angry, blood-sucking flies irked Hooley. He also didn't care for the way Phillips kept studying the tented structures surrounding him and shaking his head, as if mocking their efforts. His mind drifted to the problems surrounding their camp development, and he was barely aware that Phillips' story had come full circle. The lawman had reached the point where he was once again explaining how the other two men swam the Rio Grande to the safety of Mexico and left their partner behind.

"Should of went after them," Phillips concluded. "Doubt the Mescans want to mess around with rapscallions such as they was. But I don't have the authority. I'm a federal employee," he noted again. "As such, I'm abjugated from crossing into Mexico."

His story finished, Phillips accepted a dollop of gin—whiskey made his piles burn, he explained—and lit a small, cheap cigar. This amused Mino and set him to jabbering and pointing. Most cowboys smoked pipes or chewed tobacco, and the tiny dark stick jutted out of Phillips' fat lips like a toothpick. He observed Mino's delight for a space, then fished another from his pocket and offered it to him. Mino immediately lit it and drew the smoke deeply into his lungs, then nodded.

"Think nothing of it," Phillips said, offering what passed for a grin to Hooley.

Hooley was growing nauseous because of the rotting head. "I wish you'd take that thing off a ways," he said. He swatted a group of the black flies. "It's putting me right off my pipe."

"I got to keep an eye on it," Phillips said. "It's my responsibility. It's evidence."

"I can't imagine that anybody would want to steal it."

Phillips shrugged, rose, and lumbered off. He staked his horse, the stinking bag still in place, some distance from the tents, then wandered back. He sat down cross-legged on the ground and scraped the last of the food from a cold plate of beans and bacon.

As the afternoon began to wane, Phillips smoked another cigar and sat humming to himself, watching his hosts with growing malevolence in his misshapen eyes. It made Hooley nervous, but he forced his mind to other matters and started once more trying to explain to Mino his latest idea for bringing water to the bathhouse. The large man refused to understand Hooley's drawings and gestures, though, and Hooley's patience, of which there was never a surplus, was quickly exhausted. Soon, sweat streamed from their faces, and they were yelling back and forth in their different tongues, with Hooley providing most of the understandable profanity. It was the customary way they had of resolving their communication dilemma, and both were used to it.

After a bit, Phillips peered out through the bright sunset toward the flats, and his notice found the small cross over Mino's former partner's grave. "What's that?" he asked.

Hooley was in the middle of telling Mino what an ignorant son of a bitch he was for the fiftieth time, and he was in no mood to be interrupted by small talk. "It's a grave," he snapped.

"I can see it's a grave," the marshal said. "What I want to know is what's it doing there."

"It's got a corpse in it," Hooley said, catching his breath. "What do you think?"

"Whose corpse?"

Hooley sighed, poured himself some bourbon from his private stock and lit his pipe, then sat down and related the facts of Mino's partner's demise. The lawman listened closely and cast an appraising glance on Mino. Phillips finished his cigar, took a final drink of gin, wiped his mustache with a canvas napkin, then drew a large black revolver from his starboard holster.

"You're under arrest in the name of the law," he said to Mino.

For a moment, everything seemed frozen in the sweet orange glow of the sunset.

"What the hell for?" Hooley stepped between the gun and Mino's astonished face.

"Murder in the second degree," Phillips said. "Move, or I'll have to shoot you, too."

Hooley stepped aside. "Why do you have to shoot *anybody?*"

"For a minute there, he was looking flighty. If he cooperates and comes along quiet-like, I won't have to shoot him. I'm not fussy. I can take him dead or alive. It's all up to him."

Mino stood, astonished. His big eyes bulged like boiled eggs.

"C'mon, big'un," Phillips said. "Let's don't have no trouble now."

Mino's shoulders sagged and he stumbled forward. Phillips escorted him over to his saddlebags and pulled out a set of shackles and bound his hands.

"Where's his horse?" Phillips asked.

"He doesn't have a horse." Hooley couldn't believe what he was seeing.

"I can't take him in if he don't got no horse," Phillips said. "Whose mules is them?"

"Mine," Hooley said. "But they're not broken to ride," he added doubtfully.

Phillips looked pained, scratched his fuzzy chin. "All right. Who's the judge round here?"

"Nobody," Hooley said. "There's no town. You can see that for yourself."

Phillips turned his deep-set walleyes around the campsite. "You got buildings and a graveyard. That makes more of a town than most, especially up in Oklahoma Territory."

"It's not a town. And there's no judge. Turn him loose. He's got work to do."

"Who's the mayor? We could make do with a mayor, if there ain't no judge."

"There's not any mayor because there's not any town," Hooley yelled. He threw his hat down on the ground and stomped it. "I swear, you're a stupider son of a bitch than he is."

Phillips was unmoved. "I elect you mayor," he said. "I got the authority, being a federal employee. I appoint you by approximation. Now, we got to try this man so we can hang him."

"Hang him?" Hooley exclaimed. "You can't hang him. Hell, there's not even a tree around here tall enough to hang him on."

"We can use a doubletree." Phillips nodded toward just such an item removed from Mino's wagon. "Let's be quick about it. I got to get some shut-eye. I'm eager to get back to Oklahoma Territory and see to my wife.

She's a toothsome little thing, and I don't trust her to be without a man for too long. Lots of randy bachelors in Oklahoma Territory."

Hooley stood amazed for a moment or two, then stomped around more violently, kicking dirt and demanding that Phillips come to his senses or go to hell, whichever was more convenient. It felt good to indulge his temper, but Phillips just stood patiently, chewing on an unlit cigar, waiting for Hooley's rage to expire.

Mino appeared to have been stunned into silence by the series of events. He seemed to understand that he was shackled and that this man was the law, but beyond that, he was bewildered. His eyes beseeched Hooley for assistance.

But Hooley's daily allotment of energy was used up at last, and the euphoric pleasure of anger had also abated. He stood panting, sweating, and wishing for his pipe. "I'm not going to be a mayor *or* a judge, you stupid son of a bitch," he finally said, sighing.

"I'll be the judge," Phillips said, taking a seat. "And don't call me a son of a bitch. You're mayor, so you'll be the prosecutor. He can act as his own lawyer. Call your first witness."

"*I'm* the only damn witness. If I'd kept my mouth shut, you wouldn't know about it."

"That'd be obstructurating justice," Phillips said. "Be careful. You're under oath."

"I can't be under oath if I'm prosecuting him!"

Phillips considered this. "Is it true what you told me about him killing his partner?"

"Damn it, yes, it's true!"

"What you got to say for yourself?" Phillips asked Mino, who simply stared back in tragic bewilderment. "Cat's got his tongue," Phillips noted.

"He doesn't speak English, you stupid son of a bitch," Hooley yelled.

"I told you not to call me that no more," Phillips said. "This is your final warning."

"This is the damndest thing I've ever seen in my life," Hooley raged. His anger returned, but he forced himself to calm down. "You can't hang a man who doesn't even understand what he's been convicted of. Hell, he hasn't even been properly charged!"

"I charged him. You heard me arrest him and tell him what the charge was."

"He doesn't speak English, you stupid son of a—" He stopped when Phillips' hand dropped to the butt of his revolver. "He doesn't speak English," he finished deliberately.

"Why don't he speak no English?" Phillips asked patiently.

"Because he's some kind of foreigner."

"Mescan?"

"No. I don't think so." Hooley had never developed an acceptable theory about where Mino might have come from originally.

"Savvy espan-ol?" Phillips asked Mino, who stared dumbly. "Parely fran-sace? Sprecan-zay Dutch?" Mino looked at Hooley for translation. "Maybe he's a savage Indian," Phillips said. "Ain't supposed to be no savage Indians in Texas. Could be he's a renegade out of Oklahoma Territory. That's a federal offense, too. If he's an Indian I could tote him back, put him on trial at Fort Sill. If he had a horse." He then took thought. "What kind of Indian don't have no horse?"

"He is *not* an Indian," Hooley insisted. Then he looked at Mino. He didn't *think* he was an Indian, although Hooley's experience with Indians was minimal and limited to those he'd seen riding in civic processions or in traveling shows and circuses in St. Louis. Those, he understood, were not exactly the same as the savage Indians who still roamed the northern plains and haunted the deserts farther west. But Mino looked like neither of these. He wore regular clothes and heavy work boots, and Hooley had never heard of a savage Indian playing an accordion. Hooley also didn't think they could grow beards.

"Well, maybe he's deaf and dumb."

"That's crazier than anything you've said. You've heard him jabbering all afternoon."

"Well, why don't he speak no English or anything else? I tried everything but Chinee on him. I don't think he's a Chinaman."

"He's just a foreigner of some kind. Just not the kind you know."

"I'm trained to know foreigners," Phillips said. "I'm a deputy federal marshal." Hooley made a snorting noise. "Foreigner," Phillips repeated, and rubbed the stubble on his chin. "All right, then. And you say he killed his partner."

"I told you that. Wish I hadn't."

"Well, he's guilty, then. Here." He went to his saddle and pulled off a coil of rope. "I sentence you to be hung by the neck until you're dead," he said to Mino.

"No shit!" Mino yelled. Before he could say another thing, Phillips drew his gun again and hit him over the head with the barrel. The big man collapsed, and blood ran into his eyes.

"You idiot!" Hooley yelled. Furious indignation rose all around him like a swarm of yellow jackets. "Look what you did! There was no call for that.

Let me get something." He went for a bundle of canvas scraps and thrust one onto a bucket to wet it. Blood ran profusely from Mino's crown, covered his face. He whimpered like a whipped animal.

"I shouldn't of done that," Phillips said laconically. He inspected his pistol. "I broke a good gun last time I did that. Hard-headed rascal up near Ponca City."

Hooley pried Mino's fingers away from his wound and put the wet rag on top of his head. The big man looked up at him, fear and pain mixed with gratitude in his dark eyes. He muttered in his mysterious language words that sounded to Hooley like a plea for protection, and then muttered in a plaintive, questioning tone, "No shit?"

The tentmaker felt something snap inside him. Hooley had never had a friend or anything like a friend, and he wasn't sure that Mino was a friend, not in any way either of them could define. But in spite of the rancor that so often developed between them, Hooley acknowledged that this large, dark man down on the ground and bleeding meant *something* to him. All at once he felt the hurt and the dependency Mino was expressing in his eyes and unintelligible utterances, and all at once the anger Hooley thought was spent returned in the shape of a cold fist that clutched his heart in an icy grip.

"Should of shot him. It's easier on the gun," Phillips said, checking again for damage.

It had been a long time since Hooley had fired a weapon in anger. Not since the War, and not that much then, had he consciously aimed a weapon at another human being. In the few battles where he saw action, he usually just discharged his piece in the general direction of the charging, screaming Rebels, then turned and ran terrified. He never had any deliberate intention of killing anyone. But Phillips was pushing him past the edge of his patience and beyond reason.

"I'm making you the executor," Phillips said. "It ain't proper for me to judge him *and* hang him. I point you an adjunctive of the court." He began plaiting a noose onto the end of the rope. "Hurry and get him patched up. We can be done with this 'fore it gets full dark."

"Wait here a minute," Hooley said. He stalked over to his tented quarters, went inside and extracted his rifle from beneath his cot, came out, and shot Deputy Marshal Craggy Phillips through the surprised look in one of his misshapen eyes. He was dead before he hit the ground.

"Shit," Hooley said, deafened by the ringing in his ears.

"No shit," Mino repeated from the ground. "No shit."

They buried the marshal with his saddle and the outlaw's fly-blown head next to Mino's dead partner, but they thought better than to mark it. By lantern light, Hooley and Mino walked the oxen over it for an hour, tramping down the mound till it faded into the soil surrounding it.

The anger Hooley felt was gone and his easy, peaceful feeling returned. "Tomorrow, first light, we're taking down that goddamn cross," he said to the hapless Mino while he enjoyed a late night pipe. "Best I can see is that religious symbolism gets you into nothing but trouble."

"No shit," Mino agreed, nodding his head vigorously, but Hooley doubted that he had any idea what he was talking about.

3

THE FOLLOWING WEEK six new cowboys showed up to eat supper, drink themselves into a stupor, then find a cot for the night. They were new drovers for Rancher McPherson, who was hiring every able-bodied man he could find. Rancher McPherson was an Englishman, they averred, a man who brooked no nonsense and had little patience with impediments to his announced objective, which, they went on, was to fence in every square foot of his property. They claimed that he stated that since the open range was no longer a viable prospect, he intended to keep every blade of grass and every drop of water on his holdings completely to himself.

"The Cattleman's Association ain't too happy with him," a snaggle-toothed and terminally happy cowboy named Plunk announced. "But there ain't one hell of a lot they can do." Eventually, Hooley learned, the rancher planned to run purebred English cattle on his land, and he didn't want them inbreeding with maverick scrubs and the like. "So we got us a job of work ahead of us," Plunk concluded. "We got to round up every wild cow on the holdings and see to it that the place is cleared out for these fancy bovines."

"They won't work no way," another one of the cowboys, a slight blond boy named Jake, opined. "Texas fever'll drop them like flies soon's they get here. But I guess that's not my beeswax."

An old disturbing thought hit Hooley. He waved his arms around. "Just how much of all this belongs to Rancher McPherson?"

None knew. "It'll all be measured out sooner or later, once he gets the damn bobwire strung round it," Jake said. "But that'll be a spell. Right now, he's doing the south sections. I reckon there's a year or more's work there. He's one rich son of a bitch, though."

"He's spunky, too," Plunk offered. "Sets a toothhold on something or other and won't let go of her till she's chewed raw or eat up."

"That's likely what happened to his old lady," Jake opined. "That woman's so mean, she'd bald sheep on sight." The other boys exchanged looks that indicated a consensus.

Rancher McPherson had also built a new headquarters over in the southwest section, which meant that nearly thirty cowboys would be stopping by the camp for rest and a cooked meal.

"Surely not all at once!" Hooley exclaimed.

"Naw," Jake said. "He don't like us all bunched up. Says it might lead to mutiny. He tells us to keep moving and to find our needs as we can."

Others noted that Pease City still offered goods and services at a company rate, and they avowed that Cherokee Charlie was still cheating everybody who came by. He had hired an Indian woman who, they suspected, would service any of them for a dollar. But Hank and his pards had steered their friends to Hooley and Mino's encampment. "There ain't nothing like home cooking and warm hospitality, and you got plenty of both."

" 'Sides," Jake opined, "this is the place to be. Good food. Good liquor. And a clean place in out of the wind for the night." Hooley was as flattered as he was pleased and immediately decided to up his rates to a full dollar a night.

Jake inspected the stock Hooley kept in the corral, then inquired about the fine-looking dun mare. The marshal's mount had improved rapidly once freed of the bagged head and swarm of flies, to say nothing of the burden of the marshal's considerable weight. Another drover with the unlikely name of Algernon Chatsworth offered to buy her, but Hooley was unwilling to sell. Chatsworth seemed nettled by the refusal. "You'll change your mind," he said darkly. "I'll have that horse." He seldom spoke directly to Hooley after that.

Hank and the regulars returned that night, and Mino was moved to bring out his squeezebox and entertain them all with sad, romantic ballads he sang in his strange, foreign tongue. Soon the cowboys were singing along, though none knew what any of the words meant. Some were even weeping when the tunes turned sentimental in tone, and Hooley once more indulged himself in the warm feeling of paternity he often sensed in himself when he was surrounded by these young, idealistic men who had the whole world to explore but who apparently found nothing so pleasing as to sit around Hooley's fire and share one another's company.

HOOLIAN

1

AUTUMN DEEPENED, THE cool morning air lasting longer each day, and the men began to talk seriously of colder weather. Hooley had no idea how harsh a winter might be in such climes, but the cowboys spoke of heavy winds and high snow, and they had run out of firewood.

Hooley considered asking Heinz to freight in fuel, but Hank doubted that would be wise. "He'll have to go too far and he'd charge you for cutting and the hauling. Be high dollar."

Then Hank offered the alternative of burning cow chips. "Old-timers used to use buffalo chips," the youngster explained. "But the buff is all gone now. Cow chips ought to do as good."

Hooley had doubts, but he commissioned some cowboys to gather and pile up huge commodities of sun-dried manure. He discovered that it burned slowly and very well. There was a prodigious stench, but the men learned to build their fires downwind so that it was not so obnoxious. What firewood they had, they saved for cooking meals.

A passable bathhouse was also rigged up, with the aid of some galvanized rubber hose and a contraption called a bilge pump that Mino somehow successfully described to Heinz. The cost of a bath was set at the handsome sum of two dollars. Anytime anybody wanted to bathe, Hooley or Mino went to the well and worked the pump while the other heated the water in a large cauldron on the open fire. It was a lot of work and sapped

Hooley's energy, so he raised the price to three dollars, unless the bather had a partner who would take a turn at the pump. Few took advantage of the savings.

Heinz also began bringing letters for the cowboys, but before he could leave them legally, he claimed, they needed to name the town and apply for a postal office to service it. Hooley was stumped for a name, because all he knew was that the encampment sat on a man named Rancher McPherson's property. Heinz pointed out that wouldn't quite satisfy the federal authorities.

"Federal authorities?" Hooley asked. His mind raced to the unmarked graves up on the flats, and a quick twinge of panic gripped him.

"Yeah. They're getting sticky about who carries the mail and what happens to it," Heinz explained. "Lots of folks mail money and jewels and such, and when it don't get where it's going, you can reckon on who they're apt to blame. You got to call this place something."

"Anything around here have a name?" he asked Heinz, who was now fond of staying overnight and indulging himself in a healthy portion of the liquor that he hauled to fill Hooley's orders.

"Not so's anybody could tell," the driver said.

"What about that creek?" Hooley asked hopefully. "Most waterways have some name."

Heinz spat and gazed down into the cedar-filled breaks. "That ain't no 'waterway.' Hell, it's just barely a spring and a ditch, truth to tell. Never heard nobody call it nothing. Fact is, I didn't know it was here till you set your road agents on me and forced me here at gunpoint."

"They're not road agents," Hooley said. "They're cowhands."

Heinz drank deeply from the bottle, and belched. "That's the onliest time that ever happened to me. In all those years' service to the company," he said, "the onliest time. But, I guess we got to call this place something. Can't have no postal office without a name."

"Hooley," Mino said. Hooley gaped at him.

"Hooley?" Heinz said. "What the hell kind of name is Hooley?

"My name, goddamnit," Hooley said, stunned that Mino had spoken his name. "What the hell's wrong with it?" He thought suddenly of his mother for some reason, which irked him.

"It ain't no name for a town is all," Heinz opined. "Now maybe Hooleyville, or Hooleyburg, or something like that." He raised a hip from his recumbence and broke wind. "Maybe you could name it after your sweetie. You got a sweetie?"

"No," Hooley mumbled, distracted by Mino's articulation. What else could the man say?

"Well, then you ever *had* a sweetie? Or maybe one of them Chinese manwhores? You don't look like a fancy dan, though."

"No," Hooley bristled. "I was married. Once."

"What was her name?"

"None of your goddamn business," Hooley shot with a quick thought of Ruthie, the first he had had in a long time. "I wouldn't name a town after her, anyway. Maybe a gyp sink or a glory hole." He didn't want to think about Ruthie anymore. Or of his mother.

"Women," Heinz said sadly. "Best thing about this place is that there ain't no women around to spoil things."

"I thought you were married," Hooley said.

"I am. Sort of."

"Well, what's *her* name?" Hooley asked, enjoying Heinz's wince.

"We don't get along too good," Heinz admitted darkly. "That's why I like to come out here. I don't want no recollection of her out here."

"What's her name?" Hooley demanded, enjoying the teamster's squirming.

"Ann. Her name is Ann. But—"

"Ann," Mino repeated. "Hooley Ann."

"What?" Hooley demanded. Mino was a fount of intelligible words this evening.

"Ann. Hooleyann!" Mino said, pointing at the breaks for some reason. "Hooleyann."

"What the hell. Takes the goddamn rag off the bush," Heinz growled. "Good a name as any, and it'll remind me of why I like to come out here every time I make the trip."

"That's ridiculous," Hooley said.

"Well, it's better than just plain old Hooley."

"No shit, Gil Hooley," Mino said with a mischievous grin.

"Just how much English *do* you understand?" Hooley demanded of Mino. But whatever store of vocabulary the large carpenter owned remained his secret, and when Heinz returned, the letters he brought were addressed to Hoolian, Texas. "This is the highest degree of imbecility I've seen yet," Hooley raged. He'd gotten used to the town having his name in its title, but now that was spoiled. "Christ Almighty! They didn't even spell the first part right!"

"They got a kick out of it in Jacksboro," Heinz said.

"Well, we're not going to keep it."

But they did. The cowboys allowed that they liked the name, particularly after Chatsworth reminded them that it sounded like "Hooleyhan," a horseman's catch-up loop. Then Jake's sweetheart wrote to say that it sounded "as lyrical as any setting in one of Miss Jane Austen's romances." The young drovers all vowed to return on a more regular basis, now that they could send and receive letters from their sweethearts, mothers, and sisters in a place with such a sweet-sounding name.

2

WINTER CAME, STAYED a short time, then left. It turned out to be a mild one, with only a few days of light snow and ice, and spotty, frigid rain and sleet born on howling winds that were punctuated by short gray days that truly were harder to bear than the precipitation. On bad days, there wasn't much for Hooley to do but sit in his tent, read, smoke, and sew canvas tarpaulins to cover Mino's unused lumber. He had no idea how Mino amused himself on these blustery, gray afternoons. Business fell off so much that whole days would pass without them seeing one another except when they emerged from time to time to add fuel to the fire or met once a day to eat a meal. Even then, they only exchanged mute greetings, munched their food in sober silence, then parted.

One icy night in March, just after a heavy sleet storm threatened to deaden the tiny town's main fire forever, a party of riders arrived out of the darkness. They appeared to have been traveling for days without rest. Each of them was covered in a mantle of ice, hat brims tugged low against the frigid night. Hooley, who had just stoked up to the fire and was thinking of cooking up some bacon and cornmeal mush to stay off the chill, was startled by their sudden and stealthy appearance.

The company emerged silently and then sat without speaking. Their dark, heavily bearded faces wore no expression. Hooley stood planted where he was, staring back at them in the gloomy light. For a moment, he thought they might be ghosts—though he didn't believe in such—so still were they and so quiet. Finally, one of their number kicked his horse forward and raised a gloved hand in a casual salute to the tentmaker.

"Captain Brent Ellis," he said, "of the Texas Rangers. Frontier Battalion B Company. It's a frosty night. Be obliged if we could thaw a mite by your fire."

In the light of the flames, Hooley spied the famous five-pointed star pinned on the speaker's overcoat, snapped his mouth closed, and nodded. He had always been fascinated by dime novel stories of the famous frontier police force, and was now overawed and honored by their actual presence. "Step down," he said. "I was about to make up some bacon and mush, and I can warm up some beans, if you're of a mind to eat."

"Just coffee," Ellis said. "We'll be moving on directly." He dismounted and led his horse over to a hitching post Mino had fashioned. The others followed his example.

"Sure you won't stay the night?" Hooley was prepared to give them the cots free of charge, as no one else was using them and he expected no customers on this bleak night.

"Nope," Ellis replied. A short, one-eyed, left-handed man, he accepted a cup of coffee from Hooley. It was fresh, nearly boiling, but the Ranger drank deeply and supervised the other men as they rein-hobbled their mounts and loosened their cinches.

The Rangers each accepted a blistering-hot cup. Their clothing was frozen. As it melted in the fire's warmth, puddles of water formed beneath them. Hooley quickly ground up and boiled more coffee and made the rounds, keeping each cup topped off, accepting the Rangers' silent nods of appreciation without comment. Hooley studied the lawmen with growing disappointment. These men were far from the mental picture of Texas Rangers he had imagined, a far cry from the dashing knights of the frontier he had always believed them to be. Grim and taciturn, they spoke in gruff, vulgar cadences. Greasy, high-crowned, wide-brimmed hats, many with tattered brims and holes, shadowed dark expressions. Rather than the sleek, handsome, clean-shaven, nattily dressed, fast-on-the-draw heroes of pulp fiction Hooley had read of, this ragtag collection of scruffy, bandy-legged, unwashed men might have been taken for road agents or bushwhackers if not for the bright badges pinned to their sheepskin coats. Squatting by the fire, they bristled with guns and knives and reeked of sweat, leather, and tobacco, which they liberally shared, the chewing variety being the most popular.

Their manner thawed along with their clothing, and they began moving around, speaking among themselves, freely exchanging comments about killing outlaws, renegade savage Indians, Mexican *banditos,* cattle and horse thieves, or anyone else who got in their way, particularly if he wasn't white. As a group, they seemed self-contained, and they generally ignored Hooley and Mino as if they were no more a part of the scene than the wind or warming fire.

"I've long admired the reputation of the Texas Rangers," Hooley offered, trying to draw out the nobility he believed was hidden beneath the crusty exteriors. "You always get your man."

"We always get *some* man," one replied as he accepted a refill. His front teeth were missing, and he had a large hole in his cheek; Hooley could see his tongue working his tobacco plug through it. "We ain't paid to just ride around out here and use up good horses."

"It's all in how you use them, Coltrain," another shouted. "You'd as

soon fuck a filly as ride one!" They all laughed in gruff, growling response
to the gibe.

Hooley again offered hot food and the cots, but they again refused bed
and nourishment, as well as the liquor. Captain Ellis soon grew restless
and began wandering about, studying the tented structures surrounding
the encampment.

"What do you call this place?" he asked at last.

Hooley hesitated, then swallowed. "Hoolian," he said. It was the first
time he'd spoken the name aloud. It still sounded silly to him.

"How long you been here?" Ellis asked. Hooley explained. Ellis nodded
and continued his inspection. "Thought this land belonged to Rancher
McPherson," he said. "Big-time rancher."

A nervous pang shot through Hooley, but he suppressed it and nodded
quickly. "I've heard that, but I've not had the pleasure of his acquaintance."

"From all I hear," one Ranger remarked. "It ain't no pleasure. Goddamn
foreigner."

"I heard he was English," Hooley offered helpfully.

"Scotchman," Ellis said. "Or so I hear. Never put an eyeball on him."
He turned so Hooley could inspect that single orb. "Wants to run foreign
cattle out here, or such is the rumor."

"Never work," Hooley said authoritatively. "I hear Texas fever will drop
them like flies."

Ellis's eye brightened. He looked Hooley up and down. "You a stockman?"

"No. I just—well, I heard that."

"What is it you do?" Ellis asked, a note of contempt sounding in his
voice.

"I'm a tentmaker," Hooley said, a surge of resentment rising. "I made
all of these tents."

"Never heard of such," Ellis said. "You from *back* East?"

Hooley nodded. "St. Louis."

"You might be some kind of anarchist," Ellis observed, causing several
of the men to look up. "Hear there's lots of them *back* East. Might be
coming out here to cause some mischief."

"I am *not* an anarchist," Hooley insisted. "I'm an honest businessman.
I make tents and run this camp for . . . for cowboys. Rancher McPherson's
cowboys, now that you mention it."

"Thought you said you never met him."

"Uh, no," Hooley said. "I'm an independent businessman. The cowboys are just customers of mine. Of ours," he corrected, nodding toward Mino, whom Ellis eyed narrowly.

"Most of them'll soon be regular customers of hell, they keep working for that stingy old coot," one of the Rangers put in. "Hear he still gets a squawk out of the first eagle he ever made."

Another shook his head sadly. "That's one old boy who's riding for a fall."

"Got me a noose that'll break it," another put in, and laughed.

"But the anarchist is right about one thing," the one named Coltrain said with a laugh. "Foreign cattle ain't got a fart's chance in a high wind out here."

"I am *not* an anarchist," Hooley said quietly to Ellis, who continued to study him suspiciously. The comment brought what Hooley imagined passed for a smile from the captain, and he finally broke his survey of the tentmaker and waved his hand, dismissing the subject. Now, he put his good eye on Mino, who was squatting near the fire, gaping at the Rangers.

"He ain't a nigger," Ellis observed. "Is he tetched?"

Hooley was confused. "Uh, no . . . he's a free man so far as I know."

Ellis squinted slightly and cocked his head. "What I mean is, is he loco?"

"Oh!" Hooley said. "No, not at all. I think he's an immigrant of some kind."

The tentmaker realized the error of his choice of words immediately, as men turned their heads to examine Mino, who, suddenly aware that he was the center of attention, rose and looked plaintively at Hooley.

"What kind of immigrant? Ain't a Mescan," one of the men observed. "Too damn big."

"I'm not sure," Hooley said helplessly. "I don't know. He just came up here where I was broken down one day, and we kind of threw in together."

"He's not wanted for anything you know of?" Ellis asked.

"No," Hooley affected a look of deep thought. "He's a good carpenter," he added.

Ellis nodded slowly. "We need more carpenters out here," he said. "But we don't need more immigrants. Lots of anarchists are immigrants, or such is the rumor."

Hooley shrugged. "He's always presented himself to me as an honest man." There was an awkward silence. "He doesn't speak English, so it's hard to tell what he thinks about anything."

Ellis turned abruptly, plucked a lantern from a pole near Hooley's tent, and strode to the corral. When he returned, he inspected the tents, then asked to see ownership papers for the stock. Hooley was nervous as he brought out the ledger, which seemed only partly to satisfy the captain.

"What about that dun mare? Nice-looking horse. Got her a government brand."

"I'm boarding her," Hooley said, masking his nervousness. "The owner's a federal deputy marshal out of Oklahoma Territory. She was doing poorly when he arrived, so he decided to go on without her." That much was true, anyway, Hooley thought.

"It's not wrote down here." Ellis jabbed at the ledger. "And everything else seems to be."

"I'm doing it as a favor, not for fee," Hooley said.

Ellis's single eye studied Hooley's face, then the Ranger nodded. "White of you," he said.

"Are you looking for a stolen horse?" Hooley asked, trying to change the subject.

"Not especially," Ellis said, spitting tobacco expertly into an empty bean can. "But we do what we can whenever we can." He looked at the camp again, and just as Hooley was about to give up and decide that he would say nothing more, Ellis continued. "If we catch somebody, we get to go home. We like to go home early when the weather gets chilly. It's hard on the animals."

He shifted his weight, studied Hooley. "Truth is, we're on the trail of a bunch of bad actors. Fancy themselves to be regulators for the stockmen round hereabouts."

"Don't need no goddamn regulators if they got us," one of the men piped up.

"They been trading what they find," Ellis concluded.

Hooley spoke too quickly. "Is there a law against trading?"

Ellis's eye narrowed. "It is when goods're stolen. Been after them a year. But they're skittish. Can't get close enough to smell them. Given their descriptions, that's surprising."

"Well, I've seen nobody like that around here," Hooley averred.

"Reckon not," Ellis said, pitching his coffee into the fire. "If you had, you'd be dead as a stump. You got lots of stuff for them to steal. And, no offense, but you don't look overly bright."

"I'm bright enough not to be riding around in the dark and cold like a bunch of damn fools," Hooley said. "No offense intended," he added in a near whisper.

Ellis's face solidified into a stony mask. "None taken, but I'd watch my mouth." He thrust the ledger back into Hooley's hands. "Let's go," he said flatly.

Without further words, the Rangers dumped their coffee dregs onto the ground, stacked their cups, then mounted and rode off into the darkness and the north wind.

Hooley regretted his pique. "Come back, anytime," he called after their backs.

"Will. If you're still round hereabouts," Ellis said without looking around. "I wouldn't be, though. Bad place for anarchists."

"I'm *not* an anarchist."

"Thanks for the coffee," Ellis said, raising his hand. Then they were gone into the night.

Hooley stood watching the blackness for a few minutes, the ledger still in his hand. He decided he needed to do something about the dead lawman.

3

THE NEXT DAY, Hooley wrote to the Attorney General of Oklahoma Territory, explaining that a marshal named Craggy Phillips had come by their camp toting the severed head of a man he said was a suicidal outlaw. Hooley explained that for no apparent reason in the world, the lawman went crazy and tried to hang or shoot everyone he met, including Hooley's partner.

"He cracked the skull of an innocent immigrant who speaks no English and had done no harm to anyone," Hooley wrote with a grimace. "This official had lost his mind owing to the spicy nature of food he ate and an infestation of biting flies. He had become a menace to life and limb. Therefore, fearing for my own life as well as the life of my partner, I had no choice but to shoot him to death, there being no other recourse to law and order in these hostile climes."

He decided not to mention the Texas Rangers. After meeting them, he wasn't entirely sure they cared about law and order one way or another, or that the Attorney General of Oklahoma Territory would care about them.

He also noted that he still had Phillips' horse, and he offered to keep it until "someone in authority" could claim it. "I say this to show the good faith of myself and my partner," Hooley concluded, "and to indicate that our disposition of this officer of the law was in no way indicative of our desire for ill-gotten gain, as we are honest businessmen and law-abiding citizens."

Proud of his approximation of what he was sure was the proper phraseology for such a letter, he concluded: "It is my belief and hope you will agree that we acted prudently and within the confines of maintaining the public peace, and I remain at your service." He signed it, "Your obedient servant," with several "etceteras." Then, he noted in a postscript that among the personal effects of the deceased was a "brace of pistols" along with seven dollars and three cents, which were retained to cover the cost of Phillips' burial and the boarding of his horse.

The pistols had become Hooley's pride and joy. Peacemaker Colt's .45s, they were pearl-handled and deeply blued, as nice a pair of firearms as he'd ever seen. They rested comfortably in hand-tooled, silver-studded holsters, riding on a similarly well-made gun belt with silver conches embedded in the leather. Hooley enjoyed wearing them from time to time when no one but Mino was around to see him, and even started practicing with them during the boring winter afternoons. He was no quick draw, but he remained a good shot.

In April, Hooley received a letter back from the Attorney General of Oklahoma Territory saying that his account of things was perfectly in order. "We had numerous bad reports on this particular federal officer," the attorney general explained, "and his expense accounts have long been under scrutiny." Enclosed was an embossed and engraved commendation signed by the Territorial Governor of Oklahoma, congratulating Hooley for taking care of a "renegade lawman" so efficiently. Also enclosed was an acknowledgment of his receipt of the pistols and hard currency as compensation for the "trouble of the marshal's funeral."

Hooley showed the certificate to Mino, who nodded his head as if he could understand it.

"Guess that's the last we'll hear of Craggy Phillips," Hooley remarked.

"No shit, Gil Hooley," Mino replied. "No shit.

REGULATOR II

WHEN JEFFERSON TAY paused to consider the matter, he inwardly confirmed that he was a prudent man not given to self-indulgence. He loved good food, plentiful and well prepared, and he had been known to devour a dinner that would have comfortably satiated four or five ordinary men. But he was a large man, and he was always hungry. He enjoyed a good wine and fine brandy, but he seldom drank to excess. Any willing prostitute who indulged him without calling attention to his girth or advancing age easily satisfied his sexual tastes.

Although Tay had permitted, even encouraged, murder, rape, and torture in his work, he believed himself to be compassionate, even merciful by nature, for he never participated personally in such barbaric displays and merely observed them with objective indifference. During the late war, he developed an understanding of the value of remaining in a position of command from a position where he could observe, direct, and control the events before him. There was no profit, he believed, in becoming so involved in a thing as to lose sight of its purpose. Had he been invited to discuss the matter over a glass of good Madeira or cognac with the few men whose quality he respected, he would have lamented that the circumstances of the past few decades had led him to what many regarded as a disreputable vocation. But he also would have pointed out that even at his worst, he remained a prudent man, one often driven to drastic measures in order to guarantee profitable successes.

Such philosophical musings flitted around the edge of Tay's consciousness as he sat on a large red granite boulder in a pass of the Wichita Mountains of Oklahoma Territory and watched passively while his men laid siege to a combination way station and freight office. The stopover consisted of a stout fieldstone cabin surrounded by multiple corrals, a barn, and several other buildings. The cabin had a grass roof and small windows that doubled as shooting loops, and made a formidable fortress. Reducing it was taking far more time than Tay cared to spend in the area.

Tay lifted a cunning little telescopic spyglass, one of the few items remaining from the previous season's booty, and inspected the gunfight. Manypenny was hunkered down behind an upturned buggy, two lighted torches in his hands. He was waiting for Blasingame, Coolege, and a man named Eubanks—a relation of Coolege's, newly added to the company's complement—to subdue the defenders inside the cabin so he could set the wooden furnishings of the cabin ablaze.

Billows of black smoke from the growing fires in a half-harvested stand of corn and a hay field around the cabin rose into the cloudy spring sky and hung heavily over the scene. Tay looked upward and observed the makings of a large thunderstorm building off to the southwest, beyond the peaks of the stubby granite mountains. Lightning flashed in the boiling, green-black clouds, and coils of light gray worked in and out of the growing mass. He had no desire to be caught in the open in such a storm, so he rose from his perch and mounted his horse. It was time for him to take a personal hand in the activities below, else all could be lost.

There were four men occupying the station when Tay's men swooped down. Initially, it was Tay's idea to take the place at dawn, to come riding out of the morning sun and catch the unsuspecting defenders at breakfast. Plans were interrupted by the blast of a bugle announcing the arrival of an overland stagecoach. Blasingame was for going ahead, but Tay decided against it.

Although he disliked justifying decisions to any subordinate, he had come to rely more on the big blond man, as Coolege and his maternal relative—or whatever Eustace Eubanks was to him—were demonstrably unreliable, and Manypenny did not excite confidence. Tay explained to his deputy that both the driver and his guard were well-armed young men who looked to know their business. For another thing, there were three male passengers aboard the vehicle, and as each disembarked to stretch his legs and walk around, they clearly displayed a number of personal weapons they might well be able to use.

"Two of them look especially frisky, and we don't need to endanger our plans or take unnecessary risks by dealing with a bunch of young sports who might be crack shots," he noted.

Blasingame was not much pleased by the delay, until they saw the driver struggling to off-load a heavy metal box that might possibly contain a commodity of gold or silver coin. Tay considered abandoning the assault on the station and robbing the stage instead. But when the driver and guard resumed their positions on their seats and whistled up the team, he noted that the coach departed without reloading the heavy box.

Of late, Tay had been plagued by the worst fortune he had experienced in his entire career. He and his men seemed to be followed by disasters that had robbed them of most of their profits. The booty they collected from the series of regulatory raids on nesters that season was all collected into two wagons. While they were off scouting one final raid, though, a violent storm blew up, and lightning had apparently struck the parked vehicles, which had been secreted in a remote cedar grove. They returned to find them burned down to the metal hubs. Now, apart from the small bag of silver coins Tay kept in his saddlebags, the company had almost nothing to show for the entire season's work.

Moreover, for some reason, the ranchers who had at one time been enthusiastic about employing Tay to keep their land clear of unwanted homesteaders no longer seemed interested in regulatory services. Some actually ordered him off their property. Several evoked the name of the Texas Rangers as an incentive for Tay to quit the country immediately.

This was disturbing, as Tay's company had heretofore avoided the notice of any Texas lawmen. Now, the famous frontier law force was actively pursuing them. Tay had a grudging respect for the infamous band of constables, and he understood that if they apprehended his group, there was small chance that he would escape a noose. But being hanged by a gang of men no more refined than the prairie trash Tay presently led was most definitely not in his personal plans.

Tay considered doubling back and crossing into Mexico, at least until the Rangers lost interest, but he knew from experience that Mexico was a thoroughly miserable place to be without sufficient funds. They had to recover their losses. So they headed north by west, stopping for a few more raids on isolated settlements and ranches, trying to rebuild their plunder and escape the Rangers' persistently long reach.

The whole situation was annoying. Every time he stopped by a store or trading post to gather news, he learned that the lawmen were still after him. He also learned that the governor had approved a $1,000 reward for his capture. Tay was unaffected by the news. He had a price on his head

in so many places that one more made no difference. Still, they continued
to move northwest, seeking some kind of profit from their enterprise. A
few perfunctory raids yielded some small results and increased Blasingame's collection of bloody scalps, a practice that was becoming a dis-
gusting annoyance to Tay.

They were near Tascosa when Tay's spyglass picked out the Ranger
company behind them. The lawmen moved up their right flank, driving
them north and east, into the badlands and the sandy and uncertain terrain
of the Canadian breaks. There, just as Tay was sure he had given them
the slip by wandering back and forth over a gravelly creek bed, their
overloaded buckboards bogged down in a patch of dry sand. All was lost
as they were forced to abandon their goods and flee across the line into
Oklahoma Territory. Now, the company was growing surly with inactivity
and the constant feeling that they were fleeing an invisible enemy.

Being in Oklahoma Territory was not a pleasant prospect for Tay. He
was no more or less wanted here as anywhere else, but the territory's
posted rewards offered as much as three thousand dollars. The desperation
of men here was higher as well. Many bounty men made Oklahoma Territory home. Everyone was looking for a way to make a pile of money and
leave.

Hence, he brought Eubanks into the company. He was related to Coolege, a cousin or the husband of a cousin or nephew on his mother's side,
or something. Since Bastrop's untimely demise, Coolege had been moody
to the point of sullenness. Tay tolerated the man's impudence only because
there had been no opportunity to replace him. Such operations as they
carried out called for a minimum complement of effectives, and, as a bonus, Eubanks' presence seemed to dull the edge of Coolege's borderline
insubordination.

When Tay reluctantly gave Coolege permission to contact his mother's
cousin—or whatever he was—and enlist him into their service, the portly
regulator sent a wire from a rail depot near Washita and asked Eubanks
to join them at a rendezvous in the Wichita Mountains. He was late arriving, Tay was informed, because it took him two days to find someone
to read the telegram to him.

Tay hoped that the ugly Arkansawyer might prove to be a talisman of
good fortune, but once Eustace L. Eubanks arrived, Tay observed that the
chief difference between him and the late Zeke Bastrop was that Eubanks
seemed to wear more filth on his person, and with greater ease. When he
stood close by, the combination of fetid breath and reeking body odor
caused Tay to wonder how the man's horse stood still with his stinking
form astride him. When they accidentally came across the way station and

the mystery of the large box, however, Eubanks stepped up and proved his worth to Tay's satisfaction. For one thing, he was intensely familiar with Oklahoma Territory, where he had plied a solo outlaw trade for years.

"This here's a crossroads," Eubanks explained. His teeth were black with rot, and one eye persisted in gazing directly at the other. "The stage likely come from the railhead over to Muskogee." He focused his crossed eyes on the eastern horizon as if he could see the distant town. "That road yonder," Eubanks continued, pointing a grimy finger toward the south, "runs from down round Hobart all the way up to Cement."

"Cement," Tay corrected, noting that Eubanks pronounced the word, "Sea-ment."

"No, *Sea-ment*," Eubanks insisted. "Big ol' gypsum mine up yonder. They make plaster and such. Got 'em a payroll to meet, and I reckon that that box down yonder is their wages. Another coach'll be long directly. Local out of Hobart. Takes the money up to Cement."

Tay looked at Eubanks without showing the admiration he felt for the man's acumen. Small and stocky, Eubanks wore a thick brown beard, and from the neck of his collarless shirt a nest of curly hair sponged upward to his neck. When he removed his hat, he revealed a completely bald head circled by a thin line of greasy curls. His pate had been creased by what looked ominously like the trail of a bullet wound, a deep furrow that ran from just above his hatband line all the way over to the precise middle of the crown of his skull.

"Reckon we ought to waylay the next coach, then?" Blasingame asked.

"No," Tay said. "We require supplies, and there are saddle mounts down there we can employ." He peered at the compound through his glass. "I still see no weapons handy. But there will be an amendment: We shall delay until noon, then mount a frontal assault." He instructed Manypenny to make torches, which delighted the rodentlike man, and he put a petulant Coolege to work watering their horses at a spring about a mile away.

The attack had not gone smoothly. Manypenny began by trying to pick off one of the men with his long rifle, but he missed with every shot. This gave the alarm, and no sooner had the rest of Tay's men spurred their horses forward into the attack than the five men below had filled their hands with shotguns and rifles and retreated to their cabin, from where they mounted a blistering fire. Indeed, Tay thought, his men were lucky to find cover before they were gunned down.

That had been more than an hour before, and the time had once again come to act. Tay watched one more exchange of fire, then mounted his brindle, and worked his massive hips into a comfortable position. He glanced down to satisfy himself that the shots coming from the cabin were diminishing, although none of his men were showing any particular surge of aggression. Fire had now spread to the roof of the cabin. He spurred the horse forward and drew his saber.

Blasingame was hunched behind a water trough, using his unique weapon to suppress shooting from the two tiny windows on his side of the cabin. Coolege was typically emptying his pistol and a rifle as quickly as he could and without discernible effect, then frantically reloading, taking no time to aim when he repeated the wasteful action. Eubanks was picking his targets more carefully, but with no visible success.

Tay walked his horse down a zigzag course down to the edge of the small barn adjacent to the central structure. He paused to light his pipe, then pointed his saber toward Coolege. "Mr. Coolege," he shouted. "I believe the time has come to make an assault." Coolege looked up, stunned to see Tay sitting on his horse only twenty yards away.

"Jesus, Tay!" Coolege exclaimed. "You scared hell out of me!"

"A storm is approaching, and we don't want to be caught here in bad weather." Tay waved his saber toward the forbidding sky overhead. "It would be more practical to go ahead and rush the cabin before it burns to the ground."

"Well, just what the hell you think I'm *trying* to do?" Coolege shot back. He raised up and plastered the side of the cabin with lead but failed to score even one hit on the remaining panes of the small window. A half-dozen shots were returned immediately, splintering the overturned buggy in answer to Coolege's fusillade. "Goddamn!" Coolege cried out. "Them boys can shoot!" He started jamming more cartridges into his rifle.

"Remain calm, Mr. Coolege," Tay said sharply, then added sarcastically, "Be certain not to allow your weapon to overheat. I'll see what assistance I can find for you. In the meantime, be so kind as to suppress that fire so I can cross the yard with a measure of safety."

Coolege gaped at Tay, then finally stood up and began firing once more, now taking his time and putting some lead through the shattered window. Tay pushed the brindle forward to Eubanks' position. "I suggest we demonstrate on this flank with some expedition," he said.

"What?" Eubanks looked up at him. "What'd you say?"

"Charge the cabin, if you will."

"You're loco crazy!" Eubanks shouted. "Man could get kilt doing that."

"Please don't require me to reiterate," Tay shouted. "Mr. Blasingame, Mr. Manypenny! Shall we essay forth?"

"What the hell's he talking about?" Eubanks demanded. "Talk English, damn it!"

Blasingame didn't hesitate, though. He rose and blasted the house with both barrels of his unique weapon, reloading as he ran. Manypenny scrambled to his feet, a torch in each hand, and charged the burning structure, although to what end Tay couldn't imagine. The roof was already afire, and the main need at the moment was to recover the strongbox and any ammunition or valuables inside. Eubanks watched his two comrades move forward, then he too came to his feet when Coolege began shooting once more. Tay spun his horse and placed the reins in his teeth, as he had learned to do so long ago. He pulled one of his pistols and galloped hard toward a window where he saw a bright yellow muzzle flash from the smoke. He fired four times at the flash and was sure he saw the shadow of a figure collapse behind the dark swirls.

In seconds, his two men mashed themselves against the house's stone walls. Coolege finally saw what was happening and raced forward, firing and ratcheting his weapon. Tay rode his stallion back and forth, careful not to expose himself broadside to the small window. Finally, return fire from inside the house ceased, and the men leaned hard against the cabin and gulped air. Smoke poured freely from inside the structure, and flames licked their way through the space between the roof and walls.

"Mr. Coolege," Tay gasped, surprised to find himself out of breath. "I think we should all be gratified if you would be kind enough to fetch out that strongbox before it incinerates."

"Get it yourself," Coolege shot back. "Goddamn it! We could of been kilt charging up here like a bunch of idjits."

Thunder loud as a cannonade suddenly snapped overhead. Tay looked up into the boiling clouds above them, then returned his gaze to Coolege. The small, dirty man's rifle hung useless at his side, and his chest heaved with the effort of breathing the muggy air. "Mr. Coolege," Tay said, "I have suffered your insolence for as long as I intend to. I order you to enter that house and retrieve that strongbox. If you refuse again, I will cut you down like the mongrel you are and with no more expenditure of conscience than if you were less." He glanced at Blasingame, who had trained his piece on Coolege. Manypenny had wandered off and was happily setting fire to the barn. Another clap of thunder shattered the air.

"Ain't no call to get all riled up," Eubanks said in a heavy pant. "Great day in the morning! You two squabble worse than preachers at a banker's funeral." He stepped up to the door and kicked it. The barrier was stouter than he had anticipated, and his boot rebounded, flinging him backward into the dirt.

"Oh, hell!" Coolege shouted. "Let me do it, goddamn it." He pushed Eubanks aside, then stepped back and placed a hard kick directly on the door. It failed to give.

"Must have a bar on the inside," Eubanks said. He pulled himself up and went toward one of the windows to peer through the swirling smoke.

Coolege kicked the door again, cursed, and spluttered at his ineffectiveness. "Goddamn thing's like a rock," he said.

"Oh, hell!" Eubanks suddenly yelled. "Oh, hell!" He flung himself away from the cabin, running as hard as he could across the compound. "Run, you sons of bitches!"

Tay sat his horse in stunned amazement. Blasingame began backing away from the cabin, his weapon up and ready, his eyes slanting this way and that.

"Mr. Eubanks," Tay called toward the fleeing Arkansawyer, who flung himself down behind a water trough some fifty yards away. "Would you please make a coherent report?"

Coolege kicked the door one more time. Just as his foot made contact and splintered the door lock, forcing the heavy wooden barrier to give, lightning flashed and another clap of thunder rolled down the rocky passes of the mountains. At the same instant, the entire cabin exploded in a cloud of dust and rock.

Tay's horse reared and started falling. From the corner of his eye, he witnessed the upper half of Coolege's body sailing past him. Then Tay felt something hot strike his leg and he was tumbling backward. He saw the black toes of his boots crossing the lightning-streaked, gray-green clouds overhead. His only thought was that he hoped he didn't fall on his sword.

BOOK TWO

Margot

THE WIDOW

ONE BRIGHT JUNE morning, a young woman arrived on Heinz's freighter. Hooley's attention was immediately arrested and held by this unprecedented vision of feminine beauty. It had been well over a year since he had so much as laid eyes on a woman, and then it had only been the disheveled and dusty passengers aboard Heinz's purloined stagecoach. He had been too flustered at the time to take serious notice of female guests.

As Heinz drew his team to a halt, Hooley stepped forward and studied her closely. She wore a black dress trimmed in white, and had a pert gray bonnet on her head. She kept her hands in her lap and stared straight ahead until Heinz applied the brake, spat, and sat for a moment in sulking silence. She then casually removed her gloves and, upon spying Hooley's approach to help her down, extended long delicate fingers toward him. Her touch was soft and ran through his body like a lightning bolt, but she neither smiled nor spoke to him while he obliged her.

Once she was alighted, he assessed her to be taller than average, redheaded, buxom, and lightly freckled. Beneath the bonnet, he saw deep green eyes, white, straight teeth, and clear skin unadorned by face paint or powder. He judged her to be about twenty years old, and also guessed that beneath the rustling fabric of her dress she had well-shaped shoulders and strong arms.

Hooley discovered that it was hard not to stare at her, harder still to find anything intelligent to say. "Welcome," he stammered, when he at last found his tongue. She gave him a quick appraising glance, then looked around at the collection of tents as if he had disappeared. "I'm Gilbert Hooley," he said, moving slightly from one side to the other to keep himself in her line of sight. "I'm the proprietor of this—this camp."

She allowed her eyes to pass quickly over his face as she continued her visual inspection of the area. "My name is Margot Phillips," she said. "I've come to see my husband's grave." She gave him a quick, direct look. "Have you any accommodation suitable for a lady's privacy?"

Hooley blinked stupidly. "Uh, well . . . ," he said, glancing at the cots inside the hotel tent.

"I need to make repairs to my toilet," she clarified. Behind her, Heinz snorted, and her eyes flickered briefly. "I require privacy."

"Oh!" Hooley exclaimed, now understanding her meaning and pointing. "There's uh . . . a facility down there. I think it's what you have in mind." He felt himself grow hot beneath his beard. She seemed not to notice. With a brief nod of her head, she brushed by him and made straight for the privy, her small sharp heels ringing on Mino's boardwalk.

Hooley stepped back to watch her walk away. Confusion and shock gave way to fright, and for a moment he considered telling her that he had no idea what husband or grave she was talking about. But before he could stew over the problem, a noise startled him, and he turned to find that Heinz had dumped off a large trunk and a heavy valise along with the goods Hooley had ordered. He was apparently preparing to leave without delay.

"I got me a new customer," the teamster announced. "Rancher McPherson. He's made a contract to supply a line station down toward the salt breaks, and I got the run. Beans, coffee, tobacco, and bacon mostly, but his missus is ordering all kinds of fripperies for the ranch house she's making him build. You never seen the like of junk she's bringing out of St. Louis. But to me, it's hard money, so I best get started. You got orders, hand them over pronto."

"What about her?" Hooley called, glancing over his shoulder. He noted that her bonnet was hanging on a coat peg outside the privy's tent-flap door. "You can't just leave her here!"

"Hell I can't!" Heinz called over his rattling team. "She's bossy. And I done had a bellyful of her. Women are just panthers for trouble, tell you that! And that's the bitch-kitty of 'em all right yonder." He cracked a whip over his mules. "Never mind the orders. I got a notion of what you'll need. Two weeks, more or less," he shouted, and he was gone before Hooley even had time to think of any extraordinary merchandise he and Mino might have wanted.

Margot Phillips emerged and looked around dubiously before strolling back toward Hooley. He watched her walking, stopping to inspect this or that as she came. She carried herself well and with confidence, but there was also a fragility about her, something that invited amiability and, Hooley discovered, aroused within him a warm sensation. There seemed to be no choice but to make the best of the situation, and in spite of her moribund errand, he couldn't help but embrace the prospect of passing some time in the company of a beautiful young woman.

Hooley found a stool for her to sit on upwind of the fire, then put some coffee on to boil. She sat watching him while he searched for a clean cup. "We're not used to female company," he muttered. "Fact is, we're not used to company at all. Most of our visitors are customers."

"Customers?" she asked as she accepted the coffee, flicked a morsel of soil from the edge of the cup, sipped it, then scowled down into it.

"Cowboys mostly," Hooley explained. "Though they prefer to be called 'cowpunchers.' Come here to sleep, eat, have a drink now and then."

"I see," she said, wrinkling her brow. "Do they actually 'punch' the cattle? Are they pugilists of some sort?" Hooley tried to decide if she was being humorous. With no sign of a smile, she sniffed the coffee again, then put it down. "I guess you wonder why I'm here."

"You said—"

"Read this," she said. She reached down into the bodice of her dress, her long fingers parting her cleavage and passing between the freckled tops of her breasts. Hooley blinked. His head went light. His eyes followed her fingers, and he was instantly aroused. A sudden inner warmth spread rapidly and hollowed his entire body with a long-dormant lustful hunger.

She seemed insensitive to his stare. Her eyes fixed evenly on his face as she extracted a folded paper that proved to be a letter from the Attorney General of Oklahoma Territory, informing her of the details of her husband's death. "My experience has been that stupidity is not positively counteracted by political achievement," she said. "Indeed, I've observed that it's apt to grow prodigiously and in negative ratio to status." She gestured toward the paper Hooley still held in his hand. He made note of her vocabulary and of the fact that it seemed to match her handsome, bold demeanor. He scanned the letter again, then looked into her deep green eyes.

"That particular idiot is no longer the territorial attorney general," she continued. "He has been replaced by an even less intelligent individual of greater incompetence but with a higher capacity for avoiding meaningful accomplishment." She offered a sweet but ironic smile.

Hooley could only stare at her, unable to decide what to say.

"Who, may I ask, is that?" she asked, pointing past Hooley. He turned to find Mino standing frozen and staring at her as if she were a two-legged mule. He had been fishing, and a string of crappie hung forgotten in his hand. His trousers were wet and muddy to the knee.

"This is Mino," Hooley cleared his throat and said. "Or that's the name I've given him. He's an immigrant of some kind. Doesn't speak English."

"So few do," she said with a bright smile and flutter of her eyelashes for Mino, who blushed so deeply Hooley feared he might spontaneously combust. She then blessed Hooley with a smile and flutter of his own. The hot spot that had developed inside Hooley grew like a thunderhead on a summer afternoon.

It had been a long time since his last visit to the mulatto whores. In his travels, he had observed shaded glances of young girls, daughters and even wives of farmers. Often he saw them, barefoot and shy, sneaking peeks at him from around the corners of barns or trunks of trees, their hair hanging down on milky shoulders barely covered with dresses homemade from flour sacks. Their faces offered warm, willing smiles beneath upturned noses and sultry eyes.

Hooley was never insensitive to the possibilities residing in a soft sweet time of coupling with these robust rural lasses. But he was also alive to the risky consequences of indulging himself, and he was aware of the presence of sharp farm implements hanging in toolsheds and stables, of loaded shotguns displayed over household hearths, and of the quick tempers of the men who saw themselves as the protectors, the veritable owners of these rustic virginal sirens.

Additionally, he suspected that engaging in such pleasures would require an inordinate amount of application, and he lacked the ambition to follow the road of courtship, even for form's sake. As a widower, he buried such inclinations deep, suppressing them by forcing sour memories of Ruthie into the front of his mind. Now, however, his lust broke through and blossomed into a preternatural heat that threatened to consume him as he basked under the soft gaze of this beautiful young widow.

"Your situation reminds me of that suggested by the work of Mr. Daniel Defoe," she commented with a nod toward Mino. "He must be akin to Robinson Crusoe's Man Friday."

Hooley had no idea what she was talking about. He knew of a work of that title, but his mother had forbidden such reading in her household, deeming "French writers" such as Defoe and Trollope to be "filthy" and beneath contempt. She once threatened to burn every book in the house except the Bible, which she averred was written by "honest Englishmen."

Hooley swallowed hard. Margot Phillips smiled coyly, as if she could read his thoughts. She sniffed her coffee, frowned at it once more. "I wouldn't use this to cure tapeworm," she said.

Hooley was stung by the criticism. "I've never had any complaints before," he said.

"I doubt you'd have any tea,"she replied wistfully.

Hooley shook his head. "Not much call for it around here."

"No," she said with a sad shake of her head. "I suppose not."

Mino ultimately found the courage to break his statuelike stance and approach, and after Hooley performed a series of gestured explanations, the men escorted the lady out to show her the now completely obscured final resting place of Craggy Phillips, Deputy United States Marshal. The trio stood together for a while in silence over the blank ground. Hooley tried to sort out his feelings. A mixture of guilt and fear churned in his stomach, but at the same time, he couldn't regret what he had done in Mino's defense.

He remembered the Rangers, but he also had the paper from the now former Attorney General of Oklahoma Territory absolving him of culpability. Still, the Rangers might not want to read it, especially since the politician who sent it was no longer in office. He stared down at his dusty shoe tops, then stared at the gravesite in reverential silence, and gradually began to wonder if they were in the right spot. He had trouble remembering on which side of Mino's partner they had chosen to plant Craggy Phillips' body, and months of passage of animal and human feet had obliterated any trace of either interment. The longer he stood there, the more convinced he became that they were a good twenty-five yards off the mark.

"Piles," Margo said quietly and after a space of time had passed. "Craggy always suffered from piles when he went down too close to Mexico. Said it was the food. Too peppery."

Hooley nodded. "His last words were of you," he offered. That was mostly true, he thought. She nodded and pushed a perfumed handkerchief to her pretty nose, and Hooley felt the hollow hunger of lust once more spreading through his entire body.

This is *not* appropriate, Hooley silently lectured himself, embarrassed by the powerful urges raging through him. But as he looked at this gentle young woman, he conceded that Craggy Phillips had been right on one count, anyway: She *was* "a toothsome little thing." The word Hooley preferred, though, was "comely." She filled his mind and distracted him out of reason, pushing aside any qualms of guilt that tried to gain purchase.

It was all he could do to keep from reaching out and putting a comfort-ing—or confining—arm around her creamy shoulders, drawing her to him, kissing her. He was very nearly addled by the prospect and felt himself wanting to swoon.

Abruptly, Margot drew his thoughts back to ground when she asked to be left alone. Abashed by their lack of graciousness—and by his feelings of raw lust—Hooley led Mino away, but after they had strolled off a space, he stopped and looked over his shoulder. He saw her raise her skirts, squat down above the putative gravesite, and pee all over it.

Hooley was so shocked, he nearly stumbled into Mino. He regained his balance quickly and kept moving, breathing rapidly and feeling another flush of heat emanating from his chest. His mouth felt uncommonly dry and his mind was reeling, and all he could think to do was keep pace with Mino.

"That's a sight," he gasped, jerking his finger over his shoulder.

Mino turned, looked, then grinned. "No shit, Gil Hooley."

2

MARGOT DID NOT return to the camp directly, and Hooley was afraid she might become lost. The sun had begun to set when she appeared, her dress covered with stickerburrs and goatheads. She came up and wordlessly sat down, then spent her time picking tiny prongs off herself. Hooley fried fish and heated beans. When they finished eating, she sat back on her stool and sighed. "You think you might have a sip of bitters for a poor widow in mourning?" she asked.

Hooley practically leaped for the small shed where he kept his liquor, found a bottle, and poured a dollop into a cup, which Margot received with a grateful glance and sipped delicately. Hooley joined her with a cup of whiskey, and he drew Mino a beer from a keg. For a while, they sat once more in silence, Hooley and Mino smoking, sipping their drinks, staring into the fire.

"There's nothing for the widow of a lawman to do," she said at last with another bosom-heaving sigh. "No honest man'll have me now. I'm spoiled forever."

The now familiar fire in Hooley's groin began to kindle once more, but he put a new match to his pipe and said nothing. What did she mean, talking like this? Here she was, miles from anywhere, in a camp with two strange men, one of whom had shot her husband through the eye—something she obviously was unaware of, Hooley hoped—and she was flirting with them like a saloon girl. He tried to ignore her penetrating looks, but he couldn't help himself. Every glance he gave her quickly dropped and focused on the deep and freckled valley between the tops of her breasts.

Margot seemed insensitive to his gaze. She offered her soft stare from beneath her thick lashes, occasionally licked her lips, shifted her limbs under her skirt. No thought of occasional flirtations with farm girls or manufactured images of Ruthie could find a point of intrusion. He was almost beside himself with anxiety.

Margot sipped her drink, sighed one more time, causing her bosom to rise and fall deliciously, then continued as if she hadn't paused for the silent coquettish interlude. "Besides," she said, "I'm destitute. All we had was the house the territorial government let us live in while Craggy was a lawman. Now that's gone. Everything I own is in those traps and cases. I only came here to collect his horse. I hope that will be worth something."

She bowed her head, removed her bonnet, and unpinned her hair, allowing it to fall down across her shoulders in a rich red cascade. A tear crept into one green eye, slid down her freckled cheek, dropped into the light dusting of freckles, and rolled down to the soft cavern between her breasts. "I have nowhere to go," she sobbed.

Hooley leaned forward, his breath short. He swallowed hard, delved deep into himself to summon fortitude. "You can stay here," he said in a small, choked voice. "We ain't got much to offer, but you're welcome to share it." Mino nodded as if he could understand the words. He doubtless caught the sentiment. Both of them waited in bated silence for her reply.

"Thank you," she said, perking up and looking around quickly. The tears disappeared at once, and she flicked her hair back over her long white neck. Her face hardened slightly, and now Hooley saw something else in her countenance, something that unnerved him even more than his overwhelming attraction, but in a different way.

"What's the name of this place?" she asked.

"Hoolian," Hooley replied softly. "It's named for me."

"Not much of a place," she said. "Not much of a name, either."

"No shit, Gil Hooley," Mino muttered.

Hooley shot him an annoyed look. The soft sponginess that had dominated his insides suddenly ossified. "It's where we are. And that's what it's called."

She looked around once more, her eyes sharpening in a critical focus. "Seems to me you could use a woman's hand around here."

Hooley stared at the breasts bulging out of the fabric of her bodice and again into her face, which was different now, harder, but no less attractive. He assessed her evenly, then decided. "What we need," he said quietly, "is a whore."

In the silence that followed the remark, he felt his heart thundering inside him, anticipating her reaction. Her eyes met his directly, and her mouth partly slightly. He braced himself for an explosion of outrage, indignation, anger. But nothing was said for a long moment. She shifted a blank gaze toward Mino, then toward Hooley, and finally fluttered her eyes and smiled in a way that brought back Hooley's warming excitement in a enthusiastic reprise.

"I'll think on it," she said.

3

THE WIDOW MARGOT Phillips stayed in Hoolian to become a whore. It would take some time to adjust to the idea, she explained. She revealed that the occupation was not entirely new to her, but it had been a while since she had worked for her living and she needed to ease back into it. "I don't want to leap into anything without giving it substantial thought and planning," she said. "And there's the matter of practical preparation as well."

That announcement inspired enough anxiety in Hooley to drive him almost out of his wits. It had been his idea that she would, if compliant, remain for a few weeks, perhaps, and provide him with the carnal satisfaction his desires demanded so long as his desires demanded it, and that then she would move on. She took his invitation differently, though. To his shock and no little consternation, she clearly was implying that she would remain there indefinitely and go to work as a full-time, professional prostitute. That she had experience in the occupation shocked Hooley as much as anything else she had said or done since arriving. But he was discovering that everything she said and did was utterly impossible to anticipate. He decided that she was the most outrageous woman he had ever met—saving, of course, his mother, whose ability to surprise him had ended while he was a mere child.

Margot took stock of Hooley's reaction and explained. "I don't want you to get the wrong idea. I was reared up in a moral and upright household. But it didn't take entirely. Craggy Phillips found me working in a fancy house in Arkansas. He took a shine to me, married me, and took me to Oklahoma Territory. I was only seventeen. I'd only been a working girl for about a month, and I didn't like it much," she said, then frowned. "To be honest, though, I preferred it to being a lawman's wife in Oklahoma Territory."

In spite of Marshal Craggy Phillips' worries about roving bachelors, she insisted she remained faithful while he was away from home, which was a great deal of the time. "I didn't want for chances, mind you," she said with a coy smile. Hooley silently admitted the possibility of that. "But the truth is that only a prodigious idiot would try to take advantage of a lawman's woman." She sighed. "Especially Craggy Phillips' woman. I've never had much interest in idiotic men."

Hooley found this declaration curious, since in his view, Craggy Phillips had been about as close to pure walking idiocy as any human being he had ever encountered. He also was one of the ugliest people God ever suffered to live, Hooley thought, with a hurried wonder that any man so grotesquely limited in intelligence and appearance could woo such a lovely woman, even if she had been a whore. But he kept these thoughts to himself. He also kept quiet about the specific circumstances of the lawman's death or who his undertaker had been. Since the day at the gravesite, Margot had not mentioned her husband's untimely demise, which was fine by Hooley.

She was, though, candidly outspoken about other things: Marshal Craggy Phillips' sexual prowess, for example. Insofar as it was reputed, she averred, it was exaggerated. "Had a big old peter," she told Hooley with a shocking straightforwardness that caused the tentmaker to blush deeply. "But it seemed to surprise him when it got angry. Never knew quite what to make of it or how to use it. Always shot from the hip, if you know what I mean." Hooley knew. Just thinking about her loaded him up and made him want to shoot any way he could. "I never ridiculed him for it, though, or for anything. Maybe that's why he liked me," she concluded. "I always tried to give a man the respect he thinks he's due. Unless, of course, he's mean. A mean man is one thing I will not tolerate for any amount of comfort."

An anxious week passed before she allowed, over a hunk of roasted rabbit and plate of wild asparagus that she thought Hooley was an intelligent and a kind man. She added that she liked his looks. "You're not well educated, but you have the air of a gentleman about you," she said. "And you're not unhandsome, in a plain sort of way."

That flattered him. He was slight in the chest, but he had strong arms and nimble fingers. Though never vain, Hooley had always taken natural pride in his dark hair and deep brown eyes. Flecks of gray now appeared in his stringy beard and lengthy locks, though, and several of his teeth had been paining him of late. He also discovered that he had to squint sometimes to make sure of the consistency of smaller stitches. He was middle-aged and getting older, but Margot made him feel young again. "I'm no athlete," he said modestly, "but I try to stay healthy."

"Good health is a sign of a good mind," Margot observed idly. "But cleanliness is next to godliness. Or so I've always believed. I cannot abide a man who stinks. He might be diseased."

The comment inspired Hooley to begin sprucing himself up every evening. He trimmed his hair and cut off his beard and took to shaving twice a week, bathing as often as he could persuade Mino to man the bilge pump, and powdering himself with baking soda to quell body odor until such time as he could order Heinz to bring him some aromatic hair tonics and colognes. He did not fail to notice that the brawny and barrel-chested Mino did the same in his own fashion, except for bathing, which Hooley had never known him to do. The carpenter trimmed his thick, curly beard, began washing his heavy overalls and flannel shirts regularly, and appeared for supper with well-scrubbed hands. He also managed to reek of bay rum, although Hooley never saw a bottle of the exquisite toilet water in his possession.

Margot never remarked on the physical changes in the men. She accepted their solicitous attentions in a ladylike fashion, always dividing her flirtatious looks and seductive smiles equally between them, always keeping both jumping with an eagerness to please her and obtain a gratuitous comment. Hooley finally decided that her entire story was a ruse, that she had no intention of copulating with him—or with anyone.

When he was apart from her, he felt himself to be the world's greatest fool. He remembered the way Ruthie—and his father—had played him for a fool, and he vowed that Margot Phillips would not repeat the insult. But when he was near her, he found himself gazing on her with a heady mixture of lust and admiration. She virtually made his head swim with her seductive beauty. Her merely shifting her legs beneath her skirt or leaning over to pick up a coffee cup excited him to distraction. He discovered that studying a mental picture of her slender fingers or velvety throat could occupy his mind so completely that he might cut himself while chopping up vegetables or burn his fingers with a match he forgot to extinguish after lighting his pipe.

Nearly two weeks went by with him writhing miserably on his cot, yearning for the utterly desirable woman who slept in a small but well-made tent he and Mino had constructed for her away from the fire. He longed to broach the subject with her, to ask her when she planned on making good on her decision—if it wasn't an outright promise—but he couldn't find the courage.

Then, one night when the full moon painted the empty prairie in silvery light and the coyotes sang a raucous chorus, Margot surprised Hooley by entering his tent, where she stood in a satin gown backlit by the moonlight. He blinked to make certain he wasn't dreaming. Without a word and with only the slightest of movements, she loosened the string at the top of the gown and allowed it to fall, and then she was there, standing naked before him.

Silently, fearful that any utterance might frighten her away, he threw back his blanket, and she came to his cot and slipped in beside him. Although he had ached for nothing else in the world since the day she arrived, when she appeared, he was too gratified to speak—almost afraid to move as she snuggled next to him. She also was silent and only made small, purring noises as she nestled herself into his arms and began to run her long fingers across his skin and to kiss his hairless chest with a light, almost airy bussing. What followed was so sweet, so memorable, that he could hardly believe he hadn't imagined it.

She returned three nights in a row—each more delightful than the one before—then she stopped.

Late into the morning of the fourth day, Hooley lay on his lonely cot and stewed over the matter. He decided that she must have forsaken him and gone to Mino, and a pique of jealousy suddenly warred with a measure of satisfaction that she had come to him first. Now, though, he worried if she would ever return. What if she liked the big foreign carpenter more? Mino was obviously younger, and manlier in appearance. If that carried through to his sexual performance, then she might never return to the gentler and sweeter caresses of a lowly, aging tentmaker.

But if Mino had been with her, he made no obvious sign when Hooley finally came out into the late morning sun. As was their habit, the three of them sat in silence, sipped coffee and chewed their breakfasts, each seemingly lost in thoughts. He studied Mino and Margot for signs of a shared secret, but neither offered any, which frustrated Hooley all the more, made him feel left out of some conspiracy building against him. But then, he realized, neither he nor Margot had given any indication to Mino that they had enjoyed one another's carnal company either. That placated him for the time being, although a mild case of his dyspepsia returned when he contemplated the matter fully, something that he did with increasing vigor over the next two days.

After three nights' absence, she returned to his bed without a word about why she might have forsaken him. In fact, she came as before, with no word at all. She merely appeared, disrobed, then slid in beside him and began making love to him as if she had never been away. Three nights later, she was gone again. A pattern had been established, Hooley decided. And there was nothing he could do about it.

4

AS SUMMER WORE on, all three went about their daily chores and openly pretended that none had any special knowledge of another. Margot undertook to wash the tin dishes, but she refused to do any cooking, so Hooley and Mino took turns, although the majority of the meals fell to the tentmaker's responsibility. Although he disliked the chore, he didn't complain and worked hard to please her. It was difficult for Hooley to squelch such feelings as he had for the charms of the redheaded vixen whose affections and attentions he and his partner now apparently divided between them. He did object to the sharing, but he had no idea how he could alter things, could push Mino out of the way and claim her entirely for himself. Apart from the difficulty of discussing the matter across the abyss of their language barrier, Hooley had no idea how he could ever convince the burly carpenter to relinquish his rights anyway.

The situation ultimately seemed to settle itself. When she was in the company of both men, Margot meted out her attentions equally and never permitted either to touch her in any way that would spark any ire. Finally, Hooley convinced himself that the arrangement was fair—and it neatly avoided trouble between him and his strange partner. Even so, he often lay awake, nettled and uncomfortable, when she was not beside him, worrying that problems would eventually develop between him and Mino if his partner ever demanded a greater share of Margot's time.

Hooley discovered her prohibitions in an embarrassing way. One evening while they collected the tin plates and cups for washing after supper, he unconsciously put his hand on her forearm in a gesture of affection.

She stepped away and glared at him. "Release me!" she barked. Hooley jerked back as if he had touched something red-hot. "I will *not* permit public familiarity."

"I was only . . ." He was hot with mortification and fumbled with his words, but she tossed her head and continued to gather up the dirty dishes. He wanted to ask her what was "public" about where they were—not even Mino was nearby—but before he could ask, she was on the attack.

"I know what I've been, and what I am to become once more. But I'll not have you or any man treating me cheaply. I have my pride." She took a deep breath that made her bosom swell, then lectured him with a wagging finger. "You are never to paw at me as if I'm a dumb animal with no thought in the world but to satisfy your barbaric cravings. I will *not* tolerate it."

Hooley was hurt and frustrated. She aroused a hunger in him that he'd never known, but she always seemed to keep him off balance and on guard. He feared offending her even more than he resented the vexation she caused him. But at bottom, he was afraid that if he said or did the wrong thing, she might never come to his cot again. That, he thought, he could not bear.

At the same time, Hooley discovered that having Margot around was also entertaining in ways that began altering their lifestyle and enhancing it in a manner he had never imagined. Almost every night after supper, Mino played his squeezebox and sang lively tunes, and Hooley put aside his former objections to dancing and gave Margot a spin on the dusty ground around the large fire they kept burning at the center of the "town." When Mino wanted a turn, Hooley sang unaccompanied as best he could, often lacing the lyrics of ballads and folk songs with ribald words and phrases, prompting Margot to affect demur blushes before laughing out loud and flashing her slender ankles as she whirled around in Mino's arms.

Hooley came to love her laughter. But more than the bright smile and shining eyes and lovely mane of red hair that she often wore loose and flowing around her soft shoulders, he loved making love to her. She was the most beautiful woman he had ever imagined being with. Her body, to him, was a miracle of discovery and delight, one he never tired of contemplating when he was denied the privilege of exploring it physically. But the recollected fantasy of her naked self was never a match for the actual experience, and he delighted in discovering her revealed beauty in the flesh more than anything he had ever experienced in his life.

As he had first observed, she had long, graceful fingers, with sharply pointed nails that she kept filed with a cunning little silver rasp. She had slim dainty feet, but her legs and arms were strong and well muscled. Although once freed of the corset and stays her breasts were revealed to be modest in size, they were full, dotted with freckles and fronted by small, button-sized nipples that hardened immediately to his touch. Her belly was flat, with a protruding navel that excited him out of common sense, and he loved to wind strands of her deep red thatch of pubic hair around his nimble fingers. The mere thought of any part of her naked body caused him exquisite discomfort, wherever he happened to be. Often, he would discover himself sitting alone in his tent, his stitching forgotten on his lap, his mind filled with her white-skinned beauty, his body aching for her touch, his whole being hungering for her with a ravenous yearning that he had never before in his life imagined.

In Margo's long, strong arms, Hooley discovered the pleasures of lying with a beautiful young woman who demanded nothing from him, not even conversation. After they made love, he would often prop himself up on one elbow and in the narrow light of a moonbeam quietly look at her, immodestly naked beside him. He would run his hands up and down her skin, allowing the pads of his fingers merely to brush lightly over her features, bringing gooseflesh, which he would kiss back to smoothness. Then their eyes would meet, and unspoken feelings would seem to pass between them and caused them both to shudder with a passion that led to tight embrace and the hot wet heat of raw emotion. Some nights they merely cuddled, giggling like children who had found a secret amusement to play with, their eyes dancing in one another's reflection and the pleasure of uninhibited coupling.

He wondered if he was falling in love with her. Then he thought of Mino and decided that would be a truly stupid thing to do. Where there was love, he recalled from his reading of Shakespeare and even the Scriptures, there was anger, jealousy, eventually vengeance and death. But he couldn't help what he felt. Moreover, he thought, that, given his previous experience with Ruthie and the whores in St. Louis, he wasn't entirely certain what love was, what it felt like.

All he knew was that he was miserable whenever he was away from Margot—a misery exacerbated by his observation that she didn't seem to care whether she was near him or not—and he was especially miserable when he knew she was with Mino. His stomach was constantly in turmoil, moving from aching in utter revolt to growling with a hunger food couldn't satisfy.

He thought of telling her what he felt, derailing the plan she had to become a whore in their tiny community, offering even to marry her if that's what it would take. What held him in check, though, and reminded him of her intentions was her utter refusal to let him kiss her on the mouth, an admonition which always came, much to his dismay, accentuated by the sharpness of her tongue.

"Whores don't kiss," she said, pushing his face away from hers. "Kissing is for lovers. And a whore can never be a lover. I'm just getting back in practice so I can pay my own way. I won't be beholden to you or any man ever again."

Margot needed no practice, Hooley thought. In spite of her caveats about Craggy Phillips' sexual abilities, she was no stranger to carnal congress, and Hooley found himself learning things from her that he doubted even the mulatto whores in St. Louis could imagine. And each lesson stimulated him to yearn for more instruction—as much, he suspected, as it moved her closer and closer to a point when she would have no more need of rehearsal.

What Mino's approach to making love to Margot might have been did not enter Hooley's mind. To him, Mino was a big, happy clown. Trying to imagine him rolling around with Margot, touching her alabaster skin with his large, callused hands, was beyond Hooley's imagination. And even after several weeks of shared passion had passed, they did not "discuss" her—insofar as they could discuss anything—or exchange any gestures or signs or knowing glances.

Hooley pretended not to notice when the two of them would disappear early of an evening on the nights when she was absent from his cot. He also refused to hear the grunting, groaning, slurping laughter that sometimes came from Mino's tent and pretended not to notice the moony calf-eyes that Mino sometimes displayed over supper on the evening his three-day treat with her would commence.

Thus, in spite of his determination not to, Hooley sometimes felt the sharp prick of jealousy, but he forced himself to ignore it, to pretend that nothing was going on between her and Mino that meant anything. "She's a whore," he often reminded himself in an irritable grumble. "Just a whore who needs a place to be. And she will never be beholden to me." And, he thought with grim honesty, it would be dangerous for him to become beholden to her as well.

THE PARTNERS

———◆◈◆———

1

MARGOT COMPLETELY AVOIDED the cowboys whenever they came by. From the time the youths' dusty cloud approached and throughout their boisterous visits, Margot remained closeted in her tent and refused to come out. She even removed all corrupting evidence of her presence and kept her personal things battened down and out of sight.

"I don't want to tempt those boys to overt stupidity," she explained. "Some have been pulling their own peters for so long, they may have forgotten how to do it any other way. They need to be eased into the idea of a woman in the midst. Besides, I've never much enjoyed the company of rural workers. After their business is done, they're apt to get weepy and want mothering."

Hooley didn't complain about her ignorance of the cowboys, and he took a small pride in her assessment of them as ignorant and unsophisticated denizens of the prairie. Even so, he wondered just *who*, when she became a full-time whore, she thought would be her customers. They had no other clientele, and there were small prospects of anyone else happening by.

As for the boys, they were well enough aware of her presence. Once arrived and settled, they would sip their whiskey and cast longing looks at Margot's sealed tent as if it contained some strange creature too frightening to reveal.

As the weeks passed, the boys grew bolder and began asking Hooley about "the widow woman," but Hooley's noncommittal answers discouraged further discussion. He discovered a profound feeling of possessiveness where she was concerned, and he admitted to himself that he would happily continue to trade shelter and food for the unlimited continuation of her company, particularly her nocturnal company. He sensed, though, that she would not be long content to be his personal mistress—or rather, his and Mino's—for she had too independent a nature.

Hooley had known of several men in St. Louis who had "kept women," mistresses they set up in flats or even houses. Many of these gentlemen were married and reputed to be upstanding members of the community. He had encountered these illicit couples strolling down the street, and there was never a tinge of embarrassment or chagrin associated with the practice. But those women were mere girls, naïve and a bit silly, easily lured into their nefarious roles as concubines of wealthy men by the trinkets and gifts their lovers bestowed. Their good looks and fashionable attire made them attractive baubles for the men who supported them. Hooley had never measured much respect for any of them—or for their male keepers. He assessed the women to be mere "pets," playthings for a prosperous man's fancy, mere servants, truly, who were bred to be used and then discarded when their masters grew weary of them or when their attractiveness waned.

He could never imagine Margot in such a role. Her fierceness of temper, balanced against a determination to be taken seriously, set her apart from any other woman. He had trouble seeing her as either mistress *or* whore, and he was developing a profound affection for her that did not jibe with the notion that their union was purely sexual, a kind of business arrangement, the terms of which had never been properly articulated. More to the point, she continually referred to her "period of adjustment" as temporary and spoke of the day she would "go to work" in earnest. So Hooley decided to put the question to her directly and settle matters. He could not continue in this state of emotional limbo forever. It was time for her to declare herself.

To Hooley's enormous relief, she expressed nothing but total contempt at the prospect of bedding one of the hardworking youngsters.

"They're just a bad case of terminal imbecility walking around in boots and spurs," she snapped at him. "Half are looking for a sweetheart, and the other half just want to hurt somebody for making them cowboys. I'm not interested in either proposition. They're just little boys, hopeless as they are helpless. And I'm not prepared to take them by the hand and lead them to manhood," she declared with a finality that discouraged any further broaching of the subject. Hooley believed the matter was settled.

2

IN LATE AUGUST, Margot reversed her position entirely. She emerged one hot morning and asked Hooley if he and Mino didn't think it was about time to enlarge her accommodations. She sketched what she wanted in the ledger book, then paced off dimensions in the dusty ground while Hooley looked on with growing concern. What she had in mind would be ten times larger than her present abode.

"That's a sizable structure," he finally protested.

Margot put her hands on her dainty waist. "Well, of course," she scoffed. "What did you imagine? That I was going to entertain all of those boys in that tiny little tent? I'd die of cramp just trying to move around."

"I didn't think you were going to 'entertain' them at all," he said. "You said—"

"*What* did I say?" she challenged him. He cast into his memory for her exact words. He thought that for once, he had her. "I don't know what you *think* I said," she sniffed. "But I have a vivid memory of what *you* said. You said you wanted a whore. Isn't that the gist of it?"

"Well, yes, but—"

"Well, if you want a whore, then you want a whore*house*. You can't have one without the other, it seems to me."

Hooley surrendered silently. A pang struck his stomach. He stared at the dimensions she had sketched out. "What you're talking about seems more like a warehouse than a whorehouse."

"Don't be an idiot," she said. "Just see what you can do."

Hooley gave in. He indicated to Mino that they should get to work, and the big man happily obliged by measuring and sawing lumber, and soon the structure was framed. Hooley covered it with dyed red canvas he ordered, trading Mino's oxen to Heinz to fund the shipment. Even with Hooley's stitching with an industry uncommon to his nature, the work took several weeks.

As the tent building developed, so did Margot's interest in what she started calling "our enterprise." She inspected every activity in critical detail, changing her mind frequently and insisting that the men comply with her whims. Apart from the personal comforts she offered quietly and freely to Hooley and Mino, though, she made no contribution to their profits and had not broached the subject of the financial part of the venture and how it would be settled. This worried Hooley some, but he decided that since he had handled all the money up to this point, he would continue to be the master of the business end of the operation. Then one evening, to Hooley's astonishment, she demanded to see his ledger.

"Why, whatever for?" he asked before he thought.

"Just fetch it out here," she said and sighed. "I want to take a look at your financial condition."

He started to refuse, but her eyes slanted narrowly when he hesitated, so he followed what had developed into a habit of acquiescence to anything she demanded—quiet surrender was both preferable and safer to his ego than doing useless battle with the redheaded vixen—and brought out the volume. By the light of the campfire, she meticulously went over every entry, biting her lip in thought and muttering comments. She made some corrections in his ciphering and penmanship, then stopped and thoughtfully chewed a fingernail as she studied the balance sheet. Finally, she made a loud exclamation of disgust, slammed the book closed, clasped it to her bosom, stood up, and confronted Hooley with an outraged expression.

"How could you give that stinking Dutchman that much of your profits?" she demanded.

"What Dutchman? He's not a Dutchman." Hooley was bewildered. He thought she was talking about Mino. "Besides, he does more than his fair share—"

"I'm talking about that smelly muleskinner," she interrupted. "Heinz. He's a Dutchman if I ever saw one."

"He's a friend," Hooley protested, offended. He had come to like Heinz and the quality of goods he brought. The bandy-legged teamster was a jovial if somewhat ignorant and profane man, especially after he had a few drinks, and he always was full of news from the East. That he and Margot didn't like one another was plain, but, just as with the cowboys' visits, she secreted herself in her tent when Heinz showed up, and the wagoneer never asked about her. "If it wasn't for him," he continued, "we'd have been dead long ago. He could have left us out here to starve. For that matter, he could have reported us to the Texas Rangers and had us all hanged."

"Texas Rangers," Margot snorted. "Useless as dirt, Craggy Phillips always said. All they do is ride around the country and try to look mean, hunting for easy women and cheap whiskey or some helpless soul to dangle from the nearest limb."

Hooley felt it wise to stay with the subject. "Heinz is a friend and a partner."

"Some partner! He charges you twice what it's worth to freight your orders out here, then rakes off another ten percent when you sell it. *And* he drinks and eats for free when he's here. You probably don't even charge him to stable his mules."

"We don't have a stable," Hooley pointed out. He wondered suddenly what the going rate was for freight in this part of Texas. He'd never questioned Heinz's figures.

Margot sniffed. "If you had one, you probably wouldn't charge him."

"We couldn't survive without him," Hooley argued weakly. He realized that he had made a bad bargain with Heinz, but he didn't see any way out of it now. Besides, they were prospering. Rancher McPherson paid his men in fresh greenbacks, and a good deal of them were in Hooley's cash sack. "He's never let us down."

"Well, he's going to have to start working with us," she said. Her use of the plural pronoun did not escape Hooley's notice. "I'll speak to him," she said with a confirming nod. "I can see you're reluctant to broach the subject. Any way it falls out, we're cutting back, either on his take or on the freight fees."

"He won't like that."

"Too bad," she said, turning her eyes on him and giving them an edge as sharp as a jade knife. "You didn't *sign* anything with him, did you?"

"Sign anything?"

"Like a contract or anything?"

Hooley shook his head. "No, we just shook on it." As a matter of memory, though, he couldn't recall if they'd done even that.

"Good. Then we can negotiate something legal."

"Legal? How do you know so much about all this?"

"My daddy was a circuit court judge in Arkansas," she said with a flip of her chin. "How do you think?" Hooley shook his head. He'd never wondered about Margot's background beyond her experience in the Arkansas cathouse. "I'm a high school graduate," she said proudly. "Or nearly. Before I ran away to become a whore, my schooling was almost done. I never would have married a misanthropic jackanapes such as Craggy Phillips except to spite my daddy, which also is why I took up the soiled trade of fallen women, if you must know."

Her expression softened, and she sighed and looked into the fire. "My daddy was hardheaded. And he never came to get me as I thought he might. I guess he figured when I got tired of being a whore, I'd come home and get married to some slope-chinned, weak-tea idiot he picked out for me, have a flock of children, and grow old before my time." Her eyes flared quickly. "The way I saw it, whoring was whoring, with or without the benefit of clergy." She looked sad, suddenly. "When I sent word I'd run off with Craggy Phillips to the Oklahoma Territory, he wrote back that he never wanted to see me again. And he didn't."

Hooley didn't know what to say.

"He's dead now," she said, "my daddy. But I have all his books. And I read most of them before I had to sell them to raise a few dollars for this trip. You have no idea how hard it is to sell a book in Oklahoma Territory," she said with a sigh.

"Craggy was gone a lot, thank the Lord," she continued, "and I didn't have much else to do *but* read. But Craggy had a lot of expenses from his lawman's work, and I learned to keep ledger books. It's an honorable profession for a woman." She hugged Hooley's ledger tighter to her chest and looked sad. "But it doesn't pay much. And there are only a few men in the world with the gumption to let a woman run things for them."

Hooley nodded. He also remembered that the Oklahoma Territorial Attorney General had not thought much of Craggy Phillips' expense reports and had wondered just how adept—or trustworthy—Margot Phillips was as a bookkeeper.

"It's a handy profession for a whore, too," she noted. "Or for anybody in business. It's clear to me that you need some help, and you're going to get it." She sat down and opened the ledger, holding her pencil poised as if to make an entry. "So, what's my part of our enterprise?"

"Your part?"

"My cut. My part of the deal. You don't think I'm going to work for free, do you? You said you needed a whore, and here I am, almost ready to get down to it." Her eyes narrowed. "I think you know by now that I can shoulder my weight on that end."

Her expression was defiant and proud, and Hooley cast his eyes down, embarrassed. Although he certainly had thought of their time together as some sort of business proposition, in recent weeks he had dismissed the notion. Now, he was abashed to hear her reduce it to that level.

"I'll set my rates," she continued, oblivious to his discomfort, "and I'll throw in my share. But I need to know what I'm going to get out of it."

Hooley hadn't thought about it. In the ledger, he kept one column of figures for income, the other for expenses. At the end of each month, he deducted Heinz's portion and added up profits. He figured that when—and if—Mino and he split up, they'd divide whatever assets they had equally. A three-way split hadn't entered his mind.

"Well," he said, groping for a reasonable assessment, "you know I do the stitching and most of the cooking, and I hunt up meat now and then. Mino does the carpentering and the fishing and all of the heavy work. We both kind of brought something here, and it just fell together." He opened his hands helplessly and looked at her. "I—"

"You wonder what right I have to horn in, since all I brought here was me?"

"Well, yeah," Hooley said softly as he cast his eyes down, thought of her lying next to him, and wondered if he would ever feel her soft skin again. The gift of herself was more than enough, and he suspected that Mino would agree had there been any way to poll him on the question. He had a mental picture of himself grasping for some handle to shut this door she had so abruptly opened. "Yeah. Something like that. But not exactly."

"Well, you shot my husband down like a dog, isn't that right?"

Hooley stood still, breathless. It was the first time she revealed that she knew details of Craggy Phillips' demise. Her words hit him like a hammer in the middle of his chest. He couldn't meet her eyes.

"You didn't know I knew that, did you?"

Hooley was speechless. He shook his head.

"Well, I know. The former Attorney General of Oklahoma Territory and I go way back, you see. He's originally from Arkansas, too. And we knew each other very well, although he was a fool's own idiot." She smiled her coyest smile. "The man did have staying power, though. When he wasn't drinking," she said in a whimsical tone. Then the mask dropped in place again. "Anyhow, that gives me a toehold here. Craggy may have been an ignorant and loudmouthed fool, but he was still a United States Deputy Marshal, and I expect even a bunch of reprobated miscreants such as the Texas Rangers wouldn't take kindly if I were to tell them how you came to shoot him down in cold blood."

Hooley nodded again, fear climbing his spine like a column of red ants. "It wasn't exactly in cold blood," he muttered, but there was no heart in the correction. He was thinking of the Rangers' Captain Ellis. That one-eyed lawman would as soon hang him as piss on his fire.

"So, I'm part of the deal," she concluded. "From the start, it seems to me. We'll work out the rest, starting with that smelly idiot Heinz." She handed the ledger back. "Put that where I can find it—I want to keep a close eye on your figures. You can't add too well, though you're good at subtraction. That shows an inclination for failure in business, if you ask me." Then she gave him a quick, ironic smile and stalked off.

Heinz was right, Hooley decided. She was a panther for trouble. His gut ached horribly, and he sat down with a fresh cup of whiskey, fired his pipe, and contemplated the problem. Mino wandered up, seemed to read his mood, and sat quietly beside him.

"The only thing I'm sure of," Hooley grumbled after a spell of silence, "is that I'll do the dealing with our friend Heinz."

"No shit, Gil Hooley," Mino muttered, oblivious to the sharp look of irritation Hooley gave him.

Mino was getting on his nerves, Hooley decided. Or was it Mino? Margot was puttering around the front of her tent, and he spied the flash of long red hair when it caught the firelight. The yearning he felt for her vied with the jealousy she aroused and the total annoyance her demands and proclamations created in this otherwise tranquil existence. She had stimulated more ambition in him than he ever had in his life, and now that felt like wasted effort. He suddenly wished that he'd never laid eyes on Margot Phillips, or lain down with her, or even talked to her.

"Should have sent her on her way the very moment she got here," he muttered. This time, Mino's reply was only a sagacious nodding of his dark head.

That night, Hooley slept alone. His aching gut kept him tossing and turning until dawn. But the next day, when he saw Margot hanging out her washing on a rope—her husband's old hanging rope—strung between two poles, her face and arms blistered red from lye soap and hot water, her hair tangled wild, her firm figure pushing against her sopping shirt-waist, straining against the wet fabric, Hooley took it all back. He was very glad to have laid eyes on Margot Phillips after all, and he was gratified to know her in the other way as well.

3

HEINZ ARRIVED A few days later with his regular shipment and an uncommonly large grin. Hooley hurried out to intercept the teamster before Margot could.

"I got *no* perishables on this haul for Rancher McPherson's men," Heinz announced gleefully. He was rubbing his hands together in apparent anticipation of a long and luxurious drunk. "*And* I'm a day ahead of schedule. We can have us a good ol' time! Pour us a cup, and let's get started."

"We have business we need to talk over," Hooley said, putting out his hand and stopping the burly driver in his tracks.

Heinz looked quizzically into Hooley's eyes for a beat, then cast a suspicious squint toward Margot's tent. His shoulders sagged. "Ah, hell," he said. "I been dreading this."

As Hooley had dreaded, Heinz balked at any change in the arrangement, but the tentmaker remained firm in a way that only a man who utterly feared the woman behind him could be. Heinz protested that they had a gentleman's agreement, but Hooley, innately understanding that he had more of a chance of winning an argument with the blustering teamster than with the recalcitrant redhead, steadfastly refused to back down. Heinz, though, proved to be equally as stubborn, and tempers boiled over. After a quarter hour of bickering, the two men wound up standing in the dust of the compound and swearing in the heat, fists clenched, teeth bared, about to come to blows. Finally, they reached the end of their arguments and began covering the same ground, only this time at a shouting pitch.

"We done shook on this," Heinz yelled in frustration.

"I'm not sure we did," Hooley replied just as loudly. "And anyway, that's not a legal contract."

"Contract!" Heinz exploded. "Contract?" He brandished his fist. "I'll give you the onliest contract you need to worry about right in the middle of your goddamn nose!"

Margot had remained out of sight, but when Heinz put his fists up in front of his face, squared off, and began to dance around in front of Hooley, she emerged from her tent and rushed over. Hooley resented it, but he had to admit she was shrewd to delay her entrance until Heinz's initial anger had erupted and he resorted to physical threats. He was also relieved. The thought of having to fistfight Heinz was horrifying. Even though he was taller and younger than Heinz, he doubted he would do more than sustain serious injury at the hands of the furious muleskinner.

Before any blow could be landed, Margot came gliding up as if her feet weren't touching the ground. She put herself directly in front of Heinz's flushed face, folded her hands in front of her waist, and shook her head. "You gentlemen will pardon a woman for intruding," she said in a low, reasonable tone, "but I believe we should rehearse the facts and consider them from everyone's point of view."

"Ah, hell. Here we go." Heinz dropped his fists and spat in the dirt. "You might of let me get in a good poke at you before she come out here and stuck her nose into this."

She ignored the remark and in a calm voice pointed out that they had all come to rely on the commerce Heinz provided and that he was making a fair living. "But a fair living is all you deserve, and all you're going to receive," she said. "To take anything more is avaricious."

Heinz's small eyes blinked in confusion. "What's that mean? Are you calling me some kind of name?"

"You take it as you please," she sniffed. "To ask any more than your fair earnings would be outright greed!"

"Greed? What kind of greed is there in wrassling a bunch of mules through the wind and rain all the way out here?

"It hasn't rained in months," Hooley pointed out, but they both ignored him.

She produced a piece of paper. "Here," she said. "This will tell you what you need to know." According to the new deal, Heinz would take two percent of the profits and had to pay for any whiskey he drank. He could continue to charge premium rates for the freight and graze and water his mules without charge. If he stayed overnight, lodging and food were free, and, as a bonus, Hooley would give him the use of his mules on a permanent basis.

Heinz read over the document while his face turned darker and darker. "Why, that's no damn good!" he finally exploded in a spray of tobacco juice. "That's no damn good at all. Hooley here looks forward to my coming, so he can have somebody to drink and chew the fat with."

"That has nothing to do with it."

"It has *everything* to do with it," Heinz protested. "Why you think I come up here? For my health? A man has to have somewhere to go to. You don't know what my wife is like. She hates me and has religion clear up to the neck. Sleeps in a gunnysack to keep herself 'pure for Jesus.' Takes the rag off the goddamn bush, I can tell you! She won't let me out of the house except to work. This is the onliest place I can have a decent little time with a cup of good liquor and a friend to talk to."

"You can still do that," Margot pointed out. "But you'll pay your own way."

Heinz flapped his arms in confusion. He was learning, Hooley noted, that arguing with Margot was one of the least profitable ways to pass time anyone had ever imagined. She always won, he knew from painful experience. Now it was Heinz's turn to be similarly instructed.

The teamster paced, chewing and spitting in a fury. "This was a good place where there wasn't no damn women around to mess things up. Till lately, that is. Things was fine 'fore you showed up, wasn't they, Hooley?"

Hooley's ears took fire with shame. He felt the need to defend Heinz, and he inwardly acknowledged that the teamster was right, after a fashion. But before he could speak, Margot dropped her reasonable pose and punched a long finger into the middle of Heinz's chest.

"It makes no sense under the sun for you to charge us to haul a wagonload of liquor all the way out here and then sit around drinking it," she steamed. "You may as well drink your portion back in Jacksboro. At least you'd start home from here sober and awake. Save wear and tear on your animals, too," she added with a frown. "I never could abide a man who abuses animals the way you do."

"I do *not* abuse my animals!" Heinz shouted, momentarily confused by the sudden shift in her attack. "Do I?" he demanded of his team, who were lazing in the heat and ignoring the raging human argument. He spun around, his eyes blinking rapidly as they moved from Hooley to Margot and back again and he tried to recover the thread of the argument. "I don't know what's going on here, Hooley, but I know I don't have to take no goddamn change in the deal if I'm not a mind to." He looked at Hooley, helplessness in his eyes. Then, all the ire and anger went out of him, and his voice took on a plaintive tone. "Do I, Hooley?"

Hooley was unable to meet Heinz's gaze. He looked away and nodded. His stomach was in turmoil. He wanted to tell Heinz that he didn't have to take anything, and neither did he. But he said nothing. Mostly, he wanted to be far away from this scene, to retreat to his tent and lie down.

"You'll do what that contract says," Margot pointed out. "If you want to keep doing business here."

"And just who the hell else you going to find who's crazy enough to do business here?" he demanded. "Ain't nobody that damn stupid! Nobody!"

"Well, then, that about says it all, doesn't it?" Margot said. "But I'm sure that if we put out the word, someone would see the opportunity to cash in on a thriving enterprise."

She turned to Hooley. "Maybe we could find a Temperance Man. I know of several in Oklahoma Territory who have taken the Pledge and who have enough sense to drive a wagon around the countryside in exchange for lively profits."

Hooley gaped at her. No Temperance Man would haul liquor. "Well, I sort of like Heinz," he said. "I'm used to—"

"This isn't a matter of personal preference, Hooley," Margot said, turning her eyes once more on Heinz. "This is business, plain and simple. If this drunken lout doesn't want to make a living working with us, we'll find someone who will."

"This is *my* run, goddamn it!" Heinz yelled. "I'm the one that started it, and ain't nobody going to take it away from me! It's mine."

"It's yours so long as you sign that contract," Margot said, her voice remaining calm. "It's as simple as can be. Either you're interested in our custom or you're not."

"Well, that takes the rag off the goddamn bush!" Heinz stormed, and in a resurgence of indignation, he wadded up the contract and flung it into the dirt, then slammed his hat down. But when he looked up into Margot's hard green eyes and Hooley's embarrassed shrug, his face showed that he had now learned his lesson insofar as arguing with Margot Phillips was concerned. "Beats anything I ever seen in the name of the blue-eyed Jesus," he muttered. "Letting a woman run rough over the whole damn thing."

"You can take it or ride out," Margot said, lowering her tone again. "I'm sure we will have no problem finding some other damn fool to come out here and get drunk now and then."

"Hooley?" Heinz made one last pathetic appeal. "You going to let her get away with this?" But Hooley averted his eyes and concentrated on the river of sweat running down his back.

"Take it or leave it," Margot said. "I mean it." She looked over her shoulder at Hooley. "*We* mean it."

After a few moments of steaming silence, Heinz lowered his eyes to his boots and nodded. "Takes the rag off the bush," he muttered.

She went over the arrangement again, and Heinz put up a show of fuss about every point. Each time, he threatened to quit and appealed to Hooley, but Hooley meekly backed his female partner. It was humiliating, but there wasn't much they could do short of tying her up, putting her in the rear of the wagon, and hauling her back to where she came from. Briefly, Hooley contemplated that prospect with wistful and malicious desire, then he looked at Margot, receding from her high dudgeon and softening back into the woman he had come to know, and he realized that he could never sacrifice her so easily. That recognition made the humiliation no easier to swallow. She was a hard woman. And she was in complete control.

Later, Hooley and Heinz drank themselves into a shameful stupor. The driver left the next morning with the contract folded in his pocket and his pride stuffed down behind a wall of sulking silence. Hooley worried that he might never come again, but he made the next run, and before long he even stopped complaining about it overmuch.

Soon profits were growing and they were all prospering, not as friends or as lovers, but certainly as partners.

THE WHORE

1

MARGOT'S DIRECT INVOLVEMENT with the business of Hoolian did not stop with the new arrangements she forced upon Heinz. One warm early October morning while they broke their fasts with leftover cornbread, canned tomatoes, and bacon, she suggested that Hooley start extending credit to the cowboys.

"That's crazy," Hooley replied. Some nights, there were as many as two dozen cowboys sleeping off heavy food and drink, and there had been more than one wrangle over how much one or another of them owed when he left. Hooley had threatened to stop serving the dithering Underwood several times when the skinny young cowboy had imbibed more than he could handle and then refused to pay the proper amount. "Half of them are too drunk to pay most of the time," Hooley finished with a sigh, sensing that he was about to enter another dispute he would lose. No matter how hard he tried, he could not muster enough energy to defeat Margot in a contest of wit.

"A cowboy is basically honest," Margot insisted. "He's too ignorant to know there's not much you can do to him if he doesn't pay. I mean, he's already a cowboy. There's nothing worse than that, except maybe a lawman. Besides, when he gets a little jack in his jeans, he'd rather spend it all at once, then run up another big bill while he's feeling prosperous. When he comes in again, you can collect while he's sober."

Hooley explained that one of the boys' complaints had been about Rancher McPherson's habit of crediting the cowboys, then deducting their charges from their pay.

"That's different," she argued. "This will put the responsibility on each man. They'll be too ashamed not to pay up when they ride in again. You can trust a cowboy." She nodded and made her red curls bob in confirmation of her point. "It's not the same with a lawman, though," she added after taking thought. "Can't trust a lawman to spit straight."

"I'm still afraid we might drive them away," Hooley protested.

"Nonsense," Margot scoffed. "Where would they go other than that hog wallow, Pease City? Besides, we have other things to offer."

"Like what?" Hooley inquired. The only possible advantage he could see in their coming here was that the cots were clean and the food was decent. Hooley had discovered a grudging talent for preparing meals, but given the constant variety in their diet, a result of having to rely on whatever could be found or killed, he thought of it more as an ability to invent than cook.

"What do we offer that Pease City doesn't?" he asked, seeking any chink he could find in her rhetorical armor.

Margot didn't answer him. Instead, she straightened her skirts and changed the subject, one of her more annoying habits. "Autumn's passing," she said with a glance at the blank, blue sky. "Guess it's time I started earning my keep." She took a deep breath, making her bosom swell, then stretched her arms high over her head, linked her fingers, and made her knuckles crack. "I'm ready to go to work."

Hooley was imagining what she would look like striking the same pose naked and was working up the courage to ask her to do just that, since Mino was off fishing and they were, for once, alone in the daylight. When she spoke, though, he felt a sudden profound sadness come over him. And he admitted that she was right. If she was going to be a whore, now was a good time to start. With the change of season, the days would grow shorter, and the cowboys would be there longer and more often. The time was ripe to make some hard currency to see them through the bleak days of winter. Much as he hated to see her share her favors with the young men, he was resigned. She had announced her intention, and he knew her better than to try to talk her out of it.

Besides, he reluctantly admitted, her availability would ensure the cowboys' business. No matter what Pease City had to offer, Margot would be a draw.

The next day, Heinz arrived. It was a windy, warm Indian summer day. Dust flew everywhere when the freighter clanked up to the tent city, which now announced itself to be "Hoolian" by a big sign Margot had painted and had Mino nail up on the old doubletree. Hooley emerged from his tent and approached the teamster with a broad grin. He looked forward to smoking his pipe and sipping whiskey while the crusty driver related news of the East and tales of doings back in Jacksboro.

His plans were quickly interdicted. Instead of going inside her tent as she usually did when Heinz hove into the settlement, Margot stepped out and fell into pace beside Hooley. As they marched toward Heinz's wagon, she slitted her eyes and rolled her shoulders, as if she were preparing herself for battle. Hooley's apprehension quickly grew into dread. He lacked the ambition to endure another fight between her and Heinz. He wished she would just turn around and retreat. In the meantime, Margot's mouth took on a square shape of resolution, and he reckoned another storm was brewing and about to break over the peace of the tiny community. It was as inevitable as tomorrow's sunrise.

They reached the bandy-legged muleskinner as he alighted and turned to face them, a look of sour disappointment on his face when he observed her presence. He looked quickly at Hooley, then back to Margot. "Ah, hell. What now?" he asked, and spat in the dust.

Margot wordlessly extracted a folded piece of paper from her bodice and presented it to him. Heinz's dirty finger opened the paper, and he began reading it aloud. It was an order for a half-dozen fancy frocks, face paint, powder, and curling irons, two pairs of high-button shoes, two pairs of satin slippers, dancing pumps, and a collection of shawls, stockings, garters, petticoats, girdles, and silk bloomers. Also included were specific toiletry and makeup items, including several bottles of perfume ordered from a shop in Chicago.

"Any word there you don't understand?" she sarcastically demanded as Heinz continued his squinting examination of the list.

"This is a lot of stuff," Heinz muttered, scratching his tobacco-stained beard. "Got to have hard cash to front it."

Since the renegotiation of their deal, he had been particularly hostile toward women in general and Margot in particular. Although he seldom complained about the specifics, he waxed philosophical about the evils of what he called "the female species."

"Never knew anything that worked right when a female was involved," he would say sadly. "This used to be a lively place. Now that a woman's here, she'll be the death of us. Bet your britches."

Although Heinz's pronouncements always annoyed Hooley and created a slight stirring of anger in defense of his female partner, he always listened

to the teamster without comment. At the same time, he always felt a flush
of shame come over him for not standing more firmly beside his friend in
the face of Margot's demands. But the tentmaker considered that there
might be more to Heinz's animosity than the loss of money.

Heinz was no fool, and he wasn't blind. Hooley had explained the purpose of the large red tent, and he made no secret of Margot's future role.
Heinz could easily guess that Margot was servicing the two partners regularly, although Hooley had never confirmed or denied the fact or, for that
matter, responded at all to Heinz's frequent statement that he could see
no reason why she should not also accommodate him. The teamster finally
put the proposition to her straight, thinking that he had the upper hand
on the grounds of logic and sound mercantile practices.

Margot, though, thought differently, and stated her objections in specific
terms. She told him she would rather sleep with one of his mules than
with the greasy freighter. "They smell better," she said, "but they're not
much smarter. If you took a strap to me the way you do to them, you'd
wind up wearing it."

Heinz's pride was wounded, more by the latter remark than the former.
But he flatly refused to bathe, and Margot declined to take him into her
tent for any consideration whatsoever, even hard money. Hence, their mutual animosity had maintained a steady level of intensity, and Hooley always cringed when they exchanged even the most casual nod of
recognition. He knew that an eruption of anger was likely from either or
both with the slightest provocation.

This time, though, her direct approach to the teamster surprised
Hooley. As in everything she did, Hooley observed, she calculated her
actions to keep everyone off guard.

Heinz's squinting eyes reviewed the list. "This stuff costs real money,"
he repeated. "Who here's got that kind of geddes?"

Hooley saw Margot's face turn red. It was the first time he'd seen her
flustered.

"He does." She pointed at Hooley. "He's advancing it against my part
of the enterprise."

Hooley rocked back on his heels. He didn't mind doing that—had long
ago resigned himself to giving her anything she asked for—but she blind-
sided him with this. The canvas bag stuffed with folding money and coins
beneath his cot had become an anchor of security. His face must have
shown it, for Margo's eyes narrowed while Heinz's broadened into an "I
told you so" look.

"You will, won't you?" she demanded.

"I . . . uh . . ." Hooley trailed off and looked at the sky, searching for some way to assure her he would without losing face in front of the teamster.

Heinz was doing a poor job of hiding a smirk. "Got you hog-tied and ready for the knife," he said. "You'll be howling like a cut shoat, time I make my next run."

Hooley continued to blink and search for something to say.

Margot walked around in a tight circle, then stopped, her hands on her waist, facing Hooley. "Very well, then. I still own that dun mare, don't I?"

Hooley nodded dumbly. Mino, who finished off-loading their supplies and was observing everything closely and with his customary silence, also gave Hooley a dark, questioning look.

"Well, you keep her to back the loan," she continued. "If I don't pay you off in six months, she's yours."

Hooley was too abashed to look her in the eye. The mare wouldn't bring half of what Margot would owe on the order, and both she and Heinz knew it. "Bring the goods," he ordered Heinz in a flat tone. Then he quickly went into his tent and brought out the large canvas sack. He counted out almost all the specie he had and placed it in Heinz's fat palm. "Bring anything else she wants. If that's not enough, put it on my bill. She lives here, and she's part of the business. Full partner."

"What's that make me?" Heinz asked with a wink at Hooley.

"The village idiot," Margot snapped.

Heinz shook his head. "Beats anything I've ever seen in the name of the blue-eyed Jesus. Let a woman run you like this."

"Just bring the goddamn goods," Hooley said, his anger rising. "You got the money."

Mino looked confused as his eyes shot from man to man to Margot. He seemed to enjoy Heinz's visits and listened intently to his stories, although Hooley doubted that he understood a single word. Now, the big man stopped and studied the trio with a suspicious look on his face.

Heinz continued to grumble about the "wily ways of women," but he stuffed the money into a leather pouch. "If you come up short, I intend to take it out in trade," he warned Hooley, glancing at Margot.

"Not without a bath you won't," Margot shot back. "I can smell you coming a week before you get here."

"I done told you, I don't take no bath for no two-bit whore," Heinz declared.

Hooley's hand—fleshy, soft, and unused to hard work as it was—made a fist and jammed itself directly onto Heinz's nose. The burly teamster stumbled backward, his eyes wide in shock, and sat down hard in the dust. He started to rise, but Mino stepped forward, work-worn fists doubled up, muscles straining his flannel shirtsleeves, his bearded mouth stretched into a fierce snarl. "No shit!" he said in a menacing tone.

Heinz looked up in astonishment. "What the hell—"

Hooley had acted without thinking, but now, anger bubbled inside him. His knuckles stung. Blood ran from Heinz's nostrils. His nose was flat as a cow patty on his sunburned face. "She's not a two-bit whore," Hooley said.

"Not yet I'm not," Margot said proudly. "Not till you fill that order I'm not." She paced off a few feet and glared at him. "And you can count on the fact that I'll cost a good deal more than two bits even then!"

"You're all a bunch of damn fools," Heinz spluttered. "All three of you!" His voice was flat and sounded funny. His fingers massaged his face and came away bloody. "Goddamn, Hooley. You broke my nose! I thought you were my friend."

"I *am* your friend," Hooley said, still awash with rage. "That's why I didn't kill you."

"You're still a damn fool," Heinz repeated. He staggered to his feet. Blood ran over his mouth, saturated his beard. "Get me something to stop this bleeding, goddamnit."

Mino went for a strip of canvas, which he wet in the water while Margot paced, her arms folded in front of her.

"Hell, I don't even use whores," Heinz declared nasally. He puffed out his chest and jammed a thumb into it. "I don't *ever* have to pay for it!"

"What do you do, get them drunk and beat it out of them?" Margot shouted. Hooley saw she was fighting tears. His heart swelled, and he doubled up his fists once more, ready to hit Heinz harder if he insulted her again.

But Heinz didn't rise to the bait. He mopped blood from his beard and shook his head. "You best put a muzzle on your woman, Hooley. I never in all my life heard such talk out of a female's mouth."

"You bring the goods," Hooley said. He glanced at Mino, who nodded vigorously. "I'll take care of my—my woman." Margot spun and stared at him, her eyes wide.

"No shit, Gil Hooley," Mino said, a new, dark threat in his tone.

"I think you'd best go on," Hooley said. "This isn't a good time for a visit."

"Beats anything I ever seen in the name of the blue-eyed Jesus," Heinz muttered again. "I don't feel like drinking with you nohow. Not now. Maybe not never again."

"Those mules'll sprout wings the day you say no to a drink!" Margot hissed at him, and stalked back toward her tent.

Heinz gave her a dark look, then climbed up onto his wagon and shook his head. "The death of all of us," he said, "bet your britches."

A change of heart chased by a panic that he had stepped too far out of bounds with the teamster raced to Hooley's throat. "At least let me cook up something for you to eat," he said.

Heinz shook his head in firm rejection of the offer. "Nope. I need to put a limit on how much time I spend in the hospitality of damn fools." He glared at Margot's tent. "*And* whores," he said, "two-bit or otherwise." He then shouted at his team, whipped them alert, and left.

Hooley helplessly watched Heinz rumble away. He wouldn't get far, he knew. He'd have to stop and let the mules blow for several hours, camp out in the open, eat some jerky or whatever else he might have. He rubbed the bruised knuckles on his hand. As before, when he had shot Craggy Phillips down dead, his anger and what it made him do boosted him. It felt right at the moment. But at the same time, he wondered why he had done it, why he hadn't considered the consequences. He knew why he had killed Craggy Phillips. But hitting Heinz was clear out of the way. Margot *was* a whore, by her own proclamation. That was the deal. He couldn't get excited every time somebody pointed it out. He watched the dust from Heinz's wagon disappear in the gusty, hot afternoon wind and worried that the teamster might not ever return.

No sooner was Heinz out of sight than Margot burst out of her tent, her face flaming as red as her hair, her eyes blazing. "What are you trying to make me out to be?" she fumed. She went to a stack of cooking implements by the fire, returned, and smacked the bewildered Hooley on the arm with a long-handled spoon. Hooley reeled back from her attack as Mino stepped up beside her and tried to throw a comforting arm over her shoulders.

"Get the hell away from me, you big oaf," she yelled, and ground a heel onto his instep. He yowled and jumped back in pain, hopping on one leg.

"I am not 'your woman,' and I am not your private stock of gratification!" she shouted at the pair, brandishing the spoon like a club. "I'm white and I'm of age and I'm an honest widow. I'm educated, and I'm able. I can make my way as well as anybody!"

Hooley reeled back from the heat of her outburst, stunned nearly unconscious by her fury. His words and actions that afternoon had been automatic. He wasn't sure he could sort them out, not in any way that made sense. He had feelings for her, deep feelings, but the idea of her being "his woman" hadn't occurred to him before Heinz had brought it up, used the words. She vexed him terribly, he thought, annoyed him more than Ruthie ever had, but in a different way. If he lived to be a thousand, Hooley thought, he would never understand the ways of women.

"I'm sorry," he said, hanging his head and rubbing his arm to show that she had hurt him. "I didn't mean anything by it. I—"

"You're right, you're sorry," she cried back at him, and turned and fixed Mino with her eyes. "You, too, you Turkish idiot!" Mino shied away, holding his abused foot in both hands and falling backward.

"Turkish?" Hooley asked. "What makes you think he's Turkish?"

"What makes you think he's anything else?" she demanded. She planted her feet and studied them with a snarling sneer. "Both of you are among the sorriest and most idiotic examples of the male gender I have ever seen! I should *never* have come here. I should have gone with the territorial attorney general to Denver and made my way from there."

She took a deep breath and paced, talking rapidly. "But I didn't. I didn't have enough gumption to know what was good for me." Now Hooley saw the tears. They began at the corners of her eyes and streamed down her cheeks. "That's too bad for me. And for you. I'm here, and I'll make my own way no matter what."

She stopped her pacing and pointed at the corral where the marshal's mare stood. "If I don't, that mare's yours, and I hope she rides you to Perdition." She stalked off to her tent, leaving the two confused, abused men staring at each other through her dusty wake.

"No shit, Gilhooley," Mino said sadly.

"Why don't you learn some goddamn English," Hooley shouted at him. Mino hung his head like a scolded puppy. Hooley wondered if Margot was right, if Mino was, indeed, a refugee from some sultan's land. But the thought didn't linger. He went to his tent, found his pipe, and sat smoking hard while he angrily ripped stitches out of a piece of heavy muslin. Although he had never made clothing or tailored any garment before, he had planned to dye it green with cedar fronds, line it with rabbit fur, and make a winter cloak out of it for her. Now there would be no need, he thought, and no appreciation for his efforts.

"Bitches," he growled around the stem of his pipe while he worked. "They're *all* bitches. Twist a man in knots and leave him flopping around on the ground like a gut-shot goose. Wish she *had* gone on to Denver. Or anywhere. Women! Who the hell needs them?"

His stomach was turning over in centrifugal cramps. He clamped his teeth down hard on the pipe stem. "Best be shed of them for once and all." The memory of Ruthie's shrill laughter assaulted his ears. "I knew that once, and forgot, and it's my own damn fault." His fingers failed him, even in destruction of his work, and he flung it aside and sat fuming until full dark.

But later that night, as he lay awake and tried to will his gut to relax, he felt more than heard her slipping through the darkness. She stood beside him as she always did and let her silken garment fall silently to the ground. Then she slid next to him, her nakedness chilled by autumn-cooled prairie air. He slowly ran his hands down her sides and across her belly and made gooseflesh rise beneath his touch. He felt her narrow feet nestling between his, seeking warmth, her long fingers rubbing softly on his skin, her silky lips brushing gently against his chest.

"I'm sorry," he said, but she put her fingers to his lips, shushing him. Her other hand guided his fingers to the thick red patch covering the swell of her mons, and she whimpered with pleasure and pressed herself hard against him. Hooley's solid hostility toward her melted and flowed into a single stream of passion, and while Mino played woefully sad ballads on his concertina outside, Hooley and Margot made the sweetest love they had yet enjoyed.

He did not notice, for he was deep in a snoring sleep, when Mino's deep baritone ceased to outline the caprices of love and when Margot's strong, slender body left his side. But he did notice when he next was making entries in his ledger a curious addition in a floral, feminine hand: "Services Rendered: @2—$2.00/Margot Phillips." She had officially become a whore.

2

MARGOT MOVED FAST to make her more active partnership in the Hoolian enterprise a demonstrated reality. By Christmas, her new place was complete, in spite of occasional howling northers that suspended work and ran the skies gray with thick clouds and biting winds. With Margot providing no small amount of fussy supervision that did little more than annoy Hooley's dyspepsia, the huge tent turned out to be a masterpiece of tented architecture.

Rather than one large room, the structure contained enclosures leading off a central area, each walled with sturdy double-canvas barriers. The bright red muslin was stretched over Mino's heavy frames to form the exterior walls, and the inside was floored with thick hickory planks and tall, well-fitted shin-boards Mino had carefully measured and fitted. The building had more substance than any other construction in the tiny community. It was the largest and most imposing tent Hooley had ever dreamed of erecting. The tentmaker was as amazed by it when it was completed as he was shocked by the effort he'd spent in building it. His father, he thought, would have been speechless with pride.

Margot wasted no time admiring their handiwork. She immediately ordered the pair of artisans to construct a half-dozen beds that would handle the weight of pounding cowboys, then put Hooley to work sewing mattresses to be stuffed with dried prairie grass and had Mino build a bar and a hutch with shelves.

"What do you want that for?" Hooley asked.

"We need a proper saloon," she explained. "It will provide a parlor like a regular fancy house. A place business can be conducted in an efficient way, and where I can keep an eye on things."

"What things?" He was trying to envision Margot's idea of how all this would work. Was she planning to rent space to eight or so cowboys at a time, install them, and then move from one room to the other? His experience in brothels was limited to the whorehouse in St. Louis, where he had been met discreetly at the door by a large Negro butler who took his hat and coat, heard his preferences, then handed him a key to a particular room and wordlessly directed him to the dark stairs. He assumed there were other customers in attendance at the same time, but he never saw any. He couldn't imagine a bordello operating in such an open fashion as Margot proposed. "What do you mean?" Hooley asked.

She gave him an impatient look, then glanced at the crowded kegs and crates of bottles in Hooley's old whiskey shed. "The dispensing of liquor needs to be closely controlled," she noted. "The way you do it, anybody can just get what he wants when he wants it, and when things get busy, you can't keep account of who owes you what. Besides, you drink right along with them, and I'm not confident of your keeping your wits about you."

No one had ever questioned Hooley's ability to hold his liquor. He prided himself on his having the wherewithal to know when his senses were being impaired and to stop imbibing the moment he felt control slipping. He instantly bristled, but she cut off the reaction before it could take full shape.

"We've discussed this before, Hooley," she said. "It's a chancy way to do business."

Hooley put aside his pique and studied his methods and realized that, as usual, she had a point. He merely stacked up the barrels and kegs, bunging a new one when the old one ran dry. Then he used the old ones as stools or chairs or broke them up for firewood. The same applied to the bottled goods, which remained corked in their straw-lined crates until one was required. An empty tobacco can was provided for money and credit slips, and it was hard to tell if a customer had paid properly. For that matter, it would have been hard to tell if anyone might have dipped in and helped himself to a fistful of cash while Hooley was otherwise occupied.

But he was hurt that she automatically included a saloon in her establishment without asking him first. This time, she was going too far. The notion of his standing behind a bar and serving liquor to cowboys who were standing in line waiting their turn to have Margot all to themselves was more than he wanted to bear. He armed himself with a deep breath and roused himself from passive acceptance. He would have to hold his ground.

"I like the way I do it." He folded his arms and struck a stubborn pose. "It's handy. I was doing it this way before you showed up, and I see no reason to change."

She seemed not to notice and instead went right ahead with her gestures, instructing Mino in the dimensions she wanted for the bar by pointing to sections of the drawing, then pacing them off.

"I'm not going to come in there to sell whiskey," he insisted, raising his voice a tone or two. She still ignored him, so he changed tacks. "Is it your notion to try to compete with me?"

She turned and gave him a wry smile. "*Compete* with you? Why, Hooley, we're partners. Don't be stupid. Why would I compete with you?" She dismissed him with a wave of her long fingers, then turned back to him as if she just understood what he was saying. "It's your whiskey and your concern. For the time being, anyway. You sell it any way you want. But I'll have the saloon ready when you decide to see reason and it gets too chilly out here."

"It's been chilly right along," Hooley protested. But she had already blessed him with a bright smile of dismissal and was walking away.

"Damn it to hell," Hooley muttered and kicked the dirt. He had, for once, won an argument, but it was only because she retired the field and left him with no handy adversary. He sensed another bout of dyspepsia. "Damn all women to hell," he muttered. Mino looked at him with a sad expression, but said nothing.

3

MARGOT WAS FAR from finished with winter preparations. Although she had never met the young men she was planning to service, she ordered Hooley to persuade them to go bear hunting before the beasts fled to hibernation. They had a successful outing, returning with piles of skins and slabs of bear meat. When the hides had cured in the late fall sun, Margot hung them on the walls of the parlor and spread the tanned deerskin and cowhides on the planked floors.

When Heinz returned with her special shipment, he stood by wordlessly while Mino unloaded crates and cases. She tittered like a child over her purchases, opening boxes and fishing out items with smiles of approval while the men stood around in mute wonder. She opened colognes and asked for opinions, accepting their protesting grunts when vials were thrust under their noses as if they were expressions of high praise. She made Mino haul everything into the tent. Heinz refused to lend a hand, merely vigorously worked his plug, brooding.

"You want a drink?" Hooley asked Heinz after the silence became too much to stand.

The teamster shook his head, spat. "I only drink with friends," he grumbled. "I ain't got me no friends out here. Not no more."

Before Hooley could respond, Margot came bustling out of her red tent with a huge smile. She handed the teamster a fistful of letters to post in Jacksboro and an order for linen sheets to replace the rough canvas bedclothes. "That canvas would chafe a buffalo," she said, offering Hooley a sympathetic grin. "No offense." She also ordered a case of glassware— "For the saloon," she explained with a sideways wink toward Hooley— then explained, "A shot is a shot. Hooley can't tell how much he's pouring in those cups."

"Tell me about it," Heinz muttered. "Not that it makes no nevermind to me." That nettled Hooley, and he felt himself redden. Heinz immediately noticed. "Looks like you're running this outfit now anyway?" he commented to Margot.

"That's none of your business," Margot shot back. "All you need to do is bring our goods. We don't need some Nosy Nellie poking into our affairs."

The teamster grudgingly accepted his orders and returned in two weeks, only to be sent away again, on the same afternoon, back to Jacksboro with orders to collect a piano.

"Where am I going to find a piano?" Heinz demanded. He hadn't wet his lips with Hooley's liquor during the last two trips, and this time he arrived in better spirits, ready to let bygones be bygones, Hooley hoped. But Margot met him before his boots even hit the dirt.

He was unable to swallow his disappointment silently. "That's just not sensible," he argued.

"I remember there was one for sale in a shop near the freight office," she said blithely. "They said it had been there a while, so I expect it's still waiting. It was some used, but they only wanted five dollars. You can front the money against your bill."

"A piano," Heinz muttered. "That takes the rag off the bush."

Hooley could hardly believe she was serious. "Why do we need a piano?" Her apparent determination to run them into debt alarmed him.

"You can't have a whorehouse without a piano."

"Can you play it?"

"No," she said. "But somebody's bound to. When we start making profits, we can hire a colored man. That's a mark of distinctive class in any whorehouse I've ever heard of."

"And how many have you heard of?" Heinz snarled, eager to score a hit against her.

"More than you have, obviously," Margot shot back. "After all, you've *never* paid for it."

The old wagoneer flapped his arms in defeat, leaving them to squabble. Hooley sympathized with his frustration. There was no reasoning with her. She never gave in, never backed down, never conceded any point without obtaining some other strategic advantage in doing so. Even amongst the gross stupidity of the United States officer corps, he had never encountered such bullheadedness.

Margot followed Heinz back to his vehicle, hustled him aboard, and sent him on his way—without any ration of whiskey, sure enough. Hooley pulled up his stool and fired his pipe while he watched Heinz desultorily turn the team and put them on the long trail back to Jacksboro. If he were Heinz, Hooley thought, he wouldn't come back, not till this redheaded hooligan was gone.

Once more, Hooley wondered what he had started by asking Margot Phillips to be their whore. This was not working out at all the way he had in mind that night he had lustfully observed her sitting by their campfire. It wasn't even working out in accordance with what he understood to be her version of things. He wasn't sure, now, what he had ever wanted, but he was certain that it wasn't to be bullied and bamboozled by a shrewish woman who always managed to have her way.

Before she came, he had felt confident, superior, in charge. Now, the tables seemed to be permanently turned, and he couldn't help but think of Heinz's continual warnings that it would end badly. He felt like an employee in his own shop, afraid to speak up for fear of—of what? Offending her? She seemed offended by his very presence. Making her mad? She angered at the sight of him, it seemed, or at least every time he opened his mouth. She treated him like a recalcitrant child, a truant, a rascal who needed to be reminded of his place.

He stormed off to the whiskey shed and drew a large cup. Three times now, he had been cheated out of Heinz's fellowship. It was highly distressing, and it wasn't fair.

The whiskey went down hot. His stomach was in full revolt, and cramps forced him to lean forward. From beyond the comfort of the shed's canvas barrier, he heard her voice, shrill and demanding. She was instructing Mino in some task or other, browbeating the poor carpenter if he seemed not to understand something she said—and Hooley figured he understood none of it. Hooley's thoughts laced with visions of the shrieking harridan that Ruthie became before she left him, of the vituperative, bitter woman his mother became before she left him, of the general trouble women caused in life.

Margot was spoiling everything. Never in his life had he been pushed to such limits of endurance. Margot had accomplished what his mother and Ruthie had utterly failed to do: She had turned him into an ambitious and enterprising man. But it wasn't *his* enterprise, *his* ambition. It was hers. She was driving him forward with an inexorable enthusiasm that he neither shared nor wanted.

He thought wistfully of the complacent contentment he had enjoyed only a few months before. Margot's arrival had turned his friendly world of occasional male society into a dangerous and forbidding place full of drudgery and demands. It was like walking on a thinly frozen pond every time he talked to her, and as a result he had become even lonelier than he was before Mino arrived. In fact, he considered, he had never been so lonely in his entire life.

Moreover, he thought, taking another deep drink of his liquor, in some strange way he had become dependent on Margot. This bothered him beyond anything else. He desperately wanted her approval, found himself seeking it and mourning when he failed to obtain it. Then all at once he realized why he was afraid of offending her, of angering her. What he feared most was that she would stop coming to his bed. And, he admitted with an internal wince, he didn't like the idea of her servicing Hank and Underwood and the other cowboys—or even Mino—in the same way she came to him.

This thought, at last out in the open, bothered him more than all the rest. Could it be that in spite of all his self-directed warnings, he had fallen in love with her? Could it be that his deepest fear was that she might never love him back? "That's stupid," he declared aloud, surprised by how weak his voice sounded. "Just plain stupid," he whispered. She *was* a whore. But not in the normal sense. She didn't sell her body for money, didn't give a man a few moments' pleasure in exchange for a few coins and the promise of a return engagement. She wormed her way inside him, made him want her, desperate for her, so he would do anything to please her, then she extracted her price, and it was not a cost that could be accounted in any coin of any realm.

But damn it, she was worth it. To him. She was worth whatever price she wanted.

He took another full cup of whiskey and drank it down. He had never been truly drunk, not down-in-the-dirt-vomity-passed-out drunk. But this night, with dark thoughts of Margot's plans dancing around the campfire, and the sweet vision of her face playing across his mind, he forwent supper and drank himself onto an amber tide that washed him into a deep and dreamless sleep.

MISS MARGOT'S PLACE

1

HEINZ RETURNED TO Hoolian in a mere five days. It was some kind of record, but sure enough the burly wagoneer had a large black upright piano roped into his wagon bed. Whatever interest the instrument gathered from Hooley and Margot when they met Heinz's clattering wagon was quickly scattered by another sight: Squatting on the kegs and crates in the freighter's bed were a half-dozen extremely pretty young women.

"This time, I ain't leaving till I've had me a drink," Heinz said breathlessly as he jumped down from the wagon. "It's time we buried the hatchet, you and me," he said, rushing to Hooley and grabbing his hand to give a shake. "Now, let's have us a shot or two. I can tell you that surer than anything you ever seen in the name of the blue-eyed Jesus, I *need* me a drink!"

Heinz continued pumping Hooley's hand, but the tentmaker didn't respond or even look at the wagonneer. He could only stare at the women. They were rising from their perches among the cargo and were adjusting bonnets and clothing from the long, dusty ride.

"I been driving these females for two solid days and never touched a one of them," Heinz went on. He dropped Hooley's hand, grabbed the lapels of the tentmaker's coat. "That's hard on a man, Hooley. Makes him jumpy," he gasped. "Beats anything I ever seen in the name of the blue-eyed Jesus. Now point me toward that whiskey."

Heinz brushed past the tentmaker and made a beeline for the whiskey shed, where he downed two quick cupfuls of Hooley's private stock. Hooley paid him no mind. He remained too stunned by the women to do much more than gape.

Margot approached the wagon without hesitation, her face beaming. She helped them down and began knocking dust off their clothes while she chatted brightly and they surveyed their surroundings with doubtful eyes.

"Why, this is a tent city," a blonde beauty said. "Thought we was coming to a real town!"

"You *are* a caution, Margot," another put in with annoyance. "This is nothing but a campground! We'd best watch our step—there might be snakes hereabouts."

"More likely a preacher," another opined as she cast a suspicious eye on Hooley. "I never in my life seen a tent put up when there wasn't a preacher round about trying to get into the men's pockets and the girls' bloomers."

"This ain't Oklahoma Territory," the first one who spoke piped up. "I don't think they allow any preaching in Texas."

"That won't stop *somebody* from trying to get into your bloomers," the second one rejoined. "Salvation *ain't* the point!"

They all squealed with laughter and began milling around the wagon's tailgate.

Margot herded them into a group and pointed them toward the privy. She then climbed into the wagon bed and inspected the piano. Mino wandered up, sighted the female covey, and stopped dead in his tracks, agog when they rolled past him and left him in a low wake of flirtatious giggles. Margot obviously did not appreciate the reaction. She hopped down, grabbed him by the arm, and set him to work unloading luggage. "He's going to need help with the piano," she called to Hooley.

Hooley barely heard her. His head swam with wonder about where they had come from, what they wanted. Mino was also too dumbfounded to work. After several fumbling false starts, he unloaded all the traps and valises, then stood in the wagon bed, clearly flabbergasted by the array of rustling fabric and laughing womanhood now picking through luggage while giving him ill-concealed admiring glances.

"He's a big one, ain't he?" one asked, and shrieked a laugh.

"You'd best be careful," another piped up. "You squirm the wrong way and he's liable to squash you like a ripe cantaloupe."

This was followed by a new chorus of raucous laughter and accusations of immodesty, while Mino stood as still as a stump.

Margot interrupted the teasing and gathered the girls together and brought them, still chattering and rolling their eyes, over to Hooley for introductions.

"This is Kitty, Lulu, and Clara," she listed, "Gertie, Lora Lynn, and Ina Moon. They've come here to work for us."

"Work?" Hooley repeated dumbly. "As what?"

"Whores," Margot replied. "What did you think?" The girls fluttered like a flock of chicks. "You didn't think I was going to take on the whole countryside by myself, did you?"

"I—" Hooley's mind reeled.

"Don't be an idiot, Hooley," Margot hissed, then brightened when she turned to the giggling group. "Girls, this is Mr. Gilbert Hooley. He's my partner. *One* of my partners," she amended. "The other fool is the Turk up there in the wagon. He answers to Mino, but don't call him too quick if you want conversation."

They politely ignored her reference to Mino and offered a collective curtsy to Hooley, suddenly transforming themselves into as demure a group of young women as Hooley had ever seen having tea in his mother's parlor. None was over twenty, he assessed. Two looked much younger. And they were all comely, full-bosomed, long-limbed, and bright-eyed. His nostrils filled with perfume, and he was overcome with an illogical desire to flee. He cast an envious look toward Heinz, who was out of their range and sat astraddle a keg, furiously downing one cup of whiskey after another.

"Don't worry," Heinz growled, "I'm keeping count." He pointed toward a series of lines in the dirt. "And it's going to take a sight more than I can get down me before sundown to wash this trip out of my craw." He poured another and swallowed it. "Takes the rag completely off the goddamn bush," he muttered.

Hooley's gaze went back to the six attractive young women, who stood shyly smiling at him.

"Cat's got his tongue," Lulu, a pert brunette with flashing dark eyes and rich olive skin, offered. The others giggled in chorus.

"That's a lucky cat," Kitty, the beautiful chesty blonde with hazel eyes added without so much as a blush. The giggles became squeals of feigned embarrassment.

"Mind your manners," Margot snapped. "Aren't you going to say anything?" she asked Hooley, but he was still mute with wonder.

Margot sniffed at his apparent rudeness. She turned the girls around and shepherded them toward the red tent with instructions to pick up their satchels. "Get inside and unpack. Air out your things."

She followed them a few steps, then returned to Hooley with a look of exasperation on her face. "I swear, Hooley, you look like you're staring at a bunch of hobgoblins. Couldn't you think of anything to say? You make me look stupid, like I partnered up with two deaf dummies."

"You might have warned me," Hooley stammered.

"Warned you? About what? They're just girls, not a tribe of savage Indians."

Hooley stared after them, and Margot sighed. "They don't have a whole brain amongst them," she said. "They're pretty as sin, but dumb as a sack of feathers. Except for Kitty," she said, thoughtfully. "She's sneaky."

"Where in God's name did you find them?" Hooley couldn't imagine Margot that could mail-order prostitutes as easily as she did everything else. "I mean, how did you . . ." He trailed off into inarticulate bewilderment.

She glanced at them to make sure they were following her instructions, then explained that she had known them all in Oklahoma Territory. Like her, they had all been married to lawmen of one stripe or another, and like her, they were all widows.

"All but one," she qualified. "Ina Moon was hitched up to some young rascal who was killed by lawmen." She noted that each was pleased to be leaving the wild hills of Oklahoma Territory and to come to the civilization of the Texas prairie.

"Too many savage Indians and lawmen up there," Margot concluded. "They've got nothing to do but work all day and roll around all night with some drifter who lacks both hard money and good sense. All they get for it is a bunch of ugly young'uns and an early grave. I've already told you: Oklahoma Territory is no place for a decent widow woman. So they may as well come to Texas and be whores. It's honest work, and you don't have to mess with too many lawmen or lunatics. In Oklahoma, they're often one and the same."

"They're *willing* to be whores?" Hooley asked.

She spun on Hooley. "What else do you expect them to do, Hooley?" She slapped her hands against her skirt in exasperation. "I wrote to them and put it plain. And they came. I guess that's answer enough."

She gave a brief background on each girl, and their stories were remarkably similar. Married young to older men, they had spent their lives in the drudging labor of making a home for wandering and generally irresponsible husbands.

"Not one can write her name, except for Ina Moon, whose daddy was a missionary. Most never had anything but a dirt floor under their feet, and since Oklahoma Territory won't pay a pension to the widow of a dead lawman, they'd likely starve." She looked deep into Hooley's eyes, and he thought he saw a touch of sadness there for the briefest moment. "They had nowhere else to go, Hooley. They'd probably all become whores anyway, one way or another, if they stayed where they were." She then laughed lightly. "Here, at least, they can get paid for it."

"How much?" Hooley asked before he thought, his mind still swimming in confusion.

Margot's eyes narrowed. "That's my concern, Hooley. You sell your whiskey. I'll take care of my girls. Don't worry, you'll get your money."

Hooley was wounded. That wasn't his point. He was about to say so when Ina Moon, the girl widowed by the young outlaw, came out and stretched, arching her back, then folding her hands over her slightly rounded belly. She was Chinese, or part Chinese, or so she appeared. But she was a large girl by the standards Hooley had encountered among the females of that race. She had waist-length ebony hair, golden skin, and black eyes that slanted slightly when she smiled.

Margot was taking grim note of something that apparently didn't please her. Hooley caught her frown, then again looked at Ina Moon's shape. The girl was pregnant, and Margot was furious. She marched over and took her by the arm, questioned her briefly, then stomped back to Hooley. Ina Moon ran off toward the creek, tears spilling from her almond eyes.

"I told them not to come if they were 'encumbered,'" she fumed. "But these girls are so ignorant, I guess they don't know what that means."

The others now moved outside, carrying armloads of clothing to air out. Hooley's view was quickly blocked with corsets, petticoats and bloomers, shirtwaists and frilly nightgowns. The women laughed and chatted among themselves, having fun, as if they were about to begin a picnic, not the more sober work of prostitution.

"Anyway," Margot continued to steam, "she's full up to the brim with that young miscreant's colt, and he's holding down a hickory branch somewhere up near Tahlequah." Her mouth turned down in a thoughtful frown. "I don't know what we're going to do about that."

"We?" Hooley asked. "What *we're* going to do? I thought you said—"

"We're *full* partners, Hooley," Margot shot, walking away. "That means taking the bitter with the sweet, the barren with the fertile. I think that's in the Bible. Now, go help Mino with the piano. Then get some water boiling and start working that pump. These girls've been on the road, and they're rank. We'll deal with Ina Moon's problem later on."

2

HANK LED HIS cowpuncher pards at a gallop into Hoolian well before sundown. They arrived in a jangle of noise, whooping and hollering and firing off sidearms as if it were the Fourth of July. How they had learned of the arrival of Heinz's special passengers mystified Hooley, as none of the cowboys had been around for over a week. But they came thundering in, stirring up clouds of annoying dust and loudly announcing expectations of a rare old time in the tiny community. Not one was drunk when he arrived—a condition that was quickly remedied—but they were all reeling in their saddles, barely able to contain their enthusiasm long enough to tend to their horses.

Hooley was physically exhausted from having helped Mino wrestle the piano off the wagon and into Margot's tent, while the girls stood around giggling whenever he let loose with a spray of profanity at the ungainly and heavy instrument. Then he'd taken turns with Mino working the bilge pump and ferrying boiling water up to the bathhouse as Margot yelled at the girls to make sure that they were all inside the red tent and out of sight by the time the cowboys rode in.

Contrary to their usual habit of splashing cold water on their hands and around their necks, each cowhand was loudly clamoring for a full bath and a shave. They demanded that Mino clean their shirts and pants and good-naturedly upbraided Hooley for not having a barber's chair and a supply of witch hazel on hand. They wanted baking powder to use on their teeth, and several prevailed on him—without positive effect—to mend shirts and replace missing buttons.

Unwilling to do more service in the name of cleanliness, Hooley issued cakes of lye soap and sent the young men down to the creek to do what they could on their own. He had plenty of other things to worry him without starting to barber a bunch of exuberant cowboys.

Through it all, Margot's huge tent remained closed. No sounds came from inside, although a few of the boys worked up the courage to peer at the red canvas as if by some miracle they could gain a peek.

As the sun set, they were milling around in sopping clothes, their cheeks bright red from raw scrapings. Their hair was combed and sharply parted, slicked into high pompadours with oil, if they had it, and merely by water if they didn't. Many were so scarred and scratched from hurried self-induced applications of knives and dull razors without benefit of mirrors or hot lather that they looked as if they had been attacked by a thicket of thornbushes. But their grins were wide and their manner festive as they assaulted the whiskey shed and demanded more liquor.

It was all Hooley could do to keep up with the drinks he kept pouring. And Mino, who might have been pressed into service to help bartend, was nowhere to be seen. Hooley thought to ask Heinz to help out, but the teamster was far too gone into his own indulgence to handle the chore. He remained where he had first lit, astraddle a whiskey keg, moving only to lean down and refill his cup, each time making another mark in the dirt. Hooley kept yelling for help, but when the drunken teamster tried to rise, he stumbled and sat down hard on his tally, wiping it out completely. "Now *that* takes the rag off the bush!" he hooted.

Hooley was too harried to be disgusted. He scurried about attempting to organize his enterprise. He now saw the wisdom of moving his operation behind Margot's bar, where he could control consumption and collect payment in an orderly fashion. Previously, the boys' drinking had been intense but steady, paced over an evening. Gradually, they'd slide into blissful melancholy and sweet nostalgic memories of home, then pass out quietly. Now, there was a frenetic nature to their imbibing. They scarcely paid attention to what sloshed in their cups, but paced anxiously while they gulped down each portion and kept a close eye on Margot's tent.

Even though none had laid eyes on a single female yet—not even Margot—they behaved as if the women might vanish if the red tent wasn't constantly watched. If one of the boys suddenly perked up and took notice of the tent, the entire company would jostle into a mob, spilling whiskey as they made hasty adjustments to hair or clothing. If things hadn't been so chaotic, Hooley might have been amused.

Instead, Hooley seemed to do nothing but pour, accept an empty cup, rinse it out from a wash bucket, then pour again while cursing Mino for disappearing. Although it cooled off once the sun went down, his shirt was soaked in sweat and he had to stop often and wipe his face just to see what he was doing. Heinz had passed out in the middle of the floor, and Hooley kept tripping over his form as he moved from keg to crate to barrel. He never had time to sit down, let alone enjoy a sip of his own, and couldn't even take a moment to fire up his pipe. He had trouble keeping up with who had paid, who had change coming, who still owed him. The prepared credit slips were soon exhausted, and his shirt cuffs filled with pencil scribbles that had smeared together. When he tried to tally an individual bill in his head, he quickly lost count, and he cursed Margot for being right and vowed to swallow his pride and move his business into her red tent as soon as things quieted down.

That was going to take a while. The cowboys were becoming more rambunctious with every drink, and their conversation grew noisier. There was talk of storming the tent if festivities didn't start soon. Then, about the time things began to reach a crisis, Margot emerged.

For the second time that day, Hooley was struck mute. He knew Margot was extremely attractive, but he had never imagined how gorgeous she would appear when she emerged from the tent, all gussied up as if she were attending the music hall. She wore a sky-blue frock trimmed in cloud-white lace, cut low to expose her beautiful shoulders and gathered tightly across her bosom to lift and accentuate the freckled tops of her breasts. Her hair, curled and arranged high on her head to reveal the lightly freckled, creamy skin of her long neck, glowed scarlet in the lantern light and contrasted with the soft beauty of her face and her piercing eyes, which were complemented with dark makeup, making her lashes seem unusually large. Light pink smudges colored her cheeks, and her lips were full and red-rouged, creating the impression that the bright smile she cast toward the men was a beacon. She looked like a goddess, as if she'd stepped out of a painting, bringing with her all of the artist's talent for color and line. Hooley was unable to move for fear she would vanish.

After a long pose to allow the boys to drink in her image, she quickly tied back the flap, transforming it into a doorway. Then she stood, hands on her hips, her elbows linked behind her waspish waist by a yellow boa that matched a large feather jutting up from her curls, and inspected the waiting crowd.

Hooley continued to stand silent, an empty cup ready for refill in his hand, reminded of the female visions of St. Louis. There, on one of Ruthie's commanded outings, they would visit the opera house or pass the entrance to a fine hotel where beauties were often draped on the arm of some prosperous businessman. He had never imagined seeing Margot in such a way, never suspected that Margot's natural appeal would be so enhanced with fancy dress and face paint that it would rival that of any society woman.

As his senses returned, Hooley discovered that he wasn't the only one overwhelmed. The hubbub among the men had fallen silent. They stood like rock pillars, as if afraid that a mere breath might cause the gorgeous specter to evaporate into the prairie night.

"Boys," she said after a few beats had passed. She swung the boa as she walked on brightly polished, high-button shoes. "My name is Miss Margot, and that's my place." She gestured toward the tent. "You're welcome there. Every one of you. Meet a girl, have a laugh, take a turn on the dance floor, or do whatever else you can arrange and have the cash to support."

The men exhaled as a group, then exchanged demure looks and toed the ground. Margot's eyes went suddenly cold. "But when you walk through that door, you're my guest, and I'll expect you to behave, or you'll be asked to leave."

"I don't reckon you'll have any trouble out of us," Hank finally spoke up. "We're all pards here, and we've been looking forward to this more than anything on this green earth."

A chorus of agreeing murmurs grew until the entire company was slapping one another on the back, drinking toasts, and demanding more liquor in a rollicking attempt to swallow their nervousness along with the liquor.

Margot's smile returned, and her eyes softened while she watched them. She brought her hands together in a sharp clap, and the company fell silent instantly. "Well, there aren't many rules, but we have a few. Though my house may not be a church, I'll tolerate no nasty talk or blasphemy. You have a problem with somebody, you take it outside where you won't damage the furnishings. I'll not tolerate blood on my floors. You treat my girls like ladies and mind your manners. And,"—she once more narrowed her jade orbs and scanned the group—"a girl says 'no,' she means 'no.' You take up the problem—if there is one—with me."

She laced the boa in her crossed arms and cast a blinding smile their way. "Anybody doesn't like that, he can stay out here with Hooley! The rest of you, c'mon in. It's getting chilly!"

The men let go a lusty cheer, as Margot spun with a flourish of her feathered wrap. Hooley had trouble keeping his eyes from the swaying bustle of her skirt as she sauntered back to the tent. He figured that they would all follow her immediately. On the contrary, Margot's ceremony led to suggestions that they recharge their cups and toast the redheaded beauty.

As Hooley poured the next round, he expected an imminent stampede into the red tent. Instead, the party—some twelve or fifteen youths—continued to mill around, some demanding more liquor or beer while others formed small knots, then drifted off to one side, rolled cigarettes, and conversed in intense low tones. From time to time, they cast furtive glances over their shoulders toward the tent.

"What's the matter?" Hooley demanded of Plunk, who seemed to be eyeing the back of the whiskey shed as if it might provide him a means of sneaking away. "I thought this was what you all were waiting for."

"Hell, Hooley," Plunk replied with a sheepish grin. "Nobody wants to be first. I mean, what if it don't work out?"

"What's not to work out? They're *whores,* for God's sake. How could it *not* work out."

"Well . . ." Plunk toed the dirt as if it contained something of incredible interest. "For some of us, it's been a long time since . . . well, since . . . you know."

Hooley stared at him.

"For some of us . . . ," Plunk went on. "Well, for some of us, it might be the first time." He looked at the shuffling crowd of suddenly shy cowboys, and Hooley realized how young they were. For all their bluster and brag, most of them weren't much over eighteen. Hank, whom he always thought of as one of the older cowboys, was still a kid. They did a man's work every day, but they were mere children. The thought made the tentmaker suddenly melancholy.

"Anyway," Plunk concluded, glancing at some others standing near him, seeking support, "what if we did it wrong? Or couldn't do it at all? That could be mortifying to a man."

Several others nodded quickly. "Well, it ain't *my* first time," Tidmore announced. "But think I need me another drink or two, just in case. Then I'll be ready!"

"Not me," Hank announced. He was drunker than Hooley had ever seen him. The youngster positively swayed in the firelight. A ragged shaving cut ran down the length of his cheek, and blood spotted the white celluloid collar he had strapped around his neck. His eyes glistened in the lantern light. His shirt was clean if still damp, and his hair looked plastered to his head, but his mouth was set with grim intent. "I've been waiting for damn near ever for Hooley to get something worthwhile going around here, so I'm on my way."

He staggered toward Margot's tent, and Hooley sighed. If they went over one at a time, this could be a long night. But as Hank reached the door of the tent, he cast a look back at his pards and offered an idiotic grin. Slowly, Tidmore and Jake stepped forward. Underwood, looking ridiculously small next to the enormous Plunk, followed, all of them thumbing their belts and trying to look manly and important.

Some half dozen stayed behind, though, still seeking the fortification contained in Hooley's liquor stores. They kept at it steadily, until a couple of those who initially left returned to recharge their cups. Soon, a regular bread-and-butter line started across the compound, and to Hooley's consternation, their constant coming and going provided him with no break in the demand for alcohol at all.

Hooley returned to his steady employment. He felt he had lived a lifetime since Heinz's wagon hove into view, and his muscles cried out for relief. Additionally, he needed a drink, a smoke, to help him take his mind off Margot and what was happening inside the red tent.

He considered seeing for himself how she was handling things. Instead, because of the cowboys' unofficial decision to go over in a continuously revolving shift, the tentmaker now had his hands as full as ever. He didn't dare leave the exposed kegs and bottles. He had to remain there to collect coins and make change, memorize additions to the various bills, and pour proper dollops into the tin cups.

Hooley had had doubts that these girls knew what they were in for, but he decided they must have adjusted quickly. Comings and goings from Margot's new sporting house to his whiskey tent continued in a steady stream, and the boys' calls for more liquor increased. Hooley barely had time to consider what was happening across the way, although he heard raucous singing, rhythmic clapping of hands, and the muffled sounds of boot heels tromping out a dance on floorboards.

Throughout the evening, Mino remained out of sight. Fortunately for Hooley, none of the cowboys wanted to eat anything. They just drank, returned to the red tent, then after a bit came back for another couple of rounds. Each time they returned from the red tent, they walked with proud, strutting confidence, their hats cocked back over big winks and wide grins. Although Hooley had seen soldiers returning from bawdy houses when he was in the army, he had never seen such a display of self-satisfaction as he witnessed in these prairie youngsters. It was as if they had just done something remarkable, not merely rolled around on a canvas cot with a whore.

From time to time a brief, furious fistfight would be staged in the dusty compound. Hooley was at first alarmed by these sudden violent displays, but after a few blows were exchanged, the combatants would help one another up, throw arms around each other like lost brothers newly found, and return to the whiskey shed before, arm-in-arm, heading back to Margot's with bloody knuckles, broken noses, or black eyes.

Finally, after nearly three hours of steady traffic, things threatened to stop altogether. The boys who returned drank their liquor more calmly—seemingly aware that what money they had was rapidly depleting. Hooley found the time to collect the credit slips and to stack up emptied cups flung willy-nilly all around the compound. He hefted the cash sack as well. It had gotten far heavier. Excited, he thought immediately to show it to Margot, and actually took a few steps toward her huge red tent before he realized that it was still alive with noise.

Uproarious laughter and squealing shrieks emerged from behind the red canvas walls, and there was chorus after chorus of lively singing. When he put an ear to the night air, Hooley heard the unmistakable sounds of Mino's squeezebox. Fury came over him like a fever. While he had been half killing himself, the damned carpenter had been playing his silly instrument and doubtlessly sampling the "wares" of Margot's house. Lanterns inside the tent were lit, and he could clearly see silhouettes of dancers moving steadily to lively music cast against the outside canvas walls. Hooley took two strong strides toward the red tent. He would drag that idiotic immigrant out and thrash him.

But just as quickly as his ire rose, it evaporated. Mino's music swung into a sweet ballad, and the gentle harmonics of the concertina seemed to wash over Hooley, quench his rage, and pour raw feeling into him to fill the thirst he thought he had for his whiskey.

He returned to the shed, sat down heavily on a keg, and studied the scene before him. It was as if Miss Margot's Place, as he heard them calling it, had always been there, as if this tiny settlement was just one more town on the frontier. Although he had no sense of having caused any of it to happen, there was a profound sense of comfort about it, as if it was the most natural thing in the world for him to be playing whiskey vendor to a bunch of drunk cowboys who were spending all the money they had on women and liquor, as if they were wandering the streets of any other town. It was too fantastic to contemplate.

His musings consumed him so much he didn't even notice that Heinz had roused himself and disappeared. Hooley fished out his pipe and lit it. His body ached with exhaustion, and his eyes were gritty with fatigue. He was about to extinguish the lantern over the whiskey shed, seal up the kegs, and go to his tent when a swaying group staggered to the shed for yet another round of drinks. The pace soon quickened again, and he found himself once more scurrying to fill the demands of the drunken, sweaty revelers as they caught their second wind.

Heinz did not return, but Hooley noticed that the music from Mino's instrument, now joined by Jew's harps and mouth organs, picked up the tempo and mocked Hooley's exhausted efforts to ignore the sounds of song and dance that filled the night, so he could focus on the task at hand.

3

HOOLEY'S FINAL SHOCK of a day filled with stultifying surprises came a few hours after passages between the tents finally petered out. Most of the boys had emerged from the red tent in stumbling exhaustion, then slouched down or just sat cross-legged in the dirt, staring out of eyes blinded by alcohol and fatigue. To Hooley's disgust, some drooled, and others merely bent their heads forward and pitched their stomach's contents out into their laps.

Hooley tallied the day's take, astonished that he had sold more whiskey that evening than he did in three days of normal business. There was nearly two hundred dollars in paper money, plus generous numbers of gold and silver coins, as well as a thick bundle of credit slips. That didn't count the tallies he'd made here and there on his shirt cuffs and odd scraps of paper.

It also didn't count Heinz's consumption, he thought darkly. Then he realized he hadn't seen the mule skinner for hours. He hoped he hadn't wandered off in the darkness and been attacked by a wild animal, although Hooley observed with sour vengeance that it would serve the teamster right.

He stored the moneybag in his tent, and was just seating himself with a cup of his own private stock of whiskey and only the second pipe he had had a chance to smoke since the girls arrived when he was confronted by Hank Mitchell and Ina Moon.

The young couple strolled arm-in-arm and stood clasping one another in the firelight until Hooley acknowledged their presence. He decided they would stand there forever if he didn't do something, so he had wearily risen and found a marginally clean cup when Hank stopped him.

"That ain't what we're over here for," he said. "I've had me enough to drink for a whole lifetime. Ina Moon here's got me to take the Pledge," Hank said, an moronic grin cracking through the shaving cuts on his chin. "I ain't going to drink no more!"

"I hope she's not working on the others," Hooley grumbled. "That'd be my ruination, for sure." He remembered that Ina Moon had brought other forms of trouble to the camp.

"And that ain't all," Hank continued. "We're going to get married."

"What?"

Hank said he had taken one look at Ina Moon's dark, exotic beauty and decided to quit drinking and quit whoring on the spot. "We're going to settle down and raise a family. Starting with the young'un she's carrying in her belly right now." He beamed at her. She looked down demurely.

"Are you out of your mind?" Hooley looked at the blushing youngster. Ina Moon snuggled into Hank's side. "You're drunk as a coot right now!"

"I am *not* drunk, Hooley," Hank protested. "I puked up my guts a while ago and that sobered me up. Ain't had but a few cups since. *And* I ain't having no more. Never!" He looked into Ina Moon's dark eyes, and his chest swelled out so far that the buttons on his sweaty shirt strained. "I'm going to be a pa."

"But Hank," Hooley started, then calmed himself, trying to sound reasonable. "You haven't known this girl but a few hours." Ina Moon's gaze never left Hank's face, and he grinned idiotically down at her. "Think, man," Hooley shouted again. "She's a whore!"

She blushed deeply and dropped her eyes, but Hank's countenance darkened to a deeper hue. His eyes grew hard in the firelight. "No she's not!" he said evenly. "Ain't going to be, neither. She's just a helpless widow woman with a baby on the way. I aim to do the right thing by her, and I'll kill any man who says hold!"

Hooley's exhaustion and the frustrations and shocks of the day combined somewhere inside him and erupted. He stood up to face the calf-eyed cowboy. "You can't do this, Hank," he yelled into the youngster's face. "I won't let you," Hooley railed. "It's the stupidest damn thing I've ever heard in my life! Don't be an idiot!"

"It ain't no more stupid than what you done with Miss Margot," Hank argued, his voice rising to match Hooley's. He puffed out his chest again. "I mean, you *let* her become a whore. You *asked* her to. I ain't going to let that happen to my Ina Moon!"

"What?" Hooley's mouth dropped open. "How do you know anything about—how do you know anything about Margot?"

" 'Cause she told me," Hank said with a nod. "She told all her girls that you hired her on as a whore." He gave Hooley his best impression of a paternal look. "Now *that* was stupid."

Outrage left Hooley like an expulsion of bad gas. The young cowboy was right. Taking in Margot, allowing her to worm her way into his life may well have been the stupidest thing he'd ever done. No, he corrected, allowing her to go ahead with this harebrained scheme of setting up a whorehouse, with her as the head whore, was even more stupid. What was worse was that *she* knew it was stupid. He felt like a man who had made a foolish wager and knew he'd lost the moment he placed the bet. Opportunity had fled from his grasp like a bird taking flight, and he had not only stood by, helplessly watching it. Truly, he had urged it on its way. His stomach turned over as he looked forlornly over toward the red tent, where shadowed dancers reeled and hands clapped to keep the rhythm of Mino's music.

The thought of Margot's entertaining all those greasy young cowboys made him physically ill. The vision of their grubby fingers touching her sweet, white flesh passed before his mind's eye, then formed itself into an icy dagger that pierced his heart. "Damn it," he swore aloud, and kicked the dirt. "Goddamn it to hell and back."

But then, he looked up at the faces of the youthful couple before him and had a second revelation. What Hank proposed, poorly thought out as it may have been, was at least honest, if not downright noble. For all his apparent naiveté, Hank didn't appear to be in the least drunk, not anymore. As Hooley watched the pair staring stupidly into each other's eyes, awash with love and passion, he decided that it probably had a better chance of turning out right than anything else that might emerge from his association with Margot Phillips. Absurd as it was, right out here in the middle of the most godforsaken wilderness in the world, something genuine had happened.

"Oh, what the hell," he said, rising and drawing three drams of whiskey and handing them around. "Let's drink to it. On the goddamn house!"

"That's more like it, pard," Hank said through a fresh grin. "But we took the Pledge. For a minute there, I was afraid I was going to have to shoot you."

"For a minute there," Hooley muttered and poured two of the whiskeys back. "I almost wished you would."

Hank and Ina Moon matched Hooley's toast with coffee, then Hooley went over to Margot's tent. He stood by the open flap and called her out. She emerged with an irritable expression. "What is it, Hooley? I've got customers to tend to."

She had been dancing hard, Hooley surmised from her breathless posture. Her skin glistened with perspiration, and her coiffure was slightly mussed. He noted with satisfaction that her hair was still up, that she was still fully dressed, and that her clothes were in good repair. The exposed skin of her shoulders was alabaster in the moonlight. He struggled to fight back the urge to reach out and touch her.

She folded her arms and listened impatiently while he explained what Hank was proposing. He was wary of what her reaction would be to the betrothal of one of her girls, but she gave him a weary look of relief and took a breath that ended in a cunning grin.

"Married? Those two?" she confirmed. She looked at Hank and Ina Moon, who were still clutching one another in the glow of the firelight.

Hooley nodded. "That's what they said. Said she made him take the Pledge, too."

"Well, we have to nip that in the bud." Her frown returned briefly. "That's bad for business." She put a long finger to her chin. "I guess it's the only possible thing that could have happened. Once a whore becomes a mother, she's done anyhow," she said. She extracted a small silver flask from the pocket of her skirt and took a quick sip.

"I hope they all don't decide to do the same," he said. "We'll be out of business."

She gave him a sideways look. "You know, Hooley, sometimes it's hard to tell if you're acting stupid or whether you're really as dumb as you look." She took another sip, then once more looked across at Hank and Ina Moon. "This probably is best all round. I sure hate to lose Hank's custom," she said. "He strikes me as about the only one of these idiots with any sense."

"Once he's had a taste of marriage, my end of the business may make up for it," Hooley noted quietly.

Margot gave him another sharp look. "It's getting frosty out here, Hooley. I need to get a wrap." She then ducked back inside, and he heard her announcing the happy news.

Mino emerged, and Hooley did his best to explain the situation through gestures and mimes. It was hard for the tentmaker to concentrate, for the swarthy carpenter was decked out in ridiculous fancy dress. He was wearing a swallow-tailed waistcoat over a brocade vest that barely buttoned around his capacious belly. His neck was squashed by a high collar and thick cravat that boasted a bright red stickpin. The whole effect was topped off by an antique beaver hat, but was betrayed by the scuffed and nearly worn-out work boots he wore beneath the cuffs of his pinstriped trousers.

Hooley swallowed his temptation to burst out in derisive laughter at the carpenter's ludicrous appearance, though, and persevered in describing the situation. Once Mino grasped what was about to take place, he agreed to stand up for the groom, as the skinny Underwood, Hank's best friend, was passed out and beyond revival. Hooley was able to rouse Heinz, whom Margot, her bare shoulders now covered by a shawl, found sound asleep behind the bar inside.

When he found out what was happening, the teamster shook his head. "That's the road to hell, sure's shooting," he mourned. "Ain't one thing about being married that's worth a fiddler's fart." He bit off a chew and worked it. "Damn it. I was getting to where I sort of liked that boy. Never figured him to develop such a bad case of the dumbass."

In spite of his philosophical objections, Heinz volunteered to give the bride away. Margot, who was getting the girls properly wrapped up in shawls and cloaks, protested his participation, but the teamster prevailed when he argued that since he was the one who "toted that sweet young thing out here," he was the only one in a position to see to her "proper delivery."

"Well, the only other question is who's going to do the marrying," Heinz said as he hovered over a bracing cup of beer had demanded to help him "sober himself."

The problem hadn't occurred to Hooley, and it surprised him when Margot went to her tent and came out to hand him a Bible and tell him that he was elected.

"Me?" Hooley exclaimed, shocked. "That can't be binding. I'm not a preacher."

"Well, the girls here are convinced otherwise," Margot said with a wry grin. "They decided you're avoiding them for fear of your soul. Anyway, you don't have to be a preacher," Margot added. "Any town official can do it."

"But I'm not a town official of any sort," Hooley protested. "Anyway, there's no town."

As if he was recalling Craggy Phillips' ghost, Heinz spoke up. "There's buildings and a whorehouse and a saloon, and that makes it more of a town than most," he said. "And you are too an official. You're the post-master."

"Postmaster? When did I become postmaster?"

"Why, when you accepted the first letter I brought and agreed to hold it," Heinz said matter-of-factly and with a sidelong glance at Hank and Ina Moon, who were standing arm-in-arm off to one side, waiting for the ceremony to begin. "Too bad ol' Hank jumped the gun with her. I'd have liked a chance my own self. I've heard wondrous things about them Chinee gals."

"You're a pig," Margot sniffed.

"And you're a whore," Heinz returned flatly. "And don't go telling me different now. That takes the goddamn rag off the bush, don't it, Hooley?" He offered the tentmaker a big wink and tottered off toward the whiskey shed to organize a toast to the nuptials.

Those cowboys who could manage any degree of sobriety joined the girls in singing a ragged version of "Shall We Gather at the River." Mino captured the tune, but halfway through everyone forgot the words and merely hummed the rest. Hooley fingered the Bible and stumbled through the words. He couldn't find the right passage and was forced to rely on the dusty memory of his own nuptials with Ruthie—and to endure constant correction and emendation from Margot, who remembered her marriage to Craggy Phillips in complete detail.

"It may not have been the happiest day of my life," she said when Hooley complimented her on her powers of recall, "but you can believe it was one I have no intention of forgetting."

"That's the first thing you've ever said that's made any sense to me at all," Heinz commented.

4

THE WEDDING PARTY finished one more round of toasts, then repaired to Margot's tent for a continuation of the celebration, Mino trailing happily behind with his squeezebox. Hank and Ina Moon strolled off, arm-in-arm, cow-eyed, and deep in soughing wonder, to Mino's tent, which they were borrowing for their honeymoon. Hooley went to the whiskey shed, and took a lonely seat amidst the kegs.

He was utterly stunned by the understanding that he held an official position in the tiny township. The realization that his name was inscribed on official government documents unnerved him. The fact that his personal business and accounts might be scrutinized by some bureaucratic official frightened him. This was a more ambitious goal than he had ever imagined for himself, far more than he'd ever hoped—or wanted—to achieve. Incongruously, he wondered what his mother would think of it.

"Postmaster," he said, recalling his vigorous protest of Craggy Phillips' attempt to inflict a badge of office on him. "Who'd ever have thought up such a thing?"

From the red walls of Margot's canvas building, Heinz's braying laugh answered his question. "The man is an imbecile," Hooley muttered. But he was also shrewd, Hooley admitted to himself. Heinz had made for himself a good life and a good living. He quickly and easily maneuvered Hooley into a position of authority, cementing him to this empty spot in an even emptier prairie. There might not be a thing here but tented buildings, wind, and weather, but Heinz was making damned sure that this foothold stayed in place. Hooley admired the teamster's cunning, even if the scheme was too incredible to fathom.

Beyond the raucous music and gales of laughter coming from Margo's tent, Hooley heard the faint call of the coyotes out on the prairie. They had been his first companions on this lonely expanse, their mournful cries his only solace. Now, they seemed to grow distant, as if they were retreating from the noise and light of Hoolian, leaving it to whatever fate awaited it. It also seemed that they were laughing at him.

Margot emerged from the shadows, ducking under the canvas as she came into the narrow light inside the shed. He stood automatically, surprised by her stealthy approach. "You want to come over, have a spin on the dance floor? You look like you could use it." Her smile was mischievous and inviting, but he was overcome with a sense of futility, of melancholy so profound that he felt utterly deflated, used up, worthless. All at once, he saw her and himself for what they truly were: two damned fools stuck in the midst of helpless children in the middle of the biggest bunch of nowhere God had ever imagined.

"No," he said in a soft sigh. "It's been a hell of a long day, and I'm going to bed."

"Well, leave the lantern burning. I'll have Mino run a tally for the rest of the night."

"Rest of the night?" Hooley asked. "How much longer will all this"—he spread his arms to encompass the entire campsite—"will this go on?" He looked into her emerald eyes, saw the flicker of the fire dancing in them, and felt a stirring of passion. "How long can you go on . . . doing that?"

"Oh, Hooley," Margot said, turning and flouncing back toward her tent, her red curls bouncing against her shoulders. "Sometimes you can be such a complete and utter fool."

Irked, he sat down again, drew himself a large portion of whiskey and downed it in one gulp, then listened again for the coyotes. They were gone. Their demonstrated understanding of what he had become made him sad. But all he could think of was Margot Phillips, of the role she now played in every element of his existence. The thought scared him out of reason.

5

HOOLEY WAS AWAKENED by a chorus of loud snores echoing across new frost that covered the cold fire of Hoolian. He rose shivering and peeked out to find what resembled the results of a horrendous battle. The main flap of the red tent was down and securely tied. Cowboys were strewn all over the compound. Many boasted scars and wounds of their brief, furious altercations from the night before, and but for the heaving of chests and roar of heavy breathing, they could have been mistaken for dead men.

Most of them slept where they had finally fallen: along the boardwalk, the whiskey shed, and Margot's tent. Few were covered by so much as a slicker, but a litter of tin cups, many stepped on and dented beyond further use, lay about them. Some, Hooley observed with irony, had wrapped their arms around one another for warmth.

Briefly and with a tiny measure of jealousy, he wondered where Mino had wound up. But when Hooley looked into the larger tent that served as a hotel, he spied the big man's form under a pile of blankets and his squeezebox neatly tucked under the cot.

From the noises he heard while he pulled on his shoes, he decided that some of the cowboys were now up and stomping around to restore circulation to cold limbs. Soon he heard them staggering off toward the flats or the privy, loudly protesting their bodies' reactions to the long night of debauchery. Hacking, gagging coughs punctuated the frosty air. He placed a comforting hand on the bag of money he had stored away beneath his cot. He hadn't completely counted it, but he reckoned several hundred dollars strained the seams of the bulging sack. He would have to sew another one soon. It had been an amazing evening, and a beneficial one, although he couldn't recall ever having done so much physical labor. His arms and back ached, and his legs felt rubbery as he pulled up his braces and stepped outside.

Hank, dressed in long johns, boots, and hat, stood by the ashes of the fire. "You made coffee yet?" His breath vaporized in the chilly morning air.

"Tired of marriage already?" Hooley threw bundled dried grass on the fire, stirred the cow-chip coals to life. He found the coffeepot and began filling it from the water bucket, trying vaguely to remember if this was the same pail he had used to rinse the cups the night before.

"No, I'm not 'tired of marriage already,' " Hank mimicked in a surly tone. "Ina Moon's all tuckered out is all." He gave Hooley an impish grin. "And she's a little sick," he said with a sudden, serious look. "Women in a delicate condition get like that, you know."

"Yes, I know," Hooley snapped. "You might hurt her if you go acting the fool." He felt an unreasonable desire to wound the youngster, give him a taste of the bitterness that he felt. All night he had wondered which cowboy was enjoying Margot's body, which she had laughed the loudest with, if she had let one of them kiss her on the mouth.

"She said that didn't make no difference," Hank noted. "Where she comes from, women go about their business no matter whether they're having a baby or not. She said—"

"Sounds like you did more talking than anything else," Hooley said, enjoying a mean satisfaction in the needling. "Sounds to me like you spent the whole night jabbering away."

"Shut up, Hooley. Just get me some coffee."

As Hooley spooned fresh grounds into the boiling water, Hank's mood shifted and his face softened. He rolled a cigarette and then, after shuffling around in the dusty compound for a moment, he announced that he wanted Hooley's advice.

"About what?"

"Well, we talked it over, me and Ina Moon. And I want to open up a general merchandise store. Like the one my daddy run back in Illinois."

"Well, go ahead," Hooley said. "I'm not stopping you."

"I mean here."

"Here?" Hooley looked around the frosted tents, momentarily gratified that none was sagging under the weight of the light coat of moisturizing ice. "Here?" he asked again.

"I figure if you could build it, then I could get Mr. Heinz to bring me some shelf stock on his next trip, and I'd be in business lickety-split."

"When did he become 'Mister Heinz' to you?"

"When you're in business, it's important to show people respect," Hank lectured. "My daddy taught me that."

"When do I become 'Mister' Hooley?"

"When you agree to help me out." Hank nodded once, then looked suddenly sad. "But I always thought we was pards. It won't do for pards to call one another 'mister.' "

"Let me get this straight: You want to set up a business right here."

"Yessir." Hank nodded vigorously. "I mean, we got enough old boys coming by, and there's apt to be more when Rancher McPherson brings in his English stock."

Hooley pulled out his cold pipe and chewed on it while the coffee boiled. He knew Mino would welcome the work of building another substantial structure. So, he ruefully thought, would he. The mornings were getting colder, the days shorter, and the amount of stitching required for a store would provide Hooley with steady occupation, something to keep his mind off Margot Phillips and her doings with the cowboys.

Moreover, Hooley considered as he poured two cups of steaming, strong coffee, the notion of such an enterprise had another appeal. With a general store handling orders, responsibility for stocking a number of minor goods would shift away from him to Hank, who could then be in charge of the credit and accounts for the niggling items and necessities that the boys were forever asking Hooley to add to his orders, a practice that especially nettled Hooley and fouled up his bookkeeping. It also might remove the stigma of "postmaster" from him. If there was a store, then the storekeeper would be the logical person to handle mail. But suddenly, in a curious mental reversal, he wasn't sure how he felt about that. Now that the shock of it had worn off, the notion of being a genuine official appealed to him. He had almost decided that his mother would highly approve if she knew that he had become a person of such substance.

Still, the burden of being an official was obnoxious. It meant that some bothersome bureaucrat might show up and want to go over his books. Hooley had dealt with pesky tax collectors and city officials in St. Louis. He had no wish to do so again.

"You know anything about running a store?" Hooley asked.

"I worked for my daddy till I was past sixteen," Hank said. "I can't

read real good or cipher for beans, but Ina Moon knows how to do that
stuff fair to middling, her folks being missionaries and all. Knows it good
enough to get by, I reckon. Mostly, I know how to sell goods to people,
get what they want, and give them a good price on it so they won't go
elsewhere."

Hooley studied the icy yellow grass of the vacant prairie. He wondered
where Hank's notion of "elsewhere" might lie. The closest thing resembling a store was Pease City, and from what the cowboys told him, any
bargain made there continued to be a poor one.

"It's not a *bad* notion," Hooley admitted. "I'll talk to Margot about it
directly."

"Miss Margot already said it's a good idea. Said she'd tell you that first
thing."

Hooley felt a sharp pain in his stomach. Anger hotter than the scalding
coffee in his cup rose around it. "You mean you already talked to her
about it? *Before* you talked to me?"

"Well, yeah," Hank said. "I didn't want to proposition you, less she
thought it would work. I didn't want you to call me stupid again." He
looked at Hooley squarely. "I don't like it when you do that, Hooley. I'd
be obliged if you'd stop."

Hooley gave him an even stare. "Takes money to open a store," Hooley
said more casually than he felt. "What kind of money do you have?" He
recalled that Hank never asked for credit, always paid cash.

"I got me some saved up. Miss Margot said she'd loan me what I needed
to get started. And Mr. Heinz'll carry me for a while."

Hooley opened his mouth to protest, but then he snapped it shut. The
only money Margot had was what *they* had in the canvas bag under his
cot. He couldn't guess at how much she made last night, but he had been
in business and he knew that by the time she paid the girls, then paid off
Heinz what she owed him for the fancy goods, there wouldn't be much
left.

"I don't reckon it'd take much," Hank said. "Ina Moon said we could
get started with just the stuff the boys need: tobacco and soft goods and
the like. Everybody's always wanting a new shirt or a pair of socks, a new
axe-hammer or a sack of tobacco. Then we could add more stock. I thought
we'd put in a line of guns and knives. There's always a call for that."

"Seems you've got it all worked out," Hooley growled.

"Yep." Hank nodded. "Just need your go-ahead-on."

Hooley thought Hank might be making fun of him, but there was no
trace of sarcasm in the boy's face. Although Hooley bitterly realized he

was giving his approval of Margot's approval, he nodded. "I guess that means you're here to stay, and we'd have a stake in it."

"Well, here's where we are, and I can't think of no other place we might go," Hank said. "Besides, Miss Margot says that if we had a regular store, more folks'd just naturally show up, and this could turn into someplace real." He swept his arms around. "Not just a camp."

Hooley felt the prick of anger. "I'd say it's more than a camp." He remembered what he had said only a few hours before. He had never been so inconsistent in his life. That was another thing he could lay at Margot's feet.

"Well, sure, Hooley," Hank said, apologetically. "But a whiskey shed and a whorehouse and a tentful of cots ain't enough to make a regular town." Hank helped himself to a refill. "You know, I took the Pledge, and I'm a married man now so it's no nevermind to me, but you probably ought to move this whole deal inside Miss Margot's place and use that bar Mr. Mino built. It's sloppy the way you're doing it now."

"*Mister* Mino?" Hooley said, retrieving a stiff nod from Hank. He shook his head in response. "I guess you've already talked this over with him, too."

Hank grinned and shrugged. "Well, since he was to do the carpentering . . ."

"And just what did 'Mister' Mino say?"

"Aw hell, Hooley," Hank replied. "You know how he is. He'll go along with damn near anything, if you ask him right. He's the most neighborly man." Hooley spat into the fire. "Anyhow, you should move inside. Join the party," Hank concluded. "It'd be better for business."

"How I run my business is my lookout. I don't need any help from some green cowboy."

"If you'll give your go-ahead-on, I won't be a cowhand no more," he said. "I'll be a storekeep, good and proper."

"You'll more likely be a stupid idiot, good and proper," Hooley muttered, but Hank chose not to hear the remark, and continued to stand expectantly while Hooley thought it out.

Hooley said nothing for a while. He finished his coffee and threw the dregs into the fire. The cowboys were drifting back toward the fire now, expecting coffee, breakfast. If this kept up, he'd have to find someone else to do the cooking. He also decided he needed to start charging for food. He needed to piss, but the effort of walking off to the flats or down to the privy seemed to require more energy than the urge demanded. He almost forgot that Hank was still standing there, waiting for an answer.

"Well, what is it you want me to do, and what kind of arrangement can we make?" he finally asked. "Mino and I can't go in on your stake and do all that work for free."

"Miss Margot said she'd work out a contract, that it'd be fair."

Hooley nodded, again realizing that his fate was inexorably tied to the redheaded whore's. She was ramrodding things, and he was just a cog in her machine. If he refused, she'd either browbeat him into it or get Mino off on his own and convince him to go ahead without Hooley's help. "Well, I guess we've got a deal," he said, adding with a sarcastic tone. "If 'Miss Margot' says so."

"Reckon so," Hank said, sticking out his hand. "I'm looking forward to being your business associate, *Mister* Hooley."

The Community

1

ANK'S STORE WAS built in a month, although not before complications arose. The young cowboy-turned-merchant decided that it needed to be bigger than Margot's establishment and raised off the ground on a foundation set on large, square limestone rocks quarried from near the creek. This, Hank averred, would help protect perishable goods from rot and varmints, plus keep the structure cooler in the summer because air could circulate below the floor. He also insisted that living quarters be attached to the main room. Such a project required more materials than Hooley and Mino had ever ordered. Milled lumber was expensive to buy and freight, and canvas was going to cost a good deal. Hooley discovered that the cash they were taking in was insufficient to fund the project.

Heinz, though, saw an opportunity and offered to extend credit to make sure the store would become a reality. But when he arrived with Hooley's order things took a rancorous turn. Instead of containing the off-white, bleached cloth Hooley was used to working, the teamster's wagon roared up with stacks of brightly colored material, a mixture of old tarpaulins, thin muslin, and other inferior material. Heinz claimed he had bought the used and mismatched material at a bargain rate from a traveling Wild West show that had stumbled into Jacksboro and then gone bust.

"They was glad to let me have it at ten cents on the dollar," Heinz

explained with a broad grin. "And it's already been sewed up in places.
Ought to save you a pile of work."

Hooley's pride bristled at the idea of accepting low-grade machine-sewn
cloth. "This *makes* work for me, you idiot," he fumed. He discovered that
every prestitched seam would have to be ripped out and redone or rein-
forced with oakum-soaked twine. Most of the grommets were made of tin,
and were already rusted and broken. "This won't do, at all!" he shouted
at Heinz, who ignored Hooley's cursing and took up his customary place
in the whiskey shed. "Hell, it's just bits and pieces, covered with stains
and faded out. Most of it doesn't even match."

"It'll have to do," Heinz replied. "I can't cover your expenses every
goddamn time."

"You've never lost money coming up here," Hooley railed, feeling his
stomach revolt.

"Look, Hooley, I got this at a good price. You'll just have to make do.
Hell, that boy won't know the difference. Tell him all them fancy colors'll
draw customers. That'll put the rag on the bush if nothing else will."

Hooley wouldn't have been surprised to learn that the wily Heinz had
stolen the whole cargo, but he had no choice. The ugly, inferior material
was all he had to work with, and he figured, with an appreciative look at
the northwestern sky, that winter would soon be along in earnest, so there
was no time to waste. He set about immediately ripping out the sloppy
stitching.

Hank did not appreciate Heinz's suggestion that the garish canvas would
be an advantage, especially when Hooley was unable to find enough of the
same color to make a single wall panel. "I can make part of the roof out
of that yellow material," Hooley explained, "but every side will have a
different color. Some'll have two or three patched together."

"It'll look like a quilt," Margot put in, helpfully. "That'll make it look
more homey, don't you think? Quilts always put me in mind of my mama.
She died young."

"It'll look like a medicine show," Hank whined. "I don't want to look
'homey.' And I don't want to think about my mother. She ran off with a
traveling dentist when I was ten." He kicked the ground. "Dang it! It's a
mercantile store. It's got to look respectable, or no one'll want to come
inside. Can't you do nothing, Hooley?" The "mister" had now been
dropped for him and Heinz, Hooley noted. Margot, on the other hand,
remained "Miss Margot," not only to Hank, but to all the young men.

"No," Hooley said, losing patience. "I can't do one damn thing about
it. This wasn't my idea in the first place."

"Don't be stupid, Hooley," Margot said, putting her hand on Hank's arm. Hooley turned away to hide his frustration. She hadn't revisited his cot since the cowboys had started their regular visits, and he had no idea what her intentions were regarding that. All he himself felt was awkward confusion and an irrational desire to avoid her. Their encounters seemed always to end in an argument, one he invariably lost.

"You'll just have to accept what we have for now," she said to Hank, "and we'll try to make improvements as time goes on."

Hank finally reconciled himself to the situation, although not before he elicited a promise from Hooley that the ugly fabric would be replaced as soon as possible. He suggested openly that Hooley was trying to make it hard on him, and only Mino's enthusiasm in raising the frames pacified him.

Once the joining was done, Hooley set to stitching. Mino lined two sides of the main room with sturdy shelves, added a long counter, and built an actual door in front. He even put in window frames in the main room and covered them with cunning one-piece shutters. His craftsmanship was nothing short of amazing, and Hooley took pride in knowing that his own handiwork was joined to such a fine artisan's.

Accordingly, he did what he could to match and mix the outlandish colors of the canvas. One Saturday he sent Hank and some of the boys to fetch several travoisloads of dark red clay from the Pease River's boggy bed, and by digging a pit and mixing the clay with water, he made a runny paste in which he soaked the brighter pieces, thereby muting their loud colors. Ultimately, he did what he could to create a matched look, and when it was over, even Margot allowed that the mutlicolored, canvas-covered building complemented her red tent.

"You should think of getting colored cloth for all the tents," she advised Hooley. "It would make the whole place brighter." He didn't comment, having learned that with Margot silence was the safest and most effective rejoinder.

While the craftsmen worked, Margot's girls began sewing, using scraps of canvas to fashion curtains and creating practical little drapes Hank could pull over shelves. They also put together a large banner to fix over the front door announcing the establishment as the "Hoolian Mercantile Emporium." The building became a community effort, one that occupied every weekday and kept the small settlement's citizenry busy.

Hank was pleased enough with the effort that he stopped complaining and began making a list of his required inventory, which further strained the community money chest. After the building was finished, it took another two weeks for a grumbling Heinz to freight a tandem pair of wagons filled with dry goods of shirts, socks, and dungarees, tools, guns and ammunition, tinned fruit and meats, crackers, pickles, notions, and utensils. Finally, the new merchant's clean pine shelves were well stocked, and Hank was open for business. Two more weeks had passed when Heinz returned with a cast-iron cookstove—a wedding present, Margot said, from the three partners, although neither Hooley nor Mino had been consulted. Heinz also delivered a genuine feather mattress and a brass bed, then shocked Hooley by announcing that it was free of charge to the newly married couple.

"You never gave me one goddamn thing for free," Hooley complained after they wrestled the mattress and bed into the living quarters of the store. "Besides, you don't even like that boy."

"Can't have the first young'un born in this community come into the world on a damn canvas cot, Hooley," Heinz explained with a squinting wink. "Even if he is half Chinee."

"Never heard you complain about a canvas cot before," Hooley said.

Heinz laughed and slapped him on the back. "Don't take such offense, Hooley. We're in business together, and that's different. That bed is needed. It's my gift to the first respectable citizens of this one-horse town." Hooley snorted. "On the other hand," Heinz said, squinting at a fresh order Hooley had prepared, "we need to settle up accounts. It don't do me to make money if I don't get paid, and I brung all that stock here on your bill."

Hooley's cash sack was all but empty. There were plenty of credit slips, but those wouldn't be redeemed until the cowboys were paid. Accordingly, he offered Heinz full ownership of his mules. This satisfied him, so Hooley advised Heinz that he would be wanting more canvas to enlarge the whiskey shed. Then Margot strolled up and told Heinz to forget that notion.

"You're moving inside, Hooley. It's past time."

Hooley bristled. In the past several weeks, she had barely spoken to him, seemed constantly busy with the girls. Now, she was sallying forth to do battle with him once again, and he marshaled his forces in spite of his ready admission to himself that the fight was already lost.

"I think we decided that that was my call," he said. "Selling liquor is my part of the operation. That and the hotel. And all that's working out just fine."

"Don't be stubborn," she said, dismissing his argument with a wave of her fingers. "It's *not* working out fine. You can't keep up with demand, and we're losing money."

"That's my lookout. I manage the saloon, and that's that."

"It's not a saloon. It's just a tarp-covered shed."

"It's what there is," he snapped. "And I'm doing just fine with it. It's mine, damn it."

"No one's trying to take that away from you, Hooley," Margot said. "Don't be such a titty-baby."

She turned to Heinz for support, a gesture that stymied the teamster momentarily. "I don't know nothing about it," he muttered.

Ever since the first night of Margot's business, Heinz had been remarkably amiable in her presence. Even his usual acrimony against women in general had softened, and it had been a good while since he had said anything negative about the "plague of women" that had invaded the community. Hooley often saw him joshing and flirting with the girls and offering to bring them some "geegaw or gimcrack" they had a yen for.

Sometimes, Hooley thought, Margot was no mere woman. Sometimes, he thought she might be a witch who could cast a spell over any man who came near her, even Heinz. "This isn't any of your business," he said to the wagoneer.

Margot sniffed and homed in on Hooley. "Look, this operating out in the open just won't do. It was fine when all there was was you and a handful of cowboys, but now, things have gone too far. Besides, it's too cold out here, and your methods are costly. They're also messy. This place looks junky. Before long, the boys'll just stop drinking here, or they'll start buying their own somewhere else and bringing it in themselves. Then what'll you do?" Hooley opened his mouth to protest that there *was* no "somewhere else," but she put up her hand to silence him. "We need to keep careful records, especially since you're giving out so much credit."

"Credit was your idea!"

"And it was a good one," she affirmed. "So you'd just as well come on inside." She gave him a rare demure smile. "Besides," she added in a soft voice, "it's a lot more fun."

"No." Hooley dug in and faced her green-eyed stare. He was suddenly determined to stand his ground, no matter what the cost. "No! I don't want to come inside, and I'm not going to." He braced himself for her explosion and fired one more shot. "I'm staying right out here!"

"No, Hooley," she said softly. He wasn't prepared for a flanking attack, and he was crumbling. "There's too much inclination for mistakes out here. You might have trouble you can't handle without me or Mino handy."

"What kind of trouble?"

"Just trouble. You never know when one of these boys might pull a gun on you."

"A gun?" He'd never considered such a thing. "Why would they do that?"

"They might decide you're cheating them."

"Cheating!" Hooley exploded. "I've never cheated anybody in my whole life!"

"It's the logical thing to do," Margot said, returning him to the subject. She grinned at him, which confounded him more than ever. "Hooley. I swear, sometimes you have less sense than this squarehead." She glanced affectionately at Heinz, and to Hooley's absolute shock put her hand gently on the teamster's forearm. Heinz blushed. "Now, as soon as you can, you help Hooley move his stock on inside."

"My God!" Hooley said. "This is . . ." He stuttered off. He had no idea *what* it was.

She turned back to Hooley. "I'm not going to discuss it any more. They tell me there's a bunch of new cowboys coming in on Saturday, and we want to be ready. By the way, we're going to be wanting a second privy." Then she flounced away toward her establishment.

"Beats anything I ever seen in the name of the blue-eyed Jesus," Heinz muttered.

"Well, *you* were a fine help!" Hooley yelled, glad to have someone on whom to vent his anger. "You're supposed to be on my side. But you just puddled up and drained away."

Heinz cast his eyes away. "That woman's a panther for trouble. But I warned you, Hooley. Never say I didn't warn you."

"Shut the hell up," Hooley said, but his heart wasn't in it. He had lost once more. He wondered how much more he would have to lose before Margot Phillips was done with him.

2

SATURDAY NIGHT CAME, and because it coincided with payday, the boys were especially frisky. In spite of his best efforts to maintain a sulk, Hooley reluctantly acknowledged that the addition of even a few extra men would have overwhelmed him had he stayed out of doors. As it turned out, more than a dozen new cowboys showed up with the usual complement, most of them crowding into Hank's store and looking over his goods.

Being in Miss Margot's Place while the cowboys danced and cavorted was a chore, though. He had not been inside the red structure since he and Mino had moved the piano in over a month before, and he was surprised by the alterations the women had wrought. The bearskins on the canvas walls gave the main room a warm, solid feel, a sense of permanence. Lanterns were suspended from the triangulated ridgepoles, and there were several crude stools Mino had apparently knocked together. The piano was still jammed, dusty and unused, into the corner where he and Mino had left it, but otherwise the place had an aura of steady and prosperous business.

Just as the boys were coming in from their baths that afternoon—they all insisted on having hot baths, as it was far too cold to use the open air of the creek—Margot caught him staring at the flap-covered passageways to the girls' rooms. Each was marked by pieces of fabric and paper, dried flowers or pictures they had pinned to the rugged cloth. No two were alike, and only one doorway—the one that led to Margot's room—was without any decoration.

He was wondering what that meant when she approached wearing a bright yellow dress, cut lower than usual and accentuating her cleavage, which disappeared in a scurry of light freckles into the plunging neckline. She had a large yellow feather in her hair and wore a long boa of the same color. Her perfume filled his nostrils as quickly as the delicate beauty of her face filled his mind. Her prolonged absence from his cot accentuated his longing, made it almost painful.

"You see, Hooley, I told you you'd be happier here," she shouted over the growing hubbub caused by the rambunctious conversation and whooping of the young men, all of whom were coming inside and demanding drinks and the girls' attention. The group's coy shyness of that first night had never been repeated. Neither had Hooley's failure to let out every cot to those who had the foresight to want a place to sleep when the partying was over.

"You're going to like it much better in here." Her bright smile showed satisfaction, and Hooley resented it. He continued to pour drinks and rake bills and coins from the bar into a cigar box, a businesslike scowl fixed on his face. "You're one hardheaded man," she said to his back. The remark had a bitter edge to it. Angry as he often was with her, resentful as he usually felt toward her, when she was near him and in a happy, flirtatious mood, all his pique dissolved into butter. He now feared that she had lost patience with him. He turned around to her to respond, but all he saw was the swish of canvas and a single yellow feather floating in the wake of her departure.

His ire toward her instantly returned. The way she would say something that infuriated him, then scurry out of sight, was maddening. His stomach turned over in painful protest, but he swallowed his bile and called out to the boys he knew by name, occasionally asking one if he'd like to settle up his bill. Most obliged, so long as Hooley assured them that more credit would be extended when their cash was gone.

The drinkers and dancers soon filled the central room, which Margot had dubbed the "parlor," and strained its capacity. Although it was well below freezing outside, the air under the canvas roof was stifling with the stink of sweat and liquor mixed with smoke, expectoration, and vomit. Hooley sometimes gagged if he took a deep breath.

Mino's head was wrapped in a well-worn piece of canvas in the style of a turban, and he wore an open-throated white shirt bound by a scarlet sash. Instead of denim work pants, he had on a pair of baggy trousers that reminded Hooley of the red pantaloons worn by the Zouave regiments of the Union Army. The happy carpenter seated himself on a high stool next to the idle piano and played his concertina while the girls in their brightly colored dresses and the boys in their boots and spurs stomped up and down the planked floor, occasionally disappearing as this couple or that struck a deal for a brief sojourn to one of the back rooms behind the colored flaps. Mino never drank anything but beer, and always played his instrument and sang with gusty enthusiasm.

Hooley noticed that when the couples returned, the girls dutifully deposited their earnings into a tobacco can on the edge of the bar before engaging another cowboy for a brief turn around the floor, and that each trip behind the canvas walls seemed to diminish the amount of clothing the girls wore until finally they were cavorting and dancing while wearing little more than shimmies and bloomers. As the evening wore on, Hooley had less opportunity to observe anything because of the frantic pace of refilling glasses and wiping those that were returned. He admitted to himself that this more organized manner of commerce permitted him the luxury of resting every few minutes. He even could have had a pipe, but he didn't. Merely taking a breath was to risk choking, without his adding to the congested atmosphere.

He mopped sweat from his eyes and poured liquor, kept money and charges straight, and tried to keep an eye on Margot. She seemed to be everywhere at once: dancing with cowboys, clapping hands and stamping her feet and calling a square while Mino spun out lively tunes. She weaved through the crowd to check on a girl's welfare, offering a flirtatious toss of her red curls to a whooping cowboy, keeping a smile fixed on her face. Nothing escaped her notice, and she seemed to know all the men by name, even the newcomers. Hooley never could tell who, if any, of the cowboys she favored, or who, if any, seemed particularly to seek her out. Jealousy crawled through him like a trapped animal, scratched at the walls of his insides and clawed at his heart. But it was unable to find a place to hold on to long enough to expose the rage slowly building up along with it.

In spite of Hooley's misery, time passed quickly, although there were frequent interruptions when an argument would blow up and Margot demanded that the belligerents take their squabble outside. After a few minutes, they returned, blood streaming from a smashed nose or split lip, maybe a tooth missing, but all smiles and backslapping friends. They would buy one another a round of drinks, and the party would start over again.

Somehow, he got through the night. Things finally wound down, and Margot retired, giving Hooley a big wink as she disappeared behind her curtain. He grimaced in response, then stumbled off to his tent, alone and exhausted. He had barely collapsed onto his cot, it seemed, when loud demands for coffee jerked him awake. He pulled up his braces and staggered out to stoke the fire and began grinding the beans. There had been a light dusting of snow the night before, and everyone was shivering and slapping their sides to promote circulation.

By Sunday night, when the boys were all gone and he and Mino munched their silent way through supper, Hooley found an unexpected pleasure in his accomplishment. The next Saturday, though, the whole thing started over again, and once more, he faced the same problems, the same exhaustion, the same tax on his reserves of ambition and industry. Saturdays, he discovered as the weeks went by, became something to dread. He was continually astonished by self-realizations about his own nature as well. Although he felt no more ambitious than he ever had, Hooley ultimately realized that the indolence that had been the mainstay of his life had passed away. Maybe forever. He found himself antsy when there was no project ahead of him. He was not entirely comfortable with this new manifestation of his personality or with the responsibilities that came with it, for he discovered that as each week marched toward its end, he became filled with dread. It appeared that this would be his fate forever. To his annoyance, Margot delighted in the regularity of it, seemed actually to look forward to the Saturdays as they grew closer.

Hooley now considered moving on, putting this witch of a woman behind him along with all the burdens the settlement had placed on his shoulders. But in a practical sense, things were no different from the day he ran over the boulder and broken his axle. He had no idea where to go and no way to get there, no wagon—and now, no team and no money. Besides that, virtually all of his stock—his canvas, his thread, even his needles—was tied up in the partnership, committed to the community.

He couldn't decide whether he was trapped in Hoolian or merely stuck there.

Two months later, about the time that dread, doubt, and disgust had solidified into desperation and he was seriously contemplating merely stuffing all he could into his Gladstone bag and shouldering his rusty rifle and walking west, Margot resumed regular visits to his cot. As she had always done before, she came to him in the frigid middle of the night and wordlessly disrobed, then snuggled into his side. Hooley's surprise was complemented by his ill-concealed delight.

Even so, he steeled himself. Dozens of times since the opening night of the red tent, he had vowed never again to touch the flesh of this woman who so wantonly gave herself to any man with the price in his pocket. But after a few moments, lying there with her soft sweetness pressing into his body, her hands roaming lightly over his skin, he turned to her, wrapped her in his arms, and brought her as close to him as he could.

His ears picked up a distant braying howl of a coyote, the first he had heard in two months. She must have heard it too, for she squeezed herself more tightly next to him. "Now, Hooley," she whispered into his ear. "Isn't this much, much better?"

He had to admit that it was.

3

SHE RESUMED HER regular visits. They were passionate, albeit costly encounters—each one noted in the ledger by her slender hand—but they were no less sweet than the first time she came to him. She still visited only three nights a week, but there was never any notation in the ledger that she was also providing her "services" to the carpenter. This gave Hooley a sense of security, although he was unable to find any sign of affection in her public treatment of him. If anything, she acted as if he was an overgrown child, a person who needed constant correction and instruction. When he admitted this thought to himself, he realized that her attitude reminded him altogether too much of his mother.

In spite of this, Hooley gradually began to change his mind, once more. Margot's nocturnal attentions moved him to grow content with the notion that for a delightful space of time, he could forget what she was doing every Saturday night and focus on her time with him. He could pretend that she was there with him only because she wanted to be, not because she was charging him for the privilege. When she was there beside him, his feelings for her ran free, unfettered by the vexing way she often had, unburdened by her fierce independence and insistence that what they were about was nothing more than a business proposition.

Although Saturday nights were miseries for Hooley when he witnessed Margot all fancied and painted up, her red hair curled and piled high on her head, her eyelids and lashes heavy with color, and her smile brightening the faces of the men when they danced and joked with her, he couldn't bring himself to hold a grudge toward the young ruffians who sought her company. They came to Hoolian with their anticipations running high, their impish laughter filling the prairie air, their pockets full of money to help balance Hooley's books. Soon he did have to add another money bag.

Gradually, Hooley realized that their arrival was something he stopped dreading and started welcoming. In spite of the unavoidable jealousy that ate at him and made him feel as if he had swallowed something angry and mean, he looked forward to the rollicking music and laughter, even to the heady aromas of tobacco and whiskey breath that would fill Miss Margot's Place every week.

But he still had never danced with Margot. That was a line he couldn't make himself cross. He eventually settled into a pretense that she was actually two people—the bright and dolled-up whore who swung drunk cowboys about by the arm and flashed her long eyelashes in seductive gestures of raw sexual energy, and the soft, demure, and sometimes shy young widow who nestled herself in the crook of his arm and fell in a gentle sleep after they had made love to the baleful music of the coyotes' calls.

There was, of course, a third Margot, the Margot whose lashing tongue stung his ego and smashed his authority at every turn. This was the Margot he was fearful of encountering, the fractious she-bear of a woman who made snarling demands and caustic suggestions that often sounded absurd but, to his everlasting vexation, proved to be right most of the time. That woman was too painful to be around for Hooley to consider for long. He steadfastly refused to give that Margot a space in his mind until she emerged and demanded it, and he tried to forget that particular manifestion of her nature as soon as the encounter with her was over.

As he came to know the cowboys better, he found that to the man, they insisted that they were pleased with life. They found pleasure in spying a hawk on the wing, a rainbow across a mesa, or a massive thunderhead building across the southwestern horizon. They were an uncommonly fraternal band, seldom challenging each other's obvious lies, and unselfconsciously declaring undying friendship for one another in the midst of often brutal teasing that sometimes led to a blustering, manly defense of honor.

Only rarely did such altercations get out of hand, and when they did, Mino was always on the spot to step in and break things up by knocking a couple of heads together before anyone could do any serious harm. During the community's entire existence, there had been no genuine trouble at all, and except for the occasional reminder that up on the flats the buried bodies of a federal deputy marshal and a murdered carpenter lay decomposing beneath the prairie grass, no one would have guessed that serious violence had ever visited the tiny town of Hoolian.

4

SOME SUNDAY AFTERNOONS, the cowboys pacified their hangovers with glasses of beer laced with fresh quail eggs, when they were available, and then often went out on the flats and competed against one another in various shooting contests. Every man jack among them wore a full arsenal of weapons on his person, some sporting as many as six handguns of various calibers and sizes, stuck here and there in their clothing and tack. Margot sometimes complained that they went about more heavily armed than riverboat gamblers. She said it took a customer longer to unlimber his implements of mayhem than it did to get his clothes off.

When they competed, though, they tried each other out on fast-draw competitions and by blasting bottles and cans lofted high into the air. But in spite of the size and variety of their individual weaponry, their prowess with firearms was, to Hooley's mind, unimpressive. He suspected that apart from their occasional target practice, their weapons were more often used as hammers and clubs than as vehicles of violent confrontation, and in some of their cases, he guessed, apart from the contests they never pulled them out at all.

From time to time, the boys sought Hooley's counsel on an individual basis. He feared that they were coming to look upon him as some kind of father figure, a role he neither sought nor relished. Some asked him to write letters home on their behalf—as most of them were barely schooled or even marginally literate—to family and sweethearts. He nubbed their words onto paper while they stumbled around and sought the right way of expressing what they wanted to say, and he was sometimes astonished by their frank confessions of their hearts' contents, their admissions of loneliness and longing for those they'd left far behind.

Often, after completing such a letter, Hooley was nearly overcome with melancholy for the plight of some young towheaded youth who, in spite of his bristling weapons and rough clothes, his jawful of tobacco and swaggering gait, was truly little more than a frightened child. Eventually, he came to believe that very little he ever read in a dime novel was anywhere close to the truth.

One afternoon, the small leather packet of mail Heinz brought carried a letter to the portly cowboy Tidmore, announcing that both his father and brother back in Georgia had been carried away with cholera. The fat youngster listened while Hooley read the scrawled words from the boy's mother. Tears cut through the dust on Tidmore's chubby cheeks and his throat was contracting in rapid, gulping swallows.

"I'm sorry," Hooley said when he finished. He folded the brittle paper, then handed it to the youngster. "I know you wish you could be there for the burying."

"What for?" Tidmore barked, blinking his eyes rapidly. He stuffed the letter into his pocket and pulled out a plug and bit off a chew. "If I'd of been there, I'd likely be dead, too." He started away, then turned back, and his brown eyes became the color of dried mud. "My old man hated me 'cause I was fat, and he beat me with a hickory stick from the time I was old enough to walk," he said. "And my brother was a no-count son of a bitch who stole my girl by telling her I was nothing but a tub of lard who'd squish her if she diddled me."

His eyes were once more moist. "My ma's well shed of me, too. She never favored me, and only wrote this letter to make me feel bad." He kicked the ground. "Well, she got what she wanted, and she can go to hell."

Hooley never saw much remorse expressed by any of the boys over the sad news from their distant homes. At first, he was bewildered by their refusal to admit the futility of their lives. They were unable to save any money, for they were poorly paid and spent every dime they made, often a month in advance. The only women they knew were whores, and the only friends they had were each other. They never considered that they might be doing something more, never thought that they might return home and confront their loved ones with a prodigal desire to try to make a life for themselves while they were still young enough to do so.

At last, it occurred to Hooley why he felt such closeness to them, such kinship. It was because, like him, they were unambitious. They weren't lazy, neither were they slovenly in their manner. They were what they were. They didn't wish to be more.

Margot was wrong, he decided. They weren't ignorant or worthless.

They blamed no one for making them cowboys. They became cowboys because that was what was handy for them. It was something they could do, and it offered them the illusion of freedom and at the same time the sense of belonging. It was, Hooley thought, for much the same reason that he became a tentmaker. He lacked the ambition to do anything else.

The exception was Hank. It seemed he came almost daily to Hooley with questions about inventory, pricing, and other matters of his mercantile enterprise that were totally beyond Hooley's knowledge and expertise. Hooley was too ignorant of such matters to be of any use, but his claims of a lack of experience only increased Hank's demands for instruction.

"Miss Margot says you lived in St. Louis and ran your own business," Hank argued when Hooley pleaded that he didn't know the first thing about a general merchandise store.

"I ran a tent-and-awning company," Hooley responded.

"It's the same damn thing," Hank whined. "You just don't want to help me." Then he'd trudge off and complain to Margot that Hooley was being stubborn, and she'd return to scold him for not being patient enough with the boy.

"He's our center of respectability, Hooley," she told him. "Neither one of us is worth a tinker's dam, and we're more temporary than you think."

"Temporary?" Hooley asked her, perplexed. But in her typical fashion, she changed the subject. "Ina Moon's getting along toward her time," she said. "Hank's nervous, and he'll need a steady hand if things go bad. Be gentle with him."

"Hooley," Hank called as he marched deliberately up to Hooley's tent one crisp afternoon while the tentmaker was sitting back on his stool, leaning against a support post, trying to glean warmth from the winter sunshine. "What's your position on sprinkling and dunking?"

"What?" Hooley had been nearly asleep.

Hank explained that Ina Moon was demanding that they have the baby baptized Baptist, like her. This bothered Hank, who was, he claimed, "a Methodist by trade." He quickly added that he hadn't been inside a church since he was a tyke, and that he truly knew nothing about being either a Baptist or a Methodist, except he knew that the latter believed in getting the whole thing over with by a quick sprinkle and a few words over an infant's head, whereas the Baptists preferred to wait for a few years so they could dunk the child in some handy creek. "Seems to me a body could get drowned that away," Hank said. "I've never been underwater in my whole life."

"Well," Hooley grumbled, trying to relocate the comfort of his former position, "I don't think you need to worry about it. There's not a preacher of either stripe anywhere around here."

"You could do it, Hooley. That's sort of what we planned on."

"Don't be an idiot," Hooley said. "You may have gotten me to marry you, but I'm not about to baptize any babies."

"Well, what good are you, then?" Hank fretted. But Hooley just closed his eyes and waited until the young father-to-be went away.

When winter seemed to seize the land in a permanent grip and one gray day led only to the next, Hank's store became a popular gathering place during the cold afternoons. The girls gathered around a small stove and gossiped. Sometimes, they would sing songs—often hymns, to Hooley's initial astonishment. Hooley took a seat on a stool in the corner, smoked, and sipped coffee while he observed the warm, contented group gathered in front of Hank's well-stocked shelves, helping themselves to pickled cucumbers and soda crackers, and generally milling here and there as if they were comfortably at home.

Soon after the store opened, Hank had forsaken his cowboy duds and now wore a tightly gartered white shirt with a silk cravat over a paisley vest and long apron. He kept his hair oiled and parted in the middle and was trying with no success whatsoever to grow a mustache. Gertie, who revealed substantial talents as a cook, offered the group fresh-baked sugar cookies or possibly a pie, made with plums or quinces or, on occasion, some fresh apples Heinz brought her from Jacksboro.

As he sat in the store and watched his neighbors playing and talking among themselves, Hooley sometimes caught Margot's eye. They would exchange a knowing look, a shared, silent emotion of pride in the warm tide of life that swirled around them. He sometimes wished his mother could see him, and he smiled at the thought of how astonished she would be to observe his contentment, even though he was somehow certain that she would not have approved.

Ina Moon's baby was born on a snowy Easter Sunday morning. Margot played midwife, and Hooley provided free drinks while Mino played lively tunes to cover the mother's labor cries. Finally, Margot called Hank into the room, and shortly he emerged, a squalling infant in his arms. The tiny thing was immediately taken over by the women, who cooed and gurgled over it, arguing over whether or not it favored Ina Moon more than her late husband, whom none of them had ever met. The infant's dark chocolate eyes and mop of coal-black hair obviated the argument, but no one seemed to care. Hank's joy was boundless, and he ordered Hooley to set up drinks for everyone, forgetting his Pledge in his exuberance.

Margot finally came out, sweaty tendrils of hair raking down her forehead, and pronounced that the mother was fine and asleep at last. Hank, proud as a new dawn over his fatherhood, announced that, "on account of it being Easter," the baby would be called James, for the brother of Christ.

Hooley stood and demanded silence. He then offered a toast to the name and to the occasion, and suddenly realized that he had now been there for two full years. As he sipped his drink, his thoughts drifted quickly to the windy wilderness surrounding them, and he was struck with a painful wonder about how much longer all this could possibly last. As if in response to his silent query, he heard something rare and, to his ear anyway, foreboding. Rising above the howl of the wind came the unusual sound of a mournful coyote, crying high and shrill in broad daylight from somewhere out on the loneliness of the prairie.

REGULATOR III

JEFFERSON TAY HAD never been given to superstitious beliefs. During the war, he watched well-educated men cherish good luck charms and talismans, investing clothing or equipment or a particular horse with magical mystery that kept them alive and whole through the hellish storm of battle. Tay regarded such practices as foolish and dangerous. Relying on magical power for safety was merely religion by another name, and religion, insofar as he was concerned, was philosophical quackery. The only power Tay ever put his faith in resided in his hands and his holsters. Like Napoleon, whom he worshiped as a military genius, he believed that fortune was on whichever side had the most strength and willingness to use it.

But now, while Tay's small party made their wintry way into the tiny settlement of Enid, the aging, corpulent outlaw began to rethink the question of luck. He wondered if perhaps he needed some token to dote on, maybe even some god to pray to.

They were at the crest of a small cedar-covered ridge, and he judged the small town of Enid, Oklahoma Territory, to be about a mile away. The northwest wind whipped linen dusters around their bodies, and their horses' heads were lowered in weariness as they moved slowly toward dim points of light in the cold, gray gloom. He couldn't wait to dismount. He wanted nothing more than to sit in a plain chair with his feet on the floor and support for his aching back and throbbing leg. The desire took on a luxurious dimension.

Enid wasn't much of a town, just a railroad water stop that grew into a settlement surrounded by the usual mercantile concerns. Functioning as a stopover for cattle drovers, it boasted the barest amenities. But after nearly two months of camping out on the open prairie, his men needed to rest and refit. Their animals, including Tay's own proud stallion, were about spent, and beneath the men's tattered overcoats, their clothes were nearly in ruin. They'd had little but green meat and beans for a week. It was time to hole up, take a look at the lay of the land, figure out some way of putting things on the right track. The dwindling supply of cash in his saddlebags wouldn't carry them far, but it was better to spend quietly in a backwater outpost than to risk raising some lawman's suspicions in a larger city.

Blasingame was the only one who sat straight in the saddle. The nasty, bloodstained, scalp-filled carpetbag bounced roughly from its latigo tie. Tay wondered if the grisly trophies represented good luck for the large outlaw. Certainly, he was never discouraged, only wryly piqued when plans went awry. Tay had half expected him to take off after the way-station debacle where Coolege was blown in half, but the big blond man proved to be a rock. Leading them, wounded and bloody, away from the ruined cabin, he took them through a hammering hailstorm, found an outcropping of granite rock for shelter, then returned to scavenge bandages and food. He even came up with two bottles of half-decent whiskey, salvaged from the blasted station. What was more astonishing was that he did that even though he was bleeding badly from wounds to his neck and shoulders, the result of flying splinters of rock.

Eubanks was the only one to escape without injury, although he had become as quiet and sullen as had been his late and unlamented relative, Coolege. No sooner had they begun to warm themselves while they inspected their wounds than the short, ugly Arkansawyer openly accused Tay of bungling the whole enterprise.

"They had goddamn dynamite in there," he said. "You should of knew that, Tay, 'fore you went and let this idjit,"—he cast his crooked glare at Manypenny, who was nearest the fire, his bloody head lowered to the heat—"set fire to the whole goddamn world. Got Alvin kilt." The crease in his bald pate glowed in the firelight. "Don't know what I'm going to tell his mama."

"You can tell her he was a damned fool," Tay grumbled. He was seriously worried about himself. His back ached from the fall off his horse, and a large piece of rock from the blast had embedded itself in his left calf. Blasingame had cut it out with his massive knife, then bound it, but it pulsed with an angry throb. When he looked at Manypenny, he felt better. His narrow face was cobwebbed with thin, bloody tracks, one of which traced across his left eye in a deep, red gorge.

"It *was* stupid, Tay," Blasingame said.

"Well, that's a clear fact," Eubanks continued. "I looked in there to see what was holding the door you had us kicking on, I seen the stupid fools'd stacked up a box of dynamite against it."

"That's enough," Tay growled. "I'll hear no more about it."

"Seems to me like you need to hear—"

"Be quiet, Mr. Eubanks. I'm in some pain, and I will not hear more from you."

"I think maybe you're over the hill, Tay," the short, ugly man shot back.

Tay's hand found the butt of his Navy Colt's in the clutch holster beneath his arm. "Mr. Eubanks, I've heard quite enough." He looked at Blasingame. "That goes for all of you."

Blasingame smiled back, took out his knife, and began whetting it. He offered a narrow glance toward Eubanks, which Eubanks briefly mocked, before settling back, scowling, and muttering, "You know it's true your own damn self. We can't afford no more of this kind of thing."

"What would you know of it, Mr. Eubanks?" Tay muttered, replacing his pistol. "You're a recent arrival, barely a recruit. You don't have experience with our methods."

"Your 'methods' stink," Eubanks said. "Alvin said—"

"I think I'd shut up, I was you," Blasingame cut him off. "When Tay talks, he don't like being interrupted." Eubanks once more fell into a sulk.

That settled things for the moment, but it gave Tay pause. It was sad that things had come to this pass, almost tragic. The consideration that he had wasted most of his best years settled over him like a thin blanket.

The line of horsemen topped another rise, and the lights of Enid twinkled brightly in the gathering gloom of a wintry twilight. They were on the outskirts, and signs of civic activity were now visible near the town's clapboard buildings. Tay stopped his weary horse and called a halt. The men formed a small half circle, hunching over against the blistering wind. It was a moonless night, but the sky was clear, in spite of the crisp norther. Eubanks had a silk scarf taken from some hapless homesteader's wife wrapped around his head, and Manypenny's facial bandage was black with filth. He had lost his big rifle and had been sullen and cross ever since.

Tay began distributing coins: twenty dollars to each. It was a sizable portion of what he had, but he knew that left to their own devices, they would steal what they couldn't afford. "I want no trouble in this town," he said. He pressed a small stack of cartwheels into their outstretched palms.

"Got me a toothache," Eubanks whined.

"Move quietly and create no stir," Tay repeated. He looked at Manypenny, whose recovery he regarded as nothing short of miraculous. The bandage that covered half his face was nearly black with filth and dried blood, but he claimed he could still see out of the damaged eye socket. "It's vital to remain inconspicuous."

"Don't tell us how to act," Eubanks shot back. "We're not a bunch of green young'uns."

"I have only enough specie to repair our kits. Care is required to remain incognito."

"Why don't you talk English," Eubanks muttered. "I'll do as I please."

"I'll brook no problem from you, Mr. Eubanks."

"You're the one who's the problem, Tay," Blasingame said quietly.

Tay's head shot up, and he narrowed his eyes. He put his hand on the hilt of his sword. It was bent, and he could feel the knuckle guard biting him through his leather gauntlet. "I am obliged to ask in what context you make such a remark, Mr. Blasingame."

"Ain't no 'context,' Tay," Blasingame said. "Just saying we'll mind our manners. You got all the money, though," the blond outlaw noted. "So I reckon we got no choice but to keep you healthy." He winked, but a threat was implicit in his voice. Tay gave his self-appointed lieutenant a long look, then turned his horse and kneed him forward. Now, he had to add Blasingame to his inventory of worries.

He should have given them five dollars apiece more, he thought. But to do so now would make him appear weak. There wasn't much more, anyway. The mysterious black box in the way station had carried only a bundle of papers, which might well have been greenback dollars before they were baked to ash. There was no way to tell.

Since leaving the station, they had found little other opportunity to enrich themselves. What few farms they had raided in Oklahoma Territory were too poor to yield more than meager rations and a few head of scrawny livestock hardly worth the trouble to butcher and eat. Quality horses weren't to be found. They kept close to the territory's western environs, and Tay was grimly reminded that the only white people settling in those parts were likely as poor and dispossessed as they were. There were exceptions, of course, but more prosperous places were well guarded. He couldn't chance a major operation with a bunch that was in such bad shape.

He pondered their problems as they crossed a small wooden bridge and rode into town. The main street was surprisingly well lighted with gas lamps—an innovation Tay did not welcome. The men crossed the mid-point of the business district while people took obvious note of the sorry state of these riders and their animals. Open sores marked the horses' flanks, and the animals' eyes bulged as they half stumbled down the principal thoroughfare. Heavily armed visitors were by no means strangers to Enid, which likely had seen every conceivable level of human vagabond pass through its streets. But this group, with weapons bristling from their waist belts and saddle holsters, their ragged, bloodstained clothing and filthy bandages, their long hair tied in knots behind their heads, their unkempt beards, attracted special notice.

Tay could read disgust behind the curious faces turned toward them. He felt curiosity turn to suspicion, then wariness, but never did he read in their collective study anything like the fear he had once inspired when he rode into a town at the head of a company. Then, grown men's bowels would loosen at the mere sight of his command. Now, all he saw was chary anxiety.

The quartet reined in front of The Belle of the Plains saloon. Tay shifted his great weight, winced from the pain in his back and leg. He noticed that a few idlers scurried away hurriedly. He sighed; a man with a badge would soon appear. "Mr. Blasingame, see to the horses, if you will. There is a livery back down the street. Perhaps you can arrange a decent price for fresh mounts."

"We're *buying* horses?" Blasingame's stubbled face filled with incredulity.

"Make as good a trade as you can," Tay cut him off. "Our pockets are not deep." He ran his muddy eyes over the three men. "Remain where you can be found quickly and easily. We may have to absent ourselves without warning."

"It's been a dry month," Manypenny said. "I ain't retreating till I've had me a drink."

Eubanks looked up and revealed severely chapped lips offsetting a wind-blistered face. "Need me a hat," he said, rubbing a ragged glove over his scarred bald head. "I'm raw as green-cut cedar." He stuck a black finger into his mouth and rooted around. "*And* I got to get this chopper jerked out."

"Here comes John Law," Manypenny hissed. "Always tell by the way they walk."

A tall man in black coat, vest, and hat was moving toward them. The circular badge of a town marshal was visible on his chest. Tay dismounted heavily. He almost groaned when his bulk sank on his injured leg. He had trouble putting weight on it at all. For a moment he leaned on his weary mount and fought back the sheet of sweat that instantly covered his forehead in spite of the chilly wind. Finally, he handed his reins up to Blasingame, who scowled at the tall man and kept his hand on his weapon's stock.

"We *buy* horses here," Tay reminded him. "I want no problems with that constable." The tall man was closer. "Have I made myself clear?" Tay repeated, waiting for Blasingame's reluctant nod. "Very well. Disperse. I must deal diplomatically and expeditiously with this gentleman."

"Try talking English to him," Eubanks suggested. "Maybe that'll help."

Blasingame led the horses away, while Eubanks and Manypenny climbed onto the raised boardwalk. Tay offered his most congenial smile to the man with the badge.

"Colonel Thomas O'Halloran at your service," he said expansively, using an alias he formed years before. "To what do I owe the honor of this official greeting?"

The marshal, a handsome, trim-bearded man some ten years junior to Tay, with graying hair and piercing blue eyes, examined Tay's proffered hand but neglected to accept the gesture. "Burt Henry," he said. "Marshal of Enid."

"*Enchanté*, Marshal." Tay nodded his head and affected a shiver. "I wonder if we could repair indoors? It's breezy, and I am nearly exhausted and in need of libation." He stepped toward the saloon, fighting a tide of pain when his leg threatened to collapse, but Henry didn't move. "I would offer to stand you to a round, but I am not in funds—"

"I was just wondering who you are and what business you have here."

"Well, you already have my name: Colonel Thomas O'—"

"Colonel?"

"Retired," Tay said with a morose note. "Late of the Western Department."

Henry's eyes remained fixed on Tay. "A Reb colonel?"

"It is customary for gentlemen holding any rank above major to retain the honorific."

"Wouldn't know," Henry said. His eyes looked Tay up and down, rested briefly on his bandaged leg. "War's been over a spell. Y'all lost." Tay was determined to avoid an argument, and smiled weakly. "Want to know if you're planning any trouble here," Henry continued.

"Trouble?" Tay's eyes widened. "Why, Marshal! If washing off a bit of your brittle soil and availing myself of the best meal this fair city has to offer is trouble, that's certainly *all* I shall create." He looked down at his leg. "I may consult your local apothecary. Nasty fall, you know."

Henry glanced toward Blasingame's retreating form. The other men were now out of sight. "Looks like a rough bunch you rode in with," he observed. "All shot up."

Tay's eyes widened. "Why, Sheriff—"

"Marshal."

"Marshal, I give you my word, as an officer and a gentleman, that not one of my men is suffering from any sort of gunshot wound."

Henry nodded once and met Tay's eyes with a steady gaze.

"Them horses been put to hard use."

Tay shook his head sadly. "We have been pursued by a band of desperados for several days," he said, noting with satisfaction that Henry's eyes brightened in curiosity.

"Desperados?"

Tay nodded vigorously. "Ever since we left Kansas. Brigands purloined our wagons."

"That a fact?" Henry weighed every word.

"I should say so! They have given us no peace, although they've seldom come close enough to deal with in any direct way."

"Who was they?"

"Alas, they never exposed themselves for close inspection," Tay said. "They followed us until we escaped their notice after we crossed the Arkansas some days ago."

"The Arkansas," Henry repeated curiously, as if Tay had named a mythical waterway.

"I suspect that renegade savages may have been among them. We are fortunate to have eluded them, and we sought to come here for refuge and refitting before proceeding."

"Proceeding where?"

"To the silver mines of Colorado," Tay said with a broad smile. "My information is that a man can make a ready fortune there if he's not adverse to hard work. We shall replace our saddle mounts, purchase some fresh supplies here in your fair city."

"Got me a telegraph wire from a Texas Ranger captain name of Ellis over by Tascosa," Henry said. "Said to be on the lookout for bad actors from off the Caprock." He squinted at Tay. "Says they're coming after them."

"Indeed?" Tay beamed interrogative innocence toward Henry's face.

Henry continued, "Somebody robbed a station over in the Wichitas." Tay waited for him to say more. "What kind of work did you say you do, *Mister* . . . uh, mister?" Henry asked.

"I am presently between professions," Tay said, sighing. "I have served in many vocations since the dissolution of my military career. I have been a businessman for the most part, however. A stockman at times, and—"

"—A regulator?" Henry interrupted. "These rascals fashion themselves to be regulators."

Tay shook his head, sadly. "I cannot lie to you, Marshal. I have been so employed. In the past." Henry's eyes narrowed. Tay drew himself erect. "Your tone bespeaks disapproval."

"Never had much use for hired guns," Henry said.

"Well, I can understand your position, Marshal. But the frontier is a wild place and men are often called upon to take unusual measures in defense of their property."

"Don't much like hired guns."

"We are all limited to whatever lot fate shows us in life," Tay said. His patience with this narrow man was exhausted. "Such is the state of my talents," he went on, "that I have often been entrusted with the leadership of men." Tay opened his hands and shrugged.

"You'll be riding out tonight." It was a statement, not a question.

"Tomorrow," Tay responded. "Or the day after, if that will satisfy you. We need to recuperate. We have had a rough ordeal. Several of us had bad falls from our mounts in our attempt to escape those Kansas brigands. Each of us requires minor medical attention—the result of our adventures, *not* armed conflict—and we need to purchase fresh horses."

"Rangers could be here directly," Henry said flatly. "Ain't that far from Tascosa. Three, four days' ride, at most. Rangers'll kill good horses to run a man down." He looked at the sky, and Tay followed his gaze. "Weather's coming. Best you be gone when they get here. Rangers don't dawdle when they take a notion to hang somebody and light out ahead of a bad storm."

"I am certain you will make them as welcome as you've made me," Tay said. "But now, I do wish to retreat inside. I am in need of restorative spirits and fresh tobacco."

"Be gone tomorrow," Henry said. "Before noon. I don't much like Rangers messing around my town. Ain't supposed to come over here, but they will if they're a mind to." He looked off into the darkness. "Go anyplace they goddamn please, seems to me."

His speech was done, and Henry looked momentarily confused. Then he started off. "Be gone soon's you can," he threw over his shoulder. "Trouble from Texas ought to stay in Texas. We got enough to deal with in Oklahoma Territory. I got no use for Texas."

Tay waited for the small crowd of spectators to disperse before he hitched his belt and limped up the wooden steps and entered The Belle of the Plains. The saloon was smoky, lit only with the dim orange glow of kerosene lamps. Deserted gaming tables were lined against a back wall at the end of a long bar. He quickly spotted Manypenny sitting alone at a small table, a bottle of gin and a candle in front of him. Somehow, he'd managed to replace his filthy bandage with a clean wrapper, but it was poorly fitted. It sagged and revealed the jagged edges of his wound. The small man's dark eyes were filled by the tiny yellow flame of the candle.

"I do like a yellow fire," Manypenny said when Tay sat down. "A red or blue fire is prettier, but a yellow fire is warming."

"That was very nearly a speech for you, Mr. Manypenny." Tay waited uselessly for a smile from the ratlike man. "I am impressed. Are you considering a change of vocations? Chautauqua speaking, perhaps?" Manypenny downed his drink and poured himself another. "Where did Mr. Eubanks go?" Tay sighed and signaled for the bartender's attention.

"Went next door to get a tooth pulled. Buy a hat," Manypenny responded, keeping his eyes on the flickering flame.

A woman appeared at Tay's elbow. "You drinking or just sitting?" she asked. "Or was you interested in something more personal in the form of entertainment?"

Tay looked at her gap-toothed smile. She was short and heavily painted. Stringy blonde hair frizzed into what might have once been curls, but now looked like badly soiled pieces of hawser left to rot on some boatman's wharf. If she weighed two hundred pounds, he estimated, it was because she had starved herself for a month. Her triple chin swelled and descended into the roll of a fat neck that thickened into ponderous tops of breasts that threatened to erupt from her bodice. Tay's eyes lingered on a large hairy mole on the right one as the odor of cloying perfume struck his nostrils, and he shuddered. The thought of entering a bed with her—of viewing her naked—was revolting.

"A bottle of your best brandy, if you please." he said.

She scowled and waddled off. Tay turned to Manypenny. "Was that voluptuous siren your sister of mercy?" he asked. Manypenny gave him a confused look, and Tay clarified, "Did she change your bandage?" Manypenny nodded, lost in his study of the flame. How, Tay wondered, had he come to so low a point as to rely on a reprobated arsonist for conversation?

The woman returned with a dusty bottle and a glass. "Two dollars, silver or gold," she said. "And I got to have hard money, 'forehand. Brandy's hard to come by." Tay reluctantly fished out two flat coins. "We don't get a lot of call for it," she admitted, scooping the cartwheels from his palm. "Mostly for medicine purposes. Dropsy and the like."

Tay poured a dollop into the glass and lifted it. "I too am in need of medicinal aid," he said, nodding toward his leg. "A fresh dressing would be welcome."

"Done all the bandaging I'm 'bout to do tonight. One's my limit. I ain't no Florentine Nightingale," she said, then waited. "But how about the other?" she asked. "You feeling sparky? I charge two dollars for me, too. They's rooms upstairs."

Tay looked into her chubby face and cloudy blue eyes. Beneath the heavy powder, there was a deep scar running from her hairline down across her nose.

"No, thank you," he said. "I fear we have been on the trail for a long time, and I'm more in need of a fresh dressing, a bath, a good meal, and"— he gestured to his stained and worn uniform—"and a laundry."

"I ain't no cook and washerwoman," she said, irritably. "You think I'm a China gal?"

"I think you are interfering with my peace and quiet," Tay said, sharpening his tone. "Would you mind?" His eyes darted toward the bar, where the apron-clad attendant scowled and watched. Tay sighed. "Forgive my rudeness. But I'm in need of solitude."

"What about him?" She nodded toward Manypenny.

"He's less company than being alone," Tay remarked. Manypenny ignored them.

She shrugged and walked away, giving him a dark look over her shoulder. "Name's Goldie, you change your mind," she said.

Tay downed his drink, poured another, then pulled out his pipe and filled it with the last of his tobacco. "I had a word with the marshal," he said. "There's a possibility we might be discovered by that party of Rangers I thought we had eluded." Manypenny offered no reaction. "We depart at dawn," Tay continued. "The estimable state of Kansas is the nearest haven. I confess I haven't longed to return after so long an absence."

Manypenny's eyes stayed on the flame, the one inside the damaged socket seeming to glow beneath the scabby wound. "Kansas'll burn yellow," he said.

Tay sipped and felt the warmth of liquor spreading through him. "If you have decided against improving yourself with a bath or a decent meal, perhaps you could find Mr. Blasingame and see how he's handled the purchase of horses. We can spare no chance."

"You ask me, I think you're scared of them Texans." Manypenny shoved the bandage back into place, leaving the damaged eye exposed.

Anger swarmed about Tay's head. "I have issued an order, Mr. Manypenny," he said. "I suggest you carry it out or suffer my severe displeasure."

Manypenny raised his dark eye and stared into Tay's face for a moment. "I ain't worried about your goddamn 'displeasure,'" he said. He stood, pushed his bandage back into place. "You're running this outfit, Colonel Tay," he said. "But we ain't had a payday in a month of Sundays. When things get this skinny, I get powerful urges." Before Tay could respond, Manypenny extinguished the candle with the palm of his hand, picked up his bottle, and left.

Manypenny was a veritable fount of words this night, Tay thought. He glanced at the bar, from where Goldie watched him, then he rose, tucked the bottle beneath his arm, and hobbled out. He limped down the planked walkway to the edge of the business district, where he found a Chinese laundry next to a tonsorial parlor. There he obtained a bath and had his hair and beard trimmed while a dark-eyed Indian girl cleaned his uniform, blacked his boots, and washed and ironed his clothes. The oriental owner offered him fresh bindings for his leg, which Tay was pleased to see no longer seeped or bled.

Refreshed and feeling better about himself, he crossed the town's streets, which glowed with soft yellow gaslight, the lamps flickering in the increasing wind. While devouring a bowl of greasy chicken and dumplings in a hotel's restaurant, he began again to worry about his associates. Except for Eubanks, Tay tallied, a man who was too stupid to be crazy, his party consisted of two maniacs: one who seemed to want to set fire to everything, and another who was very likely plotting mutiny, if not some form of pointless mayhem. The situation was not comfortable, and might not be improved in the near future.

Tay finished his dinner, purchased a cigar, and stumped back to The Belle of the Plains. The saloon was now half-full of men and women, drinking, dancing. A small group sang raucously around a piano, and small knots of men gathered around the faro and chuck-a-luck tables. Goldie was nowhere evident, but Tay found Manypenny and Eubanks seated with two women, each as thin as Goldie had been fat. Neither was more inviting. Rotten teeth and bad complexions seemed to be a vocational requirement for whores in Oklahoma Territory, he observed. Eubanks had apparently found soap and water and had managed a shave, but his fore-head was smeared with a poultice of some kind. His eyes were half-closed.

"Was Mr. Blasingame successful in his endeavors?" Tay asked.

"If you call paying near a hundred dollars for a string of green-broke, sag-bellied nags 'successful,' I reckon we was," Eubanks offered. "I'm here to tell you he wasn't none too happy." He put his arm around one of the whores. "They're waiting for you to come by the livery to pay."

Tay nodded. That would leave only a few dollars in his diminishing stash. "We should resupply and depart at first light."

Eubanks turned a bleary look on Tay. "Hell, I thought you said we could lay around here for a couple days." He pulled a laudanum bottle from between his legs and drank deeply. The combination of liquor and opium ringed his eyes with blackness. "Look, we been out yonder too long already. We need to rest up some." He turned his attention to the woman next to him, grabbed her skinny breast, and almost shouted, "Ain't that right, Queenie?"

Queenie giggled and pulled him close. "You're funny," she said. Many-penny's female companion brayed out a laugh and nodded in agreement as well, although he was paying no attention to her, captured as he was, once more, by the flickering candle.

"A yellow flame's the prettiest there is," he said. "Seasoned wood and dry grass burn yellow, pure yellow. Ain't that right?" He looked at the woman next to him and grinned. Tay was astonished. In all their time together, he'd never seen the man so much as smile.

"Got that tooth pulled and doctored up," Eubanks said, tilting the lau-danum bottle. "Had me a shave, now I want me a bath." He gave Queenie another squeeze. "I *need* me a bath."

"You'll have no argument from me on that point," Tay said. "But we depart at dawn. I don't want to tarry." He looked around the barroom. "Where *is* Mr. Blasingame?"

Manypenny rolled his good eye toward the stairs leading to the second floor. "With Goldie, the one you didn't want before."

"You didn't want *Goldie*?" Queenie asked, incredulous. "You don't know what you're missing," she said with a laugh. "She's got a tongue like a cat." She looked him up and down. "You're a big ol' boy," she said, reaching out to touch the saber's hilt. "That's some sword you got." She tugged at his trousers. Eubanks reined her in and hugged her, making her squeal with delight.

"I got me a 'sword,' too, sweetie," Eubanks said. "It's a whole lot bigger than fat boy's here. I seen his—more like a busted jackknife." Queenie and her companion brayed like mules.

Tay turned and went outside. The men be damned, especially Eubanks. He would let the Rangers have them. The worst Missouri bushwhackers were less loutish.

He had no idea where he might go from here. Kansas beckoned, but now that the Rangers were pursuing him here, returning to Texas was not utterly out of the question. A lesson he had learned well was always to do what was not expected. He had observed Robert E. Lee and Stonewall Jackson tying the Union Army in knots by refusing to take the most likely course of action. His heading back into the enemy's rear was the last thing the Rangers would expect. Besides, the place he needed to reach was Mexico, and Texas was, for better or worse, on the way.

Then he sagged. The thought of setting out immediately did not appeal. Weariness weighted his body, and his leg protested his every step. And alone, without the protection even the worst of company afforded, he was vulnerable. He was a leader, not a loner. He required men behind him, even these men. Moreover, he wouldn't get far on the money he had. He needed to get organized, find something to fund their ultimate escape from the Rangers' hanging ropes.

He spied a general merchandise store's windows, still lighted against the early winter darkness, and strolled in and began buying staples. Each dime spent renewed his resentment. He emerged from the store with bundles of coffee, beans, bacon, and flour. He had ammunition for his weapons and a fresh supply of tobacco, as well as two bottles of whiskey. He had just stepped off the boardwalk when his eye caught movement right beyond the glow of the flickering gas lamps. He stepped back next to a building, and from its shadows he spied a body of men riding down the main thoroughfare: Texas Rangers.

Their horses had been ridden hard and were lathered in spite of the chill. The men wore heavy coats and bandannas over their mouths, and their broad-brimmed hats were pressed down against the cold wind. The leader wore a patch over one eye and looked neither left nor right as he passed Tay's concealed position. Their circled-star badges shone in the bright gas lamps. They had the desperate look of seasoned killers, and Tay briefly envied their one-eyed leader. He knew what it was like to lead such fearsome men, not the frontier detritus he himself commanded.

Tay's mind raced. He was helpless and alone. His men were carousing inside a saloon, and the best of them was rolling with an ugly whore in the rooms above. He waited until the company passed, then crossed the street and turned toward the livery. There was no time. He would have to go on his own, immediately. A quality commander knew to retreat when there was no hope of victory, especially if his men were being unreasonably insubordinate. It would serve them right to swing from a Ranger's rope.

Keeping to the shadows, he followed the bunch at a distance. At the livery, they dismounted, and one led their horses inside. The others stood in the middle of the street, stomping their feet to restore circulation to their legs, until their companion emerged, at which point they walked off as a body.

Tay waited until they faded into the night's gloom and their jangling spurs could no longer be heard, then walked as quickly as his aching leg would allow toward the livery. As he passed an alley opening, he was grabbed and jerked nearly off his feet. His packages went flying, and a strong grip fastened onto his right wrist.

"Unhand me, sir!" he hissed at the burly figure. The welcome heat of personal combat pushed aside all thoughts of fear and flight. "I am armed and prepared to defend myself!"

"Goddamn, Tay," Blasingame's familiar voice came back to him from the darkness. "If you're not the order-givingest son of a bitch I've ever had dealings with."

"We must be away immediately," Tay said, nodding down the street.

"Yeah, I seen them," Blasingame said. "Rangers don't come to Oklahoma Territory unless they mean to hang somebody, and I'd say we was ripe. The horses are out back the livery." He grabbed up Tay's bundles. "Guess we'll be stealing our horseflesh after all, huh, Tay? Shame the lawmen's horses is blown. Some fine animals in that string."

He stepped back into the shadows and moved off. Tay understood that control was passing to his lieutenant. But there was no time to question anything. He limped painfully after Blasingame. It was pitch black in the corral behind the livery, but in a few moments, a breathless Eubanks appeared, an absurd derby crammed over his ears, making him look shorter than ever. "I wanted me a bath," he groused. "Goddamn Texans. Can't leave a man alone for a single minute."

Tay gritted his teeth against the pain and mounted, but his poorly broken beast shied from the sudden weight and nickered loudly. He was going to miss that stallion, he thought. He settled his bulk into the saddle and drew his sword. "Where is Mr. Manypenny?" he demanded. "We must be off before those men confer with the marshal."

A shaft of light from a doorway speared the dark ground, and the small man emerged. He swung silently up into the saddle, slapped the reins, and rode off into the night. Blasingame and the others instantly followed. Flustered, Tay spurred his own horse after them, riding hard into a rising, bitter north wind that spat small flakes of ice in their faces. Tay pushed himself into the lead, then, judging them to be a good mile from the town, he slowed and picked his way, aware that hazards hidden in the dark could fatally confound them.

"We need to stop and wind the horses," Blasingame called out. "It's goddamn cold, and they're not used to this. They're nags, not worth a tin shit to begin with."

In the distance, Tay could see the dim glow from Enid's streetlamps. He reined up. "We cannot afford to tarry, gentlemen. This is a stubborn band of men who track us."

"They won't be coming in such a hurry tonight," Manypenny said. As the small man spoke, Tay realized that the glow of the town behind them was far brighter than it had any right to be, and a deeper chill than any caused by the wind thrilled through him. A high-pitched keening filled the windswept air as well, something eerie and terrifying on Tay's ear.

"What have you done, Mr. Manypenny?" A flame much brighter than gas lamps formed and grew while he stared. It cast a ghostly reflection off the low-scudding clouds.

"He took care of goddamn business," Eubanks shouted.

"My God, the horses," Tay said, his voice low, almost choking. He thought of his beautiful stallion, and tears came to his eyes. Trading him was one thing, but this was too much.

The men were now all faintly illuminated by the eerie yellow tint. The keening had stopped. The horses were dead. "Somebody had to do something," Eubanks said, "and the firebug here was the man to do it. You was getting too flighty, Tay."

"Always did like a yellow flame," Manypenny said. "Nothing burns yellow like seasoned wood."

Tay took a deep, resolving breath, pulled out his pipe, and filled it. In spite of the bitter wind blowing down his collar, he was sweating hard. He turned in the saddle and faced the arsonist. "Mr. Manypenny, my compliments. You have shown remarkable initiative."

"Like hell, Tay," Eubanks snorted. "You was too scared to know fuck from fart."

Tay wheeled his horse and put the point of the saber on Eubanks' skinny chest. "Mr. Eubanks," he said, "I am in command of this company." Eubanks' eyes flared. "One more insolent remark from you, and I will dispatch you like the inbred white trash you are." Eubanks' mouth fell open, and Tay tightened his gauntleted fist and pressed the point hard enough to force the smaller man to arch his back. "Do not mistake me," he said. "I am aware that you have the advantage of chronology and agility." He pressed harder, and Eubanks' hands flew to the cantle to steady himself. "But I have superior audacity, and I will put this blade through the coddled rancidity of your heart with no more compunction than I would spear an oyster from a shell."

Eubanks' eyes darted to Manypenny, whose face was still turned toward the flames in the distance. Tay heard Blasingame chuckle, and he relaxed his point and backed his horse away from the astonished Eubanks, who almost fell backward from his mount.

"Mr. Blasingame," Tay spoke evenly. "I am gratified by your presence of mind concerning the danger that stalks us. I feared you were overly occupied with that woman."

"No woman," Blasingame said with a shrug. "Just a whore." From inside his bloodstained coat, he removed a thick mass of hair, gore crusting on the dirty curls that, in the yellow glow of the town's firelight, looked like badly soiled pieces of hawser left to rot on some fisherman's wharf.

BOOK THREE

The Enterprise

ILL WINDS

―――◆•≍•◆―――

1

WEST TEXAS WAS always windy. Gilbert Hooley had long since developed the habit of automatically storing away anything lighter than an iron skillet as soon as he finished with it. The spring following the birth of James Moon Mitchell, the winds were particularly fierce, as if Nature herself were trying to uproot Hooley and his tiny community from their dubious foothold.

Hooley took special pride in the durability of his canvas city constructions. Thus far, no damage that couldn't be quickly fixed had been done to a single one of the structures. Hooley's expertise with needle and thread and his constant maintenance prevented the slightest rent in walls and roofs.

Hooley devoted several tedious hours each week to inspecting seams and stitches, making minor repairs, and noting spots where patches might soon be wanted. He took renewed pride in the craftsmanship his father had bequeathed to him. He thought of his mother and what a great fool she had been not to appreciate such a thing. But then, in a galling flash of bitter reality, he admitted that even if she had known about it, Bertha Hooley would have caustically pointed out that no one but a handful of cowboys and whores were present to witness the results of her son's handiwork.

Interspersed with the windy spring days were occasional calm afternoons that reminded Hooley of the ferocious heat to come later in the summer. On such evenings, flies and gnats emerged. The irritating, biting pests lit on everything, making any moment of stillness even more miserable. When sunset arrived, swarms of mosquitoes swarmed from the creek to buzz around everyone's head and create impromptu outbursts of frustrated fury from the human inhabitants. Any breath of breeze, when it came, was a blessed relief, especially if it promised rain to wash the dust from the exposed and fly-specked canvas.

But heavy winds, hot weather, and annoying insects did little to dissuade the cowboys from their weekly visits. Business rocked along while the partners prospered and—generally at Margot's demand—sought ways to improve their holdings. Such endeavors and ideas as the redheaded madam suggested, though, required the preamble of Hooley's trying to make the thick carpenter understand what was wanted. Frequent bouts of acrimonious shouting and cursing in the middle of the compound always attracted everyone out of doors to watch the burlesque.

Regardless of whether he understood the tentmaker or not, Mino's patented response, "No shit, Gil Hooley"—inflected one way for acknowledgment, another for a lack of understanding—always brought squeals of laughter from the whores' soprano chorus and greatly amused Hank and Ina Moon as well.

"I swear, you're better than a carnival show," Hank once gasped to Hooley after a particularly exhaustive effort. Hank had tears running down his youthful cheeks and invading the chin whiskers he was desperately trying to grow.

"Go to hell," Hooley shot back. "Why don't you shave. You look like a goat."

"You're a sight when you get all worked up," Hank retorted, still laughing.

In time, Hooley decided that Mino deliberately postponed apprehension of his instructions just to irk him. It provided a lengthier performance for the attractive covey of girls, all of whom fawned over the stout carpenter whenever he appeared. Hooley determined to hold his instructive sessions elsewhere, but he never managed to do so.

Work did progress, however. They extended the boardwalk to connect Miss Margot's Place to the other tents, added a second privy, and put up another structure near the well-established fire ring. Open on the lee sides from the prevailing winds, it was dubbed the "café tent." Mino knocked together several benches and tables and brought stones from the creek bed to construct a crude rock kiln for baking bread.

Hooley was eager to divest himself of the duty of cooking for the entire town, but he had small success. Gertie, the pert brunette, volunteered to handle some of it, but she wasn't much taken with it, Hooley could tell. "She didn't come all the way out here to cook for a bunch of ignorant cowhands," Margot informed Hooley. "If all she wanted to do was whip up a meal for some worthless man, then she could have stayed in Oklahoma Territory and married an outlaw or a another lawman. They both have good appetites."

In all, Hooley took an almost unconscious satisfaction in the comfortable feeling of consistency that continued to grow around the site of his original misfortune. So long as nothing taxed his natural indolence beyond toleration, he discovered a pleasing rhythm in the ebb and flow of life. And, of course, that life centered on the red tent and its beautiful young whores.

The girls, though, posed a different set of problems. He remained fumblingly confounded by the young women and their flirtatious ways, and the whole time they had been here, he had never once had a private conversation with a single one of them. He reluctantly admitted that they intimidated him with their girlish beauty, but he also was chary of exhibiting any familiarity toward them that Margot might use as an excuse to accuse him of impropriety. It was as if his home had been invaded by strangers he was forced to ignore but who were constantly in his way.

Except for the occasional social afternoons in Hank's store—which diminished in frequency as the season warmed—Hooley was only rarely able to observe them for any length of time. Keeping himself distant from them was the best position he could maintain. But the tiny town of Hoolian was far too small for anyone to remain completely isolated, and as the season warmed and the girls spent more time out of doors, Hooley grew more sensitive to the collection of beauties flitting around the tent city, and his vexation over the matter grew.

Hooley was not naïve. He knew that the nature of the business of these women abrogated personal modesty. Displaying their naked bodies was part of how they made their living. It wasn't the most *important* part, but it was a customary element of the pulchritudinous ceremony. Even so, their increasingly open displays of partial nudity always caught him off guard.

Hooley would frequently encounter one of their scantily clad forms saucily sauntering barefoot down the boardwalk, not even giving him a glance when he almost stopped and stared. To his consternation, they conducted daily chores while wearing little more than undergarments, pantalets and frilly bloomers, sometimes just thin shimmies and shifts of clingy material. They were often bare-legged and virtually bare-bottomed while they leaned over a laundry tub or athletically beat animal skin rugs on a clothesline.

And none was unattractive. Not one. He spent almost every day sur-

rounded by young, beautiful, and very much exposed female flesh. This
became increasingly unsettling for Hooley. In spite of his discomfort, he
admired Margot for keeping the women busy with housewifery during the
week: They washed linens, mended clothing, even swept the boardwalks.
But when he was outside working nearby as they busily completed some
task—their garments wet with sweat or wash water, their breasts swinging
free beneath sheer fabric, their limbs lithely moving in plain view—he
found it nearly impossible to remain nonchalant.

No day of the week was more painfully distracting than early Saturday
mornings, when they lined up at the bathhouse while Mino happily
manned the pump and Hooley toted heavy cauldrons of hot water. Afterward, they would march around in sopping-wet gowns until their tresses
dried and could be curled and coiffed in time for the boys' arrival.

What Mino's reaction to the fleshy display might have been Hooley
couldn't imagine. The perpetually happy carpenter went about with no
outward sign of perturbation, and to Hooley's dismay, the carpenter was
frequently called over to assist some scantily clad beauty with some minor
chore, but he exhibited no puerile tendencies. He might well have been
talking to his sister, Hooley thought, and he resented the large man's
indifference, pose or not, when he was in the company of some half-naked
beauty.

For Hooley, such a thing was impossible. Too often, the small, hot spot
of lust he tried to reserve for Margot was touched to life by a sideways
glance or a glimpse of a well-turned ankle or what he imagined was a wink
or a coy smile from beneath a bonnet's brim. He would then daydream
himself into a fantasy, and soon be embarrassed to discover that he was
uncomfortably aroused.

After several weeks of misery, he decided to risk Margot's temper, and
he mentioned the problem to her by suggesting that the women start covering themselves when out of doors. Things went about the way he had
feared.

"Why, Hooley, you're nothing but an old prude," Margot said with a
laugh in response to his complaint. "Whoever would have guessed?" She
gave him a mischievous smile and a wink. "*I* certainly never would have."

"I'm serious!" he protested. "I mean, I'm a *man*."

She cocked an eyebrow. "You don't say?"

"You know what I mean, Margot. Those women are running around
here half-naked."

"They're *whores*, Hooley."

"I don't care. It's not . . . decent." Margot's smile turned ironic, but he
pressed on. "I mean . . . what if somebody were to come along?"

She looked in mocking bewilderment out over the barren prairie as if surprised to discover its ubiquitous emptiness. "Who?"

"You know what I mean."

"The only 'somebody' who's apt to come along is a customer," she said with a knowing smile. "I think it's good advertising. Lets them avoid having to make hard decisions if they can see what they want right out here in the open."

"That's not the point," Hooley muttered, ready to admit defeat. Then an idea struck. "What about Heinz? What if *he* was to come along off schedule? He's unreliable. You say so yourself. What about that?" He thought the blow was well delivered. But Margot parried it easily.

"What about it? Heinz has seen every one of those girls as naked as the day they were born," she said, and winked. "And he's *paid* for the privilege. Cash, too. The only one that smelly Dutchman hasn't seen jaybird-naked is me." Her face darkened slightly and her mouth became a thin scar of determination. "And *that*, I can assure you, will *never* happen!" She smirked. "All he wants to do is look, anyway. The girls think it's sweet. But that doesn't mitigate. I *knew* he was always talk. When it came down to it, he parted with his two dollars just like every other man I've ever met."

It took a few moments for what she'd just said to register fully. "Two dollars?" His voice choked him. "You only charge them *two* dollars?"

"Well, of course. How much did you think I charged?"

"I hadn't thought about it," he admitted.

He knew she charged *him* two dollars every time she came to his cot, but figured that was a nominal sum, something to irritate him, not the standard rate that applied to every young hooligan who rode up with a few coins in his pocket and a bursting urge between his legs.

"Look at the ledger. It's all right there."

"You don't put down . . . uh . . ." She waited for him to finish, smiling and twisting a long lock of red curls around one finger. She was enjoying this entirely too much, he thought sourly. "You don't itemize," he said, satisfied with the euphemism. "You just put down totals."

"You mean I don't keep count of every poke and then make an entry for each girl, each time?" Hooley stared at her, then nodded. She replied with a laugh. "Hooley. Those are *pretty* girls! We don't have *that* big a ledger."

She sobered herself with exaggerated difficulty. "The going rate is fifty cents a whack. A dollar buys an hour. But it takes two dollars for the night when things settle down. I'd go mad trying to keep that kind of thing *itemized*." She brayed a short laugh that ended in a derisive snort. "Itemized! Oh, Hooley, the things you imagine!"

He was utterly abashed, and disappointed, and ashamed. "Well, I don't think it's right for them to be running around buck naked all the time."

"They're not 'buck naked.' " Margot sniffed.

"They might as well be!" he bellowed, pointing to Lora Lynn and Clara, who were struggling to hang one of the larger bearskins on the rope line to be beaten. Both wore loose shifts that barely came down to their bare knees. Their full hips and muscular legs were clearly visible beneath the perspiration-dampened fabric. "They're in their underwear, for God's sake."

"So are you." She pointed to his chest. As was his custom, only the top of his union suit covered him from the waist up. "You don't waste a clean shirt while you're doing chores."

"But, I—"

"You really *are* a prude, Hooley," she said. "Tell you what: You keep a sharp lookout, and if you see a bunch of preachers heading this way, set up a shout, and I'll make them get all dressed up for company."

"This isn't funny, Margot. I—"

"But if it's just a cowboy, you don't need to bother," she continued. "They've all seen it before."

"But—"

"Look, Hooley," she said, and folded her arms. "These girls only have so many serviceable garments. If they can save them by working in their underclothes, then that's money we don't spend. The way they dress is practical. It's healthy, and it's not hurting a thing. If it bothers you, then just don't look." Her rout of his argument was complete.

Thus, the girls continued their semiclothed appearances, and Hooley's frustration mounted. The only times they were fully dressed was for the opening of festivities on Saturday nights and those now rare but still delicious afternoons in Hank's store. Then, in their heavy skirts and thick shirtwaists, buttoned to the neck and secured by broaches and attractive pins, they appeared as modest as a group of schoolmarms. And they *were* pretty. With each passing week, Hooley believed, they grew prettier, more robust and desirable. From the buxom Clara's strawberry-blonde tresses and sky-blue eyes to the carrot-red, wiry curls and upturned nose of the freckle-faced Lora Lynn, they offered a veritable cornucopia of feminine appeal.

Those nights when Margot was elsewhere and he lay alone staring at the ceiling of his tent, his thoughts filled with their images. He tried to focus on other things—on his future, whatever it was—but that was too uncertain. He avoided recalling the past—too much pain there. All that was left was the girls, and more often than not, with the coyotes' distant wails mocking his fantasies, he allowed his mind to roam and his misery to compound. He blamed Margot for this, as he came to blame her for so many other things that had come to vex his life.

2

WHEN HOOLEY PUT aside the day-to-day irritations that he encountered with Mino, the girls, or anything else, he acknowledged that the real source of discomfort he had with Margot and her whorehouse was the unanswered question about her actual role in their enterprise. As proprietress of Miss Margot's Place, she was both madam and mistress. But he was unable to divine precisely how active a part she took in the business. In all the nights he worked there behind the bar, he had never seen her slip off arm-in-arm with any of the youthful drovers, never do more than share a dance or a joke. She seldom drank openly, though she often turned discreetly away for a nip from her flask. More often than not, she was in the midst of three or four of them, pulling on their cravats, punching their forearms with levity. He desperately tried to convince himself that she was only boss of the place, not an actual participant in the stock and trade of the concern.

But she still charged him for each visit she made to his cot. And she still refused to kiss him on the mouth.

On occasion, he looked up from a busy time behind the bar and discovered her missing. Anxiety instantly filled him, and he stared at the undecorated flap of canvas that served as a partition to her private quarters—or "crib," as the boys called the girls' bedrooms—as if by concentrating he could penetrate the canvas and view her in the arms of some young, sweaty, drunk thug, who would paw and fondle her and—his thoughts stopped when they approached images too painful to draw. He knew, logically, that she might have slipped out for a breath of fresh air or a quick errand to the privy. She might be calming down some cowboy who had become too rambunctious or preparing a bandage for someone's head following one of the frequent fistfights that would break out. Such thoughts did little to assuage his worries. When she was missing, his stomach instantly soured, ached, and he became snappy until she reappeared and resumed her hostess's role.

He never mentioned this. Rather, he steeled his outward reactions, contenting himself that no matter what was happening, she continued to come to his cot three times a week, and that her presence was without any sense that she had shared her delightful talents as a lover with anyone else— even if she did charge him the going rate. Indeed, he thought, their passion seemed to grow and flower as if it fed on the frequency of their couplings. But on those nights when she disappeared from the red tent's festivities, he was liable to drink far more than usual, and he always awoke the next day with a pounding headache and a revolting stomach.

It occurred to him to flat-out ask her to clarify her role in the enterprise. But he anticipated the outcome of that with foreboding. Once the words left his mouth, she'd accuse him of jealousy, of trying to run her. That *she* ran him was fine, of course, he thought bitterly. To question her activities, on the other hand, would give her too great an advantage, and he had few advantages when he dealt with her. He would have to pretend indifference, he silently lectured himself, remain phlegmatic and keep the turmoil he felt to himself. He just had to accept that she made the rules, and that she kept them, even if she didn't always tell him what they were.

Rancher McPherson's livestock enterprise apparently continued to prosper, as the number of cowboys coming each week steadily increased, and Hooley found a new worry. He became concerned about the girls' abilities to accommodate the growing custom. One night, he counted nearly thirty men in the tent, not counting Mino, or Hank, who came over to drink coffee and to stand by the piano and clap in time to the rhythms of Mino's squeezebox. Heinz, when he was present, added one more. Five women and thirty men was a burdensome ratio, Hooley thought. But the girls didn't complain that he knew of, and the money sacks under his cot bulged with cash.

That Margot was determined to make Ina Moon the last girl she lost was made clear one unusually blustery morning in early autumn. Hooley was sorting canvas scraps when he heard Margot's voice shrilly demanding that the girls come out and line up, shoulder-to-shoulder, in front of the red tent.

Dawn had brought a brisk northwest breeze that turned the open air crisp. The girls were unprepared for the shift in temperature from the sweltering warmth of the day before. They all appeared in thin wrappers, hastily thrown over very little underneath. They stood shivering in the cool air, staring apprehensively at Margot, who folded her arms under her breasts and paced irritably. At her feet was a small pasteboard box.

Mino emerged from his tent, yawning and stretching. When he spied the company assembled, he hunched his shoulders and slipped noiselessly beside Hooley.

"There's about to be some kind of storm," Hooley whispered.

"No shit, Gil Hooley," he choked out.

Hank came with an armload of dried cow patties for his stove. He stopped dead at the spectacle. He had thus far been spared the white heat of Margot's wrath, but he had witnessed its potential when it was directed toward Hooley. The young merchant dropped his load and scurried over. "What's wrong? Somebody get killed?"

"No, not yet," Hooley said chuckling. It amused him to see Margot's anger turned toward someone else, even the girls.

Margot spun and glared at the men, who suddenly found something extremely interesting to stare at elsewhere. Hooley thought he could feel heated rays from Margot's green eyes running over the three of them.

"Do you know what these are?" Margot's voice rang out, indicating that she had returned her attention to the women. She faced the line of girls, hands on her hips. The toe of her shoe touched the box. Several of the girls nodded. "I ordered them special from Chicago, Illinois. They're handmade and they didn't come cheap."

Hooley stared at the box. He had no idea what was inside it.

"You don't make the boys wear one, you'll get a baby faster than you can say 'Mama.' "

"They don't like to wear a damn sheepskin," Gertie spoke up, her black eyes blinking in the sunlight. "They say it spoils things."

"It's a sheath," Hooley said, relying on imperfect knowledge and trying to clear up Hank's quizzical look. "A man wears it when he . . . well, it stops a girl from getting a child." Hank nodded, but Hooley doubted that he understood any more than he himself did. He had only heard of such things when he was in the army. They were sometimes requested by the general officers when they went off on a toot, but their practical application mystified Hooley.

"Then you find another way," Margot said. "I provide these at my expense, just as I provide *you* at my expense, and I will not lose one of you to gross ignorance or"—her eyes went jade hard—"to deliberate and malicious subversion!"

The girls looked at one another. They obviously had no idea what she was talking about.

"I'll bet *you* don't use them," Lulu said.

Margot's eyes flared. "What *I* do is *my* business," she sparked. "And what *you* do is *my* business. And I will *not* have you sassing me." Her voice raised in exasperation. "You'd better mind your tongue, missy. I've been watching you." The wind blew strands of hair up from Margot's head, giving her an even more frightening aspect. "Ever since that baby was born, you all have been moping like a bunch of sows whose litters have died. And I know what you're planning."

A couple of the girls started to smile, but Margot's frown deepened and squelched any mirth that might have arisen. "You're all looking at Ina Moon, all glowing and fat in the prosperity of maternal health, and you're thinking she's the lucky one, that maybe you ought to latch onto one of the idiots that comes to see you every Saturday yourselves." The girls exchanged shy and embarrassed looks. "Well, I'm telling you right now that I—that *we*"—she threw a hard look toward Hooley and Mino—"*we* won't stand for it!"

The girls' heads swiveled toward the men, and Hooley was reminded of a line of mechanical ducks he had seen at a circus. Only these weren't ducks, and they certainly weren't mechanical. They were comely, buxom young women, and they were standing there in a whipping wind that often lifted the gossamer-thin fabric of their robes to reveal their naked limbs. He was suddenly embarrassed for them. But this was *not* his concern, he insisted silently.

Then he suddenly understood why she was putting this on in the open. As usual, he thought, his ire rising, when she found herself unable to handle something on her own, she dumped at least part of the responsibility on him.

"You *will* use these," she ordered, and all heads snapped back, attention riveted on the redheaded madam. "Or something else. *No* more marriages, and *no* more babies. And I will *not* pay any woman who turns up in foal and starts whining for her money!" Margot paced, working herself up even more. "If any one of you turns up encumbered," she screeched, "I will turn you out, broke as the day you showed up here, and good riddance!"

"That's not fair!" Kitty shouted. "We *earn* our money!"

"You earn it because I *let* you earn it." Margot stared them down, then evened her voice to a threatening level. "If I see even one of you so much as *look* at one of these sorry cowboys with a dripping love cast, I'll ship you back to Oklahoma Territory so fast you won't even have time to get your bloomers on!" She rose to her maximum height and pointed a finger at each one of them. "If I catch you making moony cow-eyes at some moronic miscreant in boots and spurs, or failing to take proper measures to keep from swelling up with one of their love children, you're going to wish you were in the hands of the worst savage Indian you ever heard of!"

Now, her tone softened. "Ladies," she said sadly, "you've all had hard lives, young as you are. I thought I was helping you out by summoning you here to this wilderness. But I did not bring you all the way to this godforsaken place to fall in love with some witless rustic laborer with a handful of want and a pocketful of I don't know." Again she looked at the men. "Hooley and Hank and that stupid Turkish carpenter over there are about as good a quality in a man as you'll ever encounter, and *they're* not worth a bootful of horse apples."

Hooley started. What did *that* mean?

"Hank made an honest woman of Ina Moon," she continued. "But that's Ina Moon. That's not you." She took a breath. "You are *not* here to find some paltry excuse for a good-looking peter that walks like a man. You are here to make money so you can make yourselves a life. And if you behave, money's what you'll have. Because"—she took a breath—"a life is a lot more important than any man. Take it from me."

The angry edge was back, sharpening. "You want to have a brood of young'uns, then you best get your skinny little fannies back up to Oklahoma Territory and commence living in squalor. Babies're the only crop I know of that'll grow there . . . That, and pure misery." Then she sighed. "You're whores, ladies," she said. "Soiled doves. Prostitutes. Whirlago gals! And while that may not be what you planned, I'll tell you here and now that it's better to be a whore in Texas than anything you *might* become in Oklahoma Territory."

She bent, picked up the box, and thrust it under her arm. "There's one of these in each of your cribs, and you'd better use them or give me a good reason why not. That, or pack your traps. I'm not playing midwife to any cowboy's bastard." After a long stare, she turned on her heel and went back inside the tent. The girls stood in the bitter wind, silent and still in line. It was almost, Hooley thought, as if they were waiting for someone to yell, "Dismissed."

The trio of men also remained still until, at last, the women dispersed, exchanging guilty glances while hugging their arms around themselves and milling about. The girls looked longingly at the red tent, as if they were dreading to go inside but were just as afraid to remain where they were. The wind had a bite to it, but so did Margot. And hers was worse.

Finally, Clara and Lulu joined arms and strolled toward the privy with their heads together, the gale driving them faster than they wanted to walk. Hooley imagined that they might be crying. Gertie, always the feisty loner, wandered toward the café tent and poured herself a cup of stale coffee, then stared into the cup with an empty, angry gaze. Lora Lynn, bright tresses spraying wildly in the wind, stepped toward the creek, swinging her arms akimbo in gestures of childish anger. Hooley watched her hips moving as she walked, then, embarrassed, he shifted his gaze to Kitty, a saucy blonde with a waspish waist and high, proud breasts.

Kitty hadn't moved since Margot completed her tirade. She remained near the tent's opening, shuffling her bare feet in the dust. As Hooley stared at her, he noticed as if for the first time dark eyebrows arched over almost yellow-hazel eyes and long lashes that contrasted sharply with her fair skin, which she was never afraid to display. That morning she was the least covered of all five girls.

Hank cleared his throat and removed Hooley's protracted notice from the pretty blonde. "That was a hell, uh—a *deuce* of a show," the store-keeper said, reminding Hooley that he had recently added swearing to the personal reforms Ina Moon demanded. He had also forsaken tobacco, and the rumor was that she wanted him to give up coffee. Hooley shrugged, his thoughts, like sticky cobwebs, stubbornly clinging to Kitty's shapely form, which remained where it was. Hank retrieved his cow patties and retreated to his store. Mino, who had not stopped staring at the scene of the dressing-down since it started, began humming a low tune.

"Get on about your business," Hooley said. "It's nothing to do with us."

"No shit, Gil Hooley," Mino croaked, then his shoulders sagged, and he wandered off.

"Stupid goddamn idiot," Hooley muttered to Mino's back. He was still feeling itchy as he gave Kitty one more glance. The patching chore Margot's scene interrupted no longer appealed to him, so he pulled up a stool on the lee side of his tent, a refuge he had discovered in his attempt to keep Miss Margot's Place and its inhabitants out of sight and mind. He stared at the dull-dyed stripes of the store tent and lit his pipe, determined to be alone, something he was finding harder and harder to do. Everywhere he looked there was either work to be done or someone distracting his attention. He longed for the days before Margot arrived, indeed for the days before Mino showed up, when pure indolence was a comfort to him. Something was to be said for total solitude, he thought irritably, even if it meant starving to death and being eaten by wild varmints.

He smoked and tried to calm his stomach, which was unaccountably upset. The only sounds in the camp were a howling wind that picked up cold steam and flapped unsecured canvas and the distant metallic whack of Mino's hammer as he nailed boards together for some purpose Hooley couldn't imagine. The noise irked him. He wanted a book to allow him to retreat into himself.

He was especially nettled by Margot's reference to him as counselor to her diatribe. He disliked being included without her consulting him. He also disliked her message. These were *young* women. They might be whores, but even whores were people. Why should she begrudge them respectability, even if they found it through deceit? Ruthie had trapped *him*, Hooley admitted with a painful twinge in his back teeth. Ina Moon had trapped Hank, after a fashion. And he also admitted that both he and Hank had been more than willing to be trapped. They were *all* trapped right here, and, he admitted grimly, Margot had proved a cunning trapper herself. It wasn't fair, he thought with a minor renewal of stomach cramps. But then, little about Margot was. She was a charging buffalo, a stampede, a cyclone, as irresistible as she was destructive. He wondered what match she would make against his mother. That, he knew, would be something to see.

His mood finally lightened. He considered Margot's words, sought the logic behind them. He finally conceded that, as usual, she was right. Harsh, but right again. They couldn't have these girls—these whores—having babies. Half of the young men would disappear if confronted with a pregnant whore. And how could they be sure who might be the father of a particular girl's baby anyway? That would be one thorny mess no mere postmaster could ever sort out. All that would remain here would be an orphanage for bastard children maintained by a bunch of prostitutes.

A shadow crossed in front of him, and he looked up, astonished to see Kitty, arms folded beneath her breasts, pushing them together and upward, holding herself as if she might come apart if she loosened her grasp. In the bright, cool sunlight, her simple utter beauty paralyzed him. She couldn't be more than eighteen, he thought, a vision of girlish innocence, wrapped in white gauze, childlike and in need, but at the same time seductive. He was overwhelmed by her presence, and he averted his eyes from her thinly covered nakedness and focused on her beautiful hazel eyes.

"I'm sorry you had to hear all that, Mr. Hooley," she said sadly. "It ain't right that she yelled at us like that in front of everybody. She shouldn't of done it."

Hooley nodded mutely. His tongue was stuck to the roof of his mouth. Kitty's brass-colored eyes cast themselves down toward her narrow, bare feet. Hooley followed their gaze, traced the curve of her calf as it descended past her slim ankles. She wiggled her toes in the dust, then lifted one slender instep and scratched the top of the other, and something inside Hooley stirred quickly—then rose rampant. He noted the delicacy of her features, her slightly upturned nose and the narrow dimples in her cheeks, the simple beauty of her skin and golden hair, the enticing birthmark winking at him from deep between full breasts that seemed to float beneath their thin, lacy covering. He was burning up.

"It's . . . it's not important," he said, swallowing hard, coming awkwardly to his feet, clearing his throat, then sucking hard on the dead pipe.
"Believe me, I know how she can be."

"Well, it ain't fair!" Kitty declared. "Those *things*—they're nasty! The
boys don't like them! We *all* hate them." Her eyes widened, found
Hooley's face, beseeched him for understanding. "Do you know what they
make them out of? Sheep guts!" she said before he could respond, not that
he could have with any certainty. "That's awful," she went on, softer now.
"It's worse than anything to have something like that touch you."

"I . . ." Hooley was lost in a storm of lust blasting through his chest
like a hot wind.

"When Margot sent for us to come out here," Kitty went on, "we didn't
really know what she meant!" Tears welled in her eyes. "None of us
thought she was serious."

Hooley stood, awkwardly shuffling his feet and pocketing his pipe. He
wanted to say something, but couldn't take his eyes off her breasts, so free
and full beneath the opaque fabric of her thin wrap. The outline of her
large, dark nipples, erect in the chilly air, jutted against the cloth. He
turned slightly sideways to hide his obvious display of passion, but Kitty's
tears were now flowing fully down her face. Her mouth was twisted into
an ugly tear of self-pity.

"Well, uh . . . ," he said. "She wrote to you. Told you what to expect."
His heart swelled, and he could hear it thudding in his ears. *Remember
Margot,* his mind shouted. But no other part of his body responded. "Oh,
hell, Kitty, I'm goddamn sorry she talked to you that way."

As if his words were magnetic, she moved smoothly and sweetly into
his arms, which opened automatically and folded her to him, a small,
cuddly bundle of sweet, soft skin wrapped in silky cloth against him. Sobs
racked her body, her shoulders hunching in heartrending mews. She was
now completely transformed into a girl, a child, but one with remarkable
powers. The scent of her perfume filled his nostrils, made him dizzy with
desire, solid with passion. Her breasts swelled against his undershirt, heaving with her gulping breath, her arms grasped him, pulling him so close
to her that he believed he could sense the heat between her legs as her
pelvis ground harder against him with every gasp.

"Oh, she's right!" Kitty cried bitterly. "She told us the right of things.
There *ain't* no honest way for the widow of a lawman to make it in
Oklahoma Territory, or anywhere else in this world." She pulled away
from him, looked deeply into his eyes, her own tan orbs now sultry, seeming to darken as he peered into them. "You can be a whore or a schoolmarm, but I never was no good at reading and such. I got married when

I was only thirteen. I only know how to do one thing good," she said with a deep sigh, "and you know what that is."

"I uh . . ."

"And that's the only reason Margot wanted me to come out here! To save me from being the same thing in Oklahoma Territory." Her arms tightened around his back, and she pulled him closer, tilting her head, slightly parting her mouth into an inviting opening. He saw the pinkness of her tongue, tantalizing between her straight white teeth, darting out to moisten her full lips. Margot fled from his thoughts, his feelings. He was no longer in control of his actions, his emotions. He had not kissed a woman in years, and never in pure passion. He wanted nothing more than to taste Kitty's lips. Lustful hunger clawed at his gut. He leaned forward, his mouth forming to meet hers. Her hands reached down, clutched his hips, squeezed them, pulled him closer to her sexual heat. He closed his eyes, waiting for the velvet softness of her lips.

"Well, isn't this nice?" Margot's voice cut through the windy air like an arrow. Hooley's heart stopped in mid-beat. *No,* he insisted. This *isn't* happening!

Kitty's grip was instantly gone. She was no longer touching him. It was as if she had miraculously vanished from his embrace, then reappeared behind Margot's militant stance and sardonic smile. Kitty's beautiful face, now void of the sorrowful girlish grief she had shown him only moments before, offered a sly and satisfied expression.

"Listen, Margot," he stammered. "I was—"

"Oh, Hooley." She continued to smile, but there was no warmth in it. "I don't give a hoot what you do." She nodded toward Kitty. "Or what *she* does."

Kitty gave Hooley a wink, then turned and started away. "Come on over sometime," she sang in a giggling voice. "You're a live one, Mr. 'No Shit' Hooley."

"Your turn to scrub the parlor," Margot reminded her while continuing to hold Hooley with her eyes. "Best you get to it." Kitty waved her fingers in acknowledgment as she strolled nonchalantly toward the tent. "And remember what I told you," Margot called. "Whores don't kiss." Another finger wave responded to the instruction. Kitty's hips ground in an exaggerated saunter as one bare foot followed another across the dusty compound.

On the opposite side of the compound, Hooley saw Mino, two long boards over his shoulder, stop and stare at her stroll. She waggled her fingers at the big carpenter, and for once, he blushed and turned away.

"Margot," Hooley said. "Listen to me. She came over here, and she told me—"

"I told you, Hooley. I don't care. Not a feather." He searched her eyes, but they betrayed nothing. "Although it would be better if you'd engage her on a normal basis rather than take her right out here in the open." She looked up and down the narrow alleyway between the tents. "But that's your concern. Just be sure that you put it all down in the ledger."

"Margot, it wasn't what you—"

"Hooley," she interrupted. "I'm going to tell you something about whores and women. You'd do well to learn it." She took a breath, glanced at Kitty's back disappearing into the red tent. "A woman is always a woman, no matter where she is or what she's doing. But a whore is only a whore when she's working. I can assure you that Kitty Cloud is *always* working." Hooley blinked in confusion, trying to comprehend.

"She's no good, and she never was," Margot continued. "I wouldn't have sent for her, but Gertie wouldn't come without her. They're cousins. I thought she might change when she got out here, saw the way of things, but she's the same little sneak she always was." Margot sighed and looked almost sad. "If you're going to dally with one the girls, you'd do well to avoid that one."

Hooley was barely listening. His focus was blurred. He desperately wished he could back up time and relive the last few minutes.

"It's the same as I told those girls this morning," Margot said. "They have to make up their minds whether or not they're whores. If they are, they have to decide that that's more important than being anything else. They can't have it both ways." She stepped forward and stared into his face, but again, her coldness formed a mask beneath her untamed red hair. The chilled air around them seemed warm by comparison. "What I'm saying is that loving and whoring don't mix, Hooley. And it's important for you to be able to tell the difference, especially with Kitty Cloud."

Hooley hung his head, and Margot accepted that as a response and turned to leave. Suddenly, he understood something important. "Which is it with us?" he asked, stopping her.

She fixed him with her fierce green stare, her mouth a thin scar across her pretty face. "I'm the best *woman* you'll ever find, Hooley. That's all you need to know."

As she walked away, he realized that nothing she'd ever said to him had ever been truer.

3

MARGOT DID NOT return to Hooley's cot that week, which did not surprise him, although it depressed him utterly. More irritating was her show of ignoring him. Anytime personal business brought them out at the same time, she kept her distance and avoided catching his eye. She was evading him, punishing him, keeping herself in sight, and mind, but vexingly out of reach.

To his manifest disgust, Hooley could hardly bear it. Something delicate had torn that morning, and he felt it ripping farther apart with every hour that passed. Self-recrimination ate at him like a hungry parasite. He remembered how he felt when Ruthie betrayed him, and it sickened him that he had now done the same thing to Margot. But there was nothing he could say or do without making it worse. The contradictory emotions that swirled around his head were more irritating than the flies and mosquitoes and sultry weather that returned in the wake of the light dry cold front that swept in that morning. And no wind could blow those emotions away.

Heinz showed up two days later. A blistering gale roared out of the southwest and peppered everything with fine sand. The teamster's face was covered with a bandanna, speckled muddy with tobacco juice. While he grunted with the effort of unloading the heavier items, he shouted over the howling wind what news he had regarding the continuing expansion by Rancher McPherson.

"I don't think he likes you, Hooley," he opined while he worked.

"What do you mean? He's never even met me."

"Well, he don't like what he knows," Heinz insisted. "Or that's what his missus says." He straightened up and stretched his back into the hot wind. Mino handed him a glass of beer, which the burly teamster drank down in one gulp. "Lord, that woman's a panther for work. Orders more goods every run. When it started it was all bobbed wire and sheet metal, but now it's dishes and rugs and all kinds of heavy junk. Beats anything I've ever seen in the name of the—"

"Look," Hooley said. "I need to have a talk with him."

"You're the one trespassing. He comes up here, he's like as not to bring a noose."

"A noose?" Hooley was alarmed. "Why a noose? Trespassing isn't a hanging offense."

"No shit, Gil Hooley," Mino piped up.

"Shut up," Hooley said automatically, and, as was his custom, the carpenter smiled back. "Heinz, you tell him I need to have a talk with him."

Heinz climbed back up onto his lead wagon. "You tell him yourself. Might take a notion to hang *me* if I let on I was friendly with you." Heinz spat into the gritty wind. "He *truly* don't like you, Hooley. Says he's shutting down that goddamn Pease City outfit, and you're next. Says you're corrupting his cowhands' morals with your whores."

"*My* whores? They're not *my* whores." He looked at the red tent. "You take him a message," Hooley said. "Tell him—"

"I ain't telling him nothing, Hooley. Nobody tells Rancher McPherson nothing, and they tell his missus even less. That woman's a rattlesnake with titties."

"I need to see him face-to-face."

"Get on a horse and ride on down there then." Heinz squinted in thought. "Second thought, that's a bad notion. Might shoot you on the spot. Maybe you ought to write him a letter."

"A letter? What would I say in a letter?"

"Hell, I don't know, Hooley. You're the goddamn postmaster." He strapped the reins down on the mules' backs, called them up, and he was off in a gale of dust. "Back in two weeks, if he ain't hung you by then," the teamster shouted over the rattling tack.

"Hang me," Hooley said, dumbfounded.

"No shit, Gil Hooley," Mino said, sadly shaking his head.

Hooley stalked off to his tent He was certain he was *not* going to write Rancher McPherson. The last letter he wrote brought Margot. He didn't have the courage to write another.

Hooley stewed over the problem, but no solution presented itself before the cowboys arrived for their Saturday night revelry. None of them was any help in advising Hooley on how best to deal with their employer.

"I don't believe he gives you much of a think," Jake opined over a preliminary round of free drinks Hooley set up in the old whiskey shed. Lately, the original drinking establishment had fallen into disuse, but Hooley's offer of "on the house" rounds tempted them into a detour.

"He's all het up over these new cattle that are coming in by rail to Jacksboro. Jacksboro," Underwood said. "Sometime next winter. All he talks about. All."

"That and stringing up more fence. The man has bobwire in the brainpan," Plunk commented with a sad look. "That shit's mean." He held up the palms of his hands, which were webbed with scabby scratches. "Cuts right through gloves worse than cactus."

"I need to talk to him," Hooley said. "I'm sure we can work out any differences."

"He ain't a man overly given to conversation," Tidmore wheezed. "Neither is Mrs. Rancher McPherson. She's talks good, but she don't listen worth a damn." While the others nodded, the fat cowboy suggested, "Hooley, I was you, I'd leave well enough alone. If he's got some gripe, he'll come along by and by. Just think of him like a gyp sink. Best ride around it."

The festivities at Miss Margot's Place that night were no less raucous than usual, and Hooley was soon dealing with brisk business. Margot continued to avoid catching Hooley's eye, but she was in the gleam of every cowboy's gaze. The winds had not abated after sundown, but had, if anything, grown stronger as evening deepened, so she refused to expose her scarlet coif to the elements. Instead, she'd sent Mino to fetch the boys gathering around the whiskey shed, then greeted the young men in the middle of the parlor, wearing a new lavender frock and looking lovelier than ever. Her wardrobe seemed infinite in its variety. He wondered irritably—and silently—how many of the crates Heinz toted out to the settlement were full of garments and how much she deducted from their profits to keep herself in the height of fashion. *That*, he thought, wasn't itemized in the ledger book, either.

The wind outside had shifted to the northwest and grown heavy and wet. It whipped the sides of the tent viciously, but inside it was stultifying and close. Hooley poured beer and whiskey for the thirsty drovers, and watched Margot more closely than usual. She made his heart ache, she was so beautiful. She flitted from one knot of men to the other, shouted greetings and teasing compliments over the humming crowd. Her laughter and gibes rose above the hubbub, and when she danced, her legs flew high on the spins, her feet almost flying beneath her skirt. He so longed to put things back the way they were that he was almost in physical pain, and he downed several extra whiskeys.

She kept herself aloof from him, often moving to Mino and leaning on the big carpenter's shoulders while he played his concertina and sang in his loud baritone voice. Hooley saw her taking frequent nips from the small silver flask she kept concealed in the folds of her gown. He felt sure that when his eyes were elsewhere, she was watching him as intently as he was watching her, but when he glanced her way to catch her, her attention was always elsewhere.

Hooley also watched Kitty, who was more seductively desirable than ever when she flashed her false smile and light sheens of perspiration glowed on her forehead after the exertion of a dance. She sometimes gave him a dark wink, but she never approached him. Actually, he observed, she was virtually unable to approach anyone because of the attentions of Algernon Chatsworth. He was older than the others, and fond of thick,

smelly cigars, which he always had in abundance. He was also cocky, and
Hooley had never liked him.

Chatsworth tended to stand out, Hooley thought as he poured him a
drink between dances. A sandy-haired, tall, lanky youth with a narrow,
clean-shaven jaw and extraordinarily long arms, he was a nice-looking man,
better groomed than the average cowboy. Now that he thought about it,
Hooley was reminded of some of the sons of well-heeled families he had
known in his mother's circle of friends, the sort Bertha Hooley liked to
hold up as an example of what she hoped her own son could be. Hooley
had heard comments that Chatsworth preferred Pease City and often
played two-handed poker with Cherokee Charlie.

That night Chatsworth joined the men competing for women's attentions. But the one Chatsworth seemed to concentrate on most often was
Kitty. He refused to allow her the pleasure of anyone else's company for
more than a few minutes, constantly pressing her to dance with him, and
every hour or so he was the one escorting her through the canvas partition
to her crib. Hooley decided that Margot's concerns about the girls' ulterior
intentions were well founded. Kitty seemed to have set her cap for Chatsworth, and she was making her play right under Margot's nose. The observation created a slight swell of pride in Hooley's chest. She had come
to him first, he thought. She couldn't have him, so she shifted her attentions to the handsome cowboy. There was a tinge of regret mixed in with
this realization, but it was quickly banished when Margot entered his line
of sight, and then a different, deeper regret replaced it.

The party built to a crescendo of music and general gaiety. Hooley never
lost sight of Margot. He fretted over their situation, and his frustration
mounted as he poured himself more drinks, knocked them back quickly,
and continued to brood.

Eventually, the evening began to take its toll. The constant exposure to
the suffocating tobacco smoke and fetid stink of sweating bodies and overflowing cuspidors, the extra whiskey he had imbibed gave him a throbbing
headache and a retching cough. He was utterly exhausted when the last
drink was served and no more customers were clamoring for more. Even
Mino had disappeared, and Margot, he noted with satisfaction, had retired
alone.

When he went outside, he nearly collapsed in the contrasting atmosphere. The wind had died down, and lightning in the distance revealed
large thunderheads, signaling the approach of a wet cool front. The night's
fresh damp air wrapped around him like a wet towel as he nearly staggered
with fatigue over to his tent, where he hurriedly undressed and climbed
onto his cot, ready to forget the meanness of the whole Saturday night, of

the whole week if he could. But sleep eluded him. He lay there, listening to his heartbeat. He pushed the worries about Rancher McPherson out of his mind, but his thoughts bounced from Kitty to Margot, until they finally settled on the redheaded madam and stayed there.

He had no idea how long it was before Margot's sharp voice penetrated his ear and brought him back to consciousness. "Hooley? You asleep?" she called from outside his tent.

"No," he said irritably. "What gave you that idea? What time is it?" He sat up, lit a lantern, stood, and pulled open the flap. In the wick's glow, he saw she was still in the lavender dress. She was tired, Hooley observed, and there was a concerned look on her face.

"Come on in," he said, sitting wearily on his cot, his head in his hands. Stress and the indulgence of the night hammered at his skull, and his stomach was in full revolt. His tongue was thick in his dry mouth, and his whole body seemed extraordinarily heavy.

She ducked her head inside and looked around, studying every corner of the enclosure as if she had never seen it before. Her eyes lingered on his cot, then flashed to him, racing up and down his underwear-clad form. "No, you come out. Put some coffee on." She stepped away.

"The sun's not even up yet," he protested.

"It will be in a while. Come on out here. I want to talk to you."

He was confused. For the briefest moment, he had thought this would be a reconciliation. The hope had buoyed him, but when he'd seen the serious expression on her face, his optimism had sunk. He sighed deeply, pulled on his trousers, and obliged her. As soon as he stepped out, the dewy wetness of the boardwalk outside his tent immediately soaked his socks.

"Damn it! Margot, you come inside. It's damp out here."

She looked at him and shook her head dismissively. "It wouldn't be seemly," she said. "I don't want to give anyone the wrong impression."

"Who?" As usual, a number of cowboys were lying nearby on the open ground, snoring and groaning in their sleep. He could hear a veritable roar from the hotel tent as well. Every cot was taken, he noted, picturing with some satisfaction the moneybags beneath his cot.

She followed the boards over to the café tent, picked up the coffeepot, and handed it to him. "We're partners, you know. Now, make some coffee."

He opened his mouth to argue, then remembered the invariable futility of such an exercise and snapped it shut. Ignoring the squishy wetness that soused his socks, he stoked up the fire. "What's so damned important?" he asked, when the pot was set to boil.

"We need to have a talk," she said, clasping her hands in front of her.

Hooley's heart began to beat. Here it comes: the showdown he had been both looking forward to and dreading. At last, Margot was going to reveal her feelings, her intentions. He would have to respond. His mind bounced from possibility to possibility, panicked in the realization that he had not truly considered what reaction he might offer to her declarations.

"Hooley." She sighed. "It's obvious that I have to do all the thinking and planning around here. You won't take charge of anything unless I make you, won't accept any obligation."

Caught completely off guard, Hooley almost reeled. "What does that mean?"

"Like most men, you're selfish. You're only interested in your own comfort."

"That's not true!" He thought of how much work he did around the community, how often he cursed himself for allowing so much responsibility to fall on his shoulders.

"Never mind," she said, turning away from him. "I don't want to argue with you. I should have known better than to bring up something important."

"I have no idea—," he started.

"I said never *mind*, Hooley. The boys'll be wanting breakfast soon, and I don't think Gertie's up to helping out this morning. She—all of them had their hands full last night." She peered out into the darkness. "All but one," she added in a near whisper, then seemed to catch herself and added firmly, "You're on your own."

"I was on my own when you got here," Hooley shot at her.

"That's true, Hooley. I've learned that you're often entirely on your own." She sighed. "You seem to prefer it that way, although such behavior does not show a positive propensity for success in enterprises such as ours."

In the eastern distance, he spotted the first faint blood-red light of dawn. He was furious with Margot. For some stupid, silly reason born in her never-dormant imagination, she had cost him what little precious sleep he might have had.

"Margot, you didn't come over this time of night to talk about my selfishness," he said to her back. "What do you really want?"

Finally she turned back to him, but for once, her eyes refused to meet his. "What makes you think I want anything?"

Her voice had lost its certainty, he noted, and he pounced. "You've been sliding around here ever since . . . ever since the other morning. You won't talk to me, won't even look at me. Then you come over here like this." He bit down hard on his irritation. His stomach was churning, his head pounding, but he was determined to see this through. "Besides," he said as evenly as he could, "you only come see me when you want something."

"That's not true, Hooley. I—" She stopped herself, seemed genuinely hurt. He waited. She stepped back to him, took a breath. "The truth is, Hooley, I came over here looking for Kitty." She sighed and bowed her head, giving in. "She's missing, and I'm worried as hell."

4

IT DIDN'T TAKE long to rouse the cowboys and search the area. The men, grumbling, achy, and only half-awake, stumbled off into darkness, then quickly returned to fetch lanterns and torches fashioned of scraps of board and canvas. Mino wandered around in an apparent daze, but as soon as he discovered that Margot was giving the orders, he cheerfully complied with his customary full comprehension of everything she wanted. As soon as all the men were dispatched on their individual searches, he took off toward the creek.

Hooley and Hank roamed out onto the flats and stared into the gathering morning light at the vast emptiness surrounding them. It didn't take long, though, to determine what Hooley had already suspected: Both Kitty *and* Chatsworth were missing. Also missing was Margot's dun mare, as well as food, blankets, and other supplies. "Made a regular picnic," Margot said, disgust filling her voice, when Hank reported the burglary of his merchandise.

Panic took sudden painful root in Hooley's stomach. He sprinted to his tent, leaving Margot and Hank staring in confusion. Sure enough, the overstuffed bags of cash were gone.

When Margot heard, she collapsed onto a whiskey keg and uncharacteristically took a long pull from her flask without concealment. "The little witch," she said. "I knew she was a sneak and a whore, even before she became a whore. But I never thought she'd steal from me. Not money, anyway." Hooley refused to look at her. He was still piqued that she assumed she would find the blonde whore in his tent.

"How much was there?" Hank asked.

"Thousand dollars or more," Hooley said. Margot's rapidly arching eyebrow chided him for the exaggeration. Often there was just under five hundred, the rest being in the form of credit slips the cowboys signed. "Not all in cash," he amended.

The news spread among the cowboys as they returned from their fruitless searches, eventually prompting a chorus of disgruntled mutters. "Didn't know you were getting so rich off the boys, Hooley," Jake said in a wounded tone. "That don't seem right."

"You get what you pay for," Hooley replied hotly, then sighed in frustration.

The men were all back by now. Most of them were still showing dividends of the previous night's debauch. The morning sun was now fully up, and the day was warming. Only Mino was still absent, but he could be heard shouting some inarticulate call from off in the distance. The four remaining girls had also emerged. They stood at a cautious distance, a colorful quartet wrapped in Chinese robes and crocheted shawls, hands linked, heads bowed. A funereal pall hung over the entire community. Biting flies buzzed around, lighting on any exposed skin, and thick swarms of gnats harassed every ear, making the mere act of thinking a chore.

Hooley was bone-weary, the lack of sleep and the indulgences of the night before taking their vengeance in the form of a consistent, pounding headache. His stomach was in full revolt, and every muscle seemed to be screaming. He studied the horizon. Low, dark blue clouds were building far to the northwest, teasing in their promise of rain and cooler temperatures, which, experience had taught him, the winds sometimes carried far to the north.

"If she just wanted to leave," Margot said, "she didn't have to steal us blind."

"She didn't 'steal us blind,'" Hooley snapped. He wanted to wound somebody.

"I cannot abide this kind of thing," she said bitterly. "It can spread." She nodded an affirmation. "She has to be brought back, Hooley. Otherwise every one of those girls will fill a bag with whatever she can lay a hand to and take off."

"If they figured on running for it," Hank spoke up, drawing Hooley and Margot's attention once more, "that means north. He'd be a durned fool to head south. That away, they'd run smack dab into Texas Rangers who'd hang them on the spot." The others nodded soberly and voiced a murmuring chorus of assent.

"Rancher McPherson's not going to be happy about that horse. That horse," Underwood offered. "Planned to breed him," he recalled, shaking his head. "Breed him."

"That horse come from England," Jake said. "Rancher McPherson only lets Chatsworth ride him to give him saddle time. Apt to get broomtailed if he didn't get rode every day or two."

"Why doesn't he ride him himself?" Hooley asked.

"He never rides a horse. Horse," Underwood said. "Uses a fancy buggy he rigged up."

"They'll sure light out for Oklahoma Territory," Tidmore summarized in his trademark wheeze. "Lawmen up there ain't too numerous, and most ain't too smart. Just mean."

"That's correct," Margot confirmed softly.

"As I recollect, Chatsworth's got family in Kansas or some damned place up there," Plunk offered.

"Nothing good ever came out of Kansas," Margot added dully.

"So, when you going after them, Hooley?" Hank asked.

"Me?" Hooley said, astonished. "Why me?"

"Well, you're the postmaster," Hank replied. The others nodded in vigorous agreement. "That makes you the law, or close as we got to it."

"That's too stupid to comment on," Hooley said quietly. He had a sudden urge to be off his feet. A keg was handy, so he seated himself and stared at the assembly, which seemed to be waiting for him to speak. "They're halfway there by now anyway," he said. He had no actual idea how far it was to Kansas, or even to Oklahoma Territory.

"Naw," Underwood said. "Red River's flooded. Flooded. Could catch them up easy."

"Why don't *you* go after them?" Hooley asked. "It's your boss's horse he stole."

"But it was your whore," Tidmore argued. "And your money. Have to allow that a whore's near as valuable as a horse, especially if it ain't *your* horse."

"She wasn't *my* whore!" Hooley said hotly. He shot Margot a narrow look. She rolled her eyes in response. "And the money's as much Margot's as mine, too."

"You're not saying that Miss Margot ought to go after them, are you, Hooley?" Jake tilted his hat back, "That ain't a very manly way to be."

"This is crazy," Hooley shouted at the assembly. "In the first place, we don't *know* that they went north. They could have gone to Jacksboro."

"Naw," Underwood said. "Everybody in Jacksboro knows that horse. That horse. That'd be the wrong place to go if you was on that horse. That horse."

"I wouldn't know how to find them," Hooley said, waving at the empty prairie.

"You could track them," Hank suggested.

"It's none of my damn business," Hooley went on.

"When one of our girls steals our money, it's our business," Margot said.

Hooley stared sadly at her, and flapped his hands against his legs in a helpless gesture. "Do you truly expect me to try to catch up with them, bring them back?"

Margot stared at his seated figure, looked him up and down, and the cowboys followed suit. Hooley felt entirely naked. Then she dropped her eyes. "No, I guess not," she said, a frown creasing her mouth. Then she brightened. "I can get Mino to do it." She spun around and started down toward the creek, from where the carpenter had yet to return. "It's his money, too."

Hooley stood and stepped after her. "You're going to send that idiot out to—"

She turned and gave him a fierce look. "Well, *somebody's* got to go!" she said. "And obviously, *you're* not man enough to do it."

"What about them?" Hooley demanded, sweeping his hand around the cowboys, a few of whom had succumbed to fatigue and were once more loutishly sprawled about. "They're out a horse, just the same as you are. *They're* his pards!"

"*We're* not exactly 'out a horse,' " Jake noted carefully. "Truth to tell, we don't know *who* stole what horse. Chatsworth may be on Miss Margot's horse—he was partial to mares. 'Course, he *was* in charge of the bay. We may need somebody to do some lawyering about this."

"The bay horse is a matter that young miscreant will have to answer for to his employer," Margot said. "But Kitty's a different matter. And, there's our money *and* our mare."

"*Our* mare? When did that horse become *our* mare?" Hooley nearly yelled.

"I'd say the minute you shot Deputy Marshal Craggy Phillips through the eye!" she yelled back at him. Every cowboy's eye fell on Hooley, who was momentarily stunned.

"How did you know I shot him through the eye?"

"Why, Mino told me." She nodded toward the big man, who was at last walking up, his pants wet to the waist. He apparently had taken the opportunity of the search to gig a number of bullfrogs, which hung from a line and bounced on the ground.

"Mino *told* you?" Hooley sneered. "He can't even speak English."

She glanced at the men, then blushed. It was the first time he had ever seen that reaction in her. "There's other ways of telling than talking, Hooley," she said in a low voice.

Hooley whose head was now exploding at his temples and whose stomach ached with severe cramps, looked around and noticed that silence had descended on the entire company. The cowboys stood with their mouths open in astonishment.

Finally, Underwood hitched up his pants and stepped forward timidly. "You really shoot down a deputy marshal? Marshal?" he asked. The others leaned forward to hear Hooley's reply.

He stood for a moment, his hands dangling at his sides. "Yes," he said at last. "I did. And I wish to hell I'd never even seen him."

"What kind of marshal?" Hank asked suspiciously. "Town marshal of some kind?"

"He was a *federal* marshal," Margot spat out. "A Deputy United States Marshal."

"Where'd you learn to handle a gun?" Tidmore asked, his eyes narrowing.

"I can handle a gun," Hooley snapped.

As a body, the men stepped back from him, their eyes widening. "You're funning us, right?" Jake asked nervously. "You shot a marshal? White man and everything?"

Hooley gestured toward the carpenter. "He was trying to hang Mino," he explained. "He went crazy." He looked to Margot for a reaction, but there was nothing but a small, sly smile.

"Why'd he want to hang Mino?" Tidmore asked. "Hell, Mino never hurt nobody."

"Mino knocked the brains out of his partner," Hooley said sharply. "They were arguing, and he hit him with a board. Phillips called it murder, wanted to hang him on the spot."

They all turned to stare at Mino, who grinned back, apparently unaware of the topic of conversation. "No shit," he said affably.

"But you shot him dead?" Hank stepped toward Hooley to ask.

Hooley looked at the youthful faces arrayed before him, nodded.

"Well, I'll be damned. Damned," Underwood said behind a low whistle.

Jake laughed uneasily. "We didn't know we had a *pistolero* right here in Hoolian."

"I'm not a *pistolero*, damn it," Hooley said. "He was crazy, and he was going to hurt Mino—hang him or maybe shoot him. He'd already cold-cocked him with his pistol."

Plunk, who had been sadly silent up to this point, suddenly laughed. "Bullshit!" he said. "You couldn't coldcock that man with a rock!"

"No shit!" Mino seconded. "No shit, Gil Hooley!"

"See?" Underwood cried. "He says so, too! Too!"

Hooley gave the carpenter an annoyed look. "He'd have shot me, too," he said. "It was self-defense." He saw only masks of doubt surrounding him. He turned to Margot and addressed her directly. "I didn't have any choice." He thought he saw her nod.

"Things a man'll do for a good-looking woman," Jake said, with an admiring glance at Margot. Hooley started to correct the assumption, but stopped. He'd already said too much.

Hank took a deep breath and stepped forward. "Well, what's done is done," he said. "But since you're the only one hereabouts who's put a mortal bullet in another man, I'd say that you're the one to take charge and go fetch Chatsworth and my goods back here to stand answer."

"I keep telling you, this is none of my damn business," Hooley said.

"He stole a *horse*, Hooley," Jake said. "The whore's off to one side."

"Not from where I stand she isn't," Margot commented. "I want that girl back here."

"Like as not, she talked him into the whole thing. Whole thing," Underwood offered. "Chatsworth, he never was that smart when it come to women. Women. But he stole a horse—two. Two. Can't let a man get away with that. That. Next thing you know, everybody round here will be stealing whores and horses. Then where'll we be?"

"You can find some other damn fool to go chasing after them," Hooley said irritably.

Margot moved to him as if she were floating. She put her long fingers on his forearm, looked up into his eyes. "Hooley," she said softly. "If you care for me, you'll do it."

His heart pounded in rhythm to his head as he looked down into her face. Her eyes were full of pleading, and, he thought, of promise. He looked at her slender fingers with their tapered nails on his arm and heat filled his chest, banishing the pain raging throughout his body.

"It's not for the money, Hooley," she said. "Or the damned horse. I don't care anything about that. But you have to bring Kitty back. Please, Hooley." Her fingers tightened on his arm and their pressure coursed through him like a scalding iron. "If not for my sake," she said, cutting her eyes toward the four women, who remained clustered off to one side, "then for theirs. It's for their good and ours. Please, Hooley! Don't make me beg you!" He had never hated himself more than he did at this moment, for his resolve melted in the cool moss of her eyes.

"I can't be with a man who's less than a man, Hooley," she said. "This is our responsibility, and we're partners. Partners in everything." She breathed a deep sigh, making her bosom swell, and his gaze dropped to the freckled breasts he had come to worship, then raised to the mouth he so longed to kiss. "You've got to go."

"Margot," he said. "I—"

She lowered her voice to a whisper, barely making a sound. "They expect you do something," Margot entreated him. "*I* expect you to do something, too."

Hooley looked at the anxious expressions on every face. The hammering in his head gradually returned, increased with each breath. He saw the whores, standing as if welded together, staring at him. As if prompted by some muted cue, they moved forward to hear his final answer. Mino also moved close, his mouth forming his famous phrase as he approached.

"I don't . . ." He saw the men stiffen, expecting another protest, and his determination was revived with a new idea of how to escape this absurd chore. "I don't have a horse. You sure don't expect me to go after them afoot." This, he was sure, would be the end of it. He didn't want to tell them that he hadn't ridden a horse in years, and that he wasn't any good at it even then.

"You can use my horse!" Hank offered brightly.

"If it's your horse, you ought to ride him," Hooley said quickly. "I mean, you can—"

"He can't go, Hooley," Margot urged. "He's got a wife and child to think of." Her nails were now biting into his arm through the fabric of his undershirt. "Nobody can go but you."

"She's a good horse, Hooley," Hank assured him. "Ain't been rode in months. She's a little headstrong, but she'll do you proud. I'll go catch her up."

"I—," Hooley started again, but Hank and his bride were gone. The other boys shifted around, kicked dirt, and waited for Hooley to agree. He searched for some other avenue of escape, but none presented itself. Then he took a deep breath, looked once more into Margot's pleading, promising face, and realized that, as usual, there was no choice. She had won once more.

5

HE WENT INTO his tent, found his bottle. He was sopping with sweat, and a cloud of gnats swarmed around his eyes. His hands were shaking, and his tongue felt twice its normal size. He frantically brushed away the annoying insects and drank two long, gulping swallows of the liquor in rapid succession. The headache immediately abated, but now, he felt a miserable sensation in his gut. The aching, though, wasn't caused by hunger or by his usual dyspepsia after dealing with Margot. It was nothing less than fear. His shoulders sagged, and his eyes itched with the desire to close them. The liquor hit his stomach like a fiery ball falling into a vat of oil.

He peeked out and saw her returning from Hank's store, a flour sack in her hands—supplies, he presumed. The cowboys talked quietly, occasionally glancing up, waiting for him to come out. Margot's declaration that he was the killer of lawmen elevated him in their estimation from a bumbling tentmaker to someone to be reckoned with. For the first time, they were giving him respect. And all because of a few words from an angry whore. If he hadn't been so tired, so afraid, he would have found it funny.

After one more belt of whiskey, he buttoned on a shirt and vest, then pulled on his coat, feeling the oppressive, moist heat of the enclosed tent weighing him down. He found the twin Colt's Peacemakers and hefted them, admired their workmanship. He'd kept them well oiled. He'd seen them as toys, amusements. Now, however, they took on the appearance of the dangerous tools of a lawman, bringing to mind his dime novel heroes. But this was no dime novel, and he was no lawman, no hero. He was just a tentmaker. His mother would be proud of his honesty, but she would howl over the pretension his idiocy had led him to.

He shrugged, strapped on the holsters, latched the buckle. Looking down at his faded trousers and heavy brogans, he appeared ridiculous to himself, like a little boy with wooden guns. Sweat dripped off his nose, and the empty fear inside him doubled. Some *pistolero*, he thought. For a long moment, he cast his mind about, sought some honorable way out of this. Then, he remembered the look on Margot's face, felt the impression of her fingers on his arm, heard her words echoing in his ears. To say no would be to lose her forever. He couldn't imagine it. He peeked out again and saw that Margot had added a wet canteen to the provisions for his journey. There was no way to back out now. This, he thought, was requiring more than ambition of him, more even than some effort to preserve his pride. This required raw insanity.

He took one more drink, happily noting that his stomach was numbing. He checked the pistols' loads with shaking fingers. "Shit," he muttered. "Shit, shit, shit." He wanted to weep. Finally, he pulled himself together and wiped his face with a canvas handkerchief. But he was wholly unprepared for the reaction he received from the assembly. They all fell silent. Some doffed their hats, others offered low whistles of admiration. The girls' grins were cheek-to-cheek, and Margot's mouth widened in a smile. Mino watched him with a dark and wary stare.

"Them's some six-shooters!" Tidmore offered, then timidly asked, "Them the ones you used to gun down that marshal?"

Hooley looked down at the weapons as if surprised to find them on his person. A new sensation of slight pride struck him. "No," he said, then quickly retrieved his rusty old Winchester rifle from his tent. "I used this." He looked at Margot. He wanted the record clear. "These belonged to the lawman in question," he said evenly. "I kept them in compensation for his burial and tending his horse until his widow"—he nodded respectfully at Margot—"could claim it." The men looked at Margot. "And she did," he continued. "And she stayed, and you all know what's happened since."

"You don't do a goddamn thing for free, do you?" Jake asked.

Hooley shot the young cowboy a sharp look, and Jake put his hands up in defense. "Just joshing, Hooley. Just joshing," he protested, laughing nervously.

Hank came up leading his piebald mare, neatly saddled. Mino took the reins and calmed the horse, which was irritable over having been dragged away from her morning forage. Hank fingered a coil of rawhide lariat looped around the saddle horn.

"Case you take a notion to hang him," he whispered.

"Don't be stupid," Hooley replied, "I'm not about to hang anybody."

He felt his pockets to make sure he had his pipe and tobacco. He looked at the horse and wondered if she would stand still long enough for him to mount. Beneath the alcoholic buzz, Hooley felt his embarrassment building as steadily as the storm in the northwest.

Margot handed him the sack and canteen. "I admire you for this, Hooley," she whispered. He looked past her and noticed the four girls coming up behind her, then forming a half circle of admiring, flashing eyes. The cowboys also stared wondrously at him. "I never in the world imagined that I would once more be associated with a lawman," Margot said, sighing. "And in Texas, yet."

"I'm not a lawman," Hooley hissed, fighting resurging doubt. "I'm just a tentmaker."

"Hooley," she said, giving him an openly admiring look unlike any other he had ever seen her cast toward him in broad daylight, "you sell yourself short sometimes."

Instantly, his chest expanded with confidence and pride, and he almost reached out and pulled her to him, kissed her deeply on the mouth after the fashion of a dime novel frontier knight, taking a favor from his true love before sallying forth to do battle with the forces of evil.

Before the impulse overrode his natural temerity, though, Mino spoke up. "No shit, Gil Hooley," he said in second to Margot's comment, and the girls fell into a flutter of giggles.

Irked and embarrassed, Hooley grasped the pommel and vaulted expertly into the saddle the way he'd seen the cowboys do a thousand times. He was so shocked to find that the trick worked, he almost lost his balance when the horse sidestepped under his weight. "I'll be back," he gasped as he gained control of the animal, which was considerably friskier than he had anticipated. When he felt secure, he gazed over the crowd. "And there's going to be some changes made."

"No shit, Gil Hooley," Mino said again, and there were more suppressed giggles.

"Good luck," Hank called.

"Bring him back dead or alive! Alive!" Underwood shouted. The others whooped.

Hooley suddenly once more realized precisely what he was doing but unable to see any way out of it. "Oh, to hell with it," he said in disgust. He kicked the horse out of the compound. She was eager for the freedom and loped off in a spunky canter into the maw of an approaching thunderstorm. Hooley's only real thought was that it was a big mistake not to have remembered his hat.

A POSSE OF ONE

———◆◆◆———

1

GILBERT HOOLEY HAD long since given up the habit of carrying a timepiece. Nothing much happened in his life that required precise timing, and the rhythms of the community had long ago taken shape around routines governed by circumstance rather than time of day. On another account, remembering to wind a pocket watch twice a day required the kind of systemized responsibility that Hooley always tried to avoid. For more than a year, he had reckoned the time by the position of the sun or moon, or, if the weather was cloudy, by the brightness of ambient light.

The time of day was the last thing on Hooley's mind as he tried with no success whatsoever to guide Hank's piebald pony in the face of the approaching storm. The confidence he felt when he mounted up and rode out faded rapidly once the mare found her stride and established a rapid lope. He wished he had remembered to find out if the recalcitrant beast between his legs had a name. If he could call her in some authoritative voice, he figured, the horse might respond to commands. Instead, he was at the mare's mercy. The thought tightened his mouth. It seemed that his fate was always to be at some female's mercy, and this one seemed to be taking full advantage of Hooley's ineptitude. Thus, he clung to the saddle horn and bounced along as she found her self-determined way into the wilderness.

For a long and breathless while, the pony fairly jogged through belly-high grass, tacking back and forth in what Hooley could only hope was a northern direction while he struggled to trim the reins and kicked ineffectually at her spur-toughened flanks, never able to change the mare's vague course. His only consistent locus point was the gathering storm in the northwest, the highest thunderheads of which now blotted out the sun and revealed bright flashes of balled lightning in the eerie canyons and peaks of the building cloud bank.

Every thudding step the mare took reminded Hooley of his folly. He tried to tell himself that what he was doing was important to the security of their enterprise, but he couldn't decide if that was true and what it might mean for his and Margot's future. About all he was sure of was that whatever this foolish adventure ultimately came to mean to him, it would mean something entirely different to Margot. One way or another, she would figure out how to use it against him.

The horse continued her mysterious course, and Hooley struggled to find a comfortable rhythm. He always seemed to be descending whenever the horse was rising, meaning that his skinny hips continually bounced on the stiff leather of the seat. Each equine step produced a jaw-rattling collision that caused him to bite the inside of his mouth and his tongue until they were sore and ragged. But the horse jogged on without paying any mind to his suffering rider or the massing thunderstorm or the curses Hooley screamed each time his tortured buttocks came in contact with the rock-hard saddle or his teeth jammed shut and further lacerated the inside of his cheek.

After a while, he looked over his shoulder to see how far he had actually come, but the waving grass had swallowed up the townlet. His stomach panged with a renewed discovery of hunger. He had food, he presumed, in the bag Margot had prepared, but at present, he had no choice but to cling tightly to the pommel as the horse happily cantered across the grassy prairie, bound for some destination that only her tiny brain could imagine.

The unmistakable smell of rain hit Hooley's nostrils every time he found himself on the upside of a bounce and gasping for breath to sustain himself when he collided with the beast's back. He searched the horizon for anything that might offer shelter, but nothing in the way of a grove of trees or mound of rocks presented itself. An empty ocean of grass, waving haphazardly in the increasing wind, surrounded him.

He finally regulated his involuntary movements to match the motions of the horse on the downbeat rather than in painful syncopation when the mare abruptly stopped, tossed her head, spun to the right, then took off at a running gallop across the crest of a ridge. Hooley cried out in protest, then clung to the animal until his legs ached and his fingers went numb from clutching the horse's bright mane in a desperate fist. After they had galloped flat out for a hundred yards or so, he glanced up and estimated that the ridge ran for several miles to the northeast. The horse raced along the crest for nearly the whole way before she suddenly veered off down a steep side and into the opening of a deep arroyo, where, to Hooley's relief, she slowed to a walk and clopped along as peacefully as if she were on a St. Louis street and in no hurry to arrive anywhere.

Hooley gulped air from the thick atmosphere of the deepening yellow ditch. The swirling wind did not reach the depression in the prairie, and sweat ran down into his eyes, stinging and biting. When his heart's pounding slowed, helpless frustration filled him. The mare picked its way around the casual twists of the narrow gully, the bottom of which deepened into a moist and muddy trail beneath jagged limestone rocks.

Hooley at last took stock of himself and discovered that his starboard pistol was missing. A bolt of unreasonable panic shot through him. The weapon must have jarred loose during the piebald's harebrained gallop, and he'd never recover it. The loss of the pistol so vexed him that he began loudly cursing himself, the horse, Margot and Mino, the cowboys and the whores, saving special damnation for Kitty and her cowboy lover, whom he never expected to find.

The horse happily clip-clopped along without reaction to Hooley's refrain of damning vulgarity, which irked Hooley all the more. The tentmaker ran out of breath about the time the mare rounded a sharp turn in the arroyo's bottom and discovered a deep pool of reddish water blocking the way. She stepped up to the rocky edge, lowered her neck sharply, nearly pitching Hooley off onto his head, and began to drink in loud, slurping noises. When he righted himself in the saddle, he thought of his own water and found his canteen.

"If you sit a drinking horse, you curse yourself with drowning," a voice came to Hooley from behind. Startled, he twisted awkwardly in the saddle. The action threw him off balance, and the piebald sidestepped in the opposite direction. Hooley flailed his arms, fell hard on a bed of rocky mud. The voice's laughter added insult to his embarrassment.

Hooley sprang to his feet, furiously glaring at the voice and its owner, a large man in buckskins and a tall battered beaver hat. He was, Hooley deduced, a savage Indian. He sat cross-legged under the overhang before an opening of a shallow limestone depression. Instead of the moccasins Hooley believed savage Indians always wore, the man had on a pair of high-laced boots, fairly well blackened and shiny in the gray skylight.

"Who the hell are you?" Hooley demanded hotly. "And what are you doing here?"

The man shrugged. "Might ask you the same thing, I was a mind to. I was here first."

Hooley considered drawing his pistol. His schooling in western adventures had taught him that to confront a threatening stranger unarmed was the height of folly. On the other hand, the man didn't seem threatening at all. He smiled at Hooley, although the grin was suggestive of mockery. His braids framed a clean-shaven, swarthy face, and his hands were folded neatly on the lap made of his crossed legs. To Hooley's astonishment, he was holding a long, fat cigar.

"I'm. . . . uh," Hooley started, then stopped. The piebald, now sated with water, began dropping bright green horse apples. Hooley stepped up and caught up the dangling reins, but the horse didn't seem to be going anywhere. "I'm the, uh . . ." What the hell *was* he? Hooley demanded silently of himself. He couldn't say "postmaster." That sounded too stupid. "I'm from over there." He nodded vaguely in what he hoped was a southerly direction. "My name's Hooley."

"Oh, I'd know your ashes in hell," the man said, and put the fat cigar in his mouth. "You're the son of a bitch ruined my business." He struck a lucifer and fired the end of the stogie. "Cigar?" he offered, and patted a large beaded bag that lay next to him.

"How do you know me?"

"Everybody round here knows you," the man said through a puff of gray smoke. "Even if they ain't laid eyes on you." He smiled then. "Simmer down. Ain't nobody here looking for a fight."

Hooley eyed him warily. Overhead thunder boomed and the sky was now a swirl of black and green clouds. Jagged lightning streaked angrily.

"Why don't you come on in here," the man said. "Tie up that hayburner and rest yourself under cover. It's apt to get nasty out there if a cyclone hits, and you don't even have a hat. Here, we can make room." He clamped the cigar in his teeth and scooted over. Behind him, Hooley was astonished to see, sat a woman wrapped in a blanket. Another savage Indian, Hooley thought with a sudden spring of panic. She peered at him through black eyes set narrowly over chubby and pockmarked cheeks and gave him a big gappy smile.

Raindrops began splattering around him, and he could hear the roar of the approaching squall line. Hooley was still undecided about what to do, but he realized that he was going to get soused. The rain quickened. He pulled the horse over to a clump of salt cedar and tied her off, then clamored up the side of the arroyo and scrunched himself down next to the man. As he squatted in the same cross-legged fashion as his strange host, he noticed that behind the woman the depression opened into a cave

that raced off under a ledge of rock. When he shifted his position to peer
into the hole, his legs cramped, and he squirmed around painfully and
thrust his limbs out in front of him, kneading his muscles. The Indian
ignored Hooley's exaggerated movements.

"I'm the galoot they call 'Cherokee Charlie,' " he said, but he didn't
extend his hand to shake. "Late of Pease City Store." Hooley had heard
of this man the first time Hank ever rode into his camp, but he never
expected to meet him. "This here is Loretta," the man said. "Loretta, this
is 'No Shit' Hooley, owner of the Whorehouse of Hoolian." Cherokee
Charlie flashed a sinister smile behind the thick cigar, the fumes of which
were making Hooley slightly ill. "He's the one put us out of business and
made a pile of money doing it." Loretta offered another smile.

The storm's full fury broke abruptly and doused the tiny canyon's narrow bottom with furious, whipping rain accompanied by deafening thunder. Gales blew water almost sideways down the natural corridor, loosening
lightly rooted plants in its fierceness. The mare moved closer to the yellow
walls of the deep ditch and squealed loudly when hailstones the size of
peaches clattered down into the limestone bottom and churned the red
pool into a boiling orange froth.

"This is one bitch of a storm," Cherokee Charlie yelled over the
noise, and produced an unlabeled bottle. "You want a drink?" Hooley
hesitated, then nodded. "This is nothing but homemade head-popper," he
continued, "but it'll get the job done, if you take it slow."

Hooley accepted the bottle and took a swig. The contents were liquid
fire, burning the raw bites on the inside of his mouth and searing his throat.
He immediately fell into a gagging, coughing fit as his body tried to reject
it.

"I told you to go slow," Cherokee Charlie hollered. "That shit'll blind
an owl, you drink it fast. I'm looking forward to getting back to civilization
so I can get a righteous drink." Hooley coughed some more and took a
deep breath, then another sip of the homemade brew. It went down
smoother this time, but his stomach still burned. More thunder and lightning crashed, but the hail abated and the rain began to take shape as a
sharp, steady fall. "I doubt it'll flood down here," Cherokee Charlie said.
"We ain't had a good turd-floater like this one in a good spell. Ground's
dry. It'll drink it up."

"I heard the river's up," Hooley said, remembering Underwood's words.

Cherokee Charlie nodded. "Yessir. Big rains up on the high plains. She's
full to the brim and running tight, likely. Won't last but a day or so, but
you can't get across till then. That's why we holed up here, to wait it out."
His dark eyes suddenly brightened. "You ain't lighting out too, are you?

Pulling up stakes?" Hooley shook his head. "Too damn bad," Cherokee
Charlie said. "Serve that son of a bitch Rancher McPherson right if you
left them worthless cowpunchers high and dry. But I don't blame you.
Just thought I'd ask."

"Why are you leaving?" Hooley asked.

"Rancher McPherson," Cherokee Charlie said. "Closed the damned
store. Said we couldn't turn a profit with *one* woman when you had seven,
and every one of them white."

"Five," Hooley corrected. "Actually, four," he quickly amended. "But
they're not—"

"Should of known Rancher McPherson would lie about that, too," he
said. "He lied about damn near everything. Couldn't not lie without lying.
Man's a foreigner, don't you know?"

Hooley found that statement curious coming from a savage Indian. "I've
never met him," he said. Cherokee Charlie seemed unsurprised. "He seems
to hold a grudge against me."

"Well, I don't wonder," Cherokee Charlie said. He sucked his cigar
contemplatively and watched the rain. Hooley shook his head, then thought
to fetch his pipe and lit it up. He dimly realized that this was his first of
the day, and the day had begun well before sunup. As Hooley fired his
tobacco, Cherokee Charlie took a few sips from the bottle and handed it
to Loretta, who carefully wiped the top with a grimy hand and indulged
herself.

"You said you were leaving?" Hooley asked, trying to sound sad about
it.

Cherokee Charlie nodded. He explained that a week before, Rancher
McPherson came to the store and told him he was closing it and that
Cherokee Charlie would have to find work elsewhere. "Been expecting it,"
Cherokee Charlie said. "We ain't turned a nickel's profit since you put up
that whorehouse, opened up that fancy general store."

"I didn't—"

"Don't matter," Cherokee Charlie said. "I was ready to move on, anyhow. I didn't much like the work. Time I went home."

"Oklahoma Territory?"

"Hell no," Cherokee Charlie said. "Cleveland, Ohio. I come down from
there five, six years ago." He read the astonishment in Hooley's face, then
looked at his buckskins. "Oh, I see." He laughed. "I'm called Cherokee
Charlie, but I'm no savage Indian. That was all Rancher McPherson's idea.
I'm Dutch-Irish. Mostly. Rancher McPherson thought the men would deal
quicker with a savage Indian than a Yankee whiskey peddler—that's my
old trade. He was right, too. Mostly. For a while. Then you come along

and knocked our dick in the dirt. Soft flops, store-bought whiskey, clean sheets, tasty food, regular mercantile store, and pure-white titties for them to look at!" He bit down on the cigar. "Even got music and dancing, I hear."

"I should say I'm sorry," Hooley allowed. He looked him hard in the eye. "But I'm not."

Cherokee Charlie laughed, spewing blue smoke out into the rain. "Sooner or later, things would have gone south for us," he said. "You just hurried it along. I was about tired of it anyway. Never could stay at things too long. I was at this longer than most."

He explained that Rancher McPherson was selling some cattle in Chicago when they met in a hotel's saloon where Cherokee Charlie was drumming whiskey. He was sick of the peddling business, so he accepted Rancher McPherson's proposition to come down to Texas and set up a store selling homemade whiskey to the cowboys he hired to work his ranch.

"Oh, it was a sweet deal, at first," Cherokee Charlie said. "I got twenty-five percent of the profits, and all I had to do was dress up like a savage Indian and make sure that they spent more than they made. Then, like I said, you showed up, and they mostly stopped coming. We limped along for a while, but it wasn't no good. Can't compete with a deluxe operation such as yours."

"That's competition, I guess," Hooley said.

"That's bullshit," Cherokee Charlie rejoined. "But it's all right. It wasn't ever my business. I just ramrodded it for Rancher McPherson, never did make the money you do."

Cherokee Charlie's mention of money reminded Hooley of his purpose, but he was too hungry to consider leaving until he had eaten. He hated to share his rations with this strange man, but the rain showed no signs of abating, so he fetched the soaked flour sack from the piebald that was standing patiently in the downpour, her head drooping. Inside the sack, he found a half-dozen stale biscuits—still rock-hard in spite of their dousing—potted beef, and two cans of tomatoes. Cherokee Charlie was delighted by the groceries, and he produced a large, narrow-bladed knife with a bright bone handle carved in the shape of a woman's naked leg and pried open the cans.

The utensil astonished Hooley, who noted a matching piece thrust into Cherokee Charlie's belt. The carving was remarkably lifelike, Hooley thought, right down to the bare foot and toes, with each toenail painted a different color.

"A gift from a grateful woman," Cherokee Charlie explained, and laughed. "My wife. She was so glad I left her, she sent me them as a

present. Told me if I didn't cut my own throat with one to try the other."
He held up the knife and admired it in the gray light. "Didn't count on
the river being up, so we ran out of supplies," he explained. "Ain't had
nothing to eat but prairie gopher for two days. I figured to be at a railhead
in Kansas by now." He passed an open can of tomatoes to Loretta, who
immediately fingered out a large helping and stuffed it into her mouth.

Cherokee Charlie explained that Rancher McPherson hired Loretta, a
mute half-breed he found cleaning jakes behind a saloon in Niles City, to
cook. "She took to the job quick enough," he said. Loretta smiled and
revealed a mouthful of tomato. Cherokee Charlie continued, "I tried to
work her as a whore after I heard about your setup, but she didn't take
to it." She smiled again, her black eyes full of innocence and mirth. Hooley
decided she might be deranged.

"What she *would* do," Cherokee Charlie said, "was show them her titties.
That worked out all right. I charged them two dollars a gander. But that
didn't last after you got your operation going full steam, so I lowered the
rate to a dollar, then four bits. But Loretta, sweet as she is, couldn't
compete with what you got in your stable." He winked.

"It's not *my* stable," Hooley grumbled around a mouthful of food. His
stomach clenched when the first bites arrived, but now it relaxed, accepted
the nourishment. "I got partners."

"That a fact?" Cherokee Charlie said, his eyes twinkling in mischief.
"That's not what I heard from the boys. To hear them tell it, you're the
big chief, owner, proprietor, and brains of the whole shooting match."
Hooley looked to see if he was being mocked. "Said you make a pot of
money off every Saturday night," he said. "Made them pay cash or sign
credit vouchers. That was smart. I had to deal through Rancher McPherson, and that man would cheat Satan himself." He studied Hooley's face
for a moment, but the tentmaker held his expression firm. "Boys said you
got a redheaded whore that can make a man loco, and you hired a gelded
A-rab to watch her and your personal harem, when you ain't renting them
out."

Hooley shook his head. How could they say such things? "That'd be
Mino," he muttered. "And he's no gelding, uh . . . He's a Turk. I think.
Mostly, he's a carpenter."

"Turk, A-rab, all the same thing. I read about them fellers. Thick-
peckered sons of bitches." He picked up the knife and turned it before his
eyes thoughtfully, stroked the handle. "So gelding's about all you can do
with them to keep your women healthy and appreciative."

Hooley chewed the last of the food and watched the rain grumpily.

Cherokee Charlie wiped his hands on his pants, then picked up his cigar and relit it. "It's none of my business, I don't guess. But what the hell are you doing out here? And on Hank Mitchell's mare? How is old Hank? I ain't seen him since the dawn of time. Heard he got married, though, so that'd explain it. He know you've got that horse?"

Hooley swallowed, trying to form the notion correctly. "I'm actually trying to track down one of . . . of the girls," he stammered. "She ran off last night with a cowboy."

Cherokee Charlie never blinked. "That a fact? Which one?"

"Chatsworth."

"Al Chatsworth? Prissy little dipshit son of a bitch?"

Hooley almost nodded before he shook his head. "Well, he's not that little, he's—"

"Oh, he ain't so big." Cherokee Charlie said, laughing. "Not in the ways that count. Ain't that right, Loretta?" She laughed and, Hooley thought, blushed, although it was hard to tell in the dim gray light filtering through the rain. "Can't play poker worth a damn. Owes me money, fact of the matter, but he likes a good cigar." He held up his own and admired it for a moment. "Which one he run off with? Not the redhead?"

"Uh, no," Hooley said. "The blonde. That is, *a* blonde. Named Kitty, she—"

"Aw, he talked about her, didn't he, Loretta?" Cherokee Charlie said with a wink. "That 'yellow-haired filly,' he called her. Said she was frisky! I'd say he was smitten by her, wouldn't you, Loretta?" Loretta nodded vigorously. "Had him wound up tight as a banjo string. Worst thing a man can do is fall in love with a whore," he observed. "Ain't that right, Loretta?" She smiled again and nodded. "Whores is nothing but trouble," Cherokee Charlie muttered, and a dark look crossed his face. " 'Course, all women is whores, one way or another. No matter what happens, any man who fools with one is bound to get rooky-dood."

"I'd have to agree," Hooley said irritably when he flashed on Margot's face.

"Some of them have good-looking titties, though," Cherokee Charlie said, glancing at Loretta, who shrieked out loud and held her sides in laughter. Hooley decided she *was* demented.

"So you got a notion of where they run off to?" Cherokee Charlie asked.

"Kansas, maybe," he answered vaguely.

"And they sent you to find him all by your lonesome?" Hooley nodded again, his teeth clenching painfully. "Posse of one? That's one hell of a note."

"I'm the postmaster," Hooley growled, irritated. "Seems that it was my responsibility."

"Well, you *might* catch them," Cherokee Charlie observed idly. "If they went to the river, they're still there. There's a ferry at Dutchman's Mill might be running, might not—depends on the Dutchman. Whether he's sober or not, and he's not often sober. You think *my* whiskey is rank, you ought to taste his!" He grinned. " 'Course, that might be too far to go. They could ford it if their horses could swim. If not, they drowned. No doubt to that. My guess is that they headed for the Dutchman's." He sucked on his cigar. Hooley wondered how in the world he would ever find a ferry along a river he'd never seen and had only a vague idea of how to locate.

"Let me ask you a question: Why does everybody call you 'No Shit' Hooley?"

"That's not my name," Hooley said, irked. "My name is Gil, Gilbert Hooley."

Cherokee Charlie's eyes widened, but amusement flickered behind them. "I like 'No Shit' better," he said, but Hooley's scowl discouraged further levity. "So, why you reckon them two run off, *Gilbert* Hooley?" Cherokee Charlie asked, his tone sarcastic, which further nettled Hooley. "And why do you care? It's just a whore."

Hooley decided it didn't matter. He had no expectation of finding them anyway. He watched the steady rain just outside their overhang, fought sleepiness. "They stole some bags. Full of money."

"How much?"

"Nearly a thousand dollars," Hooley admitted, wishing he hadn't mentioned it.

Cherokee Charlie laughed. "You're pulling my pecker! There ain't that much money in the whole of West Texas." Hooley didn't reply, but Cherokee Charlie was paying him no mind. He was shaking his head. "Chatsworth?" he mused aloud. "Never struck me as a thief." He looked suddenly thoughtful. "A thousand dollars, you say?"

"He also stole one of Rancher McPherson's horses." Hooley was eager to change the subject. "The one he's probably riding."

"Not the bay?"

Cherokee Charlie's presumptuous manner was irritating him. He seemed to know more than Hooley did. Then a suspicious thought struck him. "How would you know that?"

"Chatsworth was always partial to that bay," Cherokee Charlie observed. "Rancher McPherson was going to breed that stud. One fine horse, I can tell you. He'll be hopping mad if he loses that animal." He winked again. "This could go bad for you, *Gilbert* Hooley."

"Me? Why me?"

"Well, she was one of your whores. That makes you a party to stealing, seems to me."

Anger swarmed all over Hooley at once, reawakened him. "Are you crazy? How could that have anything to do with me?"

"Who's out here looking for him? Ain't Rancher McPherson, and that's a fact. Or his boys," Cherokee Charlie said, his manner unperturbed. "Whose money was it he stole?"

"*My* money! Goddamn it! You're as stupid a son of a bitch as anyone I've encountered out here yet," Hooley railed. He rose too quickly, banged his head on the opening's upper ledge. "Shit!" he cried. His eyes teared in pain.

"You're mighty free with your insults," Cherokee Charlie said. "Especially toward a man who's shared his whiskey with you and offered you a look at his woman's titties."

Hooley rubbed the knot forming on top of his head and gaped at Cherokee Charlie, then at Loretta, who smiled at him and began undoing the top of her dress.

"I have no intention of looking at anybody's . . . !" Hooley spluttered.

"I'll only charge you six bits," Cherokee Charlie encouraged him. "That's cheaper than you get over at *your* whorehouse, and I'll bet you another four bits that Loretta's titties are as good or better than any of them fancy St. Louis whores you brought down here with you, including that redhead." He turned to Loretta. "Hurry up and show him, Loretta— Chatsworth says the man likes to look at titties. Get out your money, Gilbert Hooley! If you're lucky, I might give you two peeks for the price of one."

To Hooley's horror, the woman began untying the top of her buckskin dress, all the while grinning at him. Panicked, he slid out of the cave and scrambled down from the depression into the downpour, and was instantly soaked. He found the piebald's reins and gathered them. Then he stopped. The left side of the horse was pressed against the mud-streaked wall of the ravine, and yellow clay ran in globs down onto the saddle, giving it a sticky, nasty look.

"You're not leaving already?" Cherokee Charlie sounded disappointed. "Hell, we just now shook and howdied." Hooley refused to answer. "Well, you don't have sense enough to stay out of the rain, that's your lookout. But you ought to have a hat."

Hooley stepped off, surprised when the mare docilely followed him back up the ravine.

"You're missing a sure bet in Loretta here," Cherokee Charlie called out. "You take a gander at what she's got, you'll want to tote her back, give her regular work!" Hooley didn't turn around. "Tell you what: I'll drop the freight for a look-see to four bits. Now, that's a bargain! She's worth a dollar if she's worth a dime!"

2

HOOLEY DRAGGED THE horse through the downpour, his shoes slipping and sliding in the muddy trace. Eventually, the ditch ran shallow enough to allow him to merge into the open prairie, where the thick raindrops soaked the high grass and darkened the sky. Ultimately, though, the rain washed the saddle clean and Hooley grew weary of slogging along, his head down by the horse's wet side. After three slippery, aborted attempts to duplicate his suave mounting demonstration from earlier in the day, he gave up and awkwardly hoisted himself aboard. When his weight hit the saddle, the mare instantly shied and swung around in a circle, but to Hooley's relief, she didn't buck him off.

Seating himself as comfortably as he could, he raised his bare head into the sheeting moisture and tried to get his bearings, but it was impossible. No direction presented itself logically to his instincts, and the rain was so heavy that he had no choice but to let the reins go slack and allow the horse to plod along as she would.

Thunder and lightning crashed all around him, but the rain fell straight down in a gray curtain. He was cold and wet through and the only good thing he could discover was that the mare seemed content to walk rather than run. The whiskey and meal he had consumed sapped his reserve of energy and made him intolerably sleepy. Only inertia kept him from pitching out of the saddle while the horse's plodding stride clumped dully beneath him in an unknown direction.

The encounter with Cherokee Charlie seemed like a dream, a hallucination. He was too tired to be angry, too weary to care, but the faux Indian knew far too much about everything. Hooley suddenly suspected that he had actually seen Chatsworth and Kitty, maybe was in cahoots with them. But returning to confront the lunatic in the cave was out of the question. All he wanted was to reach shelter, lie down and never get up. He lacked the ambition even to anticipate that eventuality. It was merely an idle desire that formed and remained solid in his imagination.

Now and then, the horse's path would incline slightly, and Hooley's body would shift back, then forward on the windward side of the hillock. The first few times, he jerked up straight, raised his face to the rain, and grasped for the horse's sodden mane in terror of falling off. But after a

while, he became more used to the pattern, and he developed an unconscious rhythm, and his mind slipped into a semi-sleep until the horse's
gait brought him back to consciousness. Every time he was jerked awake,
he cursed Margot for pushing him into this, but then in a short while,
he'd fall back into a half sleep and, to his consistent irritation, would dream
of her.

The rain finally began to slack off to a dull mist, but Hooley kept his
posture bent, his bare head crowned to the sky. He gradually understood
that the landscape around him was changing, becoming rougher. The grass
was shorter and coarser, and small, thorny bushes began to appear, along
with thick clumps of the deep green salt cedar and prickly pear cactus.
The soil, where it was visible, was orange-red and had turned loamy in its
muddy aspect, and large bluffs began to form around him.

The mare topped a rise, then descended into a deep draw and automatically climbed the other side. Hooley had lost all sense of direction. He
halfway hoped that if he just let her keep her head, she would find her
way back to her corral. As she climbed the other side of the draw, he
leaned forward and pressed his face into her mane to keep from keeling
backward over her rump. She topped the bluff and stopped to crop some
grass. Through the gauzy wet haze that blurred the air, he saw the Prairie
Dog Town Fork of the Red River open before him.

The river was over its banks. Bright red water boiled in the center of
what appeared to be a wide orange scar in the prairie. On the other side,
Hooley could see a few stands of deep green cedar and scrub trees amidst
more grass and rocky bluffs. But the river itself seemed angry. What would
ordinarily have been whitecaps where the rapids tumbled onto one another
or splashed around on flotsam glowed pink in the dim gray light. He had
seen the Mississippi in flood, of course, and the Tennessee and the Ohio.
But the prospect of this river running blood-red water raised hackles of
fear. On the far bank was the dreaded prospect of Oklahoma Territory, a
hell on earth from all reports, where lawmen and outlaws were indistin-
guishable.

If Chatsworth and Kitty had made it to this river, Hooley wearily
thought, it was as far as they came; no sane person would venture into
this turgid flow. But now, what was he to do? He had no idea where on
the river he might be. The culprits could be hiding anywhere in the thick-
ets of plum and high grasses that crowded into the muddy torrent. No
lawman in his reading experience had ever faced such a prospect—they
could always track their prey right to their hideouts. Reality was far different, Hooley decided.

He peered into the rainy fog behind him. He had no idea what direction he had come since leaving Cherokee Charlie's cave. He idly wondered if the pair had horses somewhere. Surely a man of Cherokee Charlie's nature wouldn't try to traverse this harsh country afoot. He looked up. The sky was little more than a low, lumpy, gray ceiling. There was no way to get a bearing. All he was certain of was that the piebald mare had somehow deduced that he wanted to go to the river. Now, she waited patiently beneath his aching legs and hips, with no idea where she should take him next. The problem, he thought, was that there was absolutely nowhere he wanted to go. He was as close to the hellish, rampaging flood below as he cared to be. If Chatsworth and Kitty were down there, more power to them. They had made good their escape, and there wasn't one damned thing he could do. But he dreaded the prospect of returning to Hoolian empty-handed and facing Margot with failure.

He pulled out his pipe and tried in vain to find a dry match, but finally gave up. Darkness was gathering, and he was exhausted, cold, wet, afraid, and utterly alone. Making a camp was out of the question, as a fire would be wanted, and he saw nothing dry enough to burn. The river, he vaguely remembered from his old map, ran mostly west to east. This meant that Hoolian—that irritatingly ridiculously named town—lay somewhere vaguely to the south.

"Hell," Hooley grumbled to the mare. "I could ride right past it and never see it. We could wind up in Mexico." For a moment, the prospect of never returning seemed inviting. "Would serve her right," he muttered. "Would serve every goddamn one of them right."

As night rapidly descended, the misty rain ended and the sky cleared. The mare walked steadily up and down the undulating and uneven ground of the cedar breaks, but the utter jet all around him vanquished any thought he had of stopping and resting for a while. He could barely make out the horse's bobbing head as she moved steadily along on what now appeared to be a direct line to somewhere he couldn't imagine. Time passed without meaning, until he spotted an unnaturally bright star rising ahead of him. He shook himself, tried to stay alert. Nocturnal animals bumped and snorted in the grass and scrub surrounding them, but he was too tired to be afraid, and in the distance, the barking snapping yelps of coyotes—his old friends—mocked his progress through the darkness.

His mind went once more to Margot. He vowed that if he lived through this, he was done with her, done forever. Then he envisioned her deep beauty, the redness of her hair, the green sweetness of her eyes. And then he thought of her naked and next to him, her soft, slender but strong body clinging to him in passion. He wondered if it was real, or merely the practiced act of a professional harridan, an accomplished whore, an evil witch who had wormed her way into his life and now cast him out to die in the wilderness's darkness, alone, friendless, and without mercy. He hated her. Then, his mind softened toward her again. He loved her. His confusion was profound, and it vexed him.

Now and then, he would sway in the saddle, then suddenly snap to, startled, his heart thudding in panic. Each time, he observed that the distant star had grown in size. It had an unusual yellow cast, and it seemed to become brighter, larger, as he watched it. He set himself toward it with a hopeless determination. His head was heavy, and his eyes and throat burned. He put his mind on his mother, wondered if she was still alive, what she might think of all this, and he fell once more into the plastic rhythm of the animal beneath him and ceased his awareness of anything but the rocking gait, the swishing sound of wet grass against the horse's belly, and the unavoidable image of Margot Phillips' face.

His half-somnambulant reverie ended when he realized the mare had stopped. The light he had seen was before him, but it was no star. It was a large campfire, at the center of which was a cedar knot, flaming brightly and casting its black turpentine into the sky. Hooley kicked his heels wearily against the mare's sides, but she didn't move. He looked down, around her sodden, dirty mane, and in the ambient light found himself face-to-face with the snaggle-toothed grin of a huge, ugly man dressed in nothing but underwear and a pistol belt around his waist. One hand held fast to the mare's bridle, the other pointed a black revolver directly into Hooley's face.

Hooley had had enough. More than enough. Enough for a day. Enough for a lifetime. A reserve of anger rose from an emotional well so deep that once aroused, it gained momentum and climbed past surprise, past fear, past any feeling but complete outrage. "I don't know who you are, you sorry son of a bitch," he croaked. "But if you don't let go of this horse, I'm going to kill you deader than Aunt Roadie's old gray goose."

The man grinned wider and turned his head slightly, exposing a huge hole in his cheek. "Hey, Captain," he yelled. "Come see what just rode in. Bless my heart if it ain't the anarchist!"

3

IT TOOK HOOLEY a few moments to realize that the man holding a pistol on him was none other than Coltrain, one of the Rangers he had met during the company's brief nocturnal visit on a frigid night nearly two years before. When understanding came over him, Hooley fairly fell off the mare in a collapse of relief and exhaustion. Coltrain gave him small time to recover. The big Texan grabbed the tentmaker by the scruff of his sodden coat and dragged him, half stumbling, into camp. The Rangers were well established around their bonfire, which was adjacent to a tiny pond that had formed in a limestone-lined depression in the prairie. The fire reflected off the rocks and lit the area for twenty yards around, revealing that the lawmen were mostly standing around barefoot in their long johns and broad-brimmed hats. Their clothing was draped over hastily cut green cedar fronds that had been placed close to the snapping pop of the flames.

"I had no idea there was this much firewood anywhere around here," Hooley commented irritably as he was led to the scowling presence of Captain Ellis.

"You got to know where to look," Ellis said. "And you can't be lazy. Wood grows where you find it, dies in the same place." He cast his single eye up and down Hooley's sodden form. "I figured you was dead a long time ago. Anarchists don't last long out here."

Hooley was too worn out to care about propriety. He looked Ellis in his one good eye. "I'm a veteran of the United States Army," he said, then added reluctantly, "and a postmaster of the United States Mail."

"Thought you were a tentmaker," Ellis said.

"I'm that, too," Hooley snapped.

"I think you're just a sad little Yankee," Ellis muttered, "and a damn fool. But that's no nevermind to me."

"I really don't give a damn," Hooley said.

"Coltrain says you threatened to shoot him."

"I didn't know who he was."

"I'll hang you as quick for shooting a Texas Ranger as I would for killing a sodbusting squarehead," Ellis said. "I might just hang you for the hell of it."

Hooley merely shook his head. There was no arguing with this man. Briefly, he wondered if Ellis could best Margot in an argument. Coltrain handed Hooley a tin cup that scalded his hand. "I don't take no offense to it," the burly Ranger said. "I'd of shot you through before you could of filled your hand anyhow. Shouldn't of called me 'sorry,' though. Bad enough that half my face is shot away, though I've got to allow that it's not many a man who can lick his own ear." He demonstrated this unique talent, grinned at Hooley. "We damn near drowned in that damn river. You been in the river, too?"

"I know that piebald." Ellis said, nodding toward the mare. "Belongs to a cowhand works for that goddamn foreigner."

"That's Hank Mitchell's horse," Hooley said. "He's not a cowhand any longer. He's a storekeeper. He loaned it to me."

"You always got a snappy answer," Ellis said. "It's wearisome. Strip down and dry out. I might decide to hang you anyway, and I won't hang a man who's uncomfortable in his clothes."

Hooley was indeed uncomfortable. He put down the coffee cup and peeled down to his underwear, then draped his clothes on the cedar fronds. A Ranger called Crowder handed him a dry blanket, and he spread it on the ground and sat on it. Ellis, who wore his badge pinned on his undershirt, came over and squatted on his haunches next to him. For a while, they drank coffee in silence. Hooley discovered that the black liquid was generously laced with whiskey.

The silence grew awkward, and the liquor made Hooley sleepier than ever, but Coltrain kept their cups brimmed up, grinning while he poured. Ellis shot him a questioning look, but the younger Ranger shrugged. "He was generous with his joe when we come through that time. And it was cold enough to freeze the balls off a buffalo." The rest of the company nodded agreement.

"They don't do a lot of goddamn anything good in Oklahoma Territory," Coltrain volunteered, "but they can brew a nice jug of corn liquor. Cuts Crowder's coffee down to size."

"And that's odd," Crowder put in. "Since I never seen a single ear of corn growing up there. Alls they got up there is chiggers and ugly fat women."

"And you tried to fuck all of both of them, Crowder," another Ranger piped up. "Only thing you got close to your pecker was chiggers. Least it looks that away from the way you're always scratching it!" Laughter was general, but Ellis didn't join in.

"I suppose I should ask what brings you back out here," Hooley finally said.

Ellis sipped, then set down his cup and began rolling a cigarette. "Well, it's none of your goddamn business, but I'll tell you anyway." He explained that they were on their way back from Oklahoma Territory when they made the mistake of trying to cross the Red River at high flood. "Ain't one of these knotheads can swim," he said. "We were half a day fishing them out of the mud downstream."

"I never had no cause to learn to swim," Crowder said. The others nodded. "Never seen enough water to worry about, truth to tell."

They lost three horses, Ellis continued. "They weren't worth much as horses, though. We lost our Texas mounts owing to an unfortunate accident of fire a few months back." He looked away suddenly. "It's hard to get good horseflesh in Oklahoma Territory."

"Why were you all the way up in Oklahoma Territory?" Hooley asked. He thought the Rangers always stayed in Texas, or so his dime novels had told him.

"That's none of your goddamn business, either," Ellis said. He nodded for Coltrain to replenish his coffee and kept staring at Hooley. "Now I'll ask the questions. What the hell are you doing out here on a stolen horse? I don't feel up to hanging you, so make a good answer."

Hooley couldn't help but bristle at the continuing accusation. "I told you: It's not stolen. It belongs to Hank Mitchell. He runs the store in . . ." He took a breath. "In Hoolian."

Ellis nodded once. "That the whorehouse I heard about? Red-tent out-fit?" Hooley nodded. "The one that's on that rancher's land—what the hell's his name? The goddamn foreigner. Man keeps turning up like a blister on my butt."

"Rancher McPherson," one of the Rangers muttered.

"McPherson." Ellis rubbed his unshaven chin. "I don't like foreigners more than I don't like anarchists."

"I'm not an anarchist," Hooley said.

Ellis looked into the fire again. The flame danced in his eye. "That's what you say, but I know that the first order of an anarchist's business is to lie about being an anarchist."

"Look—"

"It don't make no nevermind to me," Ellis went on. "We're too far from Austin or Waco for me to give a tin shit," Ellis said, "but you bear in mind that there's no place for anarchists in Texas, any more than there is for hooligans, bad actors, sneaks, road agents, and savage Indians."

"Or regulators," Coltrain put in, and Ellis shot him a look.

"Maybe we'll run *him* all the way to Kansas, too," another of the Rang-ers said.

"Crowder." Ellis's voice took on an edge, but his eye never left Hooley. "You can shut up or go to hell, whichever suits you." The Ranger humped his shoulders under his blanket and was quiet. "What mischief are you up to out here?" Ellis asked Hooley. "You out spreading your anarchy or do you have some useful purpose?" His eye narrowed as he spoke. "You don't look like much of a horseman. You've treated that animal kind of harsh."

"I didn't have much choice," Hooley said. "I don't ride too well."

Ellis nodded, satisfied. "Not many anarchists do."

Hooley started to protest again, but he held his tongue. He remembered

Margot's assessment of the Rangers' competency. The man seated on his haunches before him was a fool, but a dangerous fool. At the same time, his annoyance at the repeated implication that he was in the wrong grated on him. He stood, dismayed to hear the popping of his knees when he straightened them and to feel the soreness in his entire body from the day's riding adventure. Ellis watched him warily, one hand resting casually on his pistol's butt.

"I'm out here chasing a thief," Hooley said.

"All by yourself?" When Hooley nodded, Ellis's eye looked around the group, as if checking to see if he was the only one who found such a prospect unlikely. "What'd he steal?"

"A thousand dollars," Hooley said. "Well, more than half in cash. The rest was credit slips." Ellis's eye held him steady. "And a whore," Hooley added. "And a couple of horses."

Ellis's head lifted, alert. "Horses?"

"One, anyway. I think he had the loan of the other."

"Which one?"

The whiskey in the coffee was working Hooley hard. "Which one what?"

"What horse did he steal? The one you're riding or some other?"

"No," Hooley said. "He stole my horse." He then remembered and added quickly, "The mare I was keeping. The man who owned it . . . uh, died. His widow owns it now. We're sort of partners, so it's half mine."

"She an anarchist, too?"

"She's my partner," Hooley said. He pressed ahead, eager to stick to the subject. "This man—Chatsworth's his name—he stole it. Or the whore did. Her name was Kitty Cloud. There was another horse as well. A bay—" He stopped abruptly, realizing that he was babbling. Anger bubbled up. "Oh, what the hell! He's long gone, and so are the horses and the money—and the whore. But somebody had to try, and I'm, uh . . . the postmaster, so I—"

"Had a whore with him?" Ellis asked.

Hooley stared at him. "That's right."

"Ain't seen no whores," Coltrain put in sadly. "I'm more than half-sure of that fact."

"Not likely to, either," Ellis said. "Not till we get to Waco. Waco's a regular breed ranch for whores. Lots of Baptists there. You say he stole money?"

Hooley nodded, then narrowed his eyes. "Have you seen him, Captain? I'd like to find him, bring him back, if I can. At least get the girl and the money back. And the horse."

Hooley's words hung in silence, and he felt the eye of every Ranger on him.

"You own a knife?" Ellis asked.

"A knife?" Hooley replied. "Uh, yes. I do." He went to his drying trousers and pulled out a small, sharp folding pocketknife that had belonged to his father.

Ellis's shook his head. "I said, 'a *knife.*'"

"Wouldn't use that to pick my teeth," Coltrain grumbled in disgust.

"Well, there's some knives back at . . . uh, town," Hooley said uncertainly. "This is the only knife I ever carry. Why do you care?"

Ellis stood. "Crowder," he said, and the blanketed Ranger roused himself to find his boots. He pulled them on over bare feet. "C'mon," Ellis said. He stood, and Hooley stumbled after Crowder, Ellis, and Coltrain into the inky jet outside the firelight, down a small slope where sparse trees were slightly bunched. In the shadows of the firelight, Hooley could see the familiar white blaze on the face of Craggy Phillips'—Margot's—mare.

"You found her!" Hooley exclaimed, relief washing over him. "Did you—"

"Knew the horse right off," Ellis said, interrupting. "Figured she'd been stole."

"You could remember a horse you only saw once? Two years ago? And in the dark?"

"Never forget a horse," Ellis said. "Particularly one I suspect's been stole."

"So, where's Chatsworth?" Hooley demanded. "And did you find Kitty?"

"Kitty?"

"The whore. The whore Chatsworth ran off with. Blonde girl," Hooley explained, briefly hesitating, then continuing. "Good-looking woman. Young. Pretty. She . . ." He trailed off, realizing that all three men were standing there gaping at him. Hooley felt his knees wanting to buckle. "I'm tired," he said. "I've bounced all over the goddamn countryside looking for them."

Ellis grabbed the headstall of the mare and pulled her to one side. In the firelight, Hooley saw the body of Algernon Chatsworth sitting up against the side of a limestone boulder, his eyes staring blankly. He was wrapped in a blanket. Hooley felt something sharp and hard strike his stomach, and he stepped back, pushing into Ellis, who moved away.

"Found him that away," Crowder said. "Down by the riverbank, few miles over yonder. Gigged through the heart. Horse was running around loose, all muddy. We reckoned he tried to cross and got drowned. But then we found a fancy sticker in him, clean up to the hilt."

"It was some hilt, too," Coltrain put in.

"We'd of hung him, but he was already dead," Ellis said. "Would of him buried and done with by now but for the rain. I hate to bury a man when I'm wet." He looked at Hooley. "That's why I asked about the knife. You didn't have a snappy answer, so I decided you didn't know nothing about it." He sighed. "Ain't been dead long, I reckon. You can tote him back and bury him yourself now."

"Tote him back?" Hooley couldn't tear his view from Chatsworth's dead face. The eyes were huge. He looked as if he had just thought of something and was about to announce it.

"There was money, you say?" Ellis asked, "And a whore?" Hooley nodded. "Whore likely got the money, then, if she didn't drown, too. Money and women don't mix, even whores."

He turned back to the fire. "C'mon, anarchist or tentmaker or whatever the hell you are. He's good till morning, then you can tote him back and hang him or bury him. I doubt he's anything but past caring one way or another."

The next morning, Captain Brent Ellis and the motley assortment of well-armed frontier policemen known as Frontier Battalion B Company of the Texas Rangers escorted Gil Hooley toward the town that was named for him.

"Damn silly name for a town," Ellis opined. "Damn silly place for one, too."

"There's no such a thing as a silly place for a whorehouse," Crowder said, but Hooley gave him a dark look, so he only grinned.

They had been riding since before dawn, and Hooley was as lost as he had been the night before when, at last, he spotted in the distance a white plume from the fire of the café tent. The multicolored-peaked canvas roof of Hank's store was also visible above the waving grass. Hooley sighed with relief in spite of himself. The Rangers were probably relieved as well. The night before they'd summarily informed him that had he continued on his apparent route, he would likely have wound up in some desert and died.

"You need to leave law-manning up to them as knows what they're doing," Ellis told him. "There ain't room out here for one-man posses. Might take you for a bounty hunter and have to hang you on general principles."

Hooley couldn't have agreed more, but he was annoyed by the comment. He had no intention of explaining to the taciturn Ranger captain that he had had little choice in the matter, that a woman—a whore, no less—had talked him into it, and that a bunch of semi-idiotic cowhands had refused to go with him.

Yesterday's enforced lesson in equestrian handling had done little to make riding easier for Hooley. His hips were sore as ripe boils, and his legs ached. Every time the horse moved, he hurt. When they came closer, the mare sniffed her home territory and fairly pranced as she quickened her pace. Hooley felt the need to demonstrate some level of competence in front of the Rangers, so he kept a tight rein on her, forcing the horse to heel to command. It wasn't hard, he discovered, but keeping up with the reins and the lead rope tied to the halter trailing behind him complicated his movements. He was lucky to have at least one of the stolen horses back, he knew, but he doubted that its burden would be received with anything like a welcome. The sight of the body slung over the saddle of Margot's mare trailing behind him was hardly a comfort. There would be questions when he returned, and he had few answers.

Ellis reined up and called a halt. With some difficulty, Hooley stopped the piebald. Crowder rode to his side and handed him back his pistol and small kerchief-wrapped bundle.

"That there's the knife that stuck him," Ellis said. "You'll need it if there's an inquest."

"Inquest?"

"Ought to be one, but more often there's not."

"Aren't you coming in?" Hooley asked, slightly panicked.

Ellis shook his head. "Ought to go chase down that whore," he said. "But we can't. Not without some good horses."

"We'd sure like to stop by your place," Crowder said with a wink. "Hear tell you got some spunky little ol' things there." He shook his head. "Captain says no."

"But how—how do I explain this?" Hooley asked, sweeping his hand over Chatsworth's corpse. The wrapped knife was still in his fist.

Ellis gave him a look of raw contempt. "Word of advice, tentmaker," he said. "Get the hell out of this country. This ain't suitable for anarchists. Sooner or later, something's going to come your way that you can't wiggle out of, and I may not be around to pull your fat out of the fire. Even if I am, it's going to give me a case of the red-ass." With that, Ellis touched the brim of his hat, then wheeled his horse and galloped off into the grassy sea.

Hooley watched them until they were out of sight, then turned to look at the smoke of Hoolian trailing up into the azure sky. Finally, with a deep sigh, he tucked the bundled knife into his belt and kicked the horse on, back toward Hoolian, the noble knight of the frontier, coming home.

4

WHEN HOOLEY RODE closer to the hamlet, he noticed that a number of horses remained in the corral and that others were staked out to graze on the grassy expanse of the flats. That meant the cowboys were still there. Never before had they stayed over on a Sunday night, even when the weather turned nasty.

The thunderstorm had not spared the tent city. The ground was a quagmire, almost a swampy lake in places, although this did not encourage the cowboys to use the wooden footpaths. Most stood around in ankle-deep mud, the splatters on their trousers testimony that they were as responsible for churning the wet ground into a bog as anything else was. Several had half-full glasses of beer in hand as they gathered to greet him.

Hooley was suddenly aware that he must have been a sight, but then he was also alive to a glow of satisfaction. Even bareheaded, he decided, he made a striking figure as he guided the piebald toward the knot of men gathered in front of the café tent. He was reminded of the lawmen of his imagination, slowly making their way back to town, the bodies of their "Wanted, Dead or Alive" quarry slung over a trailing horse, a grim look of accomplishment on their faces.

The piebald slowed on her own, her hooves sucking themselves from one sinking step to another. Behind him, he heard the sloshing progress of Margot's mare as well. Chatsworth's body was fully wrapped in muddy blankets. As he passed Hank's store, the cowboy-turned-storekeeper emerged, wiping his hands on his apron. Behind him, Ina Moon, the baby on her hip, peeked outside. But there was no sign of Margot or the other girls.

Hooley noted with dismay that several tents had large holes in their slanted roofs. He assumed they were made by hailstones. Hank's store, in particular, had several jagged rips, the red tent showed two or three open tears. Even the café tent's shaded interior revealed ragged slants of sunlight coming through ragged holes in the fabric roof. But Hooley had small time to contemplate the wearying prospect of major repairs. As he reined the mare up in front of the café tent, Margot emerged from her red enclosure. Dressed in a plain black habit that reminded Hooley of widow's weeds, she shaded her eyes against the sun's brightness and studied the unlikely scene. Her hair was down on her white shoulders, and except for the bright lacquer that still adorned her nails, she looked like an innocent young woman stepping out to view a curiosity.

Hooley vainly sought to read her expression from the distance. He wanted her approval, he reluctantly admitted, but he also wanted her admiration. He did what she'd demanded of him, mostly. Kitty, the money, and the goods were gone, but he had brought back Chatsworth, and he had recovered the mare, if not the bay. In all, that wasn't a bad day's work for a tentmaker.

The girls emerged and crowded around. They were only partly dressed in shimmies and pantalets under thin wraps. Adding up the number of beer glasses in evidence, he grudgingly deduced that the boys had not spent Sunday night in any idle vigil.

"You got him?" Jake finally spoke up, breaking the silence.

"Or is it *her*?" Tidmore asked, stepping up to the wrapped corpse. "Where's the other one?" The rest of them followed, but for the moment, they kept a respectable distance.

Hooley was relishing the moment. Margot stepped out onto the boardwalk and moved toward him. Her hair flamed in the sun. Avoiding muddy tracks, she came around the walk until she stood next to him. She was looking up at him, and he discovered he liked that as well.

"My God, Hooley," she said, her tone soft, disbelieving. "What did you do?"

Hooley smiled grimly. "What you wanted." He steeled himself for a graceful dismount and stepped off the piebald. He wanted to savor the moment, to stand like a warrior returned in glory next to his trusty mount and fulfill his mental image of the hero, but he had forgotten about the mud underfoot. When his weight hit the soupy ground, his shoe sank deeply into the bog, past the ankle, and he nearly stumbled and fell headlong into the sloppy wetness. Only by holding on to the horse's saddle was he able to right himself.

"Whoa," he said softly to the sidestepping mare, hoping she wouldn't move again.

"You didn't have to *shoot* anybody, Hooley," Margot said, staring at the wrapped corpse. "Where's Kitty?"

"You shot Chatsworth? Chatsworth?" Underwood said, as if he just now understood that the blanketed bundle over the back of Margot's mare was the corpse of his old pard. "You shot him dead?" The cowboys instantly pulled the body down and began unwrapping it.

"Where's Kitty?" Gertie echoed Margot's demand from behind the red-headed madam. "She's my kinfolk, and I got a right to know what happened." The other girls came up behind her, their faces showing a mixture of dread and hopeful curiosity. "Did you shoot her, too?"

"I didn't shoot anybody," Hooley snapped. He was distracted with the problem underfoot. He extracted his foot from the mud, careful not to lose his shoe. The action sank his other foot, though, and he was doing a curious dance, trying to figure out how to get to the boards before he lost both his feet to the sticky muck. His heroic fantasy vanished, and his vexation grew as the difficulty with his balance continued.

"Well, he's deader than a stump," Hooley heard a familiar voice intone. He looked up to see Heinz standing on boards outside the whiskey shed, a cup in his hand. "See that from here. That takes the rag off the bush for good and all." He spat into the mud and grinned. "Damn, Hooley, you never told me you were such a gunman! I'd of been more careful in my whiskey count, if I'd of known that." In spite of the comment, he poured himself another generous dollop.

"I didn't kill him," Hooley said. "He was dead when I found him."

"Did you get my goods back?" Hank came wading over from his store. Hooley was annoyed to see that he had on high-laced hobnailed boots that handled the mud better than Hooley's own footwear, which, he dimly realized, was more designed for city pavements.

"To hell with that," Jake said. "What about the bay horse? Did you get the horse back?" He studied the empty distance from which Hooley had come as if he expected to see the bay stallion appear at any moment. "Goddamn it, Hooley," he said, disappointed. "Least you could of done was bring back the horse."

"Why'd you shoot him?" Margot demanded. "Where is Kitty?"

"Kitty's gone," Hooley said, "maybe drowned in the river." But no one heard him. Instead, everyone started talking at once, excitedly examining the body, and shouting questions at him, ignoring his answers and apparently uninterested in any reasonable explanations.

"Look at that! That!" Underwood yelled. "Shot him through the heart!"

"The heart!" Gertie shouted, rushing over to the group. The other girls followed, sweeping past Margot and descending on Chatsworth's corpse.

"That's not a gunshot—," Hooley started, but no one was listening. Frustration overwhelmed him, and he gave up trying to explain and snapped his mouth shut. He turned his eyes away from the group and lit on Heinz, who remained where he was, standing outside the whiskey shed with a snide smile appearing beneath his tobacco-matted whiskers. Hooley left the gaggle of shouting people and waded across the muddy compound, where the old teamster greeted him with a full tin cup of whiskey.

"For old times, Hooley," Heinz said, a twinkle appearing in his eye. "And it's on me."

"It's all on me," Hooley said, downing the drink. "It always is."

"I told you no good could come out of that redheaded panther," Heinz remarked, nodding toward Margot, whose shrill voice was blending with the others'. "Now you're a man-killer."

"I didn't kill anybody," Hooley grumbled. His legs were quivering again.

"Didn't reckon you did. But it would take a wagonload of preachers swearing on a trainload of Bibles to convince that bunch any different." His eyes twinkled. "I can't believe I was ever afraid of them. You was the one I should have kept in front of me."

"Don't be an idiot," Hooley said. Heinz grinned and spat. The group was now milling around Chatsworth's body, shouting questions none among them could answer, occasionally glancing warily at Hooley, but not approaching. Margot was now at the center of things, yelling for everyone to shut up. But no one heeded her. The girls were weeping, and the cowboys looked angry as they continued to point at Chatsworth's body and shout.

"You're a damn fool. I told you that from the get-go," Heinz said. "Beats anything I ever seen in the name of the blue-eyed Jesus. Let a female in your life, next thing you know you're a damn fool. Woman's like a tapeworm. Can't get rid of it, and sooner or later, it'll eat you up."

Hooley watched Margot lose patience with the crowd and head back to her tent. Eventually, she'd come to him to put a stop to the circus that was developing. But he wasn't ready for that. He'd had too much for one day. He sighed deeply, handed Heinz the empty cup.

" 'Nother?" the teamster asked.

Hooley shook his head. "I'll be in my tent," he said.

"Don't worry, I've kept a tab on the drinking. You likely made back whatever that young whippersnapper stole and then some. They ain't stopped drinking and poking since you left. One big hoo-rah." Hooley squinted at the teamster in disbelief. "Nothing like a scare to get a pecker hard, Hooley," Heinz opined. "I reckon your partner there was worried the rest of them would light out if they didn't keep them bare-assed naked and in arm's reach."

"That's revolting," Hooley said, and stalked away. He went into his tent and noted with disgust the sunlight that slanted down through two gaping rips in the roof. The planked floor was wet, but his cot was blessedly dry. He kicked off his shoes outside and removed the gun belt and its lonely weapon. It occurred to him that his Winchester was still in the saddle scabbard aboard the piebald, but he had no energy left to go after it.

He sat wearily on the edge of his cot, allowed the fatigue that had nagged at him for days to take over his body. Next to him was his pipe and tobacco, the wrapped knife the Rangers gave him, and the other contents of his pockets. He was too tired to smoke. Outside, the hubbub had quieted, and all he heard was a mourning dove cooing off somewhere in the distance. He remembered hearing that the birds mated for life, and that if one's mate died, the other continued to coo hopelessly until it too was dead. The thought swirled in his mind.

The tent flap opened, and Mino stood there, silhouetted against bright sunshine. He had a steaming plate of bacon and a husk of corn bread in hand. The aroma, which had been so appealing when Hooley had ridden in, was suddenly nauseating, and he waved his hand in dismissal. Mino set the plate outside and stepped in as Hooley lay his head back on his cot, welcoming the comparative cool of his canvas-covered pillow.

"I guess you want to know what the hell happened, too," Hooley muttered, finding each word a chore to form and utter. He put his arm over his closed eyes and felt rather than saw Mino squat down on the boards beside him. His ears filled with his own labored breath, and he wondered if it was possible to feel more worn out than he did at this moment. He drifted into a rising tide of sleep.

"Is she worth it, Hooley?"

The words jerked him painfully back to consciousness. Shocked, he cracked an eye and stared at the big elfin face now only inches from his own. "Did *you* ask me a question?" The words croaked out of his throat, and speaking them seemed to require every ounce of energy he could muster.

Mino only smiled. "No shit, Gil Hooley," he said.

5

WHEN HE OPENED his eyes, Hooley saw that the sky above the hole in the tent was black. The ragged strings of canvas hung down with a scowl. This nettled him, suggested shoddy workmanship. He sat up, blinking and then startled to see a figure seated on his old stool across from him. A whiff of perfume told him it was Margot.

"I guess you expect me to thank you," she said quietly.

"I don't give much of a goddamn what you do," Hooley said irritably. He moved his tongue around in his mouth, trying to summon moisture. His stomach was cramping, but from want of food, not the usual dyspepsia. "I did what you wanted, best I could. That's all."

"I didn't mean for anybody to get killed," she said.

"That didn't happen on my account," he grumbled. Every movement brought sore misery and a whispered curse. He fumbled around beneath his cot, found a bottle, uncorked it.

"Do you have to be drunk every minute you're awake?"

"I don't get drunk," he replied. "There are times I want to, but I never seem to manage." He filled his mouth with the drink, but it tasted warm, foul on his tongue, and he spat it out. "I need to eat something. Haven't had a meal in days."

"You didn't find Kitty," she said rather than asked.

He shook his head. "The best thinking is that she drowned," he said. "Crossing the river."

"I doubt it. The little sneak's too slippery to drown."

Hooley saw no point in arguing. "The bay horse is gone, too." He shook his head again, more vigorously. "I don't even know why I have the mare." Though it was dark, he could see that her face was a wall. It was pointless. She wouldn't believe him no matter what he said. "The money is either in the river or somebody else has it." He turned a dark thought briefly toward the Rangers, then let it go. Captain Ellis was too dedicated a lawman to be a thief.

She smoothed down her skirt over her knees, putting him instantly in mind of her naked body beneath the rustling fabric. She was lovely, he thought, soft and vulnerable, but utterly opaque. There was nothing of her viciousness showing, no anger, no argument, just the quiet, petty stubbornness that blunted any approach. Everything he felt for her rose to the surface of his feelings, floated there for an instant. He wanted to reach out and touch her, but he couldn't make himself do it for fear she'd vanish.

"It was a lot of money," she said.

"I didn't go after them for the money," he said. "Or the damned horse." He stared hard at her. "I want you to know that."

"She never took the money, Hooley."

"Of course she took the money. It was right here, and—"

"She never took it." She slowly removed her flask from a fold in her skirt, took a long drink. "I didn't intend for you to kill anybody," she repeated. "But I didn't think you'd go after her without the money being gone, too." She offered him the flask for a drink, but he shook his head. "I took the money. Or Mino did. I had him do it while we were searching for her. He hid the real money sacks down by the creek. I have them now. You don't have to worry."

Hooley couldn't grasp what she was saying. "I don't understand."

"I wanted the little sneak back," she said. "I needed you to bring her back. Then I could show them all that this is my outfit, my call. They'd either work for me and trust me, or they could go to hell." Her eyes took on a faraway look. "I make the rules, Hooley."

"She didn't steal the money?"

"She stole four bags of nails, washers, and wadded-up paper." She sighed. "I just wanted you to put things right between us, Hooley. Bring her back to put things right between you and me. Otherwise, it would look like I . . . Oh, what does it matter?" She leaned forward, put her hand on his arm. "I'm sorry, Hooley. I had no idea you'd have to kill anybody."

He pushed her away. "*You* took the money. You and that idiotic carpenter?"

"It *was* a foolish thing to do, Hooley. But so was bringing Chatsworth back like that. You should have buried him or something. You were just showing off."

"I thought it was the right thing to do."

"At least you could have warned me."

"How could I have *warned* you?" he railed, frustration bursting from his every pore. "I didn't know. If I had known . . ."

"You wouldn't have gone," she finished for him. "Not just for me."

For a long moment they sat in silence. "Heinz is right. I'm such a goddamn fool," he said.

"I had time to think while you were gone." She stood and paced. "I don't want to be hooked up with a lawman ever again."

"This is a hell of a note," Hooley said, reaching for his pipe. "Just one hell of a note." He held the pipe in his hand, but when he thought of lighting it, his stomach clenched.

"Seems that every time Craggy Phillips came home, he'd killed somebody some way or another. He always bragged about how he 'got his man,' just like they said in the music hall shows. All that meant was that he snuck up on some young jackanapes and shot him through the liver when he wasn't looking. I just got sick of hearing it. I can't stand going back to that."

"I didn't shoot anybody. I'm just a tentmaker, Margot." He looked up through the hole in his roof. "And not a very good one."

"We had a big storm. Hailstones big as cantaloupes," she said, typically shifting topics abruptly. "That's why the cowboys couldn't leave. Then they decided to wait for you. They were obligated."

"Obligated to drink and whore for one more night."

She shrugged. "That's our business, Hooley."

The soreness in his muscles was now crying. "I need to talk to them."

"Why, Hooley, they're gone now. They've been gone since yesterday."

"Yesterday?"

"It's Wednesday, Hooley. You've slept for two solid days. You didn't expect them to wait around here all week, did you? I just came in to see if you were still breathing. I worried that you might have been shot, too. You weren't, were you?"

"Damn it." Hooley's rising ire called for him to shout, but his strength wasn't there. "*Nobody* got shot. Hell." He pointed at the holsters lying at the foot of his cot, the single revolver in place, the other gun missing. "I even lost a gun trying to keep that goddamn horse under me."

"They took Chatsworth's body back to Rancher McPherson's ranch. To bury him, I guess." She stood now, came up to him, but not in an affectionate way. "You can tell them about the money if you want to," she said. "But they won't believe you."

"But they'll believe you?"

"Of course. I'm a whore—I'm honor-bound to tell the truth. But they don't know what to make of you, Hooley," she said. "They say you're a killer now."

"I was a killer before," he snapped. "You told them that."

"Well, you shot Craggy Phillips through the eye, didn't you?"

Hooley was too weak to argue. "I've got to eat," he said. He found his lantern and a box of dry matches. He lit it, and saw that for once, she was unadorned by makeup. Her eyes were red, her cheeks pale, and her lip ragged, as if she had been chewing on them.

"What's the matter with you?" he asked.

"I think this may have been my fault," she confessed. "Not yours."

Hooley stepped back from her. "My fault? How in hell could it be *my* fault?"

"Well, you took up with Kitty."

"I did not," he snapped at her. "You're . . . you're just wrong," he said. Then his anger swelled again. "Sometimes, Margot, it's just hard to deal with you. You know that?"

Her eyes widened in an expression he had never seen her wear before. Her eyes were huge, brimming with tears. It stunned him. "Don't be mad at me, Hooley," she said. "I couldn't stand it if you were mad at me!" Then she fled into the night.

Hooley stood alone in the sputtering lantern light. Famished, he stepped outside into the night. The stars were unusually bright and lighted the entire area with a silvery glow. All the tents were dark, quiet, even the red tent. He padded barefoot around the boardwalk to the café tent and came up with a can of peaches and bacon. He stirred the coals in the kiln, then fried the meat and ate it, dripping grease off his fingers. He found no biscuits or cornbread, but the bacon and peaches answered his hunger, and he began to relax. He stepped back around the boardwalk, silently wondering how many tents were damaged, how much patching and repair work was required. He unaccountably discovered an eagerness in himself to start repairs.

The ground between the walkways had dried out. He walked down to the privies, past Mino's tent, where he heard the big man's snores. From there, he could see the flats. In the darkness, he spied the shape of Hank's mare and a few cattle standing around the corral. He wondered why he felt this urge to fix the damaged tents. Just because he built them didn't make them his. They belonged to Margot as well, and even to the half-wit carpenter. They really had nothing to do with Hooley, but somehow, he felt a sense of proprietorship, as if they defined him.

He came back up toward the main compound. Margot's huge red tent was dark, but he went in anyway. The parlor was quiet, clean, neatened up, as if already prepared for the next weekend's festivities. A faint scent of jasmine caught his nose while he stood in the darkness and inspected the roof. He went over to the bar, pulled down a bottle, and poured himself a drink. The whiskey warmed his throat, washed into his full stomach and energized him.

In the distance, he heard a single coyote wailing. He wondered how long it would be before things went back to normal again, or if such a thing was even possible.

Alone in the darkened parlor, he felt as if none of this was connected to him, as if it belonged to some distant past. He needed something to bring it back home, to give it substance. He looked at the flap concealing Margot's crib and thought briefly of just going to her, taking her in his arms, and trying to rediscover whatever it was that they'd shared before all this happened. But he couldn't do it. It would have required him to take an action that he lacked the courage to take. He loved her—he admitted that now—but he didn't know why. And until he knew why, he couldn't do anything about it.

He left the red tent, pausing to retie the doorway flap, walked past Hank's store, then past the empty hotel tent and on to the whiskey shed. He suddenly was wide-awake and full of vigor. It was an unnatural sensation, but his whole body veritably itched for something to do. He went to his tent and pulled on his trousers, then found the canvas scraps he'd laid aside the morning Kitty approached him. Working by lantern light, he began measuring the rents in his tent's roof, and soon he'd covered it completely with neat inwoven stitching and patchwork, sealed with wax.

When he finished that, he went to the whiskey shed and worked on its four major tears. The hotel tent was in worse shape, and its size was too great to attack in the dark, but he eyed the holes for measurement, then moved back to the café tent, seated himself on one of the crude benches, and began sewing, his pipe steaming into the darkness. After a bit, he rose and went to the whiskey shed for a bottle and a tin cup, and soon he was once more at work, stitching quietly in the night, smoking, sipping his drink, and finding the contentment he'd missed. His mind shut down, focused only on the sturdy patches he made for the ragged holes left by the storm.

False dawn surrounded him with a ghostly gray light, but Hooley's concentration was so complete, he didn't notice. This was his calling, he considered between occasional pauses to listen to birdcalls from down on the creek. This was what he did and what he was. In a way, he and Margot shared that. She was what she was and doing what she did, and so was he. He was no businessman, no postmaster, no gunman, no lawman. He wasn't even much of a lover. He was a tentmaker, a tentmaker in cahoots with a whore.

The sun was fully risen when fatigue finally forced him to stop. A profound sense of earned rest overcame him. Packing up his implements, he folded the incomplete patches and strolled deliberately to his tent, where he pulled off his clothes and sat on the edge of his cot, strangely satisfied. It would be hard to sleep in the daylight, but he would try. Then tonight, when the sun set again, he would work once more, fix every damned tent in the town. Then, he would see what Margot had to say about it. If it wasn't good enough, she could just move on, take her whores and her fancy talk and move on. He didn't want to be dependent on a woman ever again.

He picked up the kerchief-wrapped knife. Even beneath the cloth, the weapon had a nice heft and balance to it. It was heavy, probably sharp. He slowly unwrapped it, being careful not to cut himself. Then, under the lantern's yellow light, it emerged in his hand, and he almost dropped it. It was a long, ugly blade, and the handle was white bone, carved in the shape of a lady's leg.

For a long moment, Hooley stared at the weapon, saw the dried blood crusted at the joint of the hilt. There couldn't be two knives like that, he thought. Then a cold panic crept up his back as he reconsidered. Yes, there *could* be; the two of them could be a matched set, in fact.

He leaped up, eager to tell someone. As he stepped outside, he was surprised to find the sun up and shadowed figures moving about in the café tent. Fresh smoke plumed from the kiln, and he could smell meat frying. He identified Margot's distinctive figure. He moved across the ground quickly, unmindful of the dust his stockinged feet kicked up as he entered the shadow of the canvas roof.

She turned, an impatient expression on her pretty face. "Good, you're up."

"Look at this," he said, holding aloft the knife.

Margot ignored the weapon. Instead, she pointed to the figure beside her, a short woman in a buckskin dress. Beads were draped around her neck and her black braids framed the round face of a savage Indian. Hooley squinted to be certain he was seeing correctly.

"You don't have to ask Gertie to help out with the cooking anymore," Margot said. "Now, we have a cook for the whole town."

Hooley's mouth hung open, and words failed him.

"Well, don't just stand there gaping." She gave him a disapproving frown. "And now *you're* the one running around in your drawers! Hooley, what's wrong with you? Just because you—oh, never mind! Sit down and eat. Mino found some bobwhite eggs, so we're in luck."

"Who?. . . . How?" Hooley asked, fumbling, staring at the woman tending the fire. She looked up at him and flashed a bright smile.

"Oh." Margot waved her hand dismissively. "That idiot Heinz found her wandering around in the rainstorm—or so he said. I have my doubts. She doesn't talk much. Her name is Loretta, and you'll be relieved to know that in addition to being a cook, she's also a whore."

REGULATOR IV

---•◆•---

J EFFERSON TAY'S MASSIVE weight sat anxiously atop a Welsh mare, a recent replacement for the two horses he had ridden nearly to death. He was no happier to be perched atop the miniature animal than she was pleased to be supporting his bulk. He hadn't been on such a small horse since he was a child, but the last place they had come across—a hard-scrabble ranch near the Kansas-Colorado line—had offered nothing in the way of livestock except two dozen head of the diminutive beasts. They would have ignored them and moved on except for the poor physical condition of their own mounts and the tenacity of an astonishingly deter-mined posse that picked up their trail a few days before. There was no choice but to abandon their exhausted mounts and shift their saddles and possibles to the smaller horses to escape the impromptu lawmen's clutches.

Tay was baffled by the rancher's motivation in making such a curious choice of livestock, but the old man was cut in two by Blasingame's pistol-gripped shotgun within seconds after becoming aware his property was in jeopardy. His scrawny wife and gangly—and possibly half-witted—son soon followed his demise with their own, so Tay was unable to obtain an explanation.

Tay's attention was suddenly distracted from his uncomfortable perch and casual contemplation of the twinkling stars in a crisp, moonlit sky. He watched with a mixture of awe and astonishment as a huge Kansas, Col-

orado & Pacific Railroad locomotive, its headlamp exploding the darkness
ahead with bright silver light, pulled to a screaming, hissing halt in front
of a tiny clapboard station with the dubious name of Ferguson Roads. It
was still hard for Tay to accept that a mere four men—harried, poorly
mounted, half-starved, and desperate as they were—could bring a gargantuan machine of such imposing proportions to a stop. More astonishing
was that they accomplished this miracle merely by stacking some furniture
from the tiny depot on the track, where the ever-efficient Manypenny then
set them afire.

It was actually one of two fires Tay's personal pyromaniac had ignited.
The first blaze was several hundred yards back down the track, but one
the engineer could safely overrun and take as a warning to slow down
before reaching the larger and more intimidating conflagration blocking
the rails. Blasingame stated he had learned the trick in Missouri. The
enormous black locomotive, steam shrilling from its jets, ground to a ca-
cophonous halt, its bell tolling loudly and smoke pouring out of its stack,
filling the night's crisp air with hot, oily stink.

Tay decided this was one of the largest things he had done since he'd
commanded a regiment of Confederate cavalry. Then, safely companioned
by well-armed—and, he recalled with a nostalgic pang, well-trained—men,
they had raided trains, but the wood-fired engines had been smaller, the
rolling stock more flimsy, usually made up of hastily constructed boxcars.
Then, it was more expedient to tear up the tracks, force a derailment.
These modern engines were veritable leviathans, fast-flying factories of
metal, smoke, and intimidating clamor. The valuables they transported in
their well-constructed carriages forbade the full-scale destruction that
would have resulted from a general derailment.

As the huge engine's wheels stopped, Blasingame emerged from the
shadows.

"What the hell's going on here?" the engineer barked. "This ain't a milk
run! You can't stop us! We're the goddamn Express. We're on a goddamn
schedule, you idiotic hayseed."

The fireman, peering out toward the blaze on the tracks, glanced up at
Tay, who sat, saber drawn, watching from his saddle. The man said something to the engineer, but before the engineer could react, Blasingame
shoved the short barrel of his weapon upward into the man's stomach and
jerked the trigger. The engineer's body flew backward from the door of
the cab and collapsed out of sight just as the fireman bailed himself off
the other side of the locomotive. The sharp report of a pistol told Tay
that Eubanks had, as planned, been waiting for him.

Blasingame leaped into the cab to bank the boiler's fire, and Tay urged his small horse down the length of the short train, which consisted of a coal tender, passenger coach, combination mail and baggage car, and caboose. Its principal human manifest, Tay understood from Blasingame's intelligence, was a group of cattle buyers en route to Emporia, Kansas. The baggage car's safe would be stuffed with the hard cash to purchase herds from late summer sell-offs.

Train robbery was not Tay's preferred enterprise. It was brazen and offered too many possibilities for calamity. He watched the shaded windows of the passenger coach until Blasingame descended from the locomotive. The big blond man was grinning widely beneath his battered straw hat. Splattered blood covered his white shirt, giving him a monstrous aspect in the flickering light of the fire. A fresh scalp was stuffed into his belt.

"Have a care, Mr. Blasingame," Tay reminded him. "We are not certain how many men are aboard or what resistance they may offer."

"I ain't worried about a bunch of Yankee beef peddlers," Blasingame announced, then added. "They might have a woman or two. Been a long time since I seen a fancy woman."

Blasingame's remarks elicited a physical shudder from Tay, but he ignored it and walked his horse along the length of the train. Eubanks moved down the opposite side and occupied the platform at the other end of the passenger coach. The windows remained shuttered and dark.

Manypenny inched his horse forward out of the darkness. His resemblance to a human rodent had, if anything, increased since his awful facial wound had healed. During the privations of the past few months, he had become unnaturally scrawny. His hands had transformed into veritable claws with long, curving yellow nails. Scars from his injury gave one side of his face a pinched look, and ragged scabs tracing down from his damaged eye socket created the effect of long whiskers. His fierce, impish aspect was only occasionally relieved by a softer, more animated countenance when he was watching a fire he himself had set.

Tay was reminded of a gargoyle as he watched the rat-faced man inspect his fire and grin in almost palpable satisfaction at the way things were going. Of all the men, he was the only one who didn't appear ridiculous aboard such a small mount. As if reading Tay's thoughts, he glanced down to his animal. "I've had dogs bigger'n this horse," he said.

Tay silently acknowledged that it was long past time for them to have finally found luck. For the past several months, the band had been constantly harassed. First, they were pursued not only by the furious company of Rangers whose horses they had burned up in Enid, Oklahoma Territory, but also by a hastily formed but nonetheless determined posse assembled by Town Marshal Burt Henry, a man Tay had seriously underestimated. It had taken the posse most of a day to gather horses, Tay surmised, but soon enough he spotted them following the outlaws' trail, with the re-mounted Rangers not far behind. Henry's party had the better mounts, Tay observed through his telescopic glass, and they soon outstripped the Rangers and very nearly caught up to the company of outlaws before they finally made the safety of Kansas.

Free of danger, Tay's company was eager to hole up for a while, but even after he was sure no one was trailing them, the corpulent commander kept them on the move, shifting them toward Colorado. Except for brief side trips into tiny settlements where they replenished their supplies, they kept away from towns, only occasionally raiding a remote trading post for ammunition and food. Such evasions did not prevent local constabularies from raising armed parties to trail them, to harry their every move and prevent them from finding a permanent camp. Word of the company's presence in a vicinity spread quickly, Tay learned. He was developing a larger reputation than he had ever enjoyed, but he took little satisfaction in the fact.

There had been too many close calls and too little profit—none, in fact. After an entire summer of narrow escapes and long, desperate flights across a dark and trackless prairie, he finally came to a momentous decision: He was going to abandon the outlaw trail forever. He had come close to mak-ing his fortune many times, but now, the emptiness of the plains and prairies that had once been his ally was being eaten up. New settlements, rural stores, and small towns were developing. One could not ride a whole day without seeing evidence of what some journalistic pundit had called "the pioneering spirit of the American agrarian," something chiefly man-ifest in the electronic telegraph poles and barbed wire fencing that bound up the prairie's frontier.

Along with the people and their infernal implements came a determi-nation to establish reliable institutions of law enforcement that threatened the free adventure of this once-open land. Dozens of times, he had picked up newspapers and seen morbid photos of itinerant scofflaws who had been gunned down or hanged by some vigilantism-inspired band of law-abiding citizens, the bullet-riddled bodies propped up in open coffins on main streets for the amusement of the self-righteous and as warnings to any who might consider violating a community's peace.

Opportunity for wealth, Tay sourly observed, was inversely proportional to civilization, and civilization was growing on the formerly unpopulated frontier like weeds in springtime. He conceded the obvious, abandoned dreams of great wealth, began to dream of more modest comforts—in short, retirement.

Retirement. The word took shape in his mind and grew with each passing day. He envisioned himself living the life of a quiet gentleman in some remote place where he could write his memoirs. He had always had a literary yearning and had long ago learned that the exploits of intrepid outlaws carried a certain cachet in the publishing environs of the East. He certainly had tales to tell, and no need to embellish his authentic eyewitness accounts with hyperbole. He had personally committed more mayhem and murder than any dozen outlaws of tabloid fame. Setting down the details might be unsavory, but it could be profitable as well.

Ultimately, he turned his ambitions to Mexico, but the last thing he wanted to do was cross the Rio Grande with empty pockets and a determined force of lawmen chasing him. When he arrived south of the border, he wanted to stay. That meant arriving quietly but with a saddlebag full of hard money. It didn't have to be a fortune, but it needed to be substantial enough to give him time to make the contacts in Boston, Philadelphia, and New York City that would enable him to launch a new and legitimate career. With this in mind, he extended his quest for a quick financial strike.

In recent weeks, though, as one of the hottest and steamiest summers of his experience passed into fall and the prospect loomed of an early winter on the trail, Tay had become despondent. The formerly deserted plains, Tay discovered, were becoming overrun with rival outlaw bands made up of angry, frustrated men, who provided a small group such as Tay's with zealous competition. Some were homegrown outfits, dispossessed farmers and ranchers who took to the outlaw trail when hopes of successful homesteading were thwarted by bank failures or by the whims of the harsh climate. Many of these were seasoned military veterans, and they were familiar with arms and tactics suitable to the local geography. He was outclassed, for once in his life—by men who were less skilled than he, but more desperate.

Accordingly, his group descended from a merely seedy and trail-worn state to ragged destitution. Ultimately, Tay came to the conclusion that if there was enough money to get them to Mexico and keep them there, it would be found in the cattle towns that dotted the Kansas prairie. Robbing a bank, though, was too daunting a prospect, even for a man with Tay's audacity. It was certainly beyond the means of such a small company. He also reasoned that if an inept lawman like Burt Henry could raise a poorly mounted posse to chase them for a week for no greater an infraction than

burning a barn, then a committee of outraged citizens from a town the
size of Emporia was apt to be even more determined, especially if a large
sum of cash was at stake.

Banks were banks, though, and trains were trains. Cattle buyers and
their money had to get to Kansas somehow, which meant that they would
be traveling by rail. Several buyers had posted bills on fence posts and a
few roadside trees announcing their intention to be in Emporia to purchase
stock at auction. Tay meditated on this enlivening prospect. Here, it
seemed, was a reasonable opportunity to obtain sufficient funds to take
him to Mexico quickly and in comfort and establish him for the rest of
his life in an artistically inspired peace.

There was also the matter of giving in to his men's increasing discontent.
Blasingame was becoming especially troublesome, and not a little dangerous. Since their flight from Enid, Tay had indulged a nagging sense that
the sly outlaw suffered rather than admired his leadership. Although he
generally obeyed Tay's orders, he now refused to address him as "Colonel." There was a sense of irony in almost every comment Blasingame
made, a contemptuous attitude the old officer recognized in his subordinate's tone and manner. Unless Tay found a way to reassert his colonelcy,
treachery from his most valuable lieutenant was a certainty.

Manypenny's complaining tone informed Tay that the small arsonist
had discovered an ally and companion in Eubanks. The pair had become
increasingly impertinent. The scarred, bald Arkansas outlaw's former lo-
quaciousness had been replaced by a sullen brooding, and he often mentioned Coolege's death and their narrow escape from Enid as evidence of
Tay's incompetence. Unlike Blasingame, Eubanks was careless about his
contempt for his fat leader. He grumbled constantly, and Tay often found
him riding apart from the others, glaring a murderous gleam from his
misshapen eyes. Tay had often watched him conferring quietly with Manypenny, who, ever since Enid, had become significantly more talkative.

A series of pistol shots indicated that Manypenny was effectively handling the crewmen in the caboose. Then Blasingame's odd gun sounded
again, and Tay kicked his small horse into movement. No return fire came
from the coach, but another series of sharp pistol barks from the opposite
end of the car indicated that Eubanks had forced open the other door.

Tay kicked his suffering mount into a stumbling lope and jogged down
the length of the train. Manypenny stood over two overalls-clad bodies
sprawled on the tracks, the blood from their wounds shining and slick in
the car's red and green lanterns. A series of final shots, punctuated by
more blasts from the passenger car, mostly from Blasingame's short shotgun, assured Tay that anyone objecting to the robbery had been subdued.

"Keep a close eye, Mr. Manypenny," Tay said. "Pay special attention to the eastward rails."

Satisfied with Manypenny's work, Tay rode up the other side of the train. The blocking blaze was dying down, and apart from the locomotive's headlamp, there was little light from anywhere but inside the passenger car, where someone had lit a lantern. Saber in hand, Tay inspected the coach through a broken window shade that had been ripped to tatters, presumably by gunfire. In the shifting shadows, he spied Eubanks' head, crowned by his battered derby, lowered over a seat. "Mr. Blasingame," Tay called. "We must put our attention to the mail coach."

Eubanks came out, his hands full of wallets and watches. "Better than some sodbuster's dugout, ain't it?" He held up a silver watch chain.

"I'll collect that." Tay stepped off of his abused animal and unfolded a cloth bag.

"Like hell," Eubanks said. "I killed men for this."

"In this company, we share and share alike," Tay reminded him. He mounted the car's high steps, annoyed to feel his breath shorten with the exertion. His leg continued to plague him. It ached from the slightest exercise or burden, and lately, the old wound had become swollen. He held open the sack. "This is for the common good," Tay said.

Eubanks glared at him, but began emptying his hands and pockets of the booty he'd stripped from the dead. "Better be a fair split," he warned. "Don't like working for nothing. Seems that's all we done here of late."

Tay looked into the coach. "Where is Mr. Blasingame?"

"He's taking hair," Eubanks said, shaking his head. "I can't see the reason. No money in that no more." He spat off into the darkness. "Truth to tell, I don't hold with it. Reminds me too much of savage Indians and such." He returned to the car.

Tay followed Eubanks inside. Bodies were strewn about the wooden seats. Eubanks returned to rifling pockets, valises, and handbags, but he was coming up with very little. The coach smelled like a charnel house. The warm, sickly sweet stench of fresh blood mixed with the stink of urine and feces, and splatterings of vomit, gore, and brains covered the coach's greenplush seats. Papers, books, and other passenger detritus were scattered about. He found another lantern and lit it, then almost wished he hadn't. The brighter light revealed Blasingame bent over a copper-haired youth, of no more than sixteen. Blasingame was expertly slicing away his scalp with his long knife.

"Mr. Blasingame, are such atrocities necessary? We have other business at hand."

Blasingame looked up with an expression that instantly chilled Tay. It had taken time to admit it, but Blasingame was the first human being Tay had ever met who frightened him. He had seen men who in the frenzy of battle became killing machines, virtual animals. He had seen bushwhackers in a high dudgeon of revenge over fallen comrades, murdered families, or ruined farms go into a mad frenzy of slaughter, rape, and mayhem. But he had never seen anyone with such deep lunacy in his eyes, and, over the past several months he was seeing it more often, particularly when the prospect of female victims was offered.

"Ain't no women here," Blasingame said. "What kind of train don't have women on it?"

"We killed everybody," Eubanks said. "They'll be after us hell for leather."

"We must see to the baggage coach," Tay replied. "And we must be timely."

When they'd ridden into Ferguson Roads at dusk, Tay had been somewhat dismayed to find nothing but a single-room depot and telegraph office. The name implied a more substantial place to his imagination. Instead, it was an out-of-the-way place, truly little more than a water stop and mail and telegraph office, just less than forty miles east of Emporia. There was no other enterprise handy, not even a livery or blacksmith, and thus no opportunity to refit themselves with regular horses. Eubanks quickly shot the dispatcher, and Manypenny cut the electronic telegraph wires, then joined the others in ransacking the office, mailroom, and depot waiting area. This was a sorry place, Eubanks announced when he found only twenty cents in the dispatcher's pockets. Meanwhile, Tay inspected the neatly chalked schedule. The Express had been on time. There was no reason to think the Local would be late. His plan was now confirmed.

As he surveyed the corpses in the passenger car, he was pleased that things seemed to be going smoothly. The cloth bag fairly bulged with handsome, city-styled wallets, and his anticipation grew at the prospect of the large banknotes that likely stuffed each one.

Blasingame added the red scalp to the other bloody trophies stuffed into his grisly belt, wiped his oversized knife blade on a dead man's coat, and stepped over the gore-covered bodies to reach the door. "No goddamn women," he repeated in a grumble.

"I think the time is well past when we could make a profit bartering females," Tay reminded him. They had taken no women—or anyone else—captive in a long time. Tay discovered that he truly didn't miss the habit. He knew he didn't miss the trouble.

"I wasn't thinking of *trading* them," Blasingame said, giving Tay a dark wink, and made his way outside. Tay stepped back to let him pass without making physical contact.

There was no denying it, Tay thought: Blasingame was utterly un-hinged. Since their escape from Enid, the big outlaw had ceased trying to conceal his homicidal hatred of women.

Eubanks stepped up and emptied two fistfuls of loot into Tay's waiting bag.

"Is this all?" Tay asked. Among the corpses, he noted a man dressed in a conductor's uniform and a Negro in a white apron. "No weapons?"

"Not one gun amongst them," he said. "Not even a rifle or a decent frog-sticker."

Tay took a precise count. There were seven men. "Cattle buyers are ordinarily men of substance," he observed. Blasingame was right, though. It seemed odd that not one woman was among them, not even a prostitute.

A clamorous shouting started outside, and they left the coach. Across the coupling, Blasingame banged on the platform door of the baggage car with an axe he had taken from the fire station at the back of the passenger coach. A metallic ring sounded with every blow.

"Ain't easy, Tay," he puffed. "This is a goddamn strongbox."

"I just hope there ain't no goddamn dynamite this time," Eubanks said. He took the axe and flailed uselessly away at the heavy steel door.

"What about the side doors?" Tay asked.

"They're ironed up, too," Blasingame said thickly. "Tighter than a Sunday virgin."

Tay inspected the car. Unlike the usual mail and baggage cars, there were no windows, not even barred openings, merely a series of sturdy ventilation louvers cut slantwise. One side door was covered by a flatiron ramp for wheeling heavy cargo aboard. The back door looked as imper-vious as the front. He mounted the abused mare, then rounded the train again.

"Best hurry up," Manypenny reminded him, then struck a lucifer and watched it burn. Tay shook his head and kicked his mount into a jog around to the other side. It had a railcar's normal sliding door, but it was also made of heavy steel. In fact, Tay noticed, the entire coach was plated with dark, rust-streaked metal.

Eubanks stood panting when Tay returned. "This beats all I ever seen," he said. "Boxed up like a rich man's coffin."

A sharp metallic sound struck Tay's ear. He looked up and saw a gun barrel poking out of a narrow port in the door. Before he could say anything, a yellow blast sparked from the barrel. Eubanks yelped and jumped back.

"Goddamn! I'm shot!" he cried. "Son of a bitch shot me!" He rolled around in the weeds, holding his leg and cursing, while the rifle spat five more shots in rapid succession.

Tay hurriedly dismounted, then moved quickly back against the side of the car, out of the line of sight of the port. He watched Eubanks scramble behind some Russian thistle piled up in the ditch alongside the track. He decided the Arkansawyer wasn't hurt too badly. A steady stream of curses confirmed the diagnosis. Experience had taught Tay that fatally wounded men were close to their own mortality and seldom said much at all. The way Eubanks was shouting blasphemies, he would live a long time. That, he thought, was a pity. He heard the scratching of boots on cinders as Blasingame approached, sticking close to the side of the coach.

"Sir!" Tay yelled. "Whoever you are in there. There is no point in resisting further, for in a few moments, your situation will be hopeless." There was no answer; instead, the slot opened and the rifle emptied again, filling the night with noise.

"Goddamn it! I'm bleeding," Eubanks yelled. "Somebody kill that son of a bitch!"

Tay drew one of his Colt's .45s and emptied the pistol at the port, with the only result that the barrel withdrew, the tiny opening slid shut, and the bullets ricocheted harmlessly off the metal door. Immediately, the port slid open again and lit the night with a half-dozen more yellow flashes. Tay jumped back. "Mr. Eubanks," Tay said, "would you stir yourself and go down and relieve Mr. Manypenny on watch? I require his services."

"Go to hell," Eubanks yelled back. "I'm bleeding like a neck-wrung rooster!"

"Mr. Eubanks, I doubt that you are so much as scratched. Follow my orders."

Eubanks didn't move. "I knew this would blow up on us. We ain't never going to get no money, and I'm going to bleed to death in Kansas. This is one hell of a note. Goddamnit, Tay," he yelled, suddenly furious. "You're nothing but a damn jinx."

Tay stepped toward the thorny bushes covering the cowering man, his starboard pistol now in hand. But Blasingame's growl interrupted his intention. "Do as he says," the blond man ordered, and the small Arkansawyer slunk away, dragging his wounded leg behind him. "Goddamn jinx," Tay heard him mutter. "Get us all kilt."

Tay grimaced, but he had no time to dwell on Eubanks' insubordination.

He awkwardly lowered himself to his knees and inspected the car. His leg ached in protest.

"We got to get inside that coach," Blasingame said. "Otherwise, all we got's a few dollars' worth of watches and junk. Not enough for a round of beers."

Tay was sure any car so well protected as this one must contain something of value. "Open the door," he called again. "I give you my word that you will not be harmed."

"Oh, *that* ought to do it, Tay," Blasingame sneered.

By way of answer, the metal shooting loop slid open again, and the barrel spat six rapid shots in various harmless directions before being withdrawn. Manypenny and Eubanks hustled up the roadbed. Eubanks was limping, but Tay supposed it was exaggerated.

Tay spoke in an exasperated tone. "Mr. Eubanks, I ordered you to *relieve* Mr. Manypenny. That means you should take over his duties and attend the watch. Now, please return yourself back to the rear of the train and keep a lookout."

"For what? Hell, Tay, ain't another living soul in miles," Eubanks said. "I'm telling you, you're a jinx. You're turning into an old woman right in front of us."

"And you, sir, are becoming intolerably impertinent," Tay said, his anger growing. "I have given you an order. Do you intend to follow it?"

"I intend for you to go to hell, fat man," Eubanks said. "You want somebody to keep watch, you do it your own self."

Tay pulled his Navy Colt's from its clutch holster and shoved it directly into the space between Eubanks' eyes, which instantly widened so the whites glowed. He flipped Eubanks' battered derby off and held the gun steady, placing his eyes on the deep scar running across the shorter man's crown. "I've had well enough of your mutinous talk, Mr. Eubanks," he said, and thumbed back the hammer.

"Don't kill him, Tay," Blasingame said quickly. "You're killing us off one by one."

Tay heard Blasingame shuffling his feet, but he kept the pistol pressed against Eubanks' forehead. "Mr. Blasingame, I do not require comment from you. You will do precisely as I say—all of you. This is still my company, my command. I have had a sufficiency of disrespectful behavior," he said. He put his eyes on Blasingame. "That comment extends especially to you, sir. If you have objection to my judgment, you are free to leave our company anytime you please."

"Simmer down, Tay," Blasingame said. "This ain't the army."

"No," Tay replied. "Were it the army, you'd be hanged, not shot." But he knew that Blasingame was right. Much as he hated to admit it, he still needed Eubanks.

"His pecker ain't big enough for him to shoot me," Eubanks said, rolling his shoulders and looking with a mocking, black-toothed grin at the big pistol still pressed against his forehead.

Tay shifted the barrel of the pistol quickly to one side and pulled the trigger, sending the bullet ricocheting off the side of the coach. The pistol's report echoed off the railroad car and then bounced off to the narrow building behind them. Eubanks jumped backward and banged his head hard against the metal wall of the baggage coach. He then stepped forward and threw a hand to his forehead. He stood for a beat, his eyes crossed, and he collapsed.

"Goddamn it, Tay," Blasingame said. "That wasn't called for."

"Mr. Blasingame," Tay ordered. "Would you please take Mr. Many-penny's place? Keep an eye on the track behind." Blasingame's eyes enlarged slightly. "When *you* are relieved, please take yourself to the steam engine. Make the train ready to move quickly, if you have the knowledge. I believe the proper term is 'build the steam.' "

"What are you reckoning?" Blasingame asked. "Make our getaway on the train?"

"Mr. Blasingame!" Tay bellowed, swiveling his position and aiming his pistol at the large man. It was the first time he had threatened him directly, and Tay discovered that the action resulted in a surprising surge of confidence. "You can do as I order you or you can join the redoubtable Mr. Eubanks in a somnambulant repose of a more eternal nature. My patience, sir, is tried past endurance!"

Blasingame stood still, as if measuring Tay's resolve. His eyes drifted down to Eubanks' unconscious body. He shifted his weight, then moved off toward the caboose.

Manypenny, who had disappeared when Tay fired his weapon, now reappeared with a bucket of water, which he dumped on Eubanks, who immediately began sputtering.

"My ears is ringing," he croaked. "Am I in hell?"

"You shall be soon enough if you disobey me one more time," Tay said. "You have your final warning." He then turned to Manypenny. "Mr. Manypenny." Tay was satisfied when the small man seemed to shrink from his gaze. "I am aware that you and Mr. Eubanks have recently formed a fraternal bond. I admire that. But your loyalty is either to me or to one another. I must ask you both to choose. I will abide no broody men in my command."

"What you want I should do, Colonel Tay?" Manypenny asked in a quiet voice.

"Please gather whatever material you require to set fire to this mail coach."

Manypenny came to himself at once, and a narrow grin crossed his pinched face. But then he looked doubtfully at the mail car. "This here is metal," he said. "Won't burn."

"I believe you'll find this unique plating does not extend to the under-carriage."

Manypenny instantly dropped to one knee. "It's all wood down here," he said. "It's oily."

"Please make haste," Tay said. "And beware that gun port." He looked up at the silent, closed slot in the door. "The man inside is a poor marks-man, but he seems determined."

"I got me a goose egg," Eubanks complained. "I can't hear a damn thing out of this ear. And I'm still bleeding. Goddamn, Tay, don't you give a damn about that?" He sat on the ground, rubbing his head, his legs thrust out in front of him, staring at what the moonlight revealed to be small amount of blood on his calf.

"You are more confounded than injured, sir," Tay replied. "Now, rouse yourself and relieve Mr. Blasingame at the caboose, or suffer a more ex-treme demonstration of my displeasure."

Grunting and groaning, Eubanks struggled to his feet, found his battered derby, then limped down the length of the train, cursing with every step.

Manypenny returned with an armload of stove wood from the box out-side the depot. He shoved it beneath the center of the mail car and then went away again for an oilcan and some rags. He busied himself dousing the fuel beneath the car, and Tay banged hard on the door. "You, inside. To save yourself from immolation, I recommend that you capitulate im-mediately."

"Colonel Tay," Manypenny said, "I don't know what any of that means, and I'm sure as hell that the son of a bitch inside that coach don't know neither."

"Will you come out now, or be burned alive?" Tay clarified.

Beneath the coach, the fire caught, and flames began to lick the metal sides as the oil-soaked rags blazed up and tendered the stove wood. There was an immediate stench of scorched wood, and Tay heard movement inside the door.

"I'm coming out, Boss-man," a voice said. "Don't shoot."

"I will not fire a shot. You have my word," Tay replied. "And neither will you, Mr. Manypenny. Hear me on this!"

After a number of clanking noises, the door slid open and an elderly Negro in the uniform of a railroad porter confronted Tay. He tossed out a Winchester '73. The weapon struck the ground, and the stock broke immediately.

"A courtesy stair, if you please," Tay said, "and be quick about it."

The man produced a rail step and Tay awkwardly mounted the car. "Keep a close eye on him, Mr. Manypenny," Tay said. "But do not harm him."

Tay inspected the car. A single lantern lighted the mail slots built into the walls amidships. They were utterly empty. He saw a stove and food cabinets at the front end, and he deduced that the vehicle also served as a galley. Then his eyes fell upon a large black safe between the mail slots and the stove. He went to it, and was about to demand that the porter open it, when he discovered that its door was ajar. Apart from one or two scraps of paper, there was nothing inside.

Sweat sheeted across Tay's forehead as he wheeled to look to the other end of the car. There, blocking off the rear of the car from view from floor to ceiling, were a number of neatly stacked crates. There could be something of value there, he thought, but smoke was now steadily drifting up from the burning floorboards and he knew it would be a near thing to sort through even part of the cargo. "Where is that porter?" he demanded.

Manypenny shoved the old man forward. His hair was mottled with white streaks and his rheumy eyes were steady on Tay, who spoke calmly. "Where have you hidden the money?"

"What money, Boss-man?"

"Do not make the mistake of trifling with me," Tay said. Smoke was thickening, irritating Tay's nostrils with an acrid stench. "I want the cash deposits this train is transporting."

"There ain't no money, Boss-man," the porter said. "We ain't shipping no 'cash deposits' I know nothing about."

"This is the Express?"

"Prairie Flyer," the porter said proudly. " 'Kansas City to Trinidad, Colorado. Eighteen hours or your money back.' "

"It stops in Emporia. That is correct?"

"Not that I know nothing about. No stops I know about, except for water and coal."

Smoke was now filled the car, and Tay and Manypenny were coughing, although the small arsonist's eyes were fixed on the smoldering floorboards, as if he eagerly anticipated the flames.

"Ain't no money I know nothing about, Boss-man," the porter repeated, also choking. "Alls I know is I heard the shooting when we pulled up, so

I quick-jumped in here. This here's a army car, attached for shipment to 'points west.' " He looked out the door. "I'm sure sorry I shot that man out there," he said. "Meant to kill him. Should of. Guess I'm getting old."

"Where's the mail clerk?"

"Ain't no mail clerk. Just me and Conductor Creighton. And the cook, Dan'l." He looked in the direction of the passenger car. "Reckon you done kilt them. Hate that. Mr. Creighton was one decent white man. Sent me back here to take care of the horse."

"What horse?" Tay looked to the rear of the car, beyond the boxes and crates. There, above the rim of boxes and crates, the dim lantern light revealed the fine head of a bay stallion bobbing in panic. Tay's heart leaped, and he started forward, but smoke now filled the car, and tears blinded his eyes. He pulled a filthy kerchief from his pocket and masked his nose and mouth. "You're sure there's no money on this train? No coin? No shipment of banknotes?"

"Not that I know nothing about," the porter said. " 'Course, they don't tell me nothing. But I reckon I was going to mail me some money—"

"Tay, Eubanks says there's a train coming." Blasingame's voice preceded him through the door and boiling smoke, and when he saw the porter his eyes narrowed. "Why's this nigger still alive?"

"Help me disembark that animal," Tay ordered, attacking the blocking stack of crates. "Open that door! Lower the ramp!" Manypenny prodded him, and the porter sprang into action, shoving aside the locks and bars, sliding the door open and pushing the ramp down. Tay cleared a space between him and the snorting, stamping animal.

He turned to Blasingame. "We need to put this train under way immediately," Tay ordered. "See to it, and at the double." Manypenny jumped out the open door. Tay reached the bay and pulled the horse forward by his headstall, admiring his gleaming coat and fine topline. "This is a splendid animal!" he coughed out, then leaped back to allow the horse to bolt through the smoke that was now pouring out both doors of the car.

Tay went to the other door, leaned out, and gasped in cold, clear outside air. A fit of coughing seized him. "There's a bay horse out there," he yelled when he caught his breath. "Someone collect him for me, if you please."

"What about the nigger? Manypenny says there's a nigger!" Eubanks yelled, limping up. "He shot me! Can't have that! I never could hold my head up in Arkansas."

"Will no one around here follow a simple order?" Tay bellowed. "Do as I say, Mr. Eubanks!" Tay looked back into the smoldering car. Flames were now visible underfoot, and they would soon spread to the rest of the train. A round of coughing once again grabbed him by the throat.

"Your choice is to remain here or to come outside," Tay choked out to the porter, who leaned against one wall. Tay's eyes were pouring water now, and his mouth was open as wide as possible to gasp what air he could from the smoke. "I gave my word you wouldn't be harmed," Tay finished, gagging and moving toward the door. Smoke billowed out as air came in. "I will keep my word, even to a Negro."

"All the same to you, Boss-man," the porter coughed, "I'll stay right where I'm at." He scrambled atop the crates. "Rather burn up than be shot by some crazy fool I should of kilt."

Tay gave him a long look, then leaped from the burning car, landing on his bad leg, which immediately collapsed and spun his bulk into gravelly cinders. Pain laced up his limb and spread throughout his massive body, clutched at his heart and conjured large black spots in front of his eyes. Aware that he was still too close to the train, he fought for consciousness, gulping air into his lungs and rubbing his eyes with the heels of his hands. With colossal effort, he set his teeth against the shooting pain in his leg and stood, drawing his sword to use as a crutch so he could hobble away. The mail car was now fully engulfed. The fire was spreading to the passenger car and caboose, consuming the oil-soaked wood of the greasy undercarriages.

He looked to the east and could see the flickering light from the approaching locomotive's headlamp atop a grove of cottonwoods. "Mr. Blasingame," he croaked. He cleared his throat, took a deep breath, then shouted, "Mr. Blasingame. I want you here. Now!"

"Tay, goddamn it," Blasingame called. "You're the order-givingest son of a bitch I've—"

"It is imperative that you go to the locomotive and start it moving," Tay wiped his eyes. "Backward. Full steam. *Back* down the track. Do you understand?" Blasingame stared, and Tay lowered his tone. "That is another order, sir. You can follow it, or be damned."

Blasingame now saw the flashing light of the approaching Local, and a grin spread across his blood-splattered face. "You're a dandified son of a bitch, but you're a fox for smart." He raced to the locomotive.

Tay brushed the gravel and weeds from his tattered coat. Then he spied the porter clamoring off the burning car, rolling down into the dust, gagging and choking. Retching coughs racked Tay's body as he limped forward and placed the point of the saber on the man's throat.

"Go on and stick me, Boss-man," the porter hacked. "I'm a dead man anyhow, but I just couldn't burn up. Reckon I'll be in hell soon enough."

"I demand to know where you put the money from that train," Tay said.

Instead of answering, the porter rolled over, shuddered, and began to vomit. Tay raised his sword, allowed the man to raise himself to his knees and retch into the weeds. Eubanks approached, leading the bay horse by his headstall.

"This the nigger that shot me?"

Tay had no time to indulge Eubanks' outrage. "Transfer my saddle to that bay. Be quick."

Eubanks' attention was immediately directed away from the porter. "Why do you get him and I don't?" he demanded. "I'm the one caught him up, and I'm shot."

"Look what I found," Manypenny's voice interrupted. The small arsonist, his pistol drawn, was escorting a man up from the blazing train. "Hiding in the caboose. Wouldn't come out till it got too hot."

"I thought you reported the caboose to be empty," Tay said. Manypenny shrugged. Tay studied the man in the fire's bright blaze. He wore a buckskin coat and long braids under a battered beaver hat. It was the attire of a civilized Indian, but Tay instantly recognized that it was a sham. A carved and highly detailed naked leg of a woman protruded from a sheath in his belt, and it took a moment for Tay to realize that it was the handle of some sort of knife.

"Disarm this savage, Mr. Manypenny," Tay ordered. As the short arsonist grabbed the knife, Tay demanded, "Why were you riding in the caboose? You're not railroad crew."

"Well, hardly, friend." The man offered a false smile, then pulled a fat cigar from the pocket of his woven vest and rolled it in his fingers. "Thought to hide till you rode off, but you fooled me." He glanced at the enflamed coaches. "Never figured you to fire the whole damn thing. I reckon you'll be taking my horse," he added with a forlorn glance at the bay.

"I should have the good horse," Eubanks said. "I'm the one that's shot."

Tay deftly lifted his saber. "Mr. Eubanks. I came close to killing you tonight. And I am presently closer. This is utterly the last time I repeat an order, not only tonight, but ever," he said. He felt the control he had missed for so many months returning to him. Confidence buoyed him above the carnage around him. "I am quite serious in that resolve, Mr. Eubanks. You will address me properly, and you will follow orders, or you can die." Eubanks studied Tay's face for an instant, then led the horse away, limping and rubbing the back of his head.

At once, the train began to roll backward, the locomotive churning white steam into the black, oily smoke of the enflamed cars. Blasingame came up from the roadbed. He stopped when he saw the man. "Who the hell is this and why ain't *he* dead?" he asked. "You're getting bad habits, Tay."

"Look, friend," the man said. "This is—" Blasingame drew his knife, and the man stepped back, his hands flying up. "Whoa!" he said. "Be careful! You might stick me!"

"I might lift your hair and piss on the bald spot," Blasingame growled.

At that moment, the porter came to his feet. "Looky there," he said. They all followed his disbelieving gaze toward the flaming train backing around the bend and disappearing into the denuded cottonwood grove. "You fixing to run that train right smack-dab into the Local," the porter commented. "If you was wanting money, why'd you do a thing like that?"

"I don't understand what you're talking about," Tay said.

"Well, it's simple as spit, Boss-man. If I was wanting to rob me some money, I'd rob the train that *has* the money. The Local. That's the mail train! They carry the money."

"What's he saying, Tay?" Blasingame demanded. He looked at the ground around them. "Where's the goddamn mail sacks?"

At that moment a thunderous explosion lit the western sky and sent a column of flame and smoke toward the stars, obliterating them from view. The noise came to their ears seconds later, just as the ground beneath their feet began to shake. Except for Manypenny, who clapped his hands in delight, everyone took one or two involuntary steps backward, awed by the force of the collision of the mail train's locomotive and the flaming caboose of the fast-rolling Express.

"Oh, my mother!" Manypenny shouted. "Look at that!"

"You mean to tell me there was *no* money on that train?" Blasingame said when he recovered himself. He grabbed the porter by the collar of his smoke-stained jacket. The porter shook his head, his eyes wide, but Tay noticed that he showed no particular fear. He reckoned himself already to be dead, Tay decided. "What about the cattle buyers?" Blasingame yelled.

"Cattle buyers?" the porter asked. "What cattle buyers?"

"These!" Blasingame demanded, drawing a handful of fresh scalps from his belt, waving them in the porter's face. "What about all the rich beef merchants on that train?"

"Oh, them!" The porter laughed, low at first, then louder. "Them wasn't no cattle buyers, Boss-man." He slapped his leg and fell into another coughing fit brought forth by the laughter. "Cattle buyers!" he choked out. "You beat all! You might as well kill me now. Done heard it all!"

"I believe, sir," the man in the Indian garb said, gathering himself and addressing Tay while keeping a cautious eye on Blasingame, "that the passengers you, uh . . . met, were hardly cattlemen. They were preachers of some kind, they said. Ministers of the Gospel—Methodist, I think they said, or maybe Presbyterian—on their way to some kind of meeting in Trinidad, Colorado. That's why we were forced to ride in the caboose. They . . . well, they took objections to my being a savage Indian, and all. The conductor was kind enough—"

"Finest white man I ever heard tell of," the porter said. "They done kilt him."

"What now, *Colonel* Tay?" Blasingame demanded. "We got nothing. No goddamn money, no nothing." Tay took a deep breath and let it out slowly as Blasingame finished his rant. "All you got is a horse, a savage Indian, and a nigger, and he's about to die."

"Now hold on there," the man in Indian dress started, and Blasingame whirled on him.

"*You're* already dead," Blasingame hissed.

Tay said nothing. He stood transfixed, his eyes on the conflagration still billowing over the cottonwood grove in the distance. The silhouette of the line of bare trees was clearly defined by the bright yellow flames, and inky smoke completely filled the night sky. He imagined that even from this distance he could hear the snap and crackle of the fire. He could almost feel its heat. But it was nothing to the heat of loss he felt surrounding him and the realization that, once again, things had quite literally blown up in his face.

"If it's money you're wanting . . ." The man swept his eyes around the company and continued in a clear tone, "I say, if it's money you want, I'm the one can show you where it's at."

"You?" Blasingame snorted. "What would a sorry son of a bitch like you know?"

"That," the man said, "is the deal I'm offering you for my life."

BOOK FOUR

Community

SOCIETY

1

GIL HOOLEY WORRIED that the tragic incident involving Kitty Cloud and Algernon Chatsworth might lead to serious repercussions, especially with Rancher McPherson. Hooley could only suppose what the fearsome stockman's reaction would be to losing not only his best horse but also the one cowboy he favored enough to trust with it. For several weeks, he fully expected the outraged rancher to appear with a bill for the missing bay in one hand and a hanging rope in the other. His anxiety nearly led him to panic. He wondered if his limited and newly acquired equestrian skills might carry him as far as Colorado, or even California. He reckoned that he could be a tentmaker anywhere, and that staying here might cost him his life.

Hooley had Cherokee Charlie's fancy knife as evidence that the young hooligan had been stabbed, not shot by the tentmaker's hand. Rancher McPherson would likely have seen the weapon in Cherokee Charlie's possession, he reasoned. The Rangers had not returned, but Hooley doubted that they would care if an "anarchist" was hanged or not. They might even help.

Whenever Hooley approached Loretta, she offered an enigmatic smile that suggested she wasn't particularly interested in coming forth with any information. Indeed, the Indian girl was deft at eluding him, and if he attempted to corner her, Margot would berate him to "leave the poor child alone."

"She's had a terrible experience, Hooley," Margot scolded. "Abandoned in the rain by some awful man who used her terribly. Are you aware that he actually beat her? I'm not generally in favor of employing savage Indians, but I will not abide mistreating them, so giving her a place to work and a friendly community to live in is the least we can do. Leave her be."

Margot's apparent intention, Hooley deduced, was to forget the entire incident of Kitty and Chatsworth. Every attempt he made to discuss it with her was rebuffed, and in a short while her attitude seemed to infect everyone. They all seemed to regard the whole episode as something of an embarrassment and best forgotten.

Even so, it was plain that Margot wanted to make amends for deceiving him. On Saturday, Mino appeared at the door of Hooley's tent with the burdened money sacks in his huge hands and a soulfully apologetic look on his thick face.

"This is a hell of a note," Hooley said, looking out beyond Mino's shuffling form. He spotted Margot near the café tent supervising the action, her eyebrows arched in an unasked question. "I don't know why this all seems to be my fault, but somehow it does," Hooley said.

"No shit, Gil Hooley," Mino muttered, and thrust the bulging sacks out toward Hooley as if they were filled with something repulsive. The tentmaker remembered the dream—if it had been a dream—in which Mino spoke to him, but when he looked into the carpenter's dark eyes and tried to elicit something more, the perpetual grin and shrug and patented response to any query discouraged further investigation.

Once the money was returned to Hooley's safekeeping, Margot refused to discuss anything about the affair. Anytime Hooley even alluded to it, she reacted with a slight wave of her long fingers, a roll of her beautiful eyes, and a spluttering noise from her lips, as if he was merely bringing up some petty minor recollection. "What's past is past, Hooley," she sang in a lilting tone. "One thing I've learned in life is that you can't go dragging up your old mistakes every time you feel colicky."

"I don't feel—"

"I'm just glad that you haven't decided to march around with those stupid guns on," she continued. "I was mistaken in that regard. You're not a lawman; you don't have the capacity for it. It would look idiotic to have an empty holster on one side—someone might have the idea that you don't know what you're doing. Which, of course, you don't."

Her remark smarted, especially since everyone else openly regarded him as a habitual man-killer now, and Hooley continued to brood over the

matter. Eager to set the record straight and have the word of his relative
pacifism passed on to Rancher McPherson, he cornered Underwood and
dragged him over to the whiskey shed. After three stiff drinks on the
house, the small cowpuncher confessed that the tentmaker's worries were
groundless. Rancher McPherson wasn't even in the state, the dithering
cowboy explained, not even in the country, having taken a boat from Galveston for England the same week the whole incident had occurred.

"He wasn't there when we took Chatsworth back and buried him. Buried him," Underwood admitted. "His missus was plum mad, though. Said
she didn't like having corpses planted all over her property." Underwood
tried to wink, but he was unable to accomplish the gesture, and both eyes
blinked instead. "She said she'd have your gonads for garters. For garters.
If she was a man. A man," he concluded.

Hooley was irritated. "Gonads? Sounds to me as if she talks like a man."

"I wouldn't cross her, Hooley," Underwood said. "She's got an edge
like a rusty razor."

At last, Hooley began to relax. And after a few weeks, the soreness in
his legs and hips receded and the cowboys' visits continued without interruption.

Loretta blended into community life as naturally as if she had been there
all along. She was more favored as a cook than a bed partner, Hooley
observed. Her sexual talents, he was given to understand, consisted mostly
of opening the top of her buckskin dress and revealing her breasts. For
this favor, she charged two bits—two more if the observer wanted to touch
them—but whether or not that was the extent of the attraction, Hooley
was unable to determine. He did learn from the cowboys' comments that
her "bosoms," as the men called them in Hooley's hearing, were well worth
the twenty-five-cent peek. "When she laughs, they look like a couple of
feed sacks filled with wiggling puppies," Tidmore opined.

Eventually, Loretta and Heinz came to apparently share a special affin-
ity. Although Hooley suspected that all that was involved was the exchange
of a quarter dollar and a long, lascivious look at her bare mammaries, the
discovery of the teamster's attachment to the Indian girl disconcerted
Hooley uncommonly, as it separated him from the one man he genuinely
liked.

After Hooley's adventure as a lawman, the cowboys gave him a wide
berth. They remained civilly courteous, but unless he made a point of
inviting them, they no longer stopped by the whiskey shed to pass time
with him. If he approached them with a casual question, they waited politely until he finished, then responded in an obsequiously respectful tone,
doffing their hats and refusing to look him directly in the eye unless they

were drunk or well on their way. Once they filled their bellies with liquor, though, they felt the need to challenge his very presence. They became brazenly patronizing, sometimes taunting him with their tone of voice if not with actual words. Whiskey-courage, Hooley thought.

Eventually, he began exhibiting a sullen pout, grudging them their inebriated attitudes and spurning their sober politeness. He worked the Saturday night parties, poured their drinks without conversation, never knowing when one of them would reach the point of inebriation where he would challenge Hooley directly. Eventually, they ignored him as they might have any working publican, paying their money and signing their credit vouchers with a casual scrawl and no personal comments.

The sticky, hot early autumn days of summer slogged on, and rain finally returned in fits and starts that did little more than settle the dust. Hooley rose every morning and searched the northwestern sky for the first norther of the season, then retreated to his tent to ply his trade. His rediscovered passion for his solitary work provided him with a satisfying personal activity. He seldom left the shade of his tent or the whiskey shed. Without ever discussing it with him, Margot took over the hotel management. She commissioned a new sign on which she painted in big red letters, "The Prairie Clipper Hotel. Cots 75¢."

"That's quite an increase," Hooley remarked, thinking that it was also a stupid name.

"You have a propensity for failure, Hooley," she said. He did not pursue the issue.

Having rid himself of the chore of the hotel, he now turned care of the animals over to Mino, who immediately set to work constructing a loafing shed that would allow up to twenty animals to stand out of the elements. Hooley was also pleased to discover that Hank was at last dealing directly with Heinz, consulting Hooley only about what liquor stocks and building materials were required, Margot was funneling her needs through Hank's tent-store, and the silent Loretta was apparently handling all orders for groceries and staples. Little by little, Hooley sensed that the small ambitions he had recently discovered in his life were fading away. He withdrew to his own company, content to sit and stitch, sip his whiskey, smoke his pipe, and wait for nightfall, when the weather would cool and the coyotes' distant mournful wails would keep him company.

Gradually, as Hooley's public connections thinned, his fractious temper came under control. His dyspepsia disappeared, and he had no more headaches or other physical ailments. He resumed regular reading, although he consigned his entire collection of dime novels to the kiln fire. He knew the truth of the West, now, and no longer wanted to read fantasies about it.

In spite of everything, Margot did not hesitate to reestablish their singular private connection. About two months after Hooley's attempt at lawman work, she returned to his cot, silently and wordlessly appearing in the darkness and spooning her soft body next to him, saying not a word about her long absence. The resumption of the habit occurred on a sweltering night, with heat lightning flashing, giving the plains an eerie ambience that even quieted the coyotes' perpetual calling. Although he had wondered if she would continue their nocturnal trysts, he had decided that he would stifle whatever passion he had once felt for their couplings.

Hence, that night when she pressed her breasts against his unyielding back, her body cool and smooth against his flesh, her nipples hard and firm against his bony spine, he made no movement, no attempt to bring her closer to him. He had promised himself to end their affair and vowed to begin the process of separating himself from her completely. But now, after a few minutes, as she lay soft and soughing against him, her small feet nestling between his and her breath caressing his skin, he couldn't bring himself to reject her, or to hurt her. He knew she was still as bristly as ever, but he now also recognized her vulnerability and need to be near him. It was a side of her she showed only to him, and only when they were utterly alone and coupling in silence. Soon, his desire for her subdued his resolve, and eventually it suppressed it utterly, and in a few months they resumed making their old sweet love three to four nights a week.

In public—or in what passed for public in the tiny town—things were entirely different. Whenever Margot encountered him in the main compound of the tiny town, she affected indifference toward him, treating him with the same diffident attitude he sensed from the cowboys, indeed from everyone but Mino, who continued to be his same, happy, half-witted self. The only time she spoke to Hooley, actually, was to criticize something he had done or failed to do or to remind him of what a dolt he was. It was wearisome and confusing, but there was no way of changing it without confronting her. Hooley had determined never to confront her again.

He also determined never to put himself completely in her power again. Such thoughts led to questions about what the future held, but he refused to let himself dwell on them, steeled himself to the moment, focused on the satisfaction of the solitary life he was learning to enjoy in the midst of his bustling community.

2

WHEN THE NORTHERS arrived, they came in rapid succession and were fiercer than usual. By then, Hooley was almost returned to the indolence and isolation he had enjoyed before Margot—or even Mino—had arrived and disrupted what had been a satisfyingly peaceful life. In spite of whipping winds and chilly evenings, a day's time passed more pleasantly, and he discovered an uncommon contentment in working four or five hours at a stretch, sewing canvas to make patches for the damaged, worn tents, and thinking idly about what other structures might be wanted if he were to rediscover the ambition to construct them. He came to regard his activities as a job, not unlike his professional responsibilities back in St. Louis. He grudgingly tolerated everything else.

The only significant change he instituted was to inform Margot she could have full charge of the saloon business. He wanted no more to do with barkeeping, and he was weary of worrying that one of the boys would get liquored up and challenge him in some stupid way. He informed his partner that he would maintain the stock and see to the orders, but would no longer work in her red tent and pour drinks for the boys.

"Why not, Hooley?" she demanded with an ironic rising of her perfect red eyebrows. "Are you tired of our company?"

"No," he lied, knowing that any attempt to explain would only lead to an argument that he would lose. He deliberately avoided her stare. He determined that her eyes were a big part of their problem with one another. If he could evade being fixed in place by them, he resolved, he could prevail. "I think it's more the other way around."

"Whatever kind of foolishness is this?" She laughed. "The boys *like* you! They call you the '*pistolero* of Hoolian.' They're half-afraid you'll turn loose and shoot them if they cross you."

"I'm just a tentmaker," he said flatly. "My days attending to the bar are over."

He was mildly surprised when she accepted the idea without further protest. "Very well, Hooley. I suppose I can get Hank to do it—I think this Temperance Society nonsense is losing its novelty for him. It's a good thing he married Ina Moon. She might have converted every one of those girls, and I'd have nothing but a tentful of psalm-singing Sunday School teachers." She spied Hank moving across the compound. "There'll soon be another baby on the way, unless I miss my guess, and he could use the income."

"What income?" Hooley asked, confused. "I never took a dime for pouring drinks."

"Well, they were *your* drinks, Hooley," she said. "If you want to hire somebody to pour them, you have to pay for the privilege." She turned and started off. "You'll be missed," she said.

"I doubt it," Hooley muttered. But she didn't rejoin, and he suspected she understood his true reasons better than he did.

In spite of his withdrawal from Hoolian's society, Hooley discovered that his role as postmaster—a duty Hank steadfastly refused, owing to his fundamental illiteracy—continued to involve him directly with the larger community. And soon, Margot's prediction of Ina Moon's influence spilling over to the others was verified. One crisp November morning, Hank found Hooley pouring himself his first cup of coffee and sauntered up, thumbs looped in outrageous paisley braces and his mustache, thin and pitiful as it was, waxed to sharp points. The storekeeper looked ridiculous dressed so formally in this frontier outpost. Hooley had long since stopped dressing for Margot—or for anyone. He felt shabby in his socks, shirtless, and in need of a shave.

"Been meaning to talk to you," Hank said to him with a nod to the ever-grinning Loretta, who brought him a cup of steaming brew.

"It's not like you have to go to a lot of trouble to find me," Hooley replied. He was in a sour mood. Without explanation or apparent cause, Margot had once more ceased coming to his cot. She hadn't appeared for a solid week, and he was trying to connect this fact to his resignation as bartender, but that made no sense. Though he had learned long ago never to try to use logic when trying to divine Margot's mind, he was still driving himself mad attempting to figure out her sudden absence. "What do you want?"

Hank's brow was furrowed in seriousness. "We need more people here, Hooley."

"Who?" Hooley asked, then, "Why?"

"We need a doctor of some kind, I think. And maybe a lawyer."

"Why on earth would we need a lawyer? That's the stupidest thing I've ever heard."

Hank looked around the compound. "We need a dentist, too," he said. "And a barber. Maybe a harness or saddle maker." Hooley snorted, but Hank was warming to the subject. "And a blacksmith. I might want to get my horse reshod. We need a lot here, Hooley."

"What we need is more common sense around here," Hooley said, resuming his stitching. "We've never had a surplus of that."

"And I want to talk to you about a new building," Hank said.

"You don't have enough business to justify the one you have," Hooley said, meanly. That was inaccurate, but the wounded look on Hank's face made the remark satisfying. "I don't have enough canvas on hand to build it anyway." The inferiority of the canvas Hooley had been forced to use to construct Hank's store was now telling, Hooley knew. No matter what he did to maintain it, the fabric was too rotten to hold up for another year. But he was disinclined to be charitable. Heinz was at fault, and Hooley felt Hank should take it up with him.

"I ain't talking about the store," Hank said. "We'll be needing a school. We'll have a regular town here soon. A school is what's needed."

"Why would we need a school?" Hooley snorted. "The only child in the whole country is yours, and he's a long way from needing schooling."

"When he needs it, I want it to be there," Hank replied, unperturbed. "I don't want him to grow up ignorant, like me. Besides, a school is the mark of a quality town."

"Schools want teachers," Hooley said. "Schoolmarms and whores don't mix." He glanced at the red tent. "First thing they'd do is shut down our only paying business. I can't see that it's in our interest to have a school in the neighborhood." He thought of Margot's words. "Next thing you know, you'll be wanting a church."

"Ina Moon can do schoolmarming," Hank said. "And she's already mentioned a church."

"A church is nothing but trouble," Hooley said, glancing out at the flats and recalling Craggy Phillips. "First sign of a steeple, and the boys will stop coming." He shook his head when a certain memory of his mother invaded his mind. "Next you'll have gardening clubs and tea parties," he muttered. "Those don't go with whorehouses either."

"We're set on having a school," Hank continued. "You be thinking of where you and Mino can build it. I think it would be handy down by the privy—you know how kids are—but that's your decision. You think on it, Hooley." Hooley did nothing of the kind.

Hank had declined the barkeeping duties because Ina Moon refused to countenance it. She didn't object to his coming over to visit with his pards on Saturday nights, but he remained steadfastly a teetotaler, although he continued to order the liquor and beer they served. Margot had finally nominated Loretta to curtail her duties in the café tent and to take over the bar. She informed Hooley that the Indian girl was also often in demand as a dancer.

"She's a wonder, Hooley," she said. "But she refuses to move into Kitty's old crib." Hooley wasn't entirely surprised. He'd read that savage Indians were superstitious about such things. "She insists on living in the cold cellar. Says it reminds her of home."

"I've never heard her say two words," Hooley remarked grimly. "She's a match for that idiotic carpenter."

"She's more a match for that filthy teamster," Margot snorted. "And him a married man!"

"From what I hear, he's not much married," Hooley replied. "He says his wife has got religion so bad she won't let him sleep in the house."

"I suspect that the big problem is his avoidance of soap and water," Margot said. "How Loretta can stand him is beyond comprehension, although savage Indians are often known to avoid sound hygienic practices."

Hooley waved away the comment. What he really wanted to discuss was Margot's prolonged absence from his cot, but he lacked the courage. "She still doesn't talk much."

"Well, she has plenty to say to anyone who'll listen and isn't interested in staring at her naked bosom all the time," Margot said accusingly.

"I've never seen—"

"I'm not talking about you, Hooley. I was talking about that filthy mule-skinner. I don't think she's charging him a nickel, either." Her eyes slitted. "You can*not* make a dollar if somebody's giving it away."

"That's true," Hooley said, agreeably.

"We ought to put a sign on that cold cellar," she said. "We could call it an annex, then make that smelly freighter pay like everyone else. He's probably eating for free, too."

The estimable establishment of the cold cellar had been enlarged over the summer and was now nearly twice its original size. Hooley put a double canvas roof over it, and Mino dug a small sluice from the creek to run through it and constructed stout shelving. They could now keep milk and the butter Loretta churned fresh longer and stock other perishables Heinz thought to bring. Loretta had also established a lively poultry flock to add to what were already tasty meals, although hawks kept harassing the hens when they ventured out of the sturdy canvas and wire house Mino had constructed near the cold cellar. A pair of roosters announced the dawn every day, and that irked Hooley, because he had taken to sleeping late. Still, there were now fresh eggs available on a daily basis, and fried chicken was becoming a regular feature of Sunday supper.

Hooley often watched the plump, silent girl cooking, cleaning, feeding chickens, working the butter churn, or taking care of other chores. But any attempt he made to catch her alone and question her was met with a toothy grin and her starting to untie the top of her buckskin dress. This invariably sent Hooley scurrying away panicked and irritated by his cowardice. "Well, what she does is her lookout," he said now. "I didn't invite her to come here."

"No, Hooley," Margot said with a narrow look. "*You* didn't invite anyone to come here, and if I know you, you never will."

He wondered what that meant, but he didn't ask for further comment.

As the days grew shorter and colder, Heinz's schedule became haphazard and unreliable. This created friction between him and Hank and further nettled Margot. She contended that the crusty old driver was growing
lazy and fat in his business and that they should renegotiate their contract.
Hooley had no interest in reopening that discussion.

At last, he learned the reason for the irregularity of the schedule. The
occasion was offered because Loretta was otherwise occupied when Heinz
arrived, so the teamster forsook his usual habit of immediately disappearing
into the cold cellar and instead rousted Hooley from his tent and demanded
whiskey. It was a blustery day, with thick gray clouds lumbering across a
sky and threatening sleet. While the tentmaker found his coat and hat, the
teamster waddled over to the shed and was on his second drink by the
time Hooley arrived.

"Colder than a poor preacher's stove out here, Hooley." He grinned.
"Need to put some toenail juice in the system to keep the pipes open."
Hooley shuffled into the wind-breaking canvas wall and found a place to
sit. "We ain't done this for a coon's age," Heinz went on, "so I figured
we ought to have a little snort or two to take the chill off."

Their sitting there was so much like old times that Hooley felt suddenly
nostalgic. "We were about to decide you might not come at all," he said.

Heinz gave him a squinting look, then poured another dollop of whiskey
into his cup. There was little alternative to the change in schedule, he
explained, since Rancher McPherson was still absent from the country and
had left his wife in charge. "She's a pistol," he said, "but not dependable.
Changes her mind with the weather. You'd think she was living in a big
old house down to Fort Worth instead of a fieldstone ranch headquarters
out in the middle of nowhere. You know she put up chintz curtains?" He
warmed to the subject, and Hooley opened his ears to any opportunity to
bridge the gap between himself and the rancher's enterprise.

"But she runs the place while he's gone?" Hooley asked.

"Oh, yeah," the teamster said, then lowered his voice. "Between you
and me and the blue-eyed Jesus, that woman's loco. Fact of the matter is,
they both are. A match for theirselves. You know, he never rides a horse.
Goes everywhere he goes in this buggy contraption he had built in New
Orleans. She goes with him, most times. It's special-sprung and closed off
from the weather. Says it's not natural for a man like him to be on
horseback. Hurts his gonads."

"Gonads?" The word seemed to be popular among the Rancher McPhersons.

Heinz nodded sagely. "You see his missus, you wonder why he wants them," he said. He then noted that Hoolian's trade had fallen off a bit with the change of seasons and he wasn't making enough money to justify a regular run.

"You're making plenty!" Hooley exclaimed, anticipating a renewal of the old contract debate.

Heinz didn't take the bait, though. He drank off his cup and sighed wistfully. "Truth is, Hooley, you're going to have to make this place grow some, get some more folks in here, more business. Elsewise, I may have to find some other line of work." He gave Hooley a telling look. "Hell, I might just retire."

Hooley wondered if Hank and Heinz had been talking. "Yep," the wagoneer said absently, "I might just take up with some gal who appreciates me." He scowled. "My old woman beats anything I ever seen in the name of the blue-eyed Jesus. Never lets me have a minute's peace. Or any other kind of piece, either," he muttered.

Heinz let his gaze drift out toward the western prairie, and his eyes took on a faraway look. "Always wanted to see me the Pacific Ocean. Maybe pan for gold in the mountains. You can't never tell what a man might do once he takes the notion." He sighed deeply. "Alls a man needs is a little ambition, elsewise he gets into a rut, stuck right where he is in life, thinking that all he's got is the onliest thing he can get." He looked toward the cold cellar. "Sometimes," he said sadly, "he don't find out what he really wants till he's damn near too old to enjoy it." He fell silent, and Hooley replenished his cup. "So, what are you fixing to do to make this place grow?" Heinz asked.

"I don't know how or why we'd want to grow," Hooley said, vexed by the idea of Heinz's taking off west. "But if you want to quit, I suppose we could all just move on." The idea had a sudden and uncommon appeal when he said it.

"Oh, I expect I'll be along for a good while." The wagoneer laughed. "I never was much for sustained travel. So I'll keep up the run for old times' sake." He extended his empty cup once more. "So long as the whiskey's pouring and Rancher McPherson keeps building."

"But Mrs. McPherson's running things at the ranch," Hooley clarified. "And she's difficult?"

"She's prickly as a goathead and mean as a jug of red ants," Heinz confirmed. "She scares the spurs off them cowboys when she goes on a tear. So they mostly stay out of sight except on payday. She's generous with their pay, as you know." Heinz sighed, then, and looked squarely at the tentmaker. "I got to tell you, Hooley. That growth thing ain't a bad notion. You can get a jump on things. Rancher McPherson's still planning to bring in them fancy English cattle. He wants to build a goddamn kingdom out here." Heinz squinted and spat. "Problem is, his missus claims she don't hold with whoring and whiskey-drinking and such. My guess is that she's the one keeps Rancher McPherson riled up over you being here. So you need some quality people here, you know what I mean. Set down some roots to keep him from running you off."

"I still don't see why he'd care what we do," Hooley said. "I have no interest in bringing more people out here. What would they do anyway?"

At that moment they were distracted when three girls emerged from the red tent and headed toward the bathhouse. Then Mino came out and happily stepped in behind them, ready to man the bilge pump and stoke up the fire to heat water. Hooley wondered idly if the girls let Mino watch them bathe.

"I think a man could find a lot to do here," Heinz said, his attention also arrested by the beautiful trio, their arms burdened with towels, their laughter crossing the chilly afternoon air. "If he knew what was here, he could, anyway."

"If some men knew what we were doing here, they'd want to shut us down."

"Who?"

"Lawmen," Hooley said, then he thought of Ellis and the ragtag cutthroats who made up his company of Rangers. "Well, preachers anyway."

"My notion of preachers is that they tend to want their ashes hauled as much as the next man," Heinz said with a wink. "A man is a man, Hooley. Don't you forget it."

Loretta suddenly hove into open view, her arms laden with a canvas bag full of dried cow chips. Her long buckskin dress accentuated her voluptuous hips and breasts. "That woman takes the rag off the bush for sure," the wagoneer said. "Margot's worked wonders with her. Wouldn't know she was a savage Indian."

Under Margot's hand, Loretta had become a plump beauty. She kept her thick black braids perfumed and decorated with ribbons, and Hooley was nearly sure she was rouging her lips. Whenever Hooley peeked into Miss Margot's Place on a Saturday night, he spotted her pouring behind the bar, her long braids swinging in rhythm to Mino's concertina, and when she would accept a dance, her moccasined feet swung her through the fetid clouds of tobacco and sweat that formed in the superheated nights inside the red tent.

With no further comment, Heinz freshened his cup once more and stepped out to meet the Indian girl. Her ear-to-ear smile revealed white, well-spaced teeth. It broadened, then she dropped her burden of fuel and opened her arms and accepted a huge hug from the burly muleskinner, seemingly indifferent to the stink of mule sweat and tobacco juice. She was also apparently uncaring about the fact that he was still resolutely married to a woman whose name formed half of the community's identity, Hooley thought sourly.

As they walked off arm-in-arm toward the cold cellar, Hooley felt depression settling over him like a mild fever. Just as he was allowing himself to admit how much he missed Margot's visits, he spied the redheaded madam emerging from her tent. In spite of the chill, she had on no cloak or shawl over her white shirtwaist, and she had her hair pulled into a bun. If he hadn't known, he would have mistaken *her* for a schoolmarm. Her loveliness was in no way diminished by her efficient garb. If anything, it made her more desirable. He desperately tried to will her to look at him, but she never cast a glance his way.

Darkness gathered as he sat and smoked and cogitated over his life. Soon, he was numb with drink, fuzzy in his mind. Everything around him had a glow that insulated him from the emotional pain of loneliness. From out on the prairie, as the moon soon rose to dispel the twilight's gloaming, he heard a lone coyote cry. He imagined that in the sour soulful wail of the animal, he heard a sadness to match his own. Hooley had never felt more isolated.

3

HEINZ'S IRREGULAR SCHEDULE resulted in there being a heavy volume of mail each time he visited. Most correspondence coming to Hoolian consisted of letters for the girls from distant relatives and friends who, Hooley suspected, had no idea what they were doing for a living. There were also letters for the cowboys from people in similar states of ignorance about the young men's wild and irresponsible lives. Hooley knew this because he was still asked to read them and write replies, one of the few vestiges of the former intimacy he had enjoyed with the pards. But they truly had little choice. Margot claimed she was too busy to be bothered assisting the mostly illiterate company, and Mino, of course, was no help.

Now, Hooley was also providing the service to the women, most of whom had at least rudimentary schooling, but only a few of whom had the language skills necessary to say what they wanted.

At the same time, Heinz began delivering an alarming amount of correspondence addressed to "His Honor, Mr. Mayor of Hoolian," and "The Esteemed Chairman of the City Council" and other nonexistent officials of the nascent community. Many had official seals and stamps from Austin and even Washington, D.C., but Hooley consigned them indiscriminately to the firebox of the café tent's kiln without opening them and hoped that if he continued to ignore them, they would stop coming. His refusal to acknowledge such missives seemed to stimulate more of them, though. Every one of Heinz's runs brought dozens of official-looking mailings from both state and federal governments, along with advertisements and catalogues. Some were of a mercantile nature, and he passed them along to Hank for Ina Moon to study, but Hooley burned the rest and felt uneasy about the attention the community was attracting.

The season deepened, the mornings became crisper, and the cowboys began their winter routines, which seemed to consist of following Rancher McPherson's electronically telegraphed instructions to clear the range utterly of maverick cattle to make way for his new breed. "He's so scared of Texas Fever, he's determined to quarantine every English cow he brings in," Tidmore remarked. "Wants us to shoot any Longhorn or common we can't catch. Hell, he don't even want a prairie dog on his range."

The cowboys began to come by Hoolian more and more during the week, showing up around dusk and sitting around the café tent drinking coffee and paying two bits a plate for one of Loretta's tasty meals, then taking a cot for the night, if they had money. Otherwise, they merely spread their bedrolls out and waited for Mino to begin a serenade. Several of them brought their own instruments now—guitars and Jew's harps— and joined in.

When Hooley questioned this new habit, Margot took offense. "Why shouldn't they come here every day if they want to?" she demanded. "You act like you don't want them here. They're our bread and butter, Hooley," she barked. "You'd best keep that in mind when you take it upon yourself to be inhospitable."

"I'm not being inhospitable," he argued weakly. "I was just curious why they don't go back to the ranch at night."

"Well," she sniffed. "That's a stupid thing to wonder. It's nearly forty miles back to the headquarters, and the weather's frosty. Plus," she added with a sympathetic frown, "the rancher's wife is bossy. Her amenities lack social companionship."

Hooley thought that no one in the world could be bossier than Margot, but he kept the opinion to himself, as he did his discomfort. Except when they needed a favor such as wanting him to read or write a letter, their pronounced deference to him was growing. It was assuming the shape of sarcasm, and they were becoming bolder, asking him where his "big-iron" was, as if they expected him to run around armed and ready for gunplay. These were no good-humored gibes such as they exchanged with one another. The snickering in their voices stung.

When the boys would settle down in the café tent, the whores would join them, but unlike the uncontrolled Saturday night revelries, the mid-evening gatherings were quiet affairs, reminding Hooley somewhat of his mother's "parlor parties," where polite people gathered for tea and sweet-meats while exchanging congenial conversation. When Hooley was young, Bertha Hooley had forced her youngest son to attend many of these affairs, and he had dread memories of sitting around in a scratchy wool suit and a stiff collar knotted to the chin with a tight cravat, and being utterly miserable for hours while his mother bragged on the prosperous future she was sure he would enjoy. That was before he became a tentmaker, of course.

Margot often joined the group, sitting quietly and pretending to listen, but Hooley suspected that she was merely keeping her ear tuned to any further plots to steal money and abscond, making sure that every comfort the cowboys derived from their visits was duly assessed, collected, and eventually consigned to the moneybags under Hooley's cot.

Hooley stayed aloof, in his tent, isolated and alone. Once in a while, he would go over to the café tent for a cup of coffee, but when he came into a crowd's midst, their jocularity died, as if he had interrupted something privileged. He felt as if he were some sort of schoolmaster who had stumbled onto a gathering of student mischief makers who were all eager for him to be gone.

He became especially irritated when someone would summon him over to settle a minor point of dispute. Reluctant as they all were to mention his onetime role as a lawman, they apparently had come to view him as some sort of bona fide official imbued with both the wisdom and the authority to adjudicate a disagreement. In spite of his resistance to the notion, he began to develop a sense that he was contributing to the welfare of the community by exercising a little common sense and logic in deciding all sorts of questions. He established that the Mississippi River was, indeed, larger than the Ohio, and that the Ozark Mountains were, technically, a set of hills. He noted that pigskin was more durable than calfskin, and he assured everybody that the electronic telegraph was the greatest marvel of the age and would never be replaced by that newfangled gadget, the telephone, which Hooley himself had never seen.

Such minor arbitrations sometimes provided Hooley with the hope that he was being accepted back into the spirit of the company, but no sooner had he rendered an opinion than the cowboys resumed ignoring him until something else came up. No one—not even Margot—ever inquired about his well-being, even on a perfunctory basis. He rarely received so much as verbal thanks for whatever service he provided, merely a satisfied nod from the winner and a derisive shake of the head from the loser that often gave birth to sarcastic gibes about his *pistolero* reputation.

Often, the cowboys would fall into a debate over some philosophical question of religion, politics, or law, and Hooley's well of knowledge was so shallow that he could offer little by way of wisdom. Margot usually sat by and smirked at his fumbling attempts to recall something he had read. He couldn't escape the sense that no matter how he responded to a question, she believed he was wrong, and he suspected that as soon as the disputants left his presence, she contradicted him. And she continued to absent herself from his bed.

Even so, they were prospering, and nearly two thousand dollars was now stored in the canvas bags. This distressed Hooley, and he finally suggested that they entrust some of it to Heinz to take back to Jacksboro and deposit in a bank for them.

"Have you lost your mind, Hooley?" Margot responded. "You honestly think I would trust that perverted reprobate with our money? I'd as soon just strap it to the back of a mule, point it toward a quicksand bog, and slap its rump."

"Heinz is honest," Hooley protested, but weakly.

"No man can resist temptation, Hooley," she sniffed. "I haven't learned much in life, but I know that for a cold fact." She put her hands in her lap. "I don't think banks are reliable, anyway," she said. "First thing you know, some bunch of bad actors will show up and rob it, and we'll be right back where we started." Her eyes sparked with a new thought. "Now, if you're nervous about keeping the money here, I can move it to my place. Might not be a bad idea anyway. That's the only source of income we have, now that you've gone lazy on us."

Hooley took offense at the notion that he was lazy, and the argument died. He had no intention of transferring the heavy bags to her tent. Besides, he found himself looking forward to their Sunday night accounting sessions, where they would assess the week's receipts. If she took away the money, those would end, and his personal contact with her would be utterly severed.

Apart from minor commerce, though, Hooley performed no official duties. Heinz's increasingly bulky mailbags ominously suggested that such a
capacity would soon have to be filled by someone. The cowboys were
clearly coming to regard Hoolian—not Rancher McPherson's ranch—as
home. Apart from Chatsworth, none had died or committed any action
that required official documentation, but Hooley decided to start keeping
records to hand over to whoever eventually emerged as the community's
civic leader. He had already recorded the marriage of the Mitchells and
the birth of James Moon Mitchell. After Margot's revelation, he decided
to include the deaths of Craggy Phillips, Deputy United States Marshal,
and of Mino's partner, whose name he merely noted to be "Carpenter
(Turkish?) NLN," for "No Last Name," after the manner of the military.
He omitted any indication of Chatsworth's death, though, for that had
happened elsewhere. Some cowboys asked him to record bills of sale for
animals and other possessions that might be presumed stolen should they
fall into the path of Texas Rangers or other impatient lawmen bent on
hanging miscreants without serious inquiry. Ambition, never his favorite
sensation, seemed to float about the community like a whimsical swarm of
gnats, occasionally gathering about his head to plague him, but easily dispersed with a wave of his hand or a pungent cloud of smoke from his
pipe.

MAYOR HOOLEY

1

ONE MORNING IN early December, Heinz's bulging mailbags brought a series of curious letters. One thick envelope in particular caught Hooley's notice. Like many before it, it was addressed to "His Honor, Mr. Mayor," but this time the title was ominously followed by his name, "Mr. Gilbert Hooley, Esq.," and was sent from an enterprising individual named Reginald T. Cooper of Monroe, Louisiana. His missive announced that he was a saddle maker. "I am also a good cobbler," he stated. "I can additionally maintain all manner of tanned goods in repair."

Cooper went on to state that he had friends in his vicinity who might also be interested in relocation. "One is a good tailor," he noted, "and is a fair barber. Another practices dentistry and treats minor physical complaints of the physique. He dispenses all manner of medicinals and refines his own opium. He is also a deacon in the Baptist Church." Cooper then noted that he was acquainted with a "highly qualified" blacksmith as well. He concluded by requesting that a "small building of commercial propriety" be erected before he arrived and enclosed ten dollars on account to secure the construction.

Enclosed with Cooper's letter was a greasy sawbuck and a well-creased piece of yellow foolscap, a handbill of some kind, Hooley determined. It was a blatant invitation to "Craftsmen, Artisans, and All Manner of Honest Christian Family Men" who might be interested in removing to "the newly opened frontier of West Texas to settle." At the bottom of the crudely printed page, Hoolian was extolled as a place where "Sobriety, Good Health, and Clean Living" offered all comers a prosperous life—and "free land to settle on." Also mentioned was the fact that the small city boasted a "variety of recreational pleasures, including a healthy climate, outdoor sporting events, and social entertainment." It concluded by stating that tradesmen and craftsmen with families and children "were especially welcome," and Hooley's name, preceded by the title "His Honor, Mr. Mayor," was neatly affixed to the last line.

Through his outrage, Hooley saw Ina Moon's hand on the drafting of the document, and Heinz's part in its distribution. He tried to imagine what Rancher McPherson's reaction would be to an advertisement for "free land." His ears burned with anger. He furiously wadded up the letter and flyer and was about to fling them into the kiln fire when he spotted Hank coming out of his store to sweep off the boardwalk. He marched over and confronted the storekeeper.

"What the hell is this?" Hooley shouted, waving the foolscap flyer. "How dare you!"

"You like it?" Hank asked brightly. "Ina Moon was proud as a fresh peach over those. She said they looked as good as an ad for any creek revival she'd ever seen."

"You stupid son of a bitch!" Hooley waved his hand over the surrounding tents. "How can you mislead people this way? We don't have a single building worthy of a name."

"They're good tents, Hooley. You say so yourself."

"I *know* they're good tents, you idiot," Hooley shouted. "But they're still *tents*. People might think they're coming to a regular town, not some tent-city on the prairie."

"Well, Hooley," Hank said, hooking his thumbs in his absurd braces and rocking back on his feet. "You said that if we was going to have a school, we'd need more kids, and I can't think of any way better to get them quick than to bring folks out here who already have them."

Hooley gathered his anger, spoke deliberately. "Hank, we're not a town."

"Will be when you build the school. You given any more thought to where you'll put it?"

"We don't need a school," Hooley snapped.

"You know, Hooley," Hank replied with a long look at Ina Moon, who had emerged and was nodding in agreement, "sometimes I don't think you're very civic-minded. You best watch your step, or we'll get somebody else to be mayor."

"That's another thing," Hooley shouted. "I'm *not* the mayor! How could you use—"

"Well, who else would be? You're the town founder," Hank shot back. "You and Mino. And an immigrant can't be mayor."

"Neither can I. And you had no right—"

"Sure you can! Of all people, Hooley, you should be glad the place is growing, putting down some roots, getting civilized. Hell—uh, heck! We can't stay a tent-city forever. I'm hoping we'll get us a brick mason or a stoneworker out here one of these days."

"Well, if we do," Hooley said, "then *I'm* out of business. I make tents, remember?"

Hank chewed on this, then finally smiled. "Aw, Hooley," he said, and grinned. "You'll get by. You're the only postmaster we got. *And* you're the mayor, like it or not. Says so right there!"

Frustrated, Hooley took the letter and handbill to Margot, but in keeping with her consistent ability to be inconsistent, she was thrilled by the prospect of civic growth. "It's about time we got new people," she said. "But we need to spruce things up. This place is getting to look too much like Oklahoma Territory to suit me. Too many ignorant cowboys and not enough stimulating conversation. Besides, new folks coming here will be good for business."

"I don't see how you can think such a thing will be good for business," Hooley replied.

"These will be workingmen," she said with a narrow look at Hooley. "It does everybody good to see a man at work. It might inspire others to be more useful."

"I'm plenty useful," Hooley said, hurt. "You wouldn't have a thing if it wasn't for me."

"Well, of course," Margot said, and sniffed. "Why do you think that everything I say is directed against you, Hooley? You need to take a broader view of life."

"Look, these are regular people. If they come, it could change everything."

"Oh, Hooley, regular people are just like everybody else. They give us respectability."

"That's what I'm worried about, and it's what you should be—"

"You can't stop progress, Hooley," she said, dismissing the topic.

Hooley found an envelope and stuffed Cooper's money into it. He scrawled out a note saying that the handbills had been born in the fetid mind of a "deranged lunatic" who was deluded as the result of torture by savage Indians, who were presently on the warpath. He addressed the letter to Cooper's return post office and sent it out with Heinz, but he didn't sign it. He wasn't sure how to do so.

2

EACH DAY WAS colder than the last, and the cowboys were now sure of a hard winter. Underwood confessed that he'd seen too many woolly caterpillars during the fall for it to be otherwise, and the sudden absence of migratory birds crossing the sky indicated that the fowl had already taken early flights south.

Mino stayed busier than ever, framing additions to existing buildings, shoring up ridgepoles and braces. Meanwhile, Hooley brought out the piecework he had done over the past several months to strengthen and patch walls and roofs that showed undue signs of wear and tear. He also enlarged and improved his own tent, sealing gaps between the crude planked floor with oakum and clay and treating himself to the extravagance of ordering a small iron stove for his tent.

The big problem Hooley realized as the cold snap continued, was their fuel supply. The year before, the availability of cow chips and the low demand for them prompted by a mild winter was in proper proportion. But now, the early cooling of the season forced conservation. As the north winds kept temperatures low and small, spitting storms of freezing rain and light snow rolled in every few days, the stockpile of dried manure was shrinking at an alarming rate. The cowboys averred that the reduction of mavericks around the immediate area had flung the search for more dried cow dung farther afield than most of them were willing to go in such cold weather.

Hooley had long ago learned that seasoned firewood was impossible to find on the treeless plains, and what little fuel could be located in or alongside creek beds was soon gathered and burned. Hooley considered borrowing Hank's piebald to relocate the cedar grove where he had met the Rangers the previous summer, but he had no true idea in what direction the place might lie, and none of the cowboys admitted to knowing where it might be.

The situation threatened to grow into a crisis with every armful of dried patties removed from the diminishing pile. Hooley estimated that the demands of the community would quickly exhaust what little combustible material remained by the first of the year. One crisp, clear afternoon, Hooley stood in front of the small stack of remaining cow chips and silently contemplated the irony that a man of his age and experience had been reduced to worrying over the size of a pile of shit as a means to sustaining his existence. He was wondering what his mother would have said to that when Mino shuffled over to stand beside him, blending his vaporizing breath with Hooley's. "No, shit, Gil Hooley," the carpenter said thought-fully, kicking the edge of the pile with one of his hobnailed boots.

Hooley's mood instantly soured even more, and he reached out and slapped Mino on the arm. "Is that *all* you can ever say?" he demanded. "I've learned more of *your* gibberish than that." This was true. The tent-maker knew most of the words to Mino's favorite songs, though he un-derstood not a one of them. "Why don't you think of something useful to do for a change?"

Mino gave him a hangdog look and shook his head, and Hooley suddenly felt sorry for him. Although he was by now convinced that he had dreamed Mino's coming into his tent and speaking clearly to him, he couldn't help but wonder if the man's inability to speak English wasn't the result of some sort of disease or mental incapacity. But before he could consider the problem further, he spotted Margot approaching with a businesslike expression. He stiffened.

The redheaded madam was wrapped in a thick bearskin robe that had been fashioned with a hood large enough to accommodate her high coif. Hooley noticed that she had taken to wearing her hair up, decorating her scarlet tresses with small, faux pearls and other fake gems. At least, Hooley assumed they were fake—he hated to think she was squandering their profits on such frippery. Her bookkeeping methods had become so con-fusing that he was utterly bewildered by the figures he found recorded in the ledger, and he had long ago abandoned any attempt to question her about them. It would be better to die bankrupt, he thought, than to live with the wrath any question of her honesty would bring down.

"Good morning, Hooley," she said formally. "I hope you've been keep-ing well during this cold snap." She cuddled deeper into the coat. The wrap was well worked and looked costly.

"That looks snug," he said. She nodded to him with an almost demure expression. "Where'd you get it?" His own thin coat was so worn that it barely held any warmth at all.

"Not that it's any of your business, but Mino gave it to me."

Hooley turned on the carpenter, who merely shrugged. He wondered if Mino was aware that he'd paid for such an obviously expensive gift, but before he could ask him, Margot was speaking again. "What have you decided to do about the bathhouse?"

"The bathhouse? What about it?"

"No one's using it. The girls say you claim it's wasteful to heat up the water."

"That's a small part of the problem," Hooley said, glancing at the pile of dried manure.

"I think it's a big problem all by itself, Hooley," she said. "I cannot abide a dirty whore. They cannot bathe in cold water. They'd catch their death. Besides, that old thing over there is falling down. The hose is leaky and the pump is inadequate. We need to build a new and proper bath-house."

"I don't think 'we' are up to it," Hooley said. She opened her mouth to protest, but he jumped in. "I mean, we could *build* it. But we don't have the materials to rig it."

"The girls need to bathe."

"We don't have enough fuel to heat water all winter," he argued, offering his trump card.

"Well, get some."

"Where?"

"Figure out something." She waved her hand casually. "I advise you to go where there's forest of some kind and cut some. If it were I—"

"But it's not 'you,' is it, Margot?" Hooley interrupted, warming in spite of the chill. "It never is 'you.' It's me. Anytime it's work to be done or a loss to absorb, it's me." She gazed at him curiously, as if he were babbling, and his anger doubled, along with an attendant internal heat. "So as usual, it's up to me to solve this problem."

"Well, only if you want to, Hooley," she said flatly. "I've never asked you to do one thing I didn't think you wanted to do or that wasn't for your own good. Or for the good of our business."

He sulked. "I just don't see why this should be my worry."

"Because you're the mayor."

"I'm not anything of the kind." Hooley sighed, weariness now flooding in to wash away the anger. "We don't have a mayor. We're not even a real town."

"We're as real as we've ever been," she snapped, suddenly on the attack, "and we're getting more real all the time. May I remind you that when I showed up there was just you and Mino sitting around a fire trying to get through the day, and now we have a real place where real people want to come?" She drew the coat more closely around her. "I do *my* part," she said angrily. "I fret over the girls, and I worry about Mino and Hank and Ina Moon, and"—she gave him a telling look—"I worry about *you*, Hooley. You need to look around more. You decided what you wanted, and you got what you wanted, and now you don't want to accept it."

"I never wanted to be mayor of anything."

She stood for a moment in the light wind, watching him. Then she softened her tone. "Hank tells me you're building a school. I think that's a good idea."

"Hank's crazy."

"Well, that's what he said. So, come up with something for us to burn," she prodded him. "Winter's coming on hard. I thought it got frosty in Oklahoma Territory, but this is chillier." She snuggled her coat around her. "You said it true: We need firewood."

"There's not any. Nowhere around here, there's not."

"There's wood all over the world, Hooley," Margot sniffed. "Oklahoma Territory is full of wood, for a start. And I'm sure there's plenty all over Texas if you'll just go get it."

"How?" Hooley asked. "I already asked Heinz, last year, and he says he won't cut it, won't haul it. He says there's no profit—"

"I'm relying on you," she said. "We all are. Lately, you've been malingering."

"Me?"

"That's right. You abandoned management of the hotel. You won't tend bar, and whenever we have a social, you go off and sull up."

"I do not—"

"I'm not going to argue with you, Hooley," she said. "We're partners, and that means you pull your own weight. I'd be mayor, but you know I can't—I'm a woman and I'm engaged in an immoral activity. That wouldn't be seemly."

"I'm your partner," Hooley protested. "That makes me as immoral as you are."

"Precisely. Which is why you have to be mayor. It's perfectly ordinary for a politician to be a partner in a whorehouse, especially when he's already the local lawman."

"Me? I'm not a law—"

"It happens all the time in Oklahoma Territory, and I'm sure Texas is no different." She put a finger to her chin. "I'd say that it's more often the case than not in Texas. It may even be some kind of requirement," she added, then fixed him with her green stare. "Find some firewood, Hooley, and quit whining about it. I'm purely sick of your whining." She stalked off.

"Damn that woman," Hooley said when she was out of earshot.

"No shit, Gil Hooley," Mino said in agreement.

"Oh, shut the hell up," Hooley snapped, and he closed his eyes, feeling a headache coming on to match the sudden wrenching in his gut. When he looked around again, Mino was gone. Hooley decided he needed a drink, but when he reached the whiskey shed, he was surprised to find Mino and Plunk, the perpetually unhappy cowboy, standing there.

"What are you doing here?" Hooley asked Plunk, who was holding a cup of coffee. "It's the middle of the week."

Plunk looked down and turned red. He appeared about to cry. "Fell off my horse," he said. The youngster took a deep breath, then blurted out, "I hurt myself, are you satisfied?"

"I don't under—"

"I hurt my backside," Plunk said, and Hooley saw the chubby young man's face transform from rage to mortification. He rubbed his hip and winced. "I can't sit a saddle. It hurts. Mrs. Rancher McPherson's put me on half pay till I can ride again."

Hooley found the situation inappropriately amusing, and he turned away to hide a smile, but before he could leave, Plunk spoke up. "So, what's the deal going to be?" he demanded.

"What deal?"

"Well, I got to take care of myself someway till I heal up. If I go find firewood, haul it back, what do I get out of it?" Hooley stared at Mino. Somehow, the ignorant carpenter had explained their need to the cowboy. "Hurry up and spit it out, Hooley," Plunk said. "I can borrow Heinz's wagons for a couple of days, I reckon. I want to be back by Saturday."

"Are you offering to go find firewood?"

"Are you hard-of-hearing, Hooley?"

"I thought you were hurt."

"I can't sit a saddle, but I can drive a wagon, I reckon." He blushed again and looked sadder than ever. "I can drive standing up. Mino here can come along and help." The carpenter nodded enthusiastically. "What about it? What's in it for me?"

"What do you want?"

Plunk thought for a moment. "Well, I can't work for money," he said morosely. "Rancher McPherson won't allow it. We only can work for him for wages, and I need the half pay. But I got to have something. Hauling back enough for this whole outfit's going to be a lot of work."

"Well, you can have a free cot," Hooley offered. "And drinks on the house for a week."

"That's not good enough," Plunk said. "We're talking hard work and a long way to go."

"What do you want, then?"

Plunk cast his eyes around until they fell on Miss Margot's Place. "Tell you what," he said. "I'll tote back wood for the whole winter, but I want ten free times with the girls."

"*Ten* times?" Hooley asked.

"Hell, Hooley, I have to go clear to the Cross Timbers for any decent wood, 'less I go up to the river bottoms. I'm apt to lose the whole damn wagon in quicksand if I do that. Then Heinz'll kill me and you'll have that my blood on your hands, too."

"There's no blood on my—"

"Anyway," Plunk continued, "up in the bottoms, all I'm likely to find is green cedar that'll smoke us all out and grease up the food. Give us all the trots." He folded his arms and frowned. "You want good firewood, I can get it. Ten times, Hooley."

Hooley looked at the red tent. "It's not my say-so. You'll have to take that up with—"

"I'm taking it up with you," Plunk said. "Makes me no nevermind how it's fixed up."

"Five times," Hooley said, trying to come to terms. "For two full wagons."

"Seven," Plunk said.

"Six," Hooley bargained. "And all with Clara." Of late, Hooley noticed, she'd been putting on weight. A double chin had developed, and she was straining what few clothes she wore around the camp in warm weather. He'd overheard several of the boys complaining that she was becoming pouty. Plunk's steady attention would be good for her.

"All with Clara?" Plunk seemed even more disappointed than he usually did.

"Clara," Hooley insisted. "That's the deal."

Plunk toed the ground and considered. "All right," he said, then turned to Mino. "Bring your sawyers and axes. Hooley, you talk to Heinz. We're on our way at first light."

Hooley was somewhat surprised to find that the mule skinner cheerfully agreed to lend out his vehicles and teams, so long as he could spend the few days' holiday in Loretta's company and not be charged for his liquor. This made the whole deal even less favorable monetarily, and Hooley didn't offer Margot any details about it. He was certain she would object to being left out of the negotiations, would complain that the price— particularly Plunk's—was too high, and would question his focus on Clara. After that, she'd find other problems. One by one, he ticked off his partner's anticipated objections.

Dread of the approaching confrontation confounded him. He isolated himself and furiously smoked and stitched more canvas, though there was no immediate need for it. Working let his mind drift away from the increasing number of problems he faced, the multitude of responsibilities. He now thought he understood why he had had no ambition before. With ambition came achievement, and with achievement came obligation. He longed for the days when the only person he was responsible for was himself.

Hooley could delay the inevitable for only so long. In a few days' time, Plunk would return and expect to start collecting. So finally, the tentmaker bolstered himself with several strong shots of whiskey and wandered over to the red tent. When Margot came out, he was momentarily stunned. She was in a fancy purple frock, cut especially low in the bodice.

"What is it, Hooley? It's still too chilly out here to stand around and gawk." Hooley swallowed and tried to remember his errand. "My face is up here, Hooley," she said sharply. "There's nothing down there you haven't seen."

He wanted to say it had been all too long since he'd seen anything at all, but her scowl discouraged him. He gathered his thoughts and told her of the deal he made with Plunk, spilling out the details quickly, then holding his breath, waiting for her reaction.

Her face opened in a broad smile. "That was using your head, for once. And Clara's a good choice. She says Plunk reminds her of her dead husband—he was a chubby thing, too—and she's stout enough to carry his weight." She tapped a finger against her pretty chin in thought. "But you tell him not to get any ideas about running off with her. I'd hate to have to send you after somebody again. We've had enough of that nonsense."

When Plunk and Mino returned on Saturday, Heinz's wagons were laden with split oak and hickory. In addition to the firewood, they had a number of stout limbs that could be hand-milled for replacement ridgepoles and other props for errant canvas. The cowboy then announced that he had struck a deal on his own authority, one that would prevent them from having to make a second trip. A woodcutter from the Cross Timbers had agreed that starting in a month's time, he would haul our shipments of fuel in exchange for ten dollars a load and five "times" with the girls.

"Five times!" Hooley exclaimed. "With who?"

"Oh, it don't matter," Plunk assured him. "He won't be picky. You ought to see his old lady. She outweighs Mino here and is ugly enough to stop a watch," he said sadly.

"But *our* deal was two loads for six times," Hooley said. "You only made one."

Plunk's face darkened. "Hooley, mess with me and I'm apt to burn that wagonload where it sits."

"Oh, what the hell." Hooley flapped his arms. "What do I care? They're not *my* whores."

Plunk's fat face turned into a rare, bright grin. "That's using your noggin. You know, you keep dealing like this, you might make a mayor of this place after all."

SOLSTICE

1

DISASTER STRUCK A week before Christmas. The northwestern sky blackened with thick, heavy clouds, and by nightfall a howling norther was ripping through the canvas community. The wind brought a horrible dirt storm, followed by pelting rain that froze when it struck the earth. The whipping gale began tearing seams apart on the older tents, especially Hank's store and its inferior cloth. Hank came to Hooley in a panic, yelling for him to come out into the windy darkness. Large rents had opened in the walls of his living quarters, and freezing rain was blowing in, and many other structures were showing alarming signs of falling apart as wind battered them with sharp, sleety projectiles. Hooley summoned Mino to help cut more patches, then impressed the girls into service as well, rapidly instructing them in how to make rapid, strong temporary stitches and how to melt the wax necessary to patch the rapidly enlarging holes.

Sleet gave way to snow about midnight. That was at first a welcome respite from the pelting pellets of frozen rain, but as the large, wet flakes swirled across the prairie, they became so dense that soon everyone was blinded to anything not in arm's reach. The temperature plummeted and the wet wind continued to howl across the naked plains. The nature of the work forbade using gloves or mittens, and fingers were soon numb.

Margot sprang into vigorous action and converted the parlor of Miss Margot's Place—the only building with no significant rips showing—into a veritable mending factory. She commissioned Loretta to ferry hot coffee, but soon Hank was forced to provide stout rawhide rope strung between buildings for people to use as guides. It was impossible to see anything, even when hooded lanterns were held up, for the light reflected off the thick flakes and added to the general confusion. As the night deepened, the temperature continued to drop, and for a while Hooley and Hank were forced to press on alone while Mino saw to the animals, making sure they were all under the loafing shed and out of the howling blizzard.

Hooley worked with mindless determination to finish the repairs. He went from seam to seam applying more wax, which hardened the moment it was taken from the cast-iron mixing cauldron and exposed to the frigid air. His thin cord coat was no match for the biting wind. His fingers fumbled when he tried to whipstitch the patches in the waving yellow lantern light. Snow continued to fall heavily, and before he knew it the entire compound was deep in drifts that covered his shoe tops and froze his feet. He ordered Loretta to build up the kiln fire so they could thaw out, but when he sat with his icy, wet shoes propped up to the blaze, he discovered a new worry: Heavy snow was building on the canvas roofs. They would have to dislodge it, or every tent in the town would collapse under the frozen weight.

For the first time since arriving, Hooley sensed how fragile the community was. Within a few hours, they could be wiped out utterly, frozen and dead beneath the screaming, snow-laden wind. He poured coffee into himself and renewed his efforts, not sure what else there was to do. He had no idea where his resolve was coming from to save this town that he had gradually come to hate. But he worked on, blindly feeling his way from rent to separated seam, burning his fingers with hot wax and slapping them against his legs when they became numb.

They had finally repaired all the rips and tears on the windward side of most of the structures, and Hooley was looking forward to rest, when Underwood and Tidmore rode in. That they had found their way in the blinding curtain of swirling white astonished the tentmaker. Although nearly frozen and miserable with the tingling pain of frostnip on the tip of his nose and tops of his ears, Hooley stepped forward, stamping his feet and beating his palms against his sides. The pards were bundled tight against the frigid night, and icicles hung from their horses' bellies, but above their scarves their eyes were wide as they peered through the blinding storm and yelled for Hooley to "come out, right goddamn now!"

"I'm already out here, goddamn it," he yelled back. It was a wonder they could see anything, so tightly wrapped were their heads and faces. He held up the sputtering lamp. "Step down. We've got coffee." As they dismounted, Harley stomped into the café tent and accepted a steaming mug from Loretta's mittened hand. The canvas snapped in the wind, and he was surprised to find the scalding beverage turning cold in his hands almost before he could drink it. Although the Indian woman was wrapped in what appeared to be a buffalo robe, from beneath it, he could see her constantly grinning face. He looked up at the rippling roof and assessed the ominous sags where the weight of the new snow rapidly collected.

"You got here just in time," he said to the pair. "We need to poke the snow off." He gestured above his head. They were wearing so many clothes they seemed twice their normal size. But they gratefully accepted the coffee and stared dumbly at the sagging roof.

"No time for that. For that," Underwood stammered out. "We run across some trouble."

Hooley looked out into the darkness. "What's the matter now?"

"A whole string of brood mares Rancher McPherson sent from England or some damn place got away," Tidmore grumbled. "Mrs. McPherson said we had to find them before they froze or got poked by some jugheaded stud." He pulled down his muffler to reveal his mustache, then sipped the coffee. "Woman's crazy," he added. "It's too cold for poking."

"That ain't the half of it. It," Underwood chipped in. The two then explained that a family named Nichols was on its way. They lost the wagon trail in the snow, Underwood said.

"They'd of froze completely if we hadn't run up on them," Tidmore said. "Lucky."

"Their horses're spavined. Spavined," Underwood complained. "Don't nobody know better than to pull a wagon with spavined horses?"

"Shouldn't pull a wagon like that with horses at all," Tidmore commented, and thrust out his empty cup for more coffee. "Damn Yankee feather merchants, you ask me."

Hooley sent Loretta to fetch Margot, and he and the boys crunched out into the snow and wind to wait for the wagon to arrive. After a long, frigid spell, Hooley was ready to give up, go inside to wait, but then he spied a flickering lantern in the distance. Soon, Jake was guiding a battered old wagon into the snowy center of town as Plunk stood on the box, reins in hand.

"These folks need help," Jake stated matter-of-factly, as if it were the most natural thing in the world to find Hooley and the others standing around in a blizzard in the middle of the night. "They're pretty near froze to death."

Margot and the girls appeared at once, although how they knew of the crisis mystified Hooley. They were prepared, though, and arrived with furs and heavy blankets. There wasn't much for the boys to do but examine the horses, which were indeed in bad shape. Mino helped him unharness them. When they returned, Hooley ignored their grumbling complaints about his bossiness and set them to work shoveling and poling snow off the canvas roofs.

Dawn came gray and cold over an alabaster winterset. To Hooley's relief, all the buildings were patched and secure from collapse. The wind abated with the arrival of the steely daylight, and the snow stopped. Hooley almost collapsed when he came into the café tent for one more cup of coffee, bacon, and biscuits. He was utterly exhausted, too numb and hollow to eat. As he began to thaw by the fire, the wetness seeped through his clothing and into his suddenly idle limbs. Finally, he found the energy to drink the coffee and light his pipe, then he waded through the snow toward the red tent, glancing at his night's work, satisfied that somehow, they had battled the storm and won. But when he arrived at Margot's door flap, she emerged to meet him with an almost angry expression and gave him the bad news: Every one of the lost and nearly unconscious travelers was sick and near death.

"They have some kind of fever, and they can't keep a thing inside them," Margot said. She added that the girls spent most of the night boiling water, emptying chamber pots, and ripping up scraps of canvas, petticoats, and linens to wash and mop the fevered brows of the suffering pilgrims. She enumerated a wife and six children of one Hiram Nichols, who was raving in a rage of fever of his own.

"They're still at it," she said in a deep sigh. "Free-flowing from both ends. They think it was something they ate. Spoiled chicken, maybe. One said all they'd had to eat for two weeks was fried dough and mush until they came across some chickens. They were dead, Hooley. They were so hungry, they ate *dead* chickens! What kind of people eat dead chickens? But I'm doubtful of that. It might be something else." She suddenly leaned forward and rested her weight on Hooley. The gesture so surprised him, his own weariness retreated as he put his arm around her, pulled her close. She didn't resist.

"Oh, Hooley, I'm so tired," she said. "Why did they have to come here? We're not properly equipped to attend sick folks."

"I don't see how we could turn them away," he said.

She pulled back from him abruptly. "Turn them away? Of course we couldn't turn them away, Hooley. Don't be mean. We had to take them in. They might be us, you know."

"I didn't mean—"

"I've heard of cholera epidemics that wiped out whole towns," she said, and resumed her former posture next to him. He felt her warmth comfortably against him until her statement registered and fear penetrated his fatigue. He looked at Nichols' wagon. It was an old army ambulance, listing to one side on broken springs. Holes in the sideboards indicated that it was worm-eaten, worn out. He swallowed hard. "I don't think it's cholera," he offered. "Could be bad food. Could be something else. Let's just hope we don't catch it."

"You always think of the other fellow first," Margot snapped, her sudden anger heating her cheeks to a rosy red. She left Hooley standing on the snow-covered boardwalk and went to the café tent for a cup of coffee. "I just hope I don't get sick and have to rely on *you* for sympathy," she threw over her shoulder at him.

By noon, snow was falling again, a dense heavy cover that froze on top of the drifts already in place. Hooley inspected his patches and repairs, then went to his tent, lit his small stove, and lay down, but within an hour Lulu came to fetch him.

"They're all dead," she said when Hooley rose groggily to meet the small brunette. She was wrapped in blankets that doubled her size, but from within the bundle he saw that her face was blotchy and her dark eyes were ringed with fatigue. "Every blessed one of them."

Hooley trudged over through the crunching snow. Although there was no wind, the cold outside was nearly painful, penetrating. He noticed that the quartet of cowboys was still there and wondered how they could bear it. They stood in the snow, smoking and hunching their shoulders against the bitter atmosphere, but when Hooley passed by, they came forward as a single, shivering body.

"We got to get back to work, Hooley," Jake said, as if Hooley had forced them to stay. "We can't mess around here too long. We got to find them horses and at least get them down into a gully or something where there's shelter or they'll every damn one of them just freeze."

"This is a big storm. Storm," Underwood noted. "Biggest this country has ever seen! And it ain't over by a sight. A sight."

"If all those brood mares die out there or turn up in foal, Mrs. Rancher McPherson'll wallpaper the bunkhouse with our hides," Jake said. "We got to get moving."

"Well, go on," Hooley said irritably, waving his hand. "I'm not holding you."

"All them folks dead in there?" Jake asked, his eyes widening slightly.

"That's the report," Hooley said.

"What you reckoned killed them?" Plunk asked. "You reckon we'll get it?"

"Not if you avoid eating chicken," Hooley said, pushing past them.

They mounted up quickly and were gone before Hooley could enter the tent.

Lulu had exaggerated the situation slightly. Nichols himself was alive. His skinny body was wrapped in blankets, his mouth was open, and he was snoring loudly. Margot, who for once looked unkempt and totally exhausted, explained that his fever had broken during the morning. Her eyes were bloodshot, Hooley noticed, and there was no spark to her look or voice. "None of the others were strong enough," she said wearily.

Hooley looked around the parlor. It was hard to imagine it as a scene of weekly festivity. The place was in chaos. He saw that all of the girls' cots had been dragged out and arranged in the middle of the room. Where it was exposed, the blank planking was stained with spills of water and vomit, and bundles of rags, overfull chamber pots, and spittoons were everywhere. Each body was neatly wrapped in a blanket.

Hooley was surprised to see Mino sitting in the corner by the dusty piano, his head down, apparently asleep. Margot studied the scene with a weary expression and spoke in a low tone. "We did what we could," she said defensively. "But they died anyway." She stepped over a pile of filthy rags. "You have to help me move them out of here, Hooley. Tomorrow's Saturday—we've got to be ready. I've used up a month's profits in linens alone." She went to the foot of one of the smaller bodies. "Come on, Hooley," she hissed in a loud whisper. "I'd ask Mino, but he's worn out from carrying water and such all day while you slept."

"I didn't sleep . . .," Hooley started, but then he trailed off. There was no point in arguing. He helped her lift the bodies and carry them outside, through the continuing white fall up onto the flats, where they lay them on the snowy ground for burial. It was dark when they finished and turned to trudge back to share a drink by the fire in the café tent. The cold was so sharp, their breath vaporized almost into solid ice when exhaled.

Hooley had remained silent during their labors. Now, he wanted to say something but didn't know what. He didn't want to argue. She was being deliberately contrary, and he had no energy left. The hissing softness of heavy snowflakes subdued what annoyance he wasn't too exhausted to feel. He refused to look at her and only sipped his coffee and allowed frustration to compete with weariness through his very bones, trying to be first to pull him down.

"How can something so pretty be so mean?" she asked at last.

"I've often asked the same question," Hooley said softly, with a glance at her.

"That man. That Nichols," she said irritably. "A fool, if I ever saw one.

And he got about what you'd expect," she added. "The imbecile drags his wife and family out here, most likely poisons them, then lets them waste away."

Hooley didn't dispute the point, but he thought that whatever it was that killed them might have killed Nichols as well. He peered through the snow-lit darkness toward the flat. A small gust of wind struck his cheek, indicating that the storm might be regaining its ferocity. That meant more work. He wondered where he would find the strength.

"He some kind of farmer?" Hooley asked to break the renewed silence.

"Some kind of idiot," Margot said, rising. "Holds on to a Bible. Says that's what kept him alive. You ask me, it was Gertie and Lulu. They're the ones who nursed him. Wiped his bottom and held his hand like he was a baby." She stood. "I'm all in, and I got a big night tomorrow night." And she was gone, quickly curtained from view by the increasingly heavy snowfall.

Hooley staggered through the snow across to his tent, clinging to the vision of his cot, his blankets, and the warmth he knew he would soon enjoy. He now remembered that in his Gladstone bag, he had an old stocking cap, one of the few legacies of his life in St. Louis and Ruthie's infernal demands for long walks in cold weather. He determined to pull it over his frozen face. He detoured through the whiskey shed for a fresh bottle, briefly wondering if the remainder of the stock might freeze. He was too tired to haul it to the cold cellar. If it froze, it froze. It would give him a good excuse to move on.

Move on. The thought was suddenly delicious to contemplate. Leave this mess behind him and just take off. He looked up into the snowy sky. Come spring, he thought. Somehow, he was moving on come spring. Then he glanced as the dim glow that came from the red tent's parlor and wondered if he really meant it, and if he did, if he had the gumption to do it.

He paused at the door to his tent to stamp his frozen feet and knock the snow off his shoes. But as he parted the flap and entered, he looked down and found that lying on his cot was Nichols, his pale face lit by a flickering lamp. "What the hell are you doing here?" Hooley asked.

Nichols raised himself up slightly, his pale eyes blinking rapidly. A small man with a large goatee, he was nearly bald, with only a ring of hair circling his pale pate. Hooley noted that he had on a ragged flannel nightshirt. "I am a lay minister of the Gospel," he said. "Primitive Baptist," he added in a qualifying clarification. His eyes shot around the tent as if he was checking for eavesdroppers. "That lady who's been so kind . . . ," Nichols whispered, then flopped back and wrapped his gnarled fingers around a worn Bible. "That woman's a harlot," he said flatly. "I cannot remain in the house of a harlot." Hooley gaped at him as snow and ice melted from his clothing and puddled around his feet. "I am not ungrateful!" Nichols said, his voice strengthening. "I am not! But it would not be seemly. So I asked to be moved elsewhere." His eyes roamed to Hooley's stark form. "I could not suffer myself to die in the home of a harlot."

"This"—Hooley gestured with his whiskey bottle—"is my bed."

"Lord help us!" Nichols exclaimed. "Does everyone in this Sodom live in tents?"

"*I* live here," Hooley yelled. "I sleep there! Right there! My bed. I made it, and it's mine." His voice rose to a quake, high-pitched and childlike. It disgusted him, made him even angrier. He swallowed, grabbed his breath. "This is my house, goddamnit."

"Oh Lord!" Nichols cried, putting his hands over his ears. "You have divested me of my family and put me into the hands of harlots and blasphemers! But I bless your name!"

"Who told you—," Hooley started, then Nichols' eyes stopped him. They were quietly defiant. He wasn't moving. Hooley stormed out of the tent and stomped through the heavy drifts of snow, which now entirely covered the boardwalks, across to Miss Margot's Place.

The flap was closed, tied from the inside, but Hooley ripped it open and entered. His intention was to go directly to Margot's room, her crib, to confront her with this latest imposition.

"Margot!" he yelled. "Margot!" He stopped in the middle of the parlor. The chaos and filth evident in his previous visit was all gone. The rude tables and stools Mino had fashioned were back in position. The carpenter's concertina was atop the ever-idle piano. But what stunned Hooley more than anything else was the warmth that filled the room. It was so warm that when the heated atmosphere hit his frozen cheek and nose, they stung. Hooley's eyes searched the room and settled on a large stove in the corner where he had last seen Mino sitting asleep. Through its door-grate he could see the red glow of coals, and beside the stove was a neat stack of wood. The appliance not only filled the entire parlor with an embracing heat, it also gave a soft light that, when reflected off the room's scarlet walls, created an orange glow.

"Margot!" he called again, remembering the purpose of his errand.

"Hooley, shut up!" Margot hissed angrily when she emerged from behind the canvas curtain concealing her crib. She stood wrapped in a bright silk robe she pulled tight around her, although it hardly concealed her nakedness. His breath caught in spite of himself. Her hair was down, and she looked so soft and lovely, he could hardly keep from reaching out for her. His purpose in being there was momentarily forgotten, but in the dim light from the small stove, her eyes flashed and reminded him that it was always dangerous to confront her with relaxed defenses.

"Those girls have had a rough two days," she said, moving over toward him. "They worked like hell to put this place in shape, and their cribs are still a mess. Tomorrow night's Saturday. What's the matter with you?"

"You put that Nichols man in my tent. In my bed!" he yelled. Our bed, he thought.

"Shhh! Hooley, for the last time!"

He lowered his tone, but felt a whine creeping into it, which irked him further. "How could you do such a thing, Margot?"

She pulled him by the arm over to the front door. "You need to get out of here. You know I don't allow any men in here on a weeknight. Those girls need their rest." She started to push him out, but he resisted stubbornly. "Where did you expect me to put him?" She sighed. "He wouldn't stay here another minute, and he'd die out there without shelter."

"Why do you care? You know what he said? He said—"

"I know what he said, Hooley. He's supposed to be a schoolteacher, but it turns out he's some kind of preacher." She put a finger to her chin thoughtfully. The gesture was so demure it superheated him. He felt himself growing sweaty. "Preachers have always been a mystery to me. They're usually the first ones to open their britches on a Saturday night, and the first ones to want to shut you down on a Sunday. I've been dreading the day a preacher would come here." She turned to the stove and held out her hands, her palms open for the warmth. "Oklahoma Territory was overrun with preachers, which was another good reason to leave it."

"He could go to the hotel tent," Hooley said.

"The Prairie Clipper's full," she whispered. "The boys came in again. All of them. Didn't you know?" She sighed. "It's cold out there, Hooley. They need their rest."

"I need *my* rest, Margot."

"Oh, Hooley. What good are you?" she demanded. "They said they'd found all the mares and that was all the work they planned to do until the weather moderated." Her eyes danced away absently, as if she was thinking. "Anyway, they're all in the hotel. Some of them are even on the floor." She smiled at him. "I upped the rate to a dollar a cot, and not one complained. What do you think of that?"

"Where am I supposed to sleep?" Hooley asked. She put her hands on her hips, a familiar pose that made him instantly sorry he had come over to confront her. He already knew how things would turn out. Then a thought struck him, and he shifted tactics. "What's that?" He pointed at the stove.

"A stove," she said. "Haven't you ever seen a stove before? If I'm not mistaken, you have one in your tent."

"Not like that one. That's a *good* stove. A big stove. Where did it come from?"

As if he had reminded her, she opened the grate and plopped in a small piece of wood. "Heinz brought it to me," she said. "Sort of a peace offering, in a way. I think he's gone sweet on Loretta," she added with a frown. "I may have to keep an eye on that, even though he's married—he could be a Mormon." Keeping her eyes on his, she lifted the back of her robe, exposing her slim, bare hips to the stove's radiated warmth. Her feet were encased in loose furry moccasins, he saw. "It's freezing, Hooley," she said. "Now go on and let me get some rest."

"And where am *I* supposed to rest?" he demanded.

"Well, not here," she said, raising her chin and moving toward him again. "Rules are rules, Hooley. And they apply to you as much as to anyone. If I start letting you sleep in here, I'll have to let everyone. Just because you're the mayor—"

"I'm *not* the mayor," he insisted. The continuing whine in his voice disgusted him. So did the bottle in his hand. He must have looked awful, he thought; he hadn't bathed or shaved in days. "I've got to lie down and sleep."

"Well, go on back to your tent and do it," she said, pushing him toward the opening.

"Where? Nichols is—"

"There's plenty of room for two," she said, giving him one final shove. "We've proved that often enough. But if you don't let me get my rest, we never will again."

The comment startled him. Did this mean she was planning to resume their love affair? The thought instantly banished his anger and frustration. At the same time, it irked him for preying on his chief weakness: her. He suddenly resolved not to admit her to his cot again, but no sooner was the declaration fixed in his mind than he recognized it for a lie.

She sniffed the icy air. "I expected Texas to be warmer than this. Get to bed, Hooley."

He stumbled through the high drifts over to the café tent, but the fire was banked, and there was nothing to eat or drink. He sucked on his whiskey bottle, sitting and hugging his body until the cold on his nose and ears became too painful to bear. A frigid hour went by before he returned to his tent and crawled beside his cot and lay down on the floor in the dark.

Nichols had employed all the good blankets, so Hooley wrapped himself in an old one he had been using as a kind of rug. He remembered the stocking cap, and began rummaging through the Gladstone bag, to no avail. He finally lit a lantern and dumped out the bag's entire contents, but the cap was missing. Frustrated, Hooley sat back, shivering in the permeating cold, and glared angrily at his unwelcome guest, only to discover that the object of his search was securely pulled down over the top of Nichols' head.

2

B Y THE TIME Hooley arose the next day, the cowboys were up, ready for a different kind of action. They announced that they didn't care what Rancher McPherson's fearsome bride might do, they were done cow-punching until Christmas came and went or the cold spell ended. "We'll go on strike if we have to," Tidmore proclaimed. "I hear they're doing it back East all the time, and if it works for a bunch of ignorant immigrants, it'll work for us."

"It ain't fit for a man to have to work out in such cold. Cold," Underwood seconded. "We're staying right here till the spring thaw!"

Hooley was alarmed by this rebellion. He tried to envision the trouble that could be caused by credit-mongering cowboys hanging around town all winter. Jake put his mind to rest. He confided that they had all received fat bonuses for clearing the range of mavericks, and that they planned to enjoy the money. "We were heading over here to do just that when those damn horses got out," he said.

"But a *strike*," Hooley pleaded, "that's just asking for trouble."

"Ah, it's just heat lightning, Hooley." Jake laughed. "Them boys wouldn't know how to do something like that. Soon as their pockets are empty, they'll be eager to get back to work. All we really have to do is go check in again next week."

Their enjoyment began slowly, but quickly picked up momentum. They started on a spree of spending freely at Hank's store, purchasing new shirts and trousers, coats and scarves, kerchiefs and bedrolls. The delighted storekeeper announced price reductions to stimulate their buying frenzy and was also taking orders for new boots and tack. Fresh duds stimulated a concern for personal hygiene and led them to the bathhouse, where they hauled coals from the café tent's kiln to thaw out the leaky galvanized rubber hose and took turns pumping and heating and hauling the water so they could bathe and shave in an astonishing assembly line of personal toilet. Then the café tent became a barbershop, as Loretta moved down a long line of shaggy heads, shearing off shoulder-length tresses.

Next, the pards, clean and highly pompadoured, demanded whole bottles of whiskey and gin, purchasing them directly from Hooley with hard coin, and finally they camped out in the café tent, where they kept Loretta busy preparing hot food. When the feast was concluded, they commenced clamoring for Margot to open up so they could start dancing and sampling the girls' favors in the "biggest Christmas shindig Texas will ever see!"

Hooley soon tired of their holiday mood—especially as none of them bothered to include him as anything more than a whiskey peddler—and he wandered out to the flats to escape their noisy merrymaking. He was soon standing beside the snow-covered and pitiful remains of the Nichols family. The small stack of bodies was clearly visible from the center of town, but no one showed any inclination to do anything about it, like bury them.

"I'm damned if I'm going to do this on my own," he said aloud. It was enough, he argued further, that he had to share his tent with the fool Nichols, who spent his waking hours muttering over his Bible and weeping. Still, the sight of the corpses stirred Hooley. He scrounged up a ragged old tarp Mino used to cover lumber, flung it over the shrouded bodies, then returned to his tent and the whining prayers of the family's patriarch.

Nichols seemed indifferent to the final fate of his family. The preacher spoke of his lost loved ones only indirectly, in one of his constant prayers, during which he also solicited help for the "blasphemer" on whom responsibility for his welfare had been placed. Hooley knew Nichols had to be going outside sometime, but there was no evidence of even a quick step out to relieve himself in the snow. How he obtained food or water was a mystery to the tentmaker. Yet somehow, Hooley observed the man was gradually recovering his strength. But he showed no inclination to abandon Hooley's tent—or his bed.

Two days later, Nichols suddenly changed his attitude. One morning, Hooley had filled the tent with pipe smoke, hoping to drive Nichols out. The milky-eyed preacher surprised Hooley by calling him the "present-day embodiment of the Good Samaritan."

"I've prayed," he said, "and the Lord told me that I should know a good Christian soul when I see one. Even if he doesn't recognize himself as such," Nichols continued, "I can spot a kindred spirit in Christ. I see you own a Bible. Have you communed with the Holy Spirit lately?"

"I'm about to commune you right out of this goddamn tent," Hooley

replied. "I am not obliged for your free hand with my personal belongings." He wanted to seize the scrawny little man by the scruff of his neck
and throw him out, but Nichols' physical frailty was too pitiful. And with
his luck, Margot and the boys would all take Nichols' side and force
Hooley to sleep out in the open. "I just wish you'd get the hell out of
here," Hooley said. "I need a good night's sleep."

"Blasphemy is a sin, my son!" Nichols rejoined. "One of your few visible
failings. I shall pray for your salvation from this road of eternal peril."
Then he opened his Bible and read aloud until Hooley was driven out into
the snow.

3

EACH DAY, THE pards arose, repaired their toilets as best they could, then
ate everything Loretta could cook. Then they recommenced their revelries in the early afternoon and continued well into the night. If they
weren't at Miss Margot's, then they were milling around in the café tent
demanding more food and hot coffee. The compound was streaked with
deep, muddy trails and stained with vomit and evidence of ill-timed self-
relief. As the week wore on, Hooley noticed that an increasing number of
the boys were merely collapsing where they found themselves, sated on
sex and liquor and tobacco, covered with icy mud and dead to the world.

Whenever Hooley was outside, he would invariably observe the Nichols
family, still pathetically unburied. The sight unnerved him, and early one
frosty evening, he decided to finally do something about it. He stormed
over to Miss Margot's Place, where he found Mino happily playing his
concertina for the amusement of the crowd. Hooley pinched the reluctant
carpenter on the ear and dragged him out to look at the corpses. For a
few days the temperature had risen, but now it was again well below
freezing. While they stood there, fresh sleet began to lay down a thick
layer of ice. Mino stood beside Hooley, staring at the tarp-covered bodies
for a moment, then said precisely what Hooley thought he would say.

"Don't you think we ought to do something?" Hooley asked. Mino gave
Hooley a curiosity-filled stare, then shrugged and returned to the red tent,
leaving Hooley to stomp around and swear at his back. But at noon the
next day, Hooley was surprised to find that the carpenter had somehow
found the time to build six coffins, which he neatly stacked next to
Hooley's tent.

Hooley's fury rose like a hot wind when he discovered the freshly constructed burial boxes left there with the clear implication that he would

be responsible for the familys' internment. But there was no one handy on whom to vent his wrath. Margot and the girls were sequestered in the red tent. The cowboys were constantly drunk or recovering from being drunk, and Mino now avoided Hooley's notice. Hank and Ina Moon remained inside their store, warm by their stove and counting their profits, Hooley reckoned. He had to take the problem to Nichols.

"Your family's lying out there in the open," Hooley said when he found Nichols in his usual posture, reading Scripture and muttering. "Who's going to see to the burying?"

"You mean they're not belowground?" Nichols asked, surprised. "I thought they were buried days ago."

"By who?" Hooley asked. Nichols stared incredulously at him. "There's a lot of work there," Hooley went on. "Somebody's got to do the goddamn work, or to pay for it to be done."

The man's watery eyes blinked rapidly, and he looked down at the Bible on his lap as if it might contain money. "I'm not in funds," he said.

"We've got a considerable amount tied up in you people," Hooley said, hating himself for putting the whole matter on a mercantile level. "Somebody needs to cover the expenses."

Nichols confessed that he had no particular talents, except for teaching, which paid little, and for preaching, which he now offered to do as soon as he was strong. Hooley considered the noise he could hear from the red tent and doubted that preaching would be wanted anytime soon. He thought about the settlers' belongings, but their horses had died or been mercifully shot by the cowboys. And Nichols' buckboard proved to be in such bad condition that Hooley relegated it to the woodpile.

"Go out there and bury them yourself." Hooley suggested. "There's coffins made."

"Oh, I'm too peekid to consider that," Nichols said. "I might not be strong enough for that till spring. But I'll say prayers, once you get them under the sod."

"Me?" Hooley shouted, filling the tent with his anger. "What makes you think *I'm* going to do one goddamn thing?" Nichols' pale blue eyes blinked at him. "That's *your* wife and children," Hooley shouted. "They're lying out there in the snow. If it wasn't so goddamn cold, the coyotes would be at them. It's a wonder they haven't been anyway."

"You're a God-fearing man," Nichols replied meekly. "A Good Samaritan. I'm sure you'll think of something. The good Lord will provide."

Hooley sat down on his stool. He wanted his cot. He wanted Nichols out of his tent. He wanted those people buried. From the red tent, music and gay laughter drifted over and made him angrier. He fetched another bottle and drank in the cold while Nichols lay back on his cot, his eyes closed, sleeping peacefully. Hooley couldn't stand it. He bundled up and went outside.

Miss Margot's Place was aglow with festive light. It was Thursday, Hooley realized. Tomorrow was Christmas Eve. The family had been dead a week tomorrow. No one cared. Why should he? In a sudden fit of rage, he flung the whiskey bottle against the icy boardwalk and stared at the shards of glass gleaming in the reflected light. "Are we a town or aren't we?" he demanded. "Are we civilized or not? What the hell kind of people are you?" He softened his voice and put his head into his frigid hands. "What the hell kind of person am I?"

The only response was Margot's laugh, high and lilting, suddenly filtering through the other noises. It reached Hooley's ear clearly, as if sent there deliberately, penetrating to touch him. It was derisive, mocking laughter, sarcastic and bitter. He stared at her tent, listened to the shouts of glee that came from inside, then heard it matched by a distant howl of a coyote somewhere off on the snowy prairie.

"Maybe the question is whether or not I'm in hell," he said aloud, and felt himself wanting to weep as he stumbled back into his tent and lay down on the bare plank floor beside the soughing Nichols, pulled the threadbare blanket over his head, and swore himself to sleep.

4

HOOLEY WAS MODERATELY surprised to see Heinz the next day. The tandem vehicles heaved up through the snowy prairie, laden with an extraordinary number of boxes and crates and whiskey barrels as well as sacks of grain for the animals. A gang of cowboys immediately appeared to off-load the cargo. The mules were covered with snow, and icicles hung from their coats and traces. The teamster's entire head was swathed in scarves and mufflers, with openings only for his sharp blue eyes and tobacco-stained mouth, which swore at the weather. Frozen juice crusted the front of the huge plaid coat that topped his heavy wardrobe.

Hooley embraced his delight in spotting the grisly freighter's lumbering form wheezing in the icy atmosphere and decided to put the problem of the Nichols family directly to him. Unfortunately, Heinz's mood was foul, for he soon discovered that Loretta was completely occupied with the ongoing celebration in Margot's tent.

"Takes the rag off the bush," Heinz complained as he stomped over and sat down next to Hooley in the café tent. It was empty for once, and the coffee was cold, but Hooley immediately stoked up the fire and put some fresh on to boil. "Come all the way out here through the snow and ice for a little Christmas cheer, and when I get here, I find the main source of that cheer too busy high-stepping with a bunch of ignert cowhands to give me a howdy-do."

"She's popular," Hooley admitted. In an attempt to soothe Heinz's anxiety, he added that all she did was *dance*, but the wagnoneer's manner remained gruff.

"My old lady threw me out," he confessed at last. "She says she's had enough of my manly ways and is going to take up the profession of nunnery."

"Nunnery?" Hooley asked.

"She's joining a goddamn convent," Heinz exploded. "Don't that beat anything you ever heard in the name of the blue-eyed Jesus?" Breath rushed out of him. "She said if I could take up with a heathen savage Indian, she reckoned she could take up with God. Waited till I got good and drunk, then sold our house and run off to San Antone. Left me a damn note!"

"I'm sorry," Hooley said. "But I thought—"

"Don't matter," Heinz said. "I been looking for it. Leastways I don't have to go find some old boy and try to shoot him for stealing her." He looked out into the swirling snow. "Don't reckon there's profit in shooting it out with God. Anyway, Loretta's got nicer titties."

"I reckon so," Hooley replied, not knowing exactly what else to say.

"Colder than a frog's ass in a dry well," Heinz concluded.

Hooley rose and fetched the coffee—lacing it liberally with whiskey to improve Heinz's disposition—and then he presented the wagoneer with the problem of what to do about the Nichols family.

"I'd advise burying them," Heinz said.

"But who's going to do it, and how much should it cost?"

"Well," Heinz remarked, warming to the drink, "costs between five and ten dollars hard money to get yourself took under in Jacksboro. The heavier freight comes if you want a marker or a choice spot in the boneyard."

"What if you don't have the money?"

"Well, if you ain't local and a member of a church or a Freemason, they have a 'pauper's funeral.' " Heinz said. "Collect a levy from the saloons. Sort of a tax. I reckon the mayor just pockets that. Anybody dies during the week and don't have the geddes, gets piled into this big old ditch out by the city dump and covered over with lime. Keeps the coyotes and hogs out of them, anyway."

Loretta suddenly appeared, and Heinz's mood brightened. Though she flashed a huge smile, Hooley could see weariness behind her dark eyes. She pretended to busy herself with preparations for the noonday meal, but Heinz's presence clearly electrified her. The effect was mutual, Hooley noticed, for the teamster's attention was becoming hard to hold. Hooley decided to act quickly. He asked Heinz if he was willing to help inter the frozen Nichols family.

"Not so you'd notice," Heinz said, finishing his coffee. "Breaking open graves out of frosty sod ain't on my list of things to do. Anyhow, digging in hard ground gets me down in my back in the best of weather. I need a good back to wrestle them mules. I need to see to them, get them under cover. Fact is, I need to get *me* under cover, too." He winked. Loretta giggled.

Heinz cut off a fresh chew and stuffed it into his mouth, then wrapped his scarves and rags around his face. "Thanks for the coffee, Hooley. It was spicy enough to be warming. I'm going to tend to my animals, then go get some shut-eye." He eyed the cold cellar, which was almost completely invisible under the snow. See you at the shindig tonight."

"What shindig?"

"The Christmas shindig." Heinz put a narrow eye on Hooley. "It's Christmas Eve, Hooley, or ain't you noticed? Margot and me is burying the hatchet." He squinted in thought. "Probably that stove done it. She invited me special to come, though I'd allow it was as much to get them goods as it was to see my handsome face."

"She invited *you?*" Hooley couldn't accept it.

"You ought to get the Christmas spirit, Hooley," Heinz said. "You're sober-sided as any undertaker I ever run up on. Maybe you *should* see to them folks' burying—can't bring you down any lower than you already are."

Christmas had never meant much to Hooley, not even when he was a child. Bertha Hooley always used it as an excuse to entertain her society friends more than anything else. She claimed not to believe in giving presents. Actually, except for the perfunctory gifts exchanged early in his marriage, he never had had a genuine present and always felt vaguely left out of the festive celebrations in St. Louis. Now, it appeared that Margot was giving him a dose of the same thing.

"Margot's feeling generous, I reckon," Heinz continued. "Free food and half-price foot-tangler, and the girls are all on for special." He squinted at Hooley through the narrow eye-slits in his garb. "I figured it wasn't your idea," he said bitterly. "I've noticed how sour you've been lately." He then gave Loretta a long, telling look, which she returned with a blushing grin, and the wagoneer crunched out of the tent and off across the snowy compound.

"That," Hooley said sourly to the ever-smiling Loretta, "does indeed take the rag off the bush." Her only reply was another giggle. Hooley fell into a sulk.

The cowboys began drifting into the café tent for their noon meal, several asking Hooley whether he would be interested in trying to man the bathhouse pump if they would go down and bust through the sheet ice. They received a surly shake of the tentmaker's head. Several seemed to find this funny, but Hooley was utterly deadened to their youthful laughter and gibes. The problem of the Nichols family remained in his mind, but a deeper wound began to hemorrhage painfully. Margot had not only failed to ask him to join her party, she hadn't even bothered to notify him of it. He was hurt. This was an insult, a clear sign that she was divorcing herself from him, separating herself entirely as both partner and person.

He wanted to be alone, to think things out. But where to go? He couldn't stomach the thought of returning to his tent and Nichols' morose presence, and the whiskey shed—his usual alternative—looked cold, dark, and lonely. He glanced at Hank's store, thought of going over to warm himself by his stove, but Ina Moon's influence on the former cowboy had made his simple company almost unbearable. He had turned smug and self-righteous, questioning Hooley's every word. He had also recently forbidden smoking in his store. He said he was afraid of fire, but Hooley saw Ina Moon's hand at work. Hank was now a new man, a woman's man, Hooley thought sourly. All the former cowpuncher wanted to discuss was the need for more civilizing influences in the community, which, Hank seemed to believe, was Hooley's responsibility and which, Hooley suspected, was Ina Moon's idea.

There literally was nowhere to go, Hooley realized. He belonged nowhere. After all this time, he was still trapped in the wilderness, surrounded by life, perhaps, but totally alone. He stepped out into the snow. Over the jocular comments of the feasting cowboys, he heard a lively rill coming from Mino's concertina. Suddenly, he realized the boys in the café tent were watching him, so he started walking. He spied Margot emerging from the red canvas structure. She was bundled in the bearskin coat and heading for the privy.

Without thinking, he stepped lively to catch up, finally attracting her attention with the noise of his footfalls in the brittle ice. He wasn't sure what he wanted to say, what he wanted her to say. He only felt the need to talk to her, to look at her, to confirm that the doubts and emptiness he felt growing inside him were genuine. When she heard him approaching, she stopped and turned, as if surprised to find him anywhere in the same world as she.

"Why, hello, Hooley," she said, tugging the hood of the furry coat more closely around her face. "Have you been hiding out again?"

Her manner was so formal, so distant, Hooley was instantly validated in his assessment of her attitude toward him. "Uh, how's business?"

"A lot you care," she said, turning from him and making her way up the boardwalk, taking small steps on the slippery footing. "Don't you worry, Hooley," she said without turning around, "I'm keeping close records. We're doing real well. I'll bring over the cash on Sunday so we can count it." She smiled coyly. "It may take all day. How's that preacher-man, Nichols?"

"He's . . . Now, see here, Margot," he said, hurrying to catch up. "We have a problem."

She kept her pace. "Nonsense," she said. "No one can have a problem on Christmas Eve. Oh, by the way." She reached the door flap of the woman's privy, then turned and gave him a bright smile. "Merry Christmas, Hooley." His heartbeat quickened in anticipation of her adding a personal invitation to join the party, but she said no more, just waited for him to return the greeting, which he neglected to do. Then she scowled and stepped inside.

He wanted to wait for her, but doing so made him feel foolish. And he wasn't sure what he would say. It was too late to wish her a happy holiday, too late to say anything that might break the ice surrounding her heart. He was utterly annoyed with himself. He was damned if he was going to beg—or even hint that he wanted—to be included in the evening's festivities. But he wished he had taken a page from Heinz's book and thought to order something special for her. That, he thought, might make her soften, make her feel guilty enough to—to what? To ask him to the party? He didn't want to go. He *wouldn't* go. He'd rather freeze to death, he told himself, than go into that tent and partake in the common revelry from which he was so deliberately excluded.

Suddenly afraid that she would come out and invite him, he hurried back to his tent. When he entered, he found Nichols sitting on the side of the cot, his head in his hands, weeping.

"This is a holy night," Nichols said sadly. "The holiest night there is."

"It's a night like any other," Hooley replied sharply.

"I just can't stand the thought that my poor family—may the Lord keep them—are still aboveground on this holy night."

"Well, why don't you do something about it," he snapped. "Seems a

man ought to take charge of his own responsibility," he said with a twinge
of guilt that made him wince.

"I'm too poorly to bury them," Nichols whined in sobbing gulps. "And
there's no one to help me." He raised his sorrowful face to Hooley. "You'll
help me. Won't you?" he pleaded. "You're a Good Samaritan. A Christian
soul, blasphemer though you are. A kindred spirit." He raised his voice
and reached for his Bible. "We're both stranded here in this wasteland.
You clearly have nothing to do with that nest of vipers across the way.
You are a good man."

"I'm a son of a bitch," Hooley growled, delighted to allow his anger to
replace the depression that had settled over him like a low-grade fever.
"And a damn fool for not chucking you out into the snow. Now, shut the
hell up."

Nichols sobbed for a while, then finally went to sleep, snoring in a
rasping, distracting manner. Hooley was disappointed. He wanted Nichols
to argue, perhaps to even try to fight him—anything to provide an outlet
for the churning sea of emotions in his gut. But there was nothing save
his rough breathing. Hooley sat on his stool and stared at Nichols until
his back began plaguing him, then lay down and stared at the top of the
tent while the afternoon faded away. He wasn't tired, wasn't sleepy. He
was confused and irritated. As always, Margot was the center of his discomfort.

If he wound up having to bury those people, he thought, then he ought
to be paid. If Mino or anyone else did it, they ought to be paid as well.
At the least, Mino should be reimbursed for building the coffins. If this
was a bona fide town, he reasoned, there would be public funds. He
thought of the money sacks beneath the cot. They were bulging, and he
speculated that the weeklong debauch in the red tent might well make
them richer. But those were not public funds. That was *her* money. *Their*
money. It was no more right for them to pay for the family's interment
than it was for Hooley to do the job all by himself. It wasn't the money.
It was the principle.

Still, he considered just going ahead and doing it on his own, then
noting the charge for his labor in the ledger, next to Margot's neat hand
recordings of "Services Rendered." But that would only start an argument,
he thought. And he had no intention of arguing with Margot Phillips ever
again.

5

HOURS SLIPPED BY, and the fire in his small stove died. Cold seeped into the tent and invaded Hooley's bones. He lay on his back, wide-awake, growing angrier and angrier, and listening to Nichols' snoring. Throughout, celebratory noises from Margot's tent assaulted his ears. They had been building to a climax, and now he heard Christmas carols along with the usual dance music and ballads. The exclusion he felt soured, turned rancid, and finally forced him to rouse himself. Snow was falling again, heavy wet flakes drifting down on a frigid windless night, filling in footprints and trails. He spied cowboys slipping and sliding around on personal errands. There were no fights or loud shouts. The men leaned on one another, cursing the uncertain footing, laughing when they fell.

Hank's store and the hotel tent were dark. Mino's tent looked abandoned and neglected under a mound of snow. Hooley pulled on his shoes, then went over to the café tent, which was deserted. He ought to eat something, he thought, but his stomach was, for the first time in months, in total, painful revolt. He picked up the coffeepot, but it was dead cold, the contents frozen. The fire was out. The music-laced merriment from Miss Margot's Place seemed to grow in volume as he sat there feeling lonely, excluded, and more and more bitter.

Whoops from the tent attracted his attention again, and he glared across at the bright light from Margot's. The time had come to take a stand on the matter of the Nichols dead. He was under no illusions: Forcing money out of people could be chancy—particularly when that money was earmarked for a different expenditure than they were used to—and it could cause them to become belligerent, especially if they were drunk. He briefly considered waiting until morning, but then decided that if a drunk cowboy was hard to handle, a hungover cowboy would be even harder.

He had best assume some formal authority, he decided. He stomped back to his tent. Nichols never stirred while Hooley strapped on the pistol belt and holsters, checking the load in the remaining Peacemaker. He put on a collar and cravat, then donned his cord coat and his hat. With a single deep breath, he left Nichols still snoring on his cot and made his way out into the white Christmas night. His purpose was resolved, and he slogged ahead, determined to see the business of the night through.

When he reached the open door of the red tent, he hesitated. Raw heat from inside had melted ice and snow in a wide semicircle made muddy with vomit and tobacco juice. With one deep breath of frosty air, he pulled back the flap and saw that every resident of the town, save those lying outside in the snow, was crowded into the parlor. Even Ina Moon was visible off to one side, surrounded by a knot of drunken cowboys. The girl's almond eyes were crinkled in mirth, her mouth wide with laughter. The music, accompanied by loud unharmonious singing, was deafening, and the stomping of heavy boots pounded out a frenetic rhythm. Hands clapped and lungs shouted. A powerful, fetid odor permeated the room under a fog of tobacco smoke.

In spite of the uncomfortable crowding and heat, everyone was having a high time. The whores were all dressed up, rather than nearly naked as they usually were at this hour of the night, and were swinging in rhythm to the music, many of them sporting sprigs of mistletoe and cedar in their hair. Loretta had red ribbons tied into her black braids. Heinz leaned drunkenly on the bar, his eyes flat and glazed with whiskey and longing. Mino sat on his stool with his squeezebox, and two cowboys plucked guitars while another beat out a rhythm on a flat rawhide drum.

Margot was standing in the back, her arms around two large men. She had on a bright scarlet dress that accentuated the redness of her hair. Curled silver ribbons shimmered in her high coif, and her eyes danced as she laughed and joked with the boys. She glanced his way when he entered, but kept her expression intact. He pushed through the crowd to the bar and climbed on top of its flat surface. As soon as there was a break in the music, he stamped his feet and held up his hands for attention. A sensation of sincere importance moved him to confidence.

Attracted by the possibility of some new entertainment, everyone quieted down immediately and turned their eyes toward the skinny man. Several cried out their delight and offered to buy him a drink, and Hooley was momentarily distracted. Then he remembered that they were drunk, and that he had come on a mission. "I hate to interrupt your fun," he announced, "but we have to make some hard decisions, and we have to make them now."

Margot pushed her way through the crowd, green eyes flashing over a disapproving frown. "Hooley!" she yelled through a false laugh. "Step down this instant! You're in Loretta's way. Somebody might want to buy a drink." A chorus of agreement followed her words.

He ignored her and raised his hands for quiet. "We have a situation," he said. "A threat to common health and a disgrace to common decency."

"What the hell would you know about decency?" a very drunk Tidmore demanded. Everyone laughed. "All you been doing is sitting in your tent with that preacher-fellow."

"Pulling each other's peckers, likely," Jake yelled. He also was weaving, and his eyes were flat with drunkenness. "Probably wishing they would grow a mite," he hooted, and received a chorus of laughs.

Hooley shot Jake a narrow, disappointed look. "I'll thank you to watch your language," Hooley said. "There's women present."

The cowboy's eyes widened and his mouth opened. "I thought this here was a whorehouse!" he declared. "If there's any women present who ain't whores yet, I'd like them to declare a price so we can get down to it."

"My wife is no whore!" Hank insisted, a husky bravado invading his voice. Hooley saw that Pledge or no, the young cowboy-turned-storekeep had been drinking.

Hooley sighed. Jake was drunk, and enjoying the attention. "Oh, I beg pardon!" he yelled at Hank. "But that lady's a *wife*, not a whore!"

"Well," Margot rejoined, "all the women here have *been* wives, one time or another. And in my experience, there's not a lot of difference."

Laughter was general, and Jake, extracted from the trouble he inadvertently started, downed a drink, then lost his footing and fell back into the arms of his pards, who pulled him away off to one side, slapping his back and congratulating him on his wit.

Hooley stubbornly stuck to his purpose. "The point is that we've got some dead folks lying out there in the weather," he continued. "We need to bury them."

"So, get after it, Hooley," Tidmore yelled. "Nobody stopping you."

"But be quiet about it. It," Underwood yelled. "We're having some fun in here."

"I don't see what all the hoorahing is over, Hooley." Plunk stepped forward, Clara hanging on his arm. "If folks need burying, somebody'll bury them."

"Who?" Hooley asked. "And who's going to pay for it?"

"Leave this alone, Hooley," he heard Margot hiss. "Have a drink."

"We have to make sure that whoever provides for the funeral is compensated."

"By who?" Hank asked, narrowing his eyes and putting his hands on his hips. "Who's going to do all this 'compensating'? I sure as hell, uh, heck ain't."

"We have to raise a levy. A tax," Hooley continued. "That's the way things are done. Heinz says so." He looked down at the freighter, who scowled and averted his gaze.

"Make way, boys," Heinz announced. "Got to go squeeze the lizard." When he reached the door, he turned. "This ain't none of my beeswax, Hooley. Don't go dragging me into it."

Hooley shook his head in disgust. "We all have to share," he said. "Pay our fair share, as we now have civic expenses that have to be met." He wasn't sure if anyone was listening, since a hubbub of conversation had begun to swell and below him Loretta was working between and around his planted feet, pouring whiskey. He spied a bucket, grabbed it, then inverted it on the bar and stood on it for greater height. His hat's brim brushed against the canvas ceiling.

Hank got up on a stool so he could see Hooley over the bobbing, mumbling heads. "Get down, Hooley," he yelled. "I ain't paying no durned taxes. I'm a merchant!"

"What if you die?" Hooley asked, trying to reason with him.

"Then bury me," the storekeeper replied. "People die, they get buried, I reckon."

"Well, those people died, and nobody's doing one thing about it," Hooley yelled back. "So I'm here to ask if we're going to bury them or not." He was pretty sure that almost no one was paying any attention to the exchange, but he needed someone to join him in his plea, and Hank was probably his best hope.

"If they die, they'll get buried," Hank yelled back, "but there's not going to be no taxes, Hooley." He climbed down and melted back into the crowd. Exasperation gripped the tentmaker. He suddenly wanted Hank's support desperately, realized that he had been counting on it. "You all can't just expect me to bury people. That's not my job."

"Then hire it done!" someone yelled, though Hooley couldn't tell who.

"But if nobody pays for it, it won't *get* done!" he pleaded, his voice rising. "People will just lay out there till they rot, you stupid sons of bitches!" His timing was off. The remark filled a sudden gap in the room's noise. Everyone stopped and looked at him again. Hank's face reappeared, right in front of him now. The storekeeper's eyes were filled with a mixture of hurt and anger.

"Who you calling a son of a bitch?" he demanded. "I done warned you about that, Hooley. You calling me out?"

"No—," Hooley started. He could see the raw anger in Hank's whiskey-reddened eyes. He had become unused to heavy drinking, Hooley thought.

"You mean to tell me if I was dead you wouldn't bury me, Hooley?" Underwood demanded. "That's a hell of a note. Note. I thought we was friends. Friends." There was a swelling murmur of angry assent. "I'd sure as hell bury *you* if *you* was dead," he went on. "Least I would till you told me you wouldn't bury Hank. Hank. *And* called him a stupid son of a bitch."

"I wasn't talking about Hank—"

"So far as I'm concerned," Underwood shouted, his face red and angry, "you can just by God bury yourself if you die, Hooley. Hooley. See if anybody here gives a tin shit. Shit." The crowd cheered and applauded the justice of the dithering cowboy's statement. He turned and took an absurd bow and nearly fell over.

"That's not the goddamn point," Hooley shouted. "I'd probably bury *you* if you died." He attempted to soften his tone, but he felt his voice rising along with his anger. "If you don't quit making threats, that's likely to happen pretty damn quick, too."

"Says who? Who?" Underwood shouted back. "You think you're man enough to do it!"

"Hooley can't make up his mind who he's calling out," Hank shouted. "Let's all go outside and settle this!"

"You can't see shit outside," offered Plunk, who had just come in from outside. "Snowing like hell out there. I say let's all choose up sides and go to bed. I'm taking Lucille here with me. I done paid for the whole night!"

"You have not, you son of a bitch," Tidmore yelled. "Ain't nobody taking Lucille anywhere for the whole night but me!"

"Who the hell's Lucille?" Hooley asked. He was confused.

"That's Lora Lynn," Margot explained from her position below his right knee. Hooley saw that she was wearing a tired expression on her face, as if she was putting up with him, but not for much longer. "She didn't like 'Lora Lynn,' so she changed her name to Lucille." Hooley saw that Lora Lynn/Lucille had also tried to dye her hair from dusty brown to yellow blonde. The result was an unappealing shade of light green. "You're causing a ruckus," Margot said. "Get down and shut up before things blow up."

"It's half price on account of Christmas, and I done paid the freight," Plunk insisted.

"Tonight's my night with Lucille, too," Tidmore protested. And a chorus of other voices joined him as several of the cowboys announced that they had had planned—and paid for—an evening's pleasure in Lora Lynn's—or Lucille's—arms.

"Hooley, why are you doing this?" Margot demanded. "You're spoiling things, and we're both going to regret it." He looked down and saw nervous uncertainty. She had obviously accepted money from more than one man for the night's rights to Lora Lynn/Lucille.

While the argument escalated, Hooley pulled out a canvas bandanna and mopped his face. Margot was right, as usual. He had severely miscalculated. Rather than being filled with generous spirits, the men were filled with alcoholic spirits, and their mood was far from civil. It had been hovering between raucous and nasty, and Hooley's interruption of the festivities had swayed the balance. The mood inside the tent was turning ugly.

"Can we stick to the point?" Hooley shouted, trying to sound determined and to bring the matter to some kind of conclusion. He now realized that this had been a terrible mistake, and he wished he could just leave. But he didn't see how. If he could collect even a few dollars, he told himself, he'd have saved face. He would go out and bury the whole damn bunch right now and be done with it.

"What *is* the point?" Margo asked ironically. "You always think there has to be a point, don't you, Hooley?" Then she shouted over the growing arguments, "*I* think the *point* is that we all need to have a few more drinks. It's after midnight, which means it's Christmas official. I'm cutting the half-price rate in half again for anybody who drinks steadily till daybreak and can still stand up. Merry Christmas, everybody!"

A raucous cheer greeted her announcement, temporarily distracting everyone from arguments over the girls. Margot gave Hooley a look so cold that it made the outside temperature seem warm by comparison. "Get the hell out of here, Hooley," she hissed at him.

"No," he shouted, turning her disapproving frown into a warning scowl. Her teeth were exposed and seemed almost pointed; he had a sudden vision of her pulling him down and ripping him apart with them. Suddenly, he was jostled from below as the men pressed in close for their first round of cut-rate beverages. Loretta was setting up a row of fresh bottles and glasses on the bar next to his bucket and was elbowing him lightly to force him to move out of the way.

"We have to decide this thing right now," he insisted in his loudest voice. "Some things have to be done for the good of everyone."

"Like what?" Tidmore asked, blinking, as if he had just now noticed Hooley standing on the bar.

"Like burying the dead, you stupid idiot," Hooley snapped.

"For a skinny old fart, you're mighty free with your insults," Tidmore rejoined.

"You still going on about that?" Hank asked, taking a drink. "Thought we settled that."

"I thought you were on a Temperance Pledge."

"Hell, Hooley." Hank laughed. "It's Christmas."

Hooley spotted Ina Moon standing way too close to a cowboy named Red, and noticed that the storekeeper was keeping a wary eye on them. "I don't see what the problem is," Hank went on. "No reason for you and me to fall out over it. Like I said: Man dies. Man gets buried."

"By who?" Hooley asked.

"Why, by anybody who's handy," Plunk put in as he shouldered up for a fresh drink. "Who buried them folks died here last week?"

"They're *not* buried! Not yet," Hooley yelled. "That's the point, you stupid—"

"They got coffins," Tidmore interrupted. "I seen Mino making them. Think you could manage to go out yonder first thaw we have and dig a hole or two?"

Hooley wiped his face again. He was dripping sweat. The problem now seemed overwhelming. "I've never seen so many stupid idiots in one place in my whole life."

"No shit, Gil Hooley," he heard. He spun around and nearly lost his balance before he spied Mino drawing a beer from a keg, then holding it up to toast him with a huge smile.

"Listen to me, all of you!" he yelled, once more silencing the hubbub. "Mino built those coffins for those folks who died. Worked right out in the cold. But nobody's buried them. He needs to be paid for that, right, Mino?" he yelled, but when he looked down, Mino was looking stupidly into Gertie's face. She was stroking his wiry, sweaty hair and talking to him, though Hooley couldn't hear her words. He suddenly had the sensation that he had somehow stumbled into a madhouse.

Jake stepped up, scratching his chin. "I think I get what you're talking about," he said.

Hooley breathed out a long sigh, finding new inspiration in the cowboy's suddenly discovered intelligence. "So, the question is who's going to pay me and Mino here for our goods? To say nothing of compensating the grave diggers, whoever they turn out to be?" He thought he saw several nods, and seized the gesture as a sign to press hard. "Goddamn it! We've got to raise a tax or they'll just lay out there till the coyotes get them or they rot!"

"They're not likely to rot in this weather," Plunk said.

"*Eventually,* they'll rot. And there's not a decent man among you who'd contribute to a Christian burial for them. Not even on Christmas Eve!"

Suddenly, the crowd became pensive. The cowboys withdrew their pawing hands from the whores, and everyone formed a semicircle around Hooley's feet.

"Well," Underwood piped up. "They got a wagon. Wagon. They got horses."

"Yeah," Plunk said. "You take that stuff and divvy up with Mino here. Whatever's inside the wagon goes to them as digs the holes when the weather improves."

"That's just fine," Hooley said sarcastically. "The wagon's eat up with woodworms, and the horses are dead. Besides, Nichols is still alive. That's his stuff."

"Well, let him tend to the cost then," Plunk said brightly. "Problem solved!"

"He doesn't have a thing," Hooley shouted, gaining momentum. "Everything he owns wouldn't pay for even one of the coffins. What's going to happen when somebody else dies? If we're going to be a town"—he shot a look at Hank—"a *civilized* town, we need a plan. Anybody might die at any time, and we'll have the same problem all over again."

"Like who?" Jake demanded. "If I didn't know better, Hooley, I'd think you was thinking of back-shooting somebody again. You seem mighty anxious to bury somebody."

"I never back-shot anybody!" Hooley shouted. He felt a dam burst and anger beginning to flow. "If I want to shoot you, I'll shoot you right through the eye."

"Yeah!?" Jake shouted at him. "Well, let's just step outside right now and give her a try!" He stepped forward, shouldering off a few hands that reached to restrain him.

"Oh hell," Hooley swore. He was off the point again. He slapped his leg in frustration. But he forgot he was wearing the pistol belt, and his palm found itself resting on the gun butt.

Jake instantly slid into a crouch and tried to jerk a pistol from his own belt. "Goddamn, goddamn!" he shouted. "Hooley's trying to shoot me! Just like he done Chatsworth." His gun hung up in the rigging, and he spun around, tugging at it and shouting.

"Jake," Hooley said in a tired voice. "I'm not trying to shoot anybody." All his anger and energy were gone. All he wanted was to have a drink, maybe smoke his pipe, then go back to his tent and sleep. He looked down at Margot and realized the impossibility of this. Nichols was in his tent, in his bed, and she wasn't. She was making money, ignoring him, leaving him to stand here and feel like a bigger fool than she always told him he was.

Jake continued to dance around, trying to free his six-shooter from the hammer-thong. "Somebody help me!" he squawked. "Hooley's gone loco! Trying to shoot me!"

"Jake," Hooley said calmly. "I am not trying to shoot you. I don't want to shoot anybody."

The slight, blond cowboy wouldn't hear it. He twisted around twice, caught his spurs on his trouser legs, and tripped. When his hips hit the planked floor, his gun went off in the holster.

Everything in the room froze as the deafening sound of the blast exploded. The acrid odor of gunpowder and fresh blood filled the room. Jake sat cross-legged, staring at the widening red stain forming on the planks beneath him.

"Son of a bitch," he said. "Hooley's kilt me." He gave Hooley a long, plaintive look, then slumped over.

REGULATOR V

⸻✦⸻

"I'M TELLING YOU," Eubanks wheezed, "it ain't going to be easy." His voice was raspy. He'd developed a deep, gagging cough that racked his body and bent him double, helplessly out of breath. Seized with another fit, he turned away from the campfire and hacked deeply, hocking up bloody phlegm and spitting into the icy darkness. He stumbled with exertion, nearly fell before he regained his balance and staggered around with an exaggerated limp. His bullet wound from the train robbery turned out to be mild, but he made the most of his discomfort.

Now, he stood swaying in front of Jefferson Tay, his face sheathed in sweat, his eyes glowing like hot coals in the reflected firelight. Tay could tell the man was in much worse shape than he had been that morning when he set out across the Prairie Dog Town Fork of the Red River. The shallow but swift waterway was frozen over under a thick blanket of snow, but in the center of the river, the ice was thin. Eubanks had been no more than forty yards from the snow-streaked Texas bank when it broke, sousing him and his Welsh mare. His curses lit up the riverbed as he made his way to the opposite side, climbed atop his shivering pony, and ridden off. He had had better luck on his return trip. The cold had deepened, and the ice held, but he was obviously chilled through.

Sending Eubanks across the half-frozen river in a blinding snowstorm to scout the fabled town had not been charitable, Tay decided as he watched the man's frozen clothing thawing and dripping by the warming fire, but there had been no alternative. He wasn't about to go blundering into some town, however small, without good intelligence, and he couldn't trust Manypenny or Blasingame to come back with reliable information. Eubanks was too cowardly to do anything foolish. But there was no hyperbole in these symptoms, Tay thought. It was beyond an ague. It was pneumonia.

"There must be fifty hard licks down there," Eubanks wheezed between gulps of air, then removed his dented derby and wiped a frozen sleeve over his head. "Most heeled to the jaw."

"By which, I presume you mean they're well armed," Tay responded, instantly deciding that planning a quick, head-on strike was out of the question.

Eubanks nodded, sneezed, removed a filthy bandanna, and wiped his nose and mouth. "Knives, guns. Cowboys, from the look of them. One at a time, they probably ain't much account. But all together . . . well, there's a bunch. And drunker than coots."

Tay painfully shifted his position. He was reclining on what had once been a rather expensive settee covered in blue brocade fabric. Now, it more closely resembled a broken-legged bench, dragged up to the muddy circumference of a bonfire and plunked down in the slush.

"They'll be gone by Sunday." The comment came from the faux Indian, who had by default become the company's most recent addition. The man was maintaining his implied identity as a savage and continued to wear a bashed-in beaver hat over thick braids. The disguise in no way deceived Tay. He addressed him as "Mr. Charles," as he regarded "Cherokee Charlie" as one of the most absurd sobriquets he had ever heard. "They have to go back to work," he continued. "They'll be gone in a day or so."

"Well, if they're still there, they ain't going to rabbit when they see a hard-luck bunch like us," Eubanks pointed out, and took a deep breath to clear his tortured lungs.

"What about women?" Blasingame asked. "You see any women?"

Tay looked past Eubanks' frozen form toward Blasingame's face. Brightly lit in the glow of the firelight, the blond outlaw's countenance appeared unnaturally red, as if washed with blood. He was smiling, but there was no humor, only madness. At his feet was the bulging carpetbag, now dyed completely black with the dried gore from its horrific contents. Lately, he had not allowed the grisly container to leave his side.

"They was there." Eubanks nodded. "I didn't see them, but I could hear them inside this big old red tent. Whole damned town's made of tents. Goddamnedest thing you ever did see. Like he said"—he gestured to Cherokee Charlie—"they got them a whorehouse and saloon, I reckon."

"You reckon?" Manypenny asked. The small man squatted on a blanket next to Tay. His tiny dark eyes never left the stream of sparks lifting from the fire into the snowy atmosphere. "It'd been me, I'd of gone inside, found some decent grub."

"They all know each other," Eubanks said. "I only got in close because of the storm. Snowing like a son of a bitch! Had to hobble that damn midget horse and come in on foot. Would of stole one, but that was against *orders*," he added with sarcasm, and tried to look to Tay for confirmation, but another fit of coughing seized him. He sat down hard by the fire, retching and gasping for breath. Sweat covered his face and mucus drained from his nose. "I would of got something to eat, but they wanted hard money even for coffee. Had them a savage Indian running the cook-shack. Now, *she* was a woman," he added with a glance at Blasingame. "She's a touch hefty. Let me thaw out some by the fire, though."

"Indian woman?" Cherokee Charlie asked, suddenly distressed. Tay looked at him. The man moved closer to the fire, there was a worried look on his face now. "Name of Loretta? Nice titties?"

"I didn't exactly shake and howdy with her," Eubanks said, then hocked and spat again. "And I didn't see no damn titties. I had me a look-see at the whole shebang, then come on back. Hell, I was froze clear through." He cleared his throat and swallowed another cough. "Damn teeth is ground down from clicking on theirselves." He straightened. "Got me a chilblain," he said, hugging himself. "Shaking worse than a leaf in a cyclone." He batted his arms around his body. "We got anything to eat?"

"Find the Negro," Tay said. "He's watching the river. He'll give you something to eat." He raised his eyes and considered the ragged, half-frozen, and sick man. "You've done yeoman work today, Mr. Eubanks," he said. "I will consider your intelligence." He smiled at the pun.

"I don't know what 'yo-man' is," Eubanks said. "Hell, half the time I don't have the first notion what you're talking about." He then stumbled off through the snow toward the charred remains of a crude cabin that had, up until the afternoon before, been Dutchman's Ferry, a sparse outpost perched on the Oklahoma Territory bank of the river. The cabin and the flatboat ferry it supported were owned by a German proprietor and his two sons, who were presently dangling together from a branch of a sturdy elm, their toes scraping the surface of skim ice on the water beneath them, their greasy scalps residing in Blasingame's bloody bag.

The hangings had not been Tay's idea. In fact, he was opposed to the very principle, believing the practice should be reserved for cowards and traitors. But the executions had been accomplished before he was on hand. He had ordered Blasingame to assault the cabin, subdue the occupants, and secure fresh mounts—apart from a pair of shaggy mules, none had been present. By the time Tay arrived, ignominiously riding in a battered Dorset buggy drawn by an ancient, scrawny mule, the men were already scalped and hanged and the buildings, as well as any provisions they might have offered, were in flames. It irked Tay enough to be removed from the big bay stallion he had captured from the train—a mount he was compelled to turn over to Blasingame—but he was further annoyed by having to turn over the company's field operations to the same blond outlaw, who, Tay had concluded, had almost entirely lost touch with reason.

Tay had swallowed his anger when he discovered the cabin in flames and resigned himself that this was just one more in a perpetual series of missteps. Had the Negro not found a hog wandering around behind the flaming cabin, they might be starving as well.

Following the debacle with the train robbery in Kansas, the company's flight south across Oklahoma Territory had been a virtual catalogue of disasters. Over the past several weeks, he sent Eubanks or Manypenny into the occasional settlement to trade the plunder—all of which turned out to be virtually worthless—they stole off the dead rail passengers. Thus, he learned that the fireman Eubanks shot during the robbery had merely played dead, then sent up an alarm as soon as the outlaws rode off. Wanted posters instantly appeared on fence posts and tree trunks, offering the estimable sum of five thousand dollars for Tay's capture—dead or alive. This meant that bands of armed vigilantes and bounty men would be roaming the Kansas countryside in search of the outlaw commander. They had no sooner crossed the line out of Kansas, and eliminated the possibility of apprehension by any pursuing lawmen, than a fierce snowstorm blasted in suddenly from the northwest, slowing their progress and causing them to become lost in the sparsely settled wilderness, as the sleet and snow obscured even the clearly marked trails. Riding for so long without rest sapped their already shallow reserves of strength. Tay's leg flared up with a renewal of agony. The limb swelled to nearly twice its normal size and turned ominously purple, and for the first time since he had been old enough to know what a horse was, Tay was unable to sit a saddle. The Negro used a hot knife to lance the festering wound, but Tay was terrified that the leg would mortify and require amputation if he didn't get to a proper doctor.

The Negro, who gave his name as "Metritous Jones," thus proved to be more than worth his own life, something Tay insisted on sparing, over Eubanks' vociferous objections. He kept Tay's leg packed with poultices concocted from roots and leaves, gunpowder and mud. That eased the pain, but Tay had no idea if the former porter's ministrations were healing or slowly poisoning him. Until that was determined, he continued to extend the Negro's life.

The morning Tay discovered that his leg would keep him from the saddle, Jones slipped off, and Tay was sure he was gone for good. But in a few hours the Negro returned with the buggy and mule. When they stopped, he proved to be a tireless guard of their camp, often standing watch all night without relief and, Tay ensured, without a weapon. Tay hated to put so much faith in a creature he truly regarded as more chattel than comrade, but necessity forced the convention. Until he more cogently defined Jones's role, he refused to call him by his name.

Tay reached down for a tin cup of chicory, all they had that resembled coffee, and about the only thing they had left by way of supplies. Raiding a homestead was beyond their present abilities. What strength they had, Tay wanted conserved, and besides, he reasoned that striking small settlements would attract the attention of the local constabulary. The robbery of Cherokee Charlie's fabulous tent-town had to be their priority.

The fake Indian's tale was fantastic, but Tay decided that it made some perverse sense. The man claimed outlaw credentials by asserting that he had tried to steal bags of cash a saloonkeeper kept hidden in his personal quarters, but he had been deceived.

"They fooled me good," Cherokee Charlie insisted. "All I got away with was nails and trash. You don't want to sell this man short. He's sneaky." He shook his head. "All I got away with was the bay, and that was pure luck."

The story was just unbelievable enough to be credible. If it was true, the tent-city would provide Tay with what he needed to reach Mexico in safety and comfort. His dream of retirement had become his primary goal. Nothing could distract him from that purpose.

The presence of women presented a problem, though. Blasingame was already speaking of a "banquet of blood." Tay had no intention of permitting him to go berserk. A general massacre would not be easily kept quiet. Every community in Texas would form a *posse comitatus* to hunt them down if people heard they'd butchered women, even whores. He also knew better than to inspire the famous police force of the Texas Rangers with anything resembling a righteousness of purpose. He glanced at Blasingame, who was whetting his knife on the sole of his boot. Tay had wearied of the large blond maniac's snide insubordination. He planned to kill him as soon as the opportunity presented itself. He looked forward to the surprise in Blasingame's eyes when he realized that Tay was more formidable than he estimated. He heard Eubanks' hacking cough in the dark distance. Eventually, he knew, he would have to kill them all.

He flexed his leg and grimaced at the lingering pain and surrounding chill and focused on the problem immediately at hand. "You previously said there were only the three men there," he said to Cherokee Charlie as if Eubanks' report had just registered in his mind. "You were lying."

"From Sunday on," Cherokee Charlie explained patiently, "there's only two men: a storekeeper, and that bartender. He's not much of a man," he said, casting a wary eye on Blasingame, who tended to grumble whenever the phony Indian spoke. "He's too skinny."

"That's two men," Tay said.

"Oh, I hear there's this carpenter. Immigrant. But he's a half-wit. Can't talk."

Tay had been trying to plumb the depths of Cherokee Charlie's potential for patented lying since the night he appeared in the light of the burning train. He wondered what scheme lay behind his plastic smile.

"I think we can handle two men and an idiot," Blasingame said.

Tay considered the situation. Discounting himself, they had only two effectives and Cherokee Charlie. And the Negro. But he had no intention of relying on either of those two. Except for the knife with the uniquely carved naked-leg handle, he kept all arms out of their newest members' hands. He'd long ago learned to turn long odds to advantage. But there was a significant difference between long odds and impossible circumstances. He had no desire to ride against fifty mounted and heavily armed cowboys.

"Those men will be gone by Sunday," Cherokee Charlie insisted.

Tay flexed his leg. A sharp pain instantly answered the gesture, but he set his teeth and refused to let it show. He would have to ride, and by morning. He could not permit this band of maladroits to attack a whole town, even one made of tents, without his direction. If they didn't immediately burn the place to the ground, they would kill anyone who might have led them to the money and make yet another wasted effort.

Eubanks, intermittently wheezing and coughing, came back to the fire with a meaty joint ripped from the butchered hog. He speared it with a stick, then thrust it over the flames.

"So, what's the plan, Tay?" Blasingame asked. "We need to think about something more than how cold it is." He tested the sharpness of his blade with his thumb and set his eyes darkly on the tip. "I'm thinking of how warming a bunch of women might be."

Tay pushed down on the ground with his sword, forced himself to stand. The leg held, but his teeth were clenched against the prickling agony the movement sent rafting up through his hips and into his chest. "I have taken stock of Mr. Eubanks' discoveries," he said.

"Eubanks is a damn fool," Blasingame said.

"Go to hell, Blasingame," Eubanks said, and poked at the meat with a dirty finger.

Tay spoke slowly, keeping his gaze steady on the dark holes that were Blasingame's eyes. "I want no mistakes this time," he said. He looked at the charred buildings of the ferry. "No more wasted opportunities. There should be horses there."

"They's plenty of damn horses," Eubanks muttered. "Cowboy horses."

"We should provision ourselves," Tay continued. "But we must be subtle in our ways. Mr. Manypenny," he said, leveling his glance at the rodentlike man. "You are not to fire those buildings until they've been thoroughly searched. We cannot afford to burn up our profits again."

"You're the one ordered me to burn the train," Manypenny said. Manypenny struck a match and stared at it, grumbling into the silence that grew around the fire. After the lucifer burned down, he lowered his rat-face's gaze to his feet.

"Mr. Eubanks, Mr. Blasingame, neither of you is to kill anyone until the money has been discovered and provisions are secured."

"What about me?" Cherokee Charlie spoke up.

"I'd fancy a braided topknot," Blasingame grumbled.

Cherokee Charlie's eyes widened. "Now wait just a damn minute—"

"Mr. Blasingame." Tay pointed his sword at the blond outlaw, who stared back, his face a mask of indifference. "This man will live—and profit—if his intelligence is reliable."

"They'd best be good intelligences," Eubanks said, licking grease from filthy fingers.

"I shall reclaim the bay," Tay said to Blasingame, who opened his mouth, then snapped it shut and nodded once. "If Mr. Eubanks is correct, there will be ample mounts tomorrow."

"Damn, Tay, you don't trust nobody," Eubanks said.

"Mr. Manypenny, go and relieve the Negro on watch. He may be needed tomorrow."

"I aim to kill *him* first chance I get," Eubanks said casually, glancing over his shoulder, then coughed deeply. "I can't go back to Arkansas with him drawing air."

"You will leave that man alone," Tay said. "I anticipate utter obedience." He waited for that to sink in. "We have an opportunity here, gentlemen. I suggest we capitalize on it."

Manypenny stared into the fire for a beat, then nodded and rose. "It's been a long ride, Colonel Tay," he said. "This better work, or we're quits."

Tay stared at him, then stumped his way on his sword crutch back toward the buggy. He would sleep there tonight, or he would try to. Mostly, he would try to anticipate what would go wrong tomorrow, and how he might forestall it.

BOOK FIVE

———◆◆◆———

Hoolian

THE PRODIGAL

1

ON CHRISTMAS DAY, Gil Hooley awoke with a thick tongue, a dry throat, and a ringing in his ears. The din didn't mimic the low, dull tone of a hangover or the annoying buzzing throb of a serious ailment. It was a loud, regular, metallic clanging that pealed with the confident certainty of some huge gong. He first became aware of it as he surfaced from the whiskey-lined depths of his sleep. A more familiar dull throb from deep inside his head banged a syncopated rhythm to the pealing noise and pressed his aching eyeballs, which seemed the size of lemons. No matter how hard he squeezed them shut, he couldn't alter the steady pain of the multiple sensations.

He rolled over in the thin blankets on the cold planks of his tent. His stomach immediately sent bile into his throat. Coming to his knees, he dragged up a bucket and started to lean over, but it was full of human waste—from the cloistered Nichols, Hooley dimly deduced. Before he was able to shove it aside, the stench attacked his nostrils and sent his cramping belly into full revolt. Blinded by pain and nausea, he scrambled about, groping for any handy receptacle. Sweat and tears oozed out as the agonized results of overindulgence utterly fled his heaving body.

It wasn't until after he recovered from a third bout of retching that he realized he had just putrefied his Gladstone bag with his stomach's acidic contents. With a spray of curses, Hooley wiped his mouth, staggered to his feet, and sought balance. He used a marginally clean scrap of canvas to mop his face. When he could focus on his surroundings, he discovered that he was alone. Nichols had at last abandoned the tent.

The events of the night before now came flooding into his consciousness. It seemed to Hooley that he explained that he wasn't trying to pick a fight with Jake a thousand times as he helped lift the bleeding young cowboy up onto the bar, where the whores fussed over him and bound his wound. No one listened. Everyone instantly developed an opinion about what had happened, formed a personal version of events, and not even their own eyewitness would contradict it. Once they had Jake out of his trousers, it became clear that the bullet had caused no serious harm, and he began rapidly replenishing his internal liquids with glass after glass of whiskey, with cheerful encouragement from all present.

When the music started up again. Hooley surrendered to the inevitable: He sat down in a corner, where he downed drink after drink and wished he had remembered to bring his pipe. Hooley remembered watching Clara's form guide the limping Jake toward her crib, his hand firmly grasping her huge hips. She was laughing and holding him tight against her when the heavy tent flap closed behind them. Hooley glanced around to see if Plunk had noticed, but the sad cowboy was slopping beer down his front and showing alarming signs of passing out where he stood. Hooley decided to beat him to it.

At some point, he remembered, Hank had accosted him. "So you want to shoot all of us."

"I didn't shoot anybody," Hooley slurred. "I was just trying to do the right thing."

"I was you, I wouldn't carry no iron around no more. You might *have* to bury yourself."

"I wouldn't sell me short," Hooley snapped. "I might be better with a gun than you are."

"Well, that wouldn't be saying much, Hooley," he said. "Heck, I'm such a rotten shot, I couldn't even hit myself in the leg the way Jake did." He looked down. "Truth to tell, If it'd been me instead of you gone after Chatsworth, I'd been the one coming in belly down and toes out."

"Hank," Hooley said as seriously as he could through the whiskey buzz, "if it had been you, not me, things would have turned out exactly the same." Hank shrugged and staggered off.

After that, things became vague. He remembered Margot's green eyes flashing mean and vengeful in his direction from time to time, and he remembered falling in the snow on his way back to his tent. For the first time in his life, he had been drunk, truly and deeply drunk.

Now he was paying for it. Steady ringing continued to torture his skull. The little stove was cold, and his teeth were chattering. He still wore the gun belt and its single pistol, but his clothing was muddy, and his shoes, which he had neglected to remove, were crusted with mud.

His head's raging was made worse by continued clanging. He glanced at the whiskey bottle, which still had a finger or two of amber liquid sitting stagnant, but the thought of swallowing it caused his gut to churn. The ringing in his ears became more urgent. After a few minutes of shivering, he realized that he was actually hearing it, not imagining it as the result of the previous night's binge. He looked outside. Mino was positioned between his own quarters and the café tent, happily jerking on a rope attached to a large brass bell mounted in the apex of a pyramid formed by three tall beams. The shiny instrument was ten feet off the ground, and the stocky carpenter was pulling its rope with a regular rhythm, causing it to ring sharply.

"Stop that!" Hooley shouted, stepping out onto the ice-covered boardwalk. Mino ignored him. He kept grinning idiotically at the bell as it swung against a solid clapper and pealed out another tooth-rattling dong. "Goddamn it," Hooley yelled. "You're going to wake the dead."

"In a way, Hooley, that's the idea," Margot said. Hooley jumped, startled to find her standing at his elbow, wrapped in her thick coat, her hands tucked into opposing sleeves. Her breath made tiny vapor puffs. "I thought you, of all people, would approve."

Hooley shot her a dark glance and shifted his attention back to Mino, who continued to ring the bell vigorously. "Where the hell did that come from?" he asked. "Goddamnit!"

"Do you really think it's proper to swear on Christmas Day, Hooley?"

He spoke deliberately. "Where the goddamn hell did that stupid son of a bitch come up with a bell like that?"

"He's had it all along," she replied, pushing back the hood slightly and wrinkling her brow in thought. "It was—" She blinked once and stared at Hooley, who was glaring furiously at the carpenter. "You really don't care, do you, Hooley?"

Hooley put his hands up to his ears, which were stinging from the cold. "Goes through my head like a knife."

"It's Christmas Day," she said. "A good time for a bell-ringing, wouldn't you say?"

"He's driving me crazy," Hooley said, then yelled, "Stop that, you stupid son of a bitch!" Mino happily continued his chore. "The man is a moron," Hooley growled.

"Oh, I don't know, Hooley," Margot said, smiling. "I think it's sweet."

Hooley scooped up a handful of clean snow and put it in his mouth. His teeth immediately protested the action, and a second stab of pain jabbed through his head, causing him to squeeze his eyes shut until it passed and left only the regular throbbing.

The morning sky was clearing, allowing patches of bright blue to appear. Heavy snow burdened the buildings, forecasting heavy work. Only the café tent had generated enough heat to melt the thick white overlay. Margot's red tent and Hank's store were in peril, and other edifices, especially the hotel, whiskey shed, and the privies and bathhouse, were also in need of attention.

"When the sun comes out," Margot said, reading his thoughts and, as usual, ready with a contradiction, "it will all melt. But this place is going to turn to pure mud. We need proper streets laid out, to put down some gravel."

"What?" Hooley stared at the snowy carpet. "Where would we get anything like that?"

"In Arkansas, they used crushed seashells," she continued wistfully. "When I was a girl, I could find tiny little seashells in the street. I collected them in a green jar." She frowned. "I always wanted to see the sea."

"The sea?"

"Craggy Phillips was going to take me down to Galveston Island," she replied absently. "But you ruined that, didn't you?" Before he could reply, her expression became serious. "I know we can't get seashells, Hooley. But we need something. I'm not grateful for all the mud everybody tracks into my house, you know."

"Margot, I don't much feel like—"

"The girls will have mud on their shoes and skirts. There's nowhere to do a decent wash until the weather clears. And we have no bootblack." She touched her chin with one finger. "Maybe Ina Moon might know some Chinese people," she said. "We need a proper laundry."

"You want us to build a laundry? Then send off for Chinamen?" He gave her a false smile. "Maybe we could put in an order with Heinz. I'm sure he could find some somewhere."

"Oh, Hooley," she said with a slight bitterness in her voice. "There's no need to be mean." Then she sighed. "Truly, I didn't want to talk about that." She smiled girlishly. "I have to say that thinking of the sea cheered me up, though. You always do cheer me up, Hooley, you know that?"

"I never noticed," he grumbled. "I didn't think I gave you any pleasure at all."

"Well, you do." She affected a pout. "From time to time, you give me the best pleasure I've ever had." She flashed a quick, pretty smile, then sobered her expression. "But that's not my concern this morning, either."

"Don't tell me you were worried about me."

Mino stopped ringing the bell, and the din ceased. He stood dusting off his hands with a satisfied grin, then stomped off. Hooley relaxed. "Where is everybody?"

"Burying those people," she said. "Having a little funeral service."

Hooley peered into the white distance. Sure enough, a line of men and women could be seen making their way toward the old graves.

"They're burying them? Now?"

"Well, we weren't about to do it last night. It was snowing a blizzard, for one thing, and everybody was having too good a time, until you showed up and ruined it."

"Who's paying for it?" he asked, bitterness invading his tone.

"We took up a collection."

"A collection," he said, stunned. "Who donated? Me, most likely," he answered himself. "Money from our 'enterprise,' Margot? All out of my share, I suppose."

"Oh, Hooley. If I was going to cheat you, I could have long ago. Everyone donated. A community effort." She formed her mouth into a thin line. "That's what you wanted, right?"

"Margot—" He was interrupted when ragged, off-key strains of a hymn came to his ears. A bunch of drunken cowboys and whores gathered around a frozen grave singing hymns, he thought. Then he spotted Mino trudging quickly toward the knot of mourners, concertina in hand. "Is there any coffee?"

She scowled at him. "I'd think you might ask how Asa is doing," she said.

"Asa? Who the hell is—"

"Asa Abernathy, Hooley. His pards—I do hate that word—call him 'Jake.'" She stared at the blank question on Hooley's face. "I thought you'd know his name. You're the one who caused him to injure himself last night."

"I didn't cause anyone to do anything. He wasn't in any pain when I saw him last."

"You are a selfish man, Hooley," she snapped. "I'm sure he will make a full recovery."

"I want some coffee," Hooley repeated.

"Always selfish," she snorted, then reinserted her hand in the folds of her coat and stepped pertly into a wide track in the snow and crossed to the café tent. Vaporizing breath steamed out of her hood, as if a steady engine were powering her. Hooley trailed after her, puffing away in the frosty air. He was gratified to find the café's fire hot, and a half-full pot of coffee. He also found a pan of cold biscuits. His stomach opened gratefully, although his throat burned so badly that swallowing was painful.

Margot poured herself a cup, produced her flask, and measured out a dollop of liquor. As an afterthought, she tipped it his way, but he shook his head. She nodded, then sipped her beverage while he moved about, shivering. As if to commiserate, she pushed back her hood. Her red hair was down, flowing onto a black lace shawl. In spite of light paint on her eyes and lips, the rouge and fake beauty mark added to one cheek, she looked like an innocent girl playing at outlandish dress-up. Her eyes were the color of new grass. She was, he reluctantly admitted, almost intolerably lovely. A preternatural heat filled his chest. It was too much, so he moved away, casting his gaze out to the flats, where with the aid of Mino's instrument the music was now harmonious.

"Everyone seems to be getting on just fine now," Hooley commented.

"Everyone gets along just fine most of the time," she said. "Except when you try to upset people. It's a trait you need to alter, Hooley. It only results in mischief." She returned to her previous topic. "The mud is going to be awful. As you refuse to provide seashells or gravel, something else will have to be done, if we are going to have this kind of weather."

She spoke as if they were sitting in his mother's drawing room, commenting on the climate over a cup of tea, rather than squatting on a crudely hewn bench under a sagging canvas tent in the middle of nowhere. Even so, he acknowledged with uncomfortable familiarity that she was right. The ground below was a carpet of frozen mud, and as the weather warmed, it would become intolerable. If the sun thawed the snow quickly, the whole town might drown in a quagmire.

"Why aren't you up there with them?" Hooley asked after a few moments of silence passed. "I thought you liked to be in the middle of things."

"Mr. Nichols is devout, but a hard man," she said. "He's not receptive to a woman in my position."

"Your position?"

"I'm a whore, Hooley. In case you forgot."

"I see the others are there."

"Oh, we had a long talk. He thinks they're all salvageable, I guess. 'Redeemable.' " She frowned into her cup. "He says I'm a 'Jezebel.' " She gave him a sudden coy smile. "She was—"

"I know who she was, Margot," Hooley said. "I'm not as ignorant as you like to pretend." He poured more coffee into his cup. His headache was gone, and his stomach was settling.

She nodded, smiled again. "He didn't think it would be right for me to be there where he's burying his wife. He sees the girls as fallen angels who can be saved, but I'm responsible for their fall." She looked off into the distance. "I'm not so sure he's not right."

"What brought about this sudden change of heart?" Hooley asked, nodding toward the flats. "Last night, I was pretty sure your friends would just leave those people for the coyotes."

"*My* friends?" she asked, an eyebrow cocking prettily. "What makes you think they're *my* friends more than yours?" Hooley didn't answer. She sighed. "You can be so stupid, no matter how intelligent you think you are." He looked away. "Actually, taking up the collection was Mino's idea."

"Mino?"

"About dawn, the snow stopped, so Mino went over and brought Mr. Nichols out for a talk. He wasn't hard to convince. You were snoring something awful, Hooley. Drunker than I've ever seen you. It wasn't dignified." Hooley scowled, but she went on. "Loretta cooked up a big breakfast, and then they went right up to get started. That's when Mino decided to put up the bell. It came off a ship. Mino *was* a sailor, you know."

"A sailor?"

"Well, a ship's carpenter or something."

Hooley shook his head. "You're telling me that after all I said and did, that idiot just smiled and said 'No shit' or something, and everyone went right along?"

"Well, there was a bit more to it than that. He can be very wise."

"And I'm just a damn fool."

"Well"—she lowered her eyes—"I can't entirely disagree." She shifted subjects rapidly. "Listen, Hooley. We've all been talking. The girls and me and Mino, and that filthy muleskinner Heinz, too—although I'm not certain he should have a say, but Loretta likes him, and she wanted him to be heard—but anyway, Hank and Ina Moon agree, and that makes it unanimous."

"What?"

She took a deep breath. "We don't think you ought to be mayor anymore."

"I never—"

"It's not that we don't like you, Hooley," she put in quickly. "Although, from my point of view, you're a hard man to like. It's just that you get . . . well, overwrought, and every time you do, somebody gets hurt."

" 'Overwrought'?! Who have I hurt?"

"You lack affability, Hooley. It's a plain fact. What's needed in a town with a future is a steady man who has an even hand. You just don't have the touch."

"Margot—"

"Now, don't sull up over this. You can still be postmaster."

"Margot, I—"

"And we count on you for the tents and all. And you manage the liquor stocks well enough, although we have to discuss some particulars in that regard."

He flapped his hands against his side, surrendering. For some reason, he wanted to laugh.

"That whiskey shed has got to go," she continued, the words rushing out in an evidently well-rehearsed speech. "We need a proper warehouse that's handy when things get busy—I can't be sending Loretta out every few minutes for another bottle, not in this intemperate weather. And"— she paused and looked at the gun belt he continued to wear—"we don't think you ought to wear a pistol anymore. You're not reliable when it comes to firearms, Hooley. You've already killed two people, and you nearly shot another man last night. Keep that up, this place will be worse than Oklahoma Territory."

"I don't suppose it would do any good to say I've only killed one man," he said, sighing. "And he was a stupid son of a bitch who deserved killing."

"I don't know what gives you the right to decide these things, Hooley," she said evenly. "But it doesn't matter. The decision is made."

"Sounds as if you had a regular town meeting."

"Well, more or less," she admitted. "It was after Mr. Nichols' sermon, actually."

"He preached a *sermon?*"

"Well, it *is* Christmas, Hooley. He wanted to preach a eulogy for his wife and family before we ate breakfast. Anyway, after he preached a while, he told us how you've treated him." Her tone sharpened. "You've been downright inhospitable, Hooley. Admit it."

"What the hell?" Hooley yelled, rising to his feet. "I gave the man my bed! Slept on the floor! I didn't even have decent blankets! I put up with his sniveling Bible-thumping for more than a week when any sane man would have thrown him out to freeze! How 'hospitable' do I have to be? *You* wouldn't have him. *I* got him. This is the thanks I get?"

"Are you saying you want to keep being mayor over our collective objections?" she asked. "That would be difficult, Hooley. It shows a propensity for stubborn behavior that's ill-suited to politics, if you ask me."

Hooley spun on her. "I'm saying, Margot, that I am *not* the mayor, and I never was. I am *not* a postmaster, and I never was. I'm just a poor dumb son of a bitch who . . ." He trailed off, watching her watch him rail. This was lunacy. "Who tried to do right by you, by everybody. And who gets knocked down every time he turns around."

"I hate it that you see it that way, Hooley," she said. "Mino said—"

"*Mino* said?" Hooley railed, feeling his anger swelling and bursting forth in a raging torrent of vitriolic sarcasm. "*Mino* said? How in the name of goddamn hell can Mino *say* anything? Am I the only sane person in this whole damned place? How can you tell me what Mino *says*? The man can't speak more than four words of English, and two of those are my goddamn name! I've seen mules with more conversation. The goddamn truth is that all he can do is nail some boards together," Hooley shouted. "He's no goddamn good for anything else."

"He's your friend, Hooley. And," she added quietly, "he's my lover."

Air rushed out of him, forming a white cloud in the frigid air. "Your lover?"

"For the time being," she snapped. "And what do you care? I'm nothing but a whore to you. *Mr. Nichols* has more respect for me than you do. And more love—if you count a preacher's love." Her jade eyes seemed to cut into Hooley's heart. "He may think I'm 'wanton and beyond salvation,' but he looks at me and sees a woman, not just a whore."

He imagined himself desperately clawing around in loose dirt, scrambling for some kind of hold on her, a way to hang on to what they had, what he *thought* they had. His stomach cramped violently. "You're not a whore to me, Margot."

"You say that now, Hooley. But when I *needed* you to say it, when you had a *chance* to say it, you didn't." She shook her head. "It's too late now. I'm a whore and you're my partner. But you cannot be mayor anymore, and that's all there is to it."

She pulled the coat over her shoulders. "I hoped you'd see reason in this," she said, "but you're as pigheaded as ever. All you want is to shoot people and stick your peter into the first pretty young thing who smiles at you, even if you have to kill her man to do it. You have no sense of loyalty, Hooley."

"That doesn't even make sense, Margot."

"You're worse than any lawman I've ever seen in Oklahoma Territory," she shot at him. "It's a pity you're such a weakling to boot."

Hooley felt something snap inside him, a resignation. The relief was immediate. "I'm leaving."

"Leaving?" she replied, dropping her anger like a casual wrapper. Her usual demeanor returned as her eyes grew large with disbelief. "Just because you can't be mayor?"

"I'm leaving, Margot." The words seemed to form in the vapor of his breath, as if he could see them. They had come too easily for him to believe he had said them aloud, so he repeated them and added, "Right now. This very morning."

"Where will you go in this weather?" Her mouth formed a thin frown of doubt. "Besides, as soon as the funeral is over, the boys have to go. Then the rest of us can sit down, have a big Christmas dinner, and—"

"I'm taking the mare," he croaked out, realizing that now that he had made the threat, he couldn't back down. His head spun with a sudden sense of freedom. "*Your* mare," he clarified. "I'm buying her." The suddenness of the decision to leave seemed to underscore its rightness. He dared not look her in the eye. "I'll buy her."

"Be sensible, Hooley."

"I want to go someplace people aren't totally out of their minds."

"You'd truly leave me, Hooley?" she asked, her eyes welling. His heart jumped and, in spite of the cold, sweat broke out on his forehead. "After all we've been to one another?"

"What, Margot?" he asked. "*What* have we been to one another?"

"I thought we might be married one of these days."

"Married?" He laughed out loud. "Us? When? When you get tired of Mino?"

She gave him a warm smile. "I'm really not 'beyond salvation,' you know. That's just a stupid preacher's notion. I can't abide preachers, to be honest. Anyway, I was a judge's daughter. I can do a good many useful things, and I'm adaptable. We'd do well to be married."

"Hell, Margot," Hooley brayed out. "You won't even kiss me."

"Whores don't kiss," she said pertly.

"Lovers do," Hooley shot back, thinking of her kissing the apish Mino.

"Well, you and I do have a certain . . . compatibility, if you know what I mean." She offered a soft smile. "But love is another matter completely. The point is that you're the one who forced me into a life of sin. What decent man would have me, the widow of a lawman from Oklahoma Territory, the whore of his killer? I'm not saying you're unkind, Hooley, though you could use lessons in graciousness. But you can't abandon me here in the middle of Texas with a bunch of ignorant cowboys. I will not tolerate that, Hooley. You owe me more." She stepped toward him as if to embrace him.

"No, Margot!" he shouted, stepping backward, dropping his coffee cup in the trampled snow. "Don't try that. It won't work." He shook his head, feeling its dull throb return to complement the storm going on in his gut. "I don't owe you anything, Margot," he said evenly. "Whatever I might once have owed you for shooting down that mad dog you were married to, I've repaid a hundred times over. We're done."

"Hooley!" she exclaimed. "I forbid you to do this! It's not seemly!"

He stomped away, leaving her bereft in the café tent. In his mind, he thought of the many times she had left him with much more to say to her retreating back and finding himself sputtering, helpless. The sensation buoyed him, floated him over the crunchy snow.

2

E GRABBED THE defiled Gladstone bag from his tent. While Margot stood silent and staring, he used fresh snow as a scour and cleaned it, then began flinging his belongings into it. He found the ledger, started to take it out to her, but thinking better of the gesture, he used the stub of a pencil to write, "$50.00 @ dun mare horse and saddle (used)."

"There," he muttered. "That's 'seemly.' " He placed the ledger on top of his cot. Somehow, to leave it where they had made such sweet love seemed fitting. Let her get it from Nichols, he thought, fury rising in him again, let the sanctimonious son of a bitch open it, read the numerous "Services Rendered" entries, learn how far beyond "salvation" she truly was.

He scurried around, gathering his belongings. He folded his needles, punches, and awls into the bag. There were other implements—cauldrons for boiling oakum and wax, boxes of grommets, his heavier tools—that he couldn't take on horseback.

He pulled out canvas bags of cash, tied at the top and bulging with coins and neatly bundled greenbacks. It was more money than Hooley had ever imagined earning, far more than a man of his limited ambition could reasonably expect to amass in his entire life. It was, he thought, probably more than Bertha Hooley had ever dreamed an indolent tentmaker might earn. But very little of it was truly his. Without Margot, he knew, he wouldn't have enough to fill a fist.

He removed a bundle of notes, about a hundred dollars, he reckoned. That was enough. The rest was hers. She could divide it with Heinz and Mino or whomever she wanted. He started to leave the cash bags next to the ledger on the cot, but then remembered Nichols. Nothing like a preacher to steal you blind, he thought, so he took them outside. Fresh prints in the snow cut a trail through the soiled white covering, indicating that Margot had gone directly to her tent. He stomped through the knee-high drifts, carrying all three bags, intent on throwing them in her face. When he reached the flap door of the tent, she stepped out to meet him with blazing eyes. She had forsaken her coat, but pulled the shawl around her shoulders, forcing the valleys of her cleavage to deepen. Hooley glanced down, then caught himself and swallowed hard.

"You're not serious about this," she said, her voice low. "It's insane."

"Here," he said. "This is nearly all of it."

"This is a foolish thing, Hooley. Think it through before you make a big mistake."

"Good-bye, Margot," he said, jamming the bags into her body, pushing her backward. "This is all you ever cared about. Now it's yours. You can make your bed with it, curl up with it. Any night Mino's too busy playing his goddamn squeezebox, it'll keep you warm."

She awkwardly hugged the bags. "What do you make me out to be, Hooley?" she demanded. "How can you just shove money at me like I'm a ten-cent chippie. How dare you!"

He crunched away in the snow. He had taken no more than five paces when he was struck in the middle of his back. He spun around, expecting her to attack him. One of the bags of money lay deep in the white drift in front of him.

"I don't want any money!" she screeched at him, and flung another bag. It whizzed over his head and landed in the snow beneath the crude tripod of Mino's bell. "I never did! I only made it for you! I was *your* whore! You hear me? *Your* whore! Nobody else's!"

He picked up the first bag and carried it to the tripod. When he bent over to collect the other, the third struck him in the buttocks.

"You go to hell, Hooley!" she shouted. "You can just go to hell!" Then she was inside, out of sight.

A deep weariness descended on him. He scooped out a hole in the snow beneath Mino's bell, then dropped the three bags into it and covered them over. Then he plowed through the snow up toward the corral. If the mourners heard the commotion, they hadn't let it bother them. More singing was drifting down. They had found a familiar melody, but the words were indistinct. Hooley dimly recorded that it was not a hymn or even a carol. Instead it was some ballad, something he had heard Mino play around the campfire back when things were more pleasant in Hoolian. The observation strengthened his resolve. "Son of a bitch probably taught them the words," he panted. "He'll talk to everybody but me."

He made his way to the corral. The horses and mules were bunched up, but Margot's mare stood off to one side. After two tries, Hooley was able to get a rope on her, then he led her back down to the storeroom by Hank's store. There, he found Craggy Phillips' old tack and started trying to put the bit on the mare's nodding head. The tangled array of cinches and straps confounded him, though, and he began cursing under his breath as he tried to figure them out.

"Going someplace?" Heinz's voice came from behind him. He turned and confronted the old teamster, who grinned and spat. Behind him, a deep fresh track trailed from the snow-buried cold cellar. "It's mighty chilly to be taking out for a trot."

"I'm leaving," Hooley said.

"I figured you'd think the rag was off the bush, start thinking about skedaddling."

"I'm not running away. I'm just leaving."

"Well, it's not often you see a mayor fired for stupidity."

"I'm not a mayor," Hooley said as patiently as he could, biting down on his temper, refusing to allow it to erupt again. "I never was. That was your doing." He looked around. "In a way, this whole thing was your doing."

Heinz shrugged, worked his plug for a beat. "I don't see how. Beats anything I ever seen in the name of the blue-eyed Jesus. I was minding my own business when you sicced your gang of road agents on me. Never been robbed one time till that happened," he reminded Hooley.

"Why aren't you at the party up there?" Hooley demanded. He finally managed to get the bridle and bit onto the animal. "I figured you'd be in the middle of it."

"Too much religion gives me the fantods. That Nichols galoot is a panther for trouble. Mark my words: Minute a preacher man shows up in the neighborhood, everything goes south. First thing they'll do is build a church house and shut down the saloons and put all the whores into the woman's auxiliary. Start a bunch of damn book clubs. 'Fore you know it, the whole place'll be overrun with ugly barefoot young'uns and feather merchants, and women'll be running the whole shebang." He grinned a blackened smile at Hooley. "Give me a choice between quilting bees and church suppers and a good honest whorehouse and a glass of whiskey, there's no contest. I can't say that you leaving might not be the most sensible thing. Next thing you know, you'll be spending half your time marrying everybody off." Hooley ignored him, worked with the saddle. "Margot know you're hightailing it?" he asked.

Hooley jerked at a strap so furiously that the whole saddle slid off the horse. "If it's any of your goddamn business, yes, she does," he shouted. "She wants me to go, so I'm going."

"Don't mind if I say that's a two–dollar load of bullshit, do you?" Heinz asked, and spat. "That woman's in love with you, Hooley."

"What the hell would you know about it? She's a whore."

"She's a woman," Heinz responded. "There's more than a shade of difference there, if you put your mind on it. You got no goddamn sense when it comes to women, Hooley," he said. "Half the time, you're ready to take a man's head off for looking cockeyed at that redhead, and the other half you're ready to throw her down the first dry well you can find time to dig. How a man could be so smart but be so stupid at the same time beats anything I ever seen. Don't say I didn't warn you the day I first laid eyes on her: That woman'll be the death of us," he concluded.

"Well, I won't be here to see it," Hooley growled, and resumed struggling with the tack. The saddle slid off the other side.

"You want some help there?" Heinz asked. Hooley stepped aside, and the bandy-legged muleskinner completed the chore. "So you're just going to leave that poor woman crying in her pillow?" he asked. "Seems harsh, Hooley."

"She knows I'm going and she knows why."

"You're a bigger fool than I always took you for," Heinz said.

"Heinz," Hooley said, turning to look into the old teamster's squinty eyes, "If you thought about it for the rest of your life, you could never imagine how big a fool I am."

"You want to have one more drink for old times' sake?" Heinz asked. Hooley shook his head. "We could always have another fight over our contract," Heinz suggested. "I ain't had my dander up in a spell. I'll let you hit me in the nose again, if it'll make you change your mind."

Hooley shook his head once more and led the horse through the snow. He stopped, turned, and started to say something to Heinz, who watched him, a bemused smile on his face. He wanted to tell the old wagoneer that he was the best friend he had had in this place, maybe the only friend he had ever had in his life. But the words wouldn't come. He tied his things to the saddle with strips of canvas. Then he fetched a fresh bottle of whiskey and thrust it into his bag, collected his pipe and tobacco, a box of lucifers, his battered Winchester, and, as an afterthought, Cherokee Charlie's bandanna-wrapped knife, which he placed in his coat pocket.

When he finished, he decided to have that drink with Heinz after all, but when he looked for him, all he saw were his tracks, tacking back to the cold cellar. "What the hell do you know about love?" Hooley demanded of the snowy trail. "Hell, you're spending Christmas looking at a savage Indian's titties."

After several abortive tries, he managed to mount the burdened animal, and from the saddle's height he spotted the crowd of mourners making their way back. Nichols and Mino were in front, walking with resolution. He didn't want to see them, not even Mino. Especially not Mino.

The clouds were utterly gone, and overhead the sky was azure. Cold shrouded him, but the horse's body heat gave him comfort. His tents—Hooley tents—stretched out around him, laden with heavy snow. They provided little more than the illusion of a town, but they represented far more than he had ever believed he would have the ambition to create. Nearly a dozen independent buildings created out of his own imagination, made by his own hand, structures that served a purpose, that provided an oasis of civilization in a stark, harsh wilderness that forgave little and demanded much more than he could give.

There was promise here, hope. But it was not his promise or his hope. It was just a pipe dream, an accident, a joke, a demonstrated lack of gumption, an inability to do anything more positive than remain where he was and make do with whatever fate brought him. That was the inevitable result of any ambition he ever tried to show. His mother was right. Ruthie was right. Even Margot was right. He was a failure, a disappointed seeker, a man without the guts to take life on directly or to seize and hold on to a woman he loved. He had fooled himself and, by doing so, had made a fool *of* himself. He had allowed himself to believe that he could find happiness in the arms of a woman who was more beautiful, more desirable than any he had ever conjured, a woman who confused, bewildered, and nettled him to distraction, even to madness. Instead of a life, all he had truly created and experienced here was pain and misery.

The horse stamped nervously as she sensed the approaching crowd. Margot *was* a whore. She was not a prostitute, not merely a woman who sold the use of her body to a man for money. She demanded payment of a more valuable coin. She wanted his sanity . . . and his soul.

He awkwardly reined the horse around to the east. He had no idea how far he would have to ride to find civilization or even shelter. But he knew what lay north—the river and the wilderness of Oklahoma Territory. And the south and the west were a mystery he had no motivation to discover. He figured he could reach Jacksboro before Heinz could catch him and try to talk him into coming back, try to convince him that things could return to normal.

"Normal," Hooley said. "What the hell is 'normal'? You're still a damn fool, Hooley."

With only the barest glance at the closed flap of the red tent, only the barest hope that she might yet emerge, give him a reason to change his mind, he gave a vicious kick to start the beast forward. "To hell with it," he muttered. "To hell with it all."

3

HOOLEY PUSHED THE plodding mare through the heavy snowdrifts of the undulating prairie for two hours before he realized that he was making such poor progress that by dark he was apt to be caught out in the middle of nowhere. The horse had grown lazy from disuse. She refused to do more than step along carefully as if the icy ground hurt her feet. She shook her head furiously every time he swore at her, something he began doing repeatedly. He pushed her on nevertheless, cursing her roundly. Soon, he was chilled through and rode with the reins wrapped around his forearms, his hands thrust inside his thin cord coat. The winter sun turned the world into a white brilliance, but after a while it crested the sky, and he watched his afternoon shadow lengthen on the crusting snow. The only thing he brought resembling food was the whiskey. All there was to do was fire up his pipe and steam along, ignoring the hunger pangs in his tortured gut.

Around him was an empty white prairie, tall grass buried by ice that was nearly blinding in its stark emptiness. The unbroken wilderness of snow—deep only in the depressions of the prairie rolls—mocked any attempt to locate a proper landmark. When he came over a rise, he often looked behind him at the straight line of the horse's tracks tracing up and down the prairie dells to a blank horizon. He kicked the horse into a faster pace, wanting to outrun the lingering thoughts of the redheaded harridan, his anger now transformed, familiarly, into nostalgic regret. But he resisted melancholy. If Margot truly loved him, she would never have let him go. She had it within her power to stop him. She had *him* within her power. She had from the moment he'd set eyes on her.

After another hour of slow walking, with no suggestion of direction from Hooley except to keep her pointed to the east, the mare suddenly topped a rise, stopped, lifted her head, and nickered loudly. Hooley gave her a violent kick, but she stubbornly refused to budge, except to try to bite him. Then he spotted a smudge on the stark white horizon. He thought he might be imagining it, but he wiped his eyes and saw that it was a mounted man sky-lined against the blue.

A thrill of fear tingled down his spine when the man stopped, then angled his mount toward Hooley's position. This could mean trouble, he knew. Who else but some outlaw would be a big enough fool to be out here on such a winter's day? He thought to run, but all around him there was only an immense alabaster blankness. Given the mare's performance thus far, he grimly estimated, he could make better time on foot. The rider plowed through the snow directly toward him. Hooley loosened his pistol in its holster. He was prepared to be friendly, but was damned if he was going to be waylaid by a road agent after all he'd been through.

Hooley now saw it was a Negro man mounted on a mule. He had no saddle or blanket, was bareheaded, and wore the all-white uniform of a railroad porter under a ragged quilt knotted across his chest and pulled up to tuck around himself. Gray bristles sprouted on his cheeks, and the white in his hair matched the snow. The man reined in his furry mount, flashed a brilliant smile.

"Afternoon, Boss-man," he said. "It sure enough takes a world of work to push an animal through all this snow. A mule makes for a hard ride for an old man's backside." Hooley stared back. "I'm purely gratuitous to run up on somebody out here." He ignored Hooley's demonstrated astonishment. "Metritous Jones is the name." Hooley swallowed and nodded slightly. Jones nodded back in an obsequious manner. "I'm hating to bother you on such a fine day, but I'm discombobulated by all this snow. I'm hoping you can tell me where I might find a whorehouse round these parts. Kind of a tent, I hear tell."

Hooley was vaguely insulted that anyone, especially a Negro, would regard the nascent community as nothing more than a whorehouse. "Why would you want to know? There's no colored people there. No colored women, anyway."

Jones nodded his head. "Oh, my days of plowing the pleasurable female furrows is long past, Boss-man." He laughed. " 'Sides, I got me an old fat wife back up in Missouri. I'm a Christian man, more or less, and that woman of mine gets feisty if she thinks I'm out cathousing around."

"You're not a piano player, are you?" Hooley asked suspiciously.

"Can't say as I am. I used to pick a little banjo, but that was a long time ago. You looking to meet up with a piano man out here?"

"It was just something somebody said once," Hooley muttered, slightly embarrassed.

Jones smiled again. "Nossir. I can't play no piano. Just looking for that whorehouse."

"Why?"

Jones's eyes narrowed slightly. "Take it from me, Boss-man, you don't want to know."

Hooley was offended by such effrontery. "I do want to know. In fact, I insist on it."

Jones looked Hooley up and down, and a spark of hope invaded his face. "You ain't the laws, are you?" Hooley set his jaw and shook his head. Jones's face fell. "I didn't reckon so. Could sure use me some laws. But they is scarce in this neighborhood."

"You might say that," Hooley said with a deep pang.

Silence fell between them. "Where the hell did you come from?" Hooley asked finally.

"Last night, I was with some white men up the other side of the river, but I shucked them off 'fore daybreak." He patted the mule's neck. "Should of took me a horse, but what they had was too comical for a growed-up man to ride, truth to tell," he said. "The mule seemed more likely. He ain't much for hurry, but he's a dog for work."

"Who were these white men?" Hooley asked, looking at the blank horizon beyond Jones.

Jones's face darkened. "Truth to tell, they ain't much account."

"Who were they?" Hooley demanded.

"I'd say *who* they is ain't important." He studied Hooley. "I done said enough."

"I don't think you've said half enough," Hooley said, his voice rising.

"Well, I don't mean to be uppity, Boss-man," he said, grinning again, "but I ain't at license to say my own business, exactly." He winked. "Can't you tell me where this whorehouse place is at? I reckon I lost my way in all this snow. I didn't know it snowed like this in Texas."

"I need to know what you want there," Hooley said. "In that town."

"You from there?"

Hooley nodded. "I have, uh, associations there," he said slowly.

Jones sighed deeply. "Well, I need to get there ahead of them folks I was with."

Hooley studied the vacant horizon. "I haven't seen anybody else."

"Don't mind my saying so, Boss-man, but you best be glad you ain't," Jones said. He looked around. "You know how to get to this whorehouse place, I'd sure be obliged if you'd just say so. It's not getting no warmer sitting here this way." Hooley realized the man was shivering. "And . . . well, the folks I'm trying to catch up ain't exactly the most patient bunch. They like as not finish their business and light out, if I don't shake a leg."

"What business?" Hooley demanded, mystified. "What business do they have there?"

"That ain't nothing to do with me, truly," Jones replied evasively.

"They just heading that away, and I need to get there ahead of them. Got to finish something I started."

Hooley stared hard at the Negro's smiling countenance. He seemed harmless enough, but his words befuddled the tentmaker and roused dark suspicions. Then he decided that this was more of Hank's nonsense, another party of settlers and tradesman the storekeeper invited. Hooley sighed. "You follow that trail," he said, pointing to the mare's tracks leading back through the snow to the west. "I'd say two or three hours. For me it was, anyway."

"That's a good thing, Boss-man," he said. "I'm near froze out here." He made no move to ride on. "Don't reckon you'd like to swap animals with me? A mule'll carry a load, and I can see that you're traveling in leisure."

Hooley shook his head. "No," he said. "I'll keep the horse."

"I was kind of fearful you'd say that, Boss-man." Jones shook his head and kicked the mule forward. "It was just a notion." Hooley relaxed slightly, but as soon as Jones came close, the Negro pulled his hand from beneath his quilt and revealed an ugly weapon. It looked like a shotgun that had been sawed off and turned into a side arm. Hooley's mouth gaped open, and he vaguely realized he'd just dropped his pipe in the snow.

"Purely hate to do this," Jones said. "Truth to tell, I wouldn't make a wart on a good highwayman. But I got to have that horse."

Hooley's hand dropped to his pistol.

"Nope," Jones said firmly, lifting the barrel. "Druther you not do that. I got to say, I never shot this thing, but I reckon it'd blow a hole in you I could walk through."

Hooley was rigid. His mouth was suddenly dry, and his chest heaved with deep breaths of panic. "They hang men for horse theft in Texas," he said. "And you should know that I'm on personal acquaintance with the Texas Rangers."

"Oh, that's all right, Boss-man," Jones said. "That bunch'd as soon hang a nigger as take a shit." His grin dropped. "Mainliest thing is that you throw that side gun off yonder."

Hooley waited a beat, but Jones gestured with the weapon one more time. "Boss-man, I'm going to have that horse and saddle one way or other, and I can't have you back-shooting me." Slowly, Hooley tossed his single Peacemaker off about twenty yards.

"Now," Jones said, "ride off yonder a ways, and get off." Hooley stayed still for a beat. "I had me a hard night." Jones sighed. "Hard week, truth to tell. I'm supposed to be back home in Missouri with my old woman.

It's Christmas, if I reckon right. But I ain't home. I'm in Texas. I'm trying to do a thing against my best judiciousness, and you're in my way."

His face lost all its affable obsequiousness and formed a serious mask. "Now, be a gentleman, and do like I tell you. They'll hang me if they catch me, so it don't make no nevermind to me if it's for stealing a horse or killing a white man." He cocked the twin hammers on the weapon. "Now, I'm asking polite: Move that horse over yonder and step down."

Hooley kicked the mare forward. Jones followed her as she walked off about fifty yards and stopped. "I'm truly much obliged," he said. "Now, step down, and mind the ice."

Nearly blinded by rage, Hooley did as bidden. He watched as Jones slid down off the mule, drew a knife from his trousers, and cut the ties holding Hooley's bag from the mare's saddle, all the while keeping him covered with the short shotgun.

"I ain't exactly stealing nothing," Jones said. "We're just swapping animals."

"I don't seem to have much choice," Hooley said, embarrassment working in him like a thunderstorm. Beneath his rage and embarrassment, something else was bothering him as well, though he couldn't tell what.

Jones laughed and swung up into the mare's saddle. To Hooley's astonishment, she neither sidestepped nor bucked. Jones grinned down at him. "Make note, Boss-man: I ain't leaving you afoot out here," he said. "I'm leaving you this here mule and all your possibles." Jones looked around from the superior height of the mare. "I got to say I never seen so much of ice-cold nowhere in my whole life, and I can't wait to get back to Missouri. This chore's got me sidetracked, and I'm anxious to be done with it."

"What 'chore'?" Hooley demanded. "I want to know. You owe me that much."

Jones reined the mare around and kicked her hard back down her tracks toward Hoolian. To Hooley's aggravation, the horse responded and stepped lightly through the snow, nearly prancing off, with the bobbing Jones riding high in the saddle. "Oh, it's nothing too much, truth to tell," he said, his toothy smile broader than ever. "They's just a man there I got to kill."

It wasn't until he disappeared that Hooley realized what had been bothering him. The knife in Jones' hand had a bone handle carved in the shape of a woman's naked leg.

BAD ACTORS

⸻◆⸻

1

THE WESTERN HORIZON was awash with a bright red sunset that reflected off the snow and nearly blinded Jefferson Tay and his company when they finally reached the top of a low rise on the prairie. Tay's ponderous weight sat uncomfortably atop the muddy and abused bay stallion. The animal was much the worse for wear, and Tay now worried about its capacity to take him as far as Mexico. He worried more about his ability to ride that far on any animal.

He drew the rein in tight, wincing from shooting pains in his leg. They spread instantly with any motion, and the past several hours' riding had been excruciating. He refused to complain. An effective leader never showed weakness, never allowed his men to see him suffering, he believed. He removed a worn gauntlet and scraped around in his ragged tunic's pockets to locate enough scraps of tobacco to fill his stubby pipe, then lit it slowly and contemplated the brilliant sky. The mixtures of bright colors seemed to mock his purpose, suggested that what he sought was shining just beyond some distant fall of wasteland. They were hours behind schedule and were, collectively, in the worst condition of their recent career.

"Would you look at that," Manypenny said when his own panting pony had climbed parallel to Tay. "Wish I could set a flame like that. Looks like the whole world's on fire."

Tay had no patience for aesthetic observations at the moment, no time to contemplate nature's magnificence in this blank wilderness of wintry misery. His leg was in agony, and even the effort of drawing on the pipe sent sharp splinters racing throughout his body like miniature lightning bolts, sometimes nearly blinding him with their exquisitely ragged edges.

Blasingame, Eubanks, and Cherokee Charlie forced their weary animals into line. Cherokee Charlie was mounted on the old mule from the abandoned buggy, and Eubanks had been forced to accept the remaining shaggy jenny from the corral at Dutchman's Ferry. Their other animals were gone, run off or stolen by the treacherous Negro.

Eubanks had, predictably, exhibited the strongest reaction against the porter's treason when they awoke to discover that all their mounts but the bay, which Tay had carefully tied to the buggy, were missing, and that most of their weapons were gone as well. The ailing outlaw stomped around swearing vengeance against the departed Negro and reminding Tay that none of this would have happened had he been given free rein against the porter to begin with. But the Arkansawyer's rage was soon tempered by his deepening illness. During the daylight hours, it had become so bad that he lay upon rather than rode the mule that carried him. Every breath Eubanks took was audible, his body shuddered with fever, and his eyes were glazed with sickness. Tay was determined to leave him behind if he fell off his mule, without even the courtesy of a *coup de grace*.

In the early morning hours, Metritous Jones had cunningly permitted Manypenny to stand watch for only a few hours before returning to relieve the small arsonist. He had complained that he couldn't sleep anyway and that he wanted to cut some side meat off the butchered hog so they could have a "good breakfast." Without consulting Tay, who was finally able to ignore his throbbing leg long enough to doze off, Manypenny got into his bedroll. When they awoke, they discovered Jones' desertion.

Blasingame was the most philosophical of them in his acceptance of the calamity. Although Jones had somehow crept up and stolen the big blond outlaw's patented side arm and had been brazen enough to purloin Cherokee Charlie's fancy knife right out of his belt, Blasingame had actually brayed when they took account of what was missing. "I swear, Tay," he chortled, "you're the only Reb I've ever heard of that would trust a nigger." He veritably danced a jig while tears of mirth rolled down his unshaved cheeks, all but confirming Tay's conclusion that his chief lieutenant was completely insane. Any doubts that might have lingered were dispelled when Blasingame instantly sobered and looked darkly at Tay. "If he'd took my trophy bag, I'd start my new one with yours."

Although the animals hadn't wandered far, it took most of the morning to locate the two Welsh ponies, who were found browsing the tops of weeds poking up through the snow in a cottonwood grove some two miles from the burned-out ferry. The other horses and the missing mule were not handy, but tracks led down the riverbed and then to the east, confirming Jones's escape.

Tay was concerned that the brazen Negro might locate a party of Texas Rangers and alert them to the company's criminal goal. He wasn't sure how much credibility the Sons of the Confederacy who protected Texas might give to the tale of some wild-eyed man of color, for of late, he had observed that many veterans of Ulysses Grant and Bill Sherman had relocated to Texas. It was still a chancy prospect to trail Jones. He insisted they ride out at once.

"That's fine for you," Eubanks had weakly protested through throaty wheezes. "You got the only righteous horse." Tay would have rebuked him, but a renewed fit of coughing seized the bald man and brought him to his knees in whimpering helplessness. No one else said a word while Tay heaved his sizable form aboard the big stallion, his teeth clenched against the sea of pain that swept over him from the effort.

The loss of weaponry was a sorer point. Tay had his pistols and his saber, but all their long arms were gone. Manypenny retained his side arm, and Blasingame had his large knife, which he admitted in a dark mutter would be "good enough for the need," but Eubanks was entirely without a weapon. Cherokee Charlie remained unarmed, for whatever trust the phony Indian had earned in the company was now compromised by the Negro's treachery. The braided man said little, merely pulled his battered beaver hat low on his forehead.

Once mounted, with Eubanks feverish, wheezing and hacking wretchedly, they made their way upriver and tried to cross, but the sun's warming effects created rapidly thinning ice that sent them back twice, panicked lest they fall in and completely douse themselves in the frigid flow. Eubanks' exhortations that it hadn't killed *him* to fall in went unheeded, particularly as they were punctuated with fits of coughing that left him nearly inarticulate. It was well past midday before they found a place where the water was shallow enough to permit a safe fording. At that point, they stopped and ate what was left of the meat which Jones had apparently fortuitously forgotten, then began making their way southwest across the snowy landscape.

Tay assessed their situation carefully. Without their complement of weapons, they would have to proceed with care, evaluating opportunities as they were presented. To his mild satisfaction, his men seemed undeterred from the day's purpose, in spite of their reduced potential, something which assured that the risk of casualties would be high. With a bit of good fortune, he would soon be sipping quality brandy and penning his memoirs in the warmth of Old Mexico.

As they rode, his leg began swelling, and the pain became severe. At last he was obliged to use a clasp knife to cut a slit in the rotting fabric over the bandages covering the oozing lesion, in order to relieve pressure on the wound. The Negro's poultices and bandages had turned black with leaching blood. An obnoxious odor occasionally assaulted Tay's nostrils, but he elected not to worry about it. There would be time for medical attention after this was over, and if things went well, there would be ample funds to ensure the silence of whatever surgeon he could find to treat the leg properly, even if he had to abduct the man and haul him by force all the way to Mexico.

Cherokee Charlie's increasingly vague directions led them in a south-westerly direction, up and down a snow-covered prairie, for most of the afternoon, until finally, just as the sun was setting, they came in sight of their goal, now but a few miles distant. Tay pulled out his telescopic spy glass and studied the red glow of the horizon. Silhouetted against the crimson brilliance, he observed were some humped shapes and a column of smoke coming from them.

"I take it that that is our objective," he said with a glance at Cherokee Charlie.

The fake Indian pushed back his smashed hat, squinted into the fading light, and nodded. "Well, I can't say for sure, but it looks like it."

"You can't say for sure?" Blasingame spoke up, surprising Tay. The huge gap-toothed outlaw had been virtually mute since they crossed the river, only humming slightly beneath his breath, his eyes clouded and cast down as if he was lost in deep, dark thoughts. "You been there before, right?" Blasingame demanded. "You *said* you tried to rob the place."

"Well, not exactly," Cherokee Charlie admitted. "I had partners, you see. They actually came from there. They did the actual robbing."

"Tay," Blasingame said evenly. There was no trace of madness now. The game was afoot, and he was suddenly all business. "Sure as you're born, this bastard's lying."

"Great day in the morning," Eubanks wheezed weakly. "Let's move or die standing."

Tay looked at Cherokee Charlie. "Sir," he said. "I recommend that you tell us what we can anticipate. Mr. Eubanks' reconnaissance was limited. What, precisely, can we expect?"

"Well, I never did say I actually *been* there," Cherokee Charlie con-fessed, addressing Blasingame, not Tay. "But I *know* there's a whorehouse.

Chock-full of beauties." He glanced around at the men. "And there's money. Thousands."

"If this goes awry," Tay said, putting his hand on his saber's damaged hilt, "I will cut you into twenty pieces and feed you to prairie wolves while you are still alive."

"Not before I'm done with him," Blasingame said.

"Like I said, there was bags of money. *Bags* of it." Cherokee Charlie cast a fearful eye toward Blasingame. "Now, I been gone a while. Things change."

"Doubtful, sir. Doubtful," Tay said. "My experience has been that change in this part of the world is difficult to effect and rarely comes rapidly."

"Tay," Eubanks gasped. He was slumped over the neck of his mule. His derby had been lost. "After today, I hope to God I never hear you say another word." He dropped his scarred, bald head, shiny with sweat, back down to his animal's neck. His mouth hung open, streaming drool.

"We shall ride in as if we are seeking ordinary custom," Tay said calmly, gritting his teeth against the hurt in his leg. "Remember your orders." He looked into Manypenny's eyes. "No flames until the money is secure." Then he looked at Blasingame, whose dark irises were focused on the dying sun, which in return gave his unshaven face a bloody tone. "And no killing," Tay said.

"Hell you say." Blasingame snapped our of his reverie and stared at Tay.

"The *hell* I say, Mr. Blasingame," Tay countered. "Our fortune has been in peril, and I absolutely insist that you follow orders. Otherwise, I shall dispatch you here and now."

"You ain't man enough to 'dispatch' me, Tay," Blasingame said, "and I doubt they can find a rope stout enough to haul your fat ass off the ground."

"That will do, sir," Tay said. "I shall brook no more impudence." He took a deep breath. "Mr. Blasingame," he said, taking advantage of the blond outlaw's apparently lucidity, "I rely on you, but do not be mistaken. One iota of disobedience, and I shall slay you with impunity."

"What the hell's an 'impunity'?" Eubanks asked with a weak chuckle.

"I am a man of honor, sir." Tay continued to look at Blasingame. "And I am a man of my word. If this gentleman"—he nodded at Cherokee Charlie—"is correct, we still stand to profit from this enterprise. Nothing would suit me more, I can assure you. But do not assume that you are indispensable. You may facilitate the outcome. You by no means guarantee it."

Blasingame slowly nodded. "If they're women there, they're mine. All of them."

"Money, then decent horses, then supplies," Tay said. He shifted his voice to a conciliatory tone. "Those are the priority objectives. Then, we shall see what other amusements may be offered." He offered the blond outlaw a patronizing smile. "I somehow doubt you will be disappointed, Mr. Blasingame." Blasingame's scowl suddenly reversed into a lunatic grin

"Let's proceed, gentlemen," Tay said. "And may Providence, for once, be on our side."

2

FULL WINTER DARKNESS was relieved only by the silvery glow of a rising moon when Gilbert Hooley stumbled into the center of the town that was accidentally named for him. He had no idea where he was, only that for the first time in hours, he was not on his frozen feet.

Forever, it seemed, he had been plodding dumbly along, face bent to the snow-covered ground, eyes mindlessly focused on the double set of tracks created by Craggy Phillips' mare. He feared losing the tracks in the growing darkness, but as the sun set, the full moon had come up behind him, and he used his shadow as a compass.

He pushed on steadily, drawing energy from the warmth of his exertion. Sweat ran from under his hat, then froze, and cemented his skin to the collar of his coat. A light wind made his eyes water. Tears froze on his cheeks, broke off, and were replaced by more. Gripped by the single purpose of putting one foot in front of the other, he thought only of returning to warmth, food, and, annoyingly enough, Margot.

Her scowling face had swum before his eyes. Her sharp voice had assaulted his frozen ears, scolding him for a fool. And he had silently answered, confessing that she was right. She was always right. She would be right forever. He didn't care. He desperately wanted to know she was safe. She—all of them—were his responsibility. He had abandoned them. It was up to him to save them. And, with luck, he could find that Negro Jones and kill him for abandoning him with an idiot mule, for making him walk through this frozen white hell.

No sooner had Metritous Jones disappeared over the curve of the prairie along the mare's original track than Hooley, furious beyond reason, leaped to action and tried to mount the mule. For nearly half an hour he tried to make the beast stand so he could jump upon its bare back, but every time he tried to throw a leg over the animal, the mule casually stepped aside, leaving Hooley sprawled in the snow, breathlessly cursing while the mule moved away, mutely observing the tentmaker's foolishness with what Hooley interpreted as an ironic expression.

Hooley finally forced himself to calm down. He used his trouser braces and the gun belt to tie the Gladstone bag and bedroll around the mule's neck. Then he searched for the pistol, but numerous failed attempts to mount the animal had trampled the snow around the entire area, and he was unable to find it. His pipe was also lost. A quick study of the sky told him he was wasting time, so he took hold of the mule's rein and led it through thigh-high drifts at the bottom of depressions and up the other sides. Exhaustion took up a pace beside him. He could feel it as certainly as a companion tracking him back to Hoolian. He didn't look around, didn't look back.

He then recalled what had bothered him so when Jones was robbing him. It was the unique knife in the Negro's hand. There could be no doubt that it was the matching piece to the one presently riding in his own pocket. But as he stalked along through the snow, holding his trousers up with one hand and grasping the mule's lead with the other, Hooley concluded that Cherokee Charlie was coming, and not alone. He apparently had a gang of bad actors with him to take the bags of money Margot had decoyed Kitty and Chatsworth out of.

It was all clear to Hooley. The three of them had been in cahoots. Kitty and Chatsworth were probably hiding in the cave behind Cherokee Charlie and Loretta when Hooley stumbled upon them in the arroyo shelter. Or they were nearby, hiding with the bay horse and other mounts. When Cherokee Charlie discovered that the bags had nothing in them but trash, he killed Chatsworth—maybe Kitty, too. Where, exactly, Loretta and a railroad porter fit into all this, Hooley couldn't fathom. His head swam with possibilities. Desperation pushed him faster through the snow.

Thirst and hunger soon joined exhaustion in step with Hooley's progress. They were so tactile in their presence that he believed he could hear their voices behind him, but when he glanced backward, the horizon was dark and empty. He filled his mouth with snow, but the effort made him colder and brought a quick excruciating headache when the icy mass touched his palate. His fingers, cramped from grasping his trousers or the mule's rein, grew stiff, but he pushed on, leading the burdened mule behind him, switching hands so he could give one and then the other a turn at being thrust inside his pants for warmth.

He had no idea when he lost the mule. Feeling was virtually gone from his digits, and when he decided that a swallow or two of whiskey could not hurt him, he turned and realized he was no longer holding the leather rein. The animal was nowhere in sight. After spending too much energy cursing any god that could make such a creature—a species fundamentally responsible for his being out in this wilderness to begin with—Hooley plodded on, blinded to all but his mission. When he fell in the center of the compound, it was the first time he had been off his feet for hours. He assured himself that after a few moments' rest, he would be able to rise and continue.

"So, you've finally come back," Margot's voice penetrated the icy fog shrouding his ears. "It took you long enough." It was the same voice he had been hearing for hours, so he silently steeled himself for her verbal attack. "I never thought I'd say this, Hooley, but I'm glad to see you." He lay still, soaking up the luxury of not moving. His breath roared in his ears, and he could feel his heart beating. "Are you just going to lie there wallowing in the snow? At least roll over. It's highly disconcerting to speak to a man's backside."

Always obedient to her, even to this command of her specter, he wearily complied. As before in the fatigue-blinded visions of his trek, her face was fixed in a stern expression of admonition, her green eyes peering out of the hood of her bearskin coat. But her image had no aura of was no hazy dreaminess this time. He shook his head and blinked. She was real.

He swallowed dryly to clear his throat. "Margot, there's some men—"

"There're always *some* men," she said with an idle wave of her long fingers. "It's one of the principal things wrong with the world. Now, get up. I don't know what took you so long. I was anticipating your arrival before dark."

Stumblingly Hooley found his feet. They were soaked and numb. He stomped them to revive circulation. "I'm frozen," he muttered. "And starved."

"You don't ever change, do you, Hooley?" she snapped. "Always thinking of yourself first." She looked at him in the dim light of a lantern hanging in the café tent. He had actually walked blindly past Hank's emporium and fallen on his face right in front of it. He noticed she had his rusty old Winchester in her hand.

"And you are hardly starved," she corrected. "You *may* be famished. Your tendency to exaggerate may well be the cause of most of our difficulties." She stood back and assessed him. "Where are your guns?"

Hooley looked down at his waist. The absence of his braces caused his trousers to bag, and he was vaguely conscious of having had to hold them up to keep from stumbling out of them. "There's this stupid nigger—"

"I'll thank you to speak more respectfully of Mr. Jones," she said. "I'm no fonder of people of color than you are—although they often make loyal employees—but he's gone out of his way to alert us to the pending danger. I offered him a job, but he doesn't play piano."

Hooley brushed muddy snow from his clothing and looked around. The buildings still sagged under the weight of their snowy covers. No one had done a thing about it, he sourly noted.

"He tells me there seems to be some scheme to rob us by a bunch of Kansas outlaws—although he thinks they may well be from Oklahoma Territory. I wouldn't put it past people from either place. I've never found much to admire in Kansas."

"It's Cherokee Charlie," Hooley blurted out. "He's got a gang, from all I can figure out."

"Who?"

"Cherokee Charlie," Hooley repeated. "He killed Chatsworth. Kitty, too, most likely."

"Hooley, we have no time for fanciful stories," she sniffed.

"Look!" Hooley insisted, fishing into his baggy pockets and coming up with the bandanna-wrapped blade. "Jones has one just like it." He held it up and showed the handle to her. "They're a matched set, and when I last saw Cherokee Charlie, he had the pair."

"I've seen better craftsmanship," Margot said, glancing at the carved naked-leg handle. "I don't know what you're talking about. All I am sure of is that we appear to be in some peril."

"We need to get organized," Hooley said.

"There's no one here, and I doubt they'll arrive tonight," she said, pointing at the bright stars overhead. "It's too cold, and it's still Christmas. What kind of people do such things on Christmas?"

Hooley looked around. His stomach was now cramping violently, demanding food. He was cold, shivering. He went to the café tent. A full pot of coffee bubbled on the kiln stove, and he hurriedly poured a cup, sloshing it onto his fingers, scalding them. But he didn't feel it.

"I'm nearly dead," he said, gulping the boiling brew. "I think I've walked forever."

"Hooley, your propensity for hyperbole has always undermined your credibility," she said. "It's a sorry trait in a politician, and a worse one in a lawman."

He spied a pot of beans. He grabbed a spoon and began eating them directly from the cooking vessel.

"You've only been gone half a day, and you've lost what few manners you had. If you're that hungry, sit down and I'll fix something."

Hooley took another mouthful, talked around the food. "Margot, you've got to listen to me. Cherokee Charlie was the one who put Chatsworth and Kitty up to stealing the moneybags. It was what she wanted all along—with me, I mean. Don't you see? The nig—"

"That's ridiculous," she said. "I don't even know the man, and I'm sure that Kitty Cloud never associated with anyone with so silly a name." She offered a thin smile. "Your defense of your own actions is original, though. I'll give you that."

"He's coming," Hooley insisted. "There's men with him. The nig—Jones said—"

"I'm aware of the situation," she interrupted. She cast her gaze out into the darkness.

Hooley suddenly became aware that there was no light from any of the other tents. "Where is everybody?" he asked, surprised.

"Who?"

"Everybody!" Hooley demanded, coming to his feet. "Hank, Mino? The pards?"

Margot explained that mid-afternoon, Metritous Jones had ridden in on "*my* mare"—the emphasis was not lost on Hooley—and warned them that some "bad white men" were coming. "He said they were bent on rape and robbery," she said. "He told us what happened at Dutchman's Ferry, wherever that is. Does anything around here have its original name?"

"What? What happened?"

"Oh, Hooley, if you can't keep up with the news, I can't be responsible. The point is that you are our only lawman, and—"

"I think I was fired from that job," Hooley said, irked.

"The least you could have done was stay on until you were replaced," she sniffed. "Anyway, you raced out of here like your trousers were on fire, so we had to get some help."

"Where could you go for help?" Hooley demanded.

"Well, that wasn't easy to decide," she said pensively. "Heinz said there was a company of Texas Ranger riding into Jacksboro when he left, and he knows they object to riding abroad in inclement weather, so they might still be there. He rode off on my mare to see if they'd come—for all the good they'll do. He had an idea he might see you on the way, but I guess he didn't."

"What about Hank?"

"Hank decided he should go see if Rancher McPherson was back yet. He thought he might send the pards over to help us."

" 'Might'?" Hooley said, looking out into the darkness. "And why didn't they just *stay*?"

"They were already gone when Mr. Jones arrived," she said. "They said they'd taken a week off and they had to get back to work."

"They're gone?"

"Of course, Hooley," she said. "How many times do I have to tell you? Anyway, it's not their fight. It's ours. Or mine and Mino's, since you left. Hank took Ina Moon and the baby, as well on one of those odd rigs—a travois, I think it's called. I didn't think it was smart, as it's apt to be bumpy and I suspect that she's encumbered again." She sighed. "Asa will probably be hard to convince to come to your assistance, particularly since you shot him."

"I didn't shoot him!" Hooley shouted. "My God, Margot, do you even pay attention to what goes on right in front of you?"

"Those boys are no more reliable with firearms than you are, to be honest."

"Well, there's still that Nichols—"

"Well, I wouldn't count on him. Mr. Nichols didn't think that he could do much, as a preacher and all. He said experience has taught him that road agents don't respond well to scriptural messages, so he went with the girls. They'll come back when things quiet down."

"Cowards," Hooley said, a new anger rising to match the one that had driven him all afternoon. He was sore, and tired, and, now, seriously afraid. "Every goddamn one of them's a coward."

"Don't you *dare* say that, Hooley. They didn't run off and leave me helpless. You did."

"You've never been helpless in your life, Margot," he snapped. "Where *are* the girls?"

She smiled cunningly, "Mino took them down to the creek in Heinz's wagon to hide."

"We need him here," Hooley said.

"There you go again being selfish. He can't be involved in a fight, not since he's a convicted felon and a fugitive."

"A felon? Who's a felon?"

"Why, Mino!" she exclaimed. "You said he only escaped hanging because you shot Craggy Phillips through the eye while he was trying to perform his lawful duty."

As always, her reasoning flummoxed him. He sighed. "So you really are all alone."

She lifted the rusty rifle. "Waiting for you," she said.

"You *knew* I'd come back?" This was too incredible. "Margot, if that nigger hadn't robbed me—where is he, anyway?"

"Calm down, Hooley. His name is Mr. Jones. He warned us, and then he left."

"Left? Where?"

"I'm sure I have no idea," she said. "Do you expect me to keep track of everyone who comes through here? I'd need a chalkboard to do that, and I don't have the time." Hooley studied the darkness surrounding the tiny community. In the distance he heard the familiar wail of a coyote, baying at the silver disk of a moon above the snow.

"Why can't you keep your trousers up?" she asked. "It's distracting to talk to a man who holds his pants all bunched up that way."

"I used my braces to tie my goods to the mule," Hooley said quietly. "No saddle."

"Where is that mule, by the way? And you never did say where your guns were."

"We've got to get out of here, Margot," Hooley said flatly. "We've got to go, now."

"Don't be silly. I'm not about to walk off and leave all this to a bunch of miscreants." She stepped out into the compound. "We earned that money, and I will not hand it over to a gang of cretinous scofflaws bent on thievery."

"These may be desperate men, Margot. You don't—"

"I know that you're either going to protect us, or you won't. And if you won't, then I'll have to protect myself. You forget that I am the widow of a lawman from Oklahoma Territory. I know a thing or two about self-preservation." The moon was high in the clear sky, and Hooley could see her plainly in the silvery glow off the snow. "You're my knight in shining armor, Hooley," she said in a softer tone. "Is that what you want to hear? You're my Lancelot. Now, find something to hold your pants up, and let's see what you can do to save me."

"I hardly think that would be appropriate, madam," a voice came from an enormous man in the ragged and filthy tunic of a Confederate officer. He emerged from the darkness and pushed his large horse toward them. His cavalry hat was greasy and tattered, and his gauntleted fist gripped a saber's broken hilt. "I fear," he said as his mount came up to Margot, "that your salvation will depend as much on yourself as on anyone."

Margot spun on the man and pulled up the Winchester, but Hooley saw the flash of the long blade in the moonlight. "Margot!" he cried, hurling himself forward, striking the chest of the big bay. The horse balked, reared, and caused the corpulent rider to miss in his swipe at the redheaded madam. Margot dropped the rifle and raced off into the darkness in the same instant Hooley recognized the animal as the same one he had last seen prancing under the muscular thighs of a proud Algernon Chatsworth. Then everything before his eyes went black.

3

JEFFERSON O'HALLORAN TAY was caught off guard by the sudden assault of the skinny man he had followed across the snowy prairie. His assumption was that the individual was utterly exhausted, and from the conversation he overheard between him and the bearskin-coated beauty who was presently intent on shooting Tay with a rusty rifle, he also doubted the man's tendency to do anything more than scamper away when confronted with adversity. The woman was an altogether different matter. She was feisty and eager to defend herself in a manly fashion. When her defender's impetuous collision with the bay stallion caused the weary horse to rear, Tay had been off balance, as he swung his blade to disarm her. He instinctively tightened his grip on the animal, eliciting such pain in his suffering leg that he saw black spots before his eyes and bile filed his mouth. When he regained control, the man lay facedown in the snow, but the woman had fled.

Manypenny now rushed forward from behind a tented structure and inspected the prone figure. He held a piece of milled lumber and had apparently been fashioning a torch from strips of cloth. "He's coldcocked, but I don't reckon he's dead." The small man turned his scarred face toward Tay and gave him a drunken smile. "Can I set him on fire?"

Tay spat to clear his mouth's acidic contents and inspected a set of tracks leading off into the darkness beyond the tents. "No," he said. "He may be of value."

Cherokee Charlie now slunk out from the shadows and looked down at the man on the ground. "It's No-Shit Hooley," he said, "the saloon-keeper."

Tay's leg was alive with pain. He nodded toward the tracks and spoke through clenched teeth. "Mr. Manypenny, please see what you can do to retrieve that woman."

"What woman?" Manypenny peered into the icy darkness. "Damn it, Colonel Tay," he whined. "Let me catch something alight. You can't see shit out here."

"She escaped in that direction." Tay pointed with his sword. "I suspect she may be the *madame-doma* of the reputed brothel. She certainly speaks with more impudence than any mere prostitute. Now, if you please, sir. Be swift."

Tay breathed hard, keeping a close eye on Cherokee Charlie, who stood dutifully beside the man he had identified and peered around the settlement. "Settlement" was about all it was, Tay observed. All his doubts about Cherokee Charlie's veracity concerning a significant fortune came to the fore. If Mr. Charles had lied, Tay vowed, he would spend his last few breathing hours wishing for death.

Shortly after they spied the town, their progress was blocked by a pile of ice-covered granite rocks too slippery for the animals' hooves. This forced them to seek a detour. Fading daylight and the unbroken sea of snow then confused Cherokee Charlie's navigational abilities. After a half hour of wandering vaguely toward the southwest, he confessed that he was lost.

"Let's just kill him now and be done with it," Blasingame had suggested.

"You're not careful," Cherokee Charlie protested, "you'll ride clear past it."

Blasingame immediately declared his intention to scalp the phony Indian alive, but Tay postponed him. Then they came across a wandering mule laden with baggage. Tay recognized it as a twin to the animal Eubanks was riding, which meant that Metritous Jones was in the vicinity. This stimulated all of them—even Eubanks, who was slipping in and out of reasonable lucidity—to continue. After securing a fully loaded Colt's Peacemaker, a full bottle of whiskey, and a small bundle of greenbacks— all of which perplexed Tay, as he could not imagine where the traitorous Negro had obtained such goods—they followed the animal's tracks, bent on recapturing and summarily executing Jones. Blasingame and Many-penny—but not Cherokee Charlie, despite his entreaties—immediately be-gan sharing the bottle. Tay nominally objected, but he estimated that any attempt at discipline would result in mutiny.

Just as the final rays of the sun disappeared, they spied Hooley's lone form stumbling blindly through the snow, and Cherokee Charlie declared that the figure was none other than "No-Shit Hooley," another of the curious sobriquets Tay found incredibly annoying and refused to utter.

Because Eubanks' health had deteriorated to the point that he could no longer maintain a decent pace, Tay elected to follow the staggering pe-destrian, especially since he was progressing in the direction that Cherokee Charlie now insisted the town should lie. They fell in behind the man, keeping a decent distance but holding his form in view by the light of the moon. To Tay's astonishment, the man kept plodding on mechanically, only occasionally stopping for short rests, and rarely looking back, even though his men, particularly the pair sharing the bottle, were making ample noise in their arguments over the liquor as they became more and more inebriated.

When they reached a snow-encrusted sign that announced the town, they moved off and fanned out, although the man on foot didn't vary his speed but proceeded at the same stumbling gait toward the snow-laden tents in the near distance. Tay commissioned Blasingame to scout for fresh horses. He then handed Eubanks the captured Colt's and ordered him to hold his position—as if he could do anything else—and guard their retreat.

"Keep an eye out for that Negro," Tay recommended. "He may reappear at the least opportune time."

"I'll bring you his balls," the bald man muttered, waving his hand weakly.

Tay scowled at him. Eubanks was too sick to be of any use. He ordered Blasingame to give him the rest of the whiskey, hoping that the stimulation would keep him somewhat alert. Then, with Manypenny and an increasingly nervous Cherokee Charlie in tow, he circled the village and entered from behind a large canvas canopy where light and smoke were in evidence.

Tay was concerned by the complete lack of movement in the tent-city. Eubanks' intelligence affirmed a lively commerce, but the buildings were empty and dark, save for the single lantern-lit structure, from which smoke continued to emerge. By easing his stallion in close behind it, he had decided that apart from the two squabbling people, there was no one else about, and indeed, no one but the lone assailant had come forward to defend the woman.

Tay now observed that his unwitting guide might well be dying, as a pool of blood had stained the snow beneath his head.

"Tay!" Blasingame's voice came through the frigid darkness and was soon followed by the large outlaw himself, still mounted on his diminutive horse. "Corral's up there, but there ain't no horses. Just mules. Wagon mules, from the look of them." His speech was overloud and slurred, but Tay's disappointment was too severe for him to care. He silently cursed Eubanks for a liar. Bad luck.

Blasingame was swaying in the saddle. He cast his dark eyes around the snow-shrouded tents. "Hell," he said. "There ain't no whorehouse. This looks like some kind of Mescan army outfit. Just a bunch of goddamn tents!" He looked down at the form on the ground. "Not enough hair to braid a quirt," he snorted.

Tay took another breath against the pain and collected his emotions. "This is precisely what Mr. Charles foretold." He looked down for confirmation from Cherokee Charlie, but he had disappeared.

"This ain't no proper town," Blasingame insisted.

"I would hazard that that structure is the brothel." Tay used his sword to outline an unusually large red tent, then shifted the point. "And that must be the general mercantile Mr. Charles spoke of. Note the sign. My estimation is that any specie they have will be cached in one of those curious erections," Tay continued. "Begin with the disorderly house, and report anything you find. We need to be hastily absent. Something strikes me as being amiss. Be quick, sir!"

Blasingame looked dubiously at the tents and swayed dangerously. "Tay, you're still the order-givingest son of a bitch I ever run across."

"Have a care, Mr. Blasingame," Tay warned. "There are individuals in the area unaccounted for. The Negro, for one."

"That nigger is dead. He just don't know it yet," Blasingame growled, and rode his horse toward the red tent, shouting, "But there better be some goddamn 'unaccounted' women in that whorehouse, or there's going to be hell for breakfast, and I can name one savage Indian whose hair I'll have in my bag quicker than a cat can lick his ass!"

"Mr. Charles," Tay called, guiding his horse around a tripod with an enormous bell hanging at its apex. "Show yourself!" Tay shouted. Cherokee Charlie peeked out from behind a flap of canvas, his gaze fixed on Blasingame's back. "If you would be so good as to inspect the emporium," Tay ordered.

"I'd be careful of him," Cherokee Charlie said, looking down at the man on the ground. "He can be sneaky." Then he lumbered off through the snow, his braids flopping in the moonlight.

Tay took a long look at the prostrate figure on the ground, decided he was dying if not dead, then turned his horse and rode the length of the town, assessing the major structures and smaller canvas constructions, obviously individual quarters. It shouldn't take long to search them, he thought. He made note of the neat boardwalk and the even spacing of the buildings. They were not positioned in any haphazard fashion but deliberately arranged, with an almost military precision. In spite of its modest appearance and material flimsiness, this was indeed a town of some substance and permanence. He felt a sudden optimism about finding hard money.

As he passed the large red tent again, he heard the sounds of ripping canvas and breaking glass, indications that Blasingame was at work. Something seemed to be going right, at least. If indeed the women had fled, the big man would focus on locating the secreted funds. Tay returned to the meager light of the large canopy, which apparently was some kind of dining hall fashioned like an officers' field mess, with bench tables and a functional stone oven.

"Colonel Tay, I got her, but she's a bitch-kitty to handle," Manypenny squawked as he emerged, holding the woman by her long red hair. His unlit torch functioned as a club with which he prodded her forward. Her fur coat had been stripped from her and reversed. The garment's sleeves were tied behind her arms, a prudent precaution. Even in the dim light of the lantern, Tay could see that those parts of Manypenny's face not scarred by the injury were scratched and bleeding. "She was hunkered down behind a woodpile," Manypenny gasped. "Come at me like a catamount. I didn't have no rope, so I used that fur. I put a claim on it, too. I earned it."

The woman glared jade hostility at Tay. Her low-cut dress was muddy and wet, and her bosom heaved with anger. Manypenny pushed her forward, causing her to fall to her knees. "I warn you," she spat out. "If any harm comes to me, you will answer to Gilbert Hooley."

"And who, may I ask, is that worthy?" Tay inquired, somewhat amused.

"He's the main lawman of Hoolian," she said, struggling to put her feet under her and rising. Her defiance impressed Tay. "He recently retired, but he is still formidable. He won't be intimidated by a gang of Oklahoma Territory white trash who would abuse a harmless woman."

"Harmless!" Manypenny exclaimed, running a hand over his lacerated face. "Woman's got claws like a bobcat! Let me burn her, Colonel Tay!"

"You come near me, you little rodent, and I'll rip you to shreds!" she spat at him. "I cannot abide ugly men!" she declared. "And you're drunk!" She returned her glare to Tay. "I demand to be released," she said. "Gil Hooley will not tolerate this!"

Tay smiled, impressed by her manner of speech. "I think you'll find that the gentleman in question is indisposed." He nodded toward the form on the ground.

"He's resting," she said. "He's an excellent shot. He's apt to get up and gun you down at any moment." Tay just laughed, and Margot took a deep breath. The action seemed to calm her, and her tone utterly changed. "I'll have you know that I am not only his close personal friend and business partner, I am also the daughter of an Arkansas circuit judge and the widow of a United States Deputy Marshal. I also have a personal friendship with the former Attorney General of Oklahoma Territory. You are sadly mistaken if you think you can manhandle me and not answer for it!"

She spun on Manypenny, who stumbled backward to escape her wrath. "Get away from me!" she ordered, and then, turning awkwardly back to Tay, she explained in a businesslike voice, "This man reeks. I've smelled more fragrant slaughterhouses."

"My name is Colonel Jefferson O'Halloran Tay. And as an officer and a gentleman I would love to say that I am at your service, but most clearly, the opposite is the case."

She sniffed the air between them. "You also smell. I cannot abide a filthy man."

A smashing noise from the red tent reminded him of the larger situation.

Blasingame had lit a lantern inside. He was now throwing things out the front flap of the structure—bottles, it appeared.

"Whoever that is," she stated, "will be charged for breakage. I'm holding you responsible," she said to Tay.

"I recommend you extend your fullest cooperation," Tay said, still amused by her spunk. "If you do so, you will not be harmed."

"*I* recommend that you vacate the area this minute," she shot back. "I will not countenance such rude behavior from smelly obese drunks, and neither will Gil Hooley."

"Mr. Manypenny," Tay said. The small arsonist was dancing from foot to foot, clearly eager to be about his destructive craft, but keeping his distance from the woman even though her arms were tightly bound. "Would you kindly inspect that structure?" He pointed toward another large tent, where some cots were visible through the open flap. "Once you've determined that it contains nothing of value, you may put fire to it." Manypenny's narrow grin widened, and he raced off.

"I should warn you that I am intolerant of obese men," she said. "It's a sign of laziness."

"Madam," Tay said sternly. "Please try to concentrate on what I am saying. We are here to collect a commodity of cash I understand you have amassed."

"Cash? You mean money?"

"I most certainly *do* mean money," Tay replied. He now saw Blasingame's form emerge from a hole he had sliced through a wall of the red tent. He came out with a bottle in his hand, took a deep drink, and furiously kicked the snowy ground.

"If you relinquish the funds without protest," Tay continued, "we shall collect what other necessities we require and will bid you adieu without further inconvenience. You will not be molested. I give you my word."

"There's no money here," she laughed—veritably cackled, Tay thought.

"Certainly, there is. I am quite well informed on the matter. Therefore—"

"There ain't no women in there." Blasingame came up, his huge knife in one hand, the ugly stained carpetbag in the other, the liquor bottle under his arm. "Ain't nobody in there."

"There's no money here," the woman repeated. "We work on barter and credit."

"Damn, Tay," Blasingame said in a long expulsion of breath when he spied the woman. He dropped the bag and moved toward her. Tay actually saw him lick his lips. "While you had me sorting ladies' drawers, you been out here with the real prize all along." He continued to step toward her, his knife at the ready. "She's mine."

Tay kicked the horse forward, setting his jaw against the immediate pain in his leg. The flat of his sword fell on Blasingame's chest, halting him just out of reach of the glaring redhead, who thrust her jaw forward as if defying the big blond outlaw. "I shall have the money, madam," Tay said calmly. "Or he shall have you. That is your alternative."

"I'll give *you* an alternative," she said hotly. "You ride out right now, and I won't send Gil Hooley after you." She looked down at her coat. "But you may owe me for damages. I won't know until I take an inventory."

Behind Tay, a whoosh of flame announced the ignition of the tent with the cots. Tay turned and looked briefly as Manypenny, his crudely made torch in one hand and a container of some sort in the other, raced across the compound toward the store, whooping and shouting, "I found coal oil, Colonel Tay!"

"Mr. Manypenny," Tay yelled. "Restrain yourself! The search of that edifice is not completed!" The small pyromaniac skipped across the snow up onto the porch of the store and inside. "Stop him!" Tay ordered Blasingame, whose dark eyes had not left the woman's form. "That's our hope of provision, and the money may well be secreted in there!" Blasingame did not move. "Go after him, Mr. Blasingame!" Tay bellowed. "That is an order!"

"I can't stop him," Blasingame said in a low, calm voice. His eyes totally focused on the woman, who stared defiantly back. "He's crazy as a shit-house rat. This is a real fancy lady," he muttered. His eyes went dark and blank. "And she's mine."

"Does every person in your employ routinely roll in fresh offal to acquire a personal stench?" the woman asked. "If you're the boss of this outfit, I'm not impressed with your efficiency."

Tay put his sword on Blasingame's shoulder and touched the point to his cheek, pricking it, drawing blood. The blond outlaw instantly came to and shifted his gaze to Tay, but there was no fear in his eyes, no acknowledgment that Tay could slice his nose away with a flick of his wrist. There was only madness. In spite of the torture he was being put through by his injured limb, Tay leaned forward. "Hear me on this, Mr. Blasingame," he hissed rapidly. "Do not harm this lady. She has my word."

"Your word don't mean shit, Tay," Blasingame said in the same flat voice.

"Follow orders, sir, or I will geld you and leave you for carrion. Do not mistake me," Tay said, then wheeled the bay around and spurred toward the flaming store.

"*That's* what he smells like!" the woman called at his back. "Carrion!"

Flames were active inside the store tent. Tay spied Cherokee Charlie leaping through a smoky window into a snowdrift. "Goddamn it," the Indian shouted through a cough when he spotted Tay. "Why'd you let him set fire to everything? Hell, there's valuable goods in there!"

Tay quickly surveyed the compound. Blasingame continued to stand there as if transfixed by the woman in front of him, who glared back at him, holding her ground, her arms still held fast by the unique bearskin binding. "Mr. Manypenny!" Tay shouted. "Report to me this instant!"

As if in answer, an adjacent structure suddenly erupted in flame. The bay horse stamped nervously and tried to wheel away from the fire. Manypenny swept around the side of the sudden blaze and scampered under the legs of the stamping bay, causing the skittish animal to begin to buck and nearly unseat Tay.

"This place is a tinderbox, Tay," he shouted gleefully. "Nothing but old canvas! Might get them all going at once! And it's yellow flame! Who'd of thought?" He began wrapping a piece of stove wood with strips of canvas and marched deliberately toward the red tent.

Tay had no breath to spend on the small arsonist. He was blind with pain and fighting to control his horse. The animal wheeled, nearly stomping Cherokee Charlie, who was rushing around grabbing unsuccessfully at the bay's bridle. Finally, Tay slapped the horse's rump with his sword and sawed viciously at the reins to jerk the animal into form. He leaned forward, taking deep breaths to fight off the splintering agony that raced throughout his body as the big stallion stomped and quivered beneath his throbbing leg. He then spied Manypenny emerging from the red tent, whipping his new torch. He also held a small concertina, which made an angry whine as the rodentlike man dropped it and gave it a vicious kick, launching it back inside the tent.

"There's all kinds of liquor," he shouted. "I splashed some over these old hides. Nothing burns like whiskey and hair! Watch her go up in one big shot. That'll be a sight!"

"No! Mr. Manypenny," Tay gasped, then he saw a huge, ape-shaped form flying across the snow toward the arsonist. "Be alert, Mr.—"

The figure tackled the smaller man, knocking him backward into the red tent, where flames were gathering. Tay tried to urge his horse forward, but the mount balked. He spurred the animal, bracing himself against the agony in his leg, but another fiery explosion, this time from the store behind him, boomed, sending the horse into a wild bucking run, flinging the corpulent commander from his saddle, and landing him hard on the ground, which was already turning into a loblolly beneath the rapidly melting snow.

Tay lay still, panting, seeking strength. Oddly, he no longer felt anything from his leg. Nor could he hear anything besides a steady pounding in his ears. His eyes were strangely focused on the firmament overhead, and he could suddenly see shooting stars, hundreds of them, racing across the sky beyond the moon's glow.

Then his view of the heavens was blocked by Cherokee Charlie. "I caught up the bay, Colonel." He looked down at Tay, and his dark eyes grew large. "I don't reckon you'll be needing him anymore." He peered around, his swarthy face illuminated by the fires, "Found my Loretta down in a root cellar," he said. "That's no place for a good woman. So if you don't mind, I think I'll take her and we'll just move along." Then he was gone.

Tay lay silent for few moments, and then the pounding in his ears became intolerable and he tried to sit up. Although he felt no pain, when he looked down past his massive belly he saw that his sword was thrust upward through his body. The blade, broken and jagged, ran out of his groin, the hilt buried beneath the bulk of his huge hips, sticky blood flowing from his body and into the muddy slush. The pounding, he now knew, was his heart, pumping his life out.

"Providence is a whore, and death the only remedy for bad fortune," he observed, and satisfied with the articulation of what he realized was a wonderful epigraph for the book he would never write, he lay back and watched the shooting stars streaking in the moon-washed sky.

4

MARGOT, WHOSE ATTENTION had been entirely focused on the big blond outlaw who stood holding her in the focus of his two dark, dead eyes, was late in becoming aware that the heart of the town's commerce, the red tent, Miss Margot's Place, was on fire.

"You idiots!" she shrieked when she saw flames through the tent's front door, "You stupid, stupid idiots!" Her words crackled with rage, and, as it always had before, her angry voice pierced Hooley's stupor, jarring him back to a painful reality. It also had a profound affect on her appointed guardian, whose face flickered with sudden awareness. He seemed to discover her anew, and stepped forward with a menacing snarl on his lips.

Hooley pulled himself to his knees. His face was alive with hurt, and blood poured from a badly broken nose. He vaguely recollected the horse's hoof glancing through the darkness toward his face, then nothing. He resisted the urge to retreat into mindless darkness. Everywhere he looked, the world was on fire, and it took him a moment to determine that he had not died and gone to hell. In the center of this blazing vision, he saw Margot, her red hair tangled and wild, her green eyes wide in a mixture of rage and terror, her mouth open in a continuing moan of angry protest, and her arms bound in some incredible wrapping that looked all too much like her fine bearskin coat, turned inside out and tied securely around her arms.

He tried to stand but nearly fell backward. He touched his damaged proboscis, then quickly drew away bloodied fingers when sharp shooting pains seemed to send lightning into his brain, nearly blinding him. As he tried to assemble his thoughts, he became aware that his redheaded partner was not alone. Stepping deliberately toward her was a gargantuan man with long, greasy locks. She was slowly backing away from the point of a butcher knife he held out toward her, moving it teasingly as if trying to decide exactly where he would jab it into her.

Automatically, Hooley leaped toward the man and struck him on the side with the weight of his whole body. So solidly built was his adversary that the main effect of the tentmaker's assault was merely to rock him slightly, Hooley bounced off the giant's muscular bicep and fell back into the snowy mud.

"Don't be stupid, Hooley!" Margot scolded. "He's drunk, and he might be dangerous. Do something useful! My tent is on fire!" The big man, his balance and purpose regained, moved toward her again. She stepped backward once more, then tripped and fell over.

Hooley regained his feet, gathered his pants, and yelled, "Stay away from her!"

The giant gave a long look at Margot's stockinged legs kicking in the air over her head, then swerved toward Hooley. He flashed a predatory grin and swiped viciously with the blade, neatly catching the front lapels of Hooley's coat, slicing deep enough to cut through his shirt.

Hooley looked into the man's face, which was blood red in the firelight and filled with raw insanity. His stomach hollowed with a fear that matched the pain of his broken face, and his skin tingled as he began to slowly retreat, one hand holding up his pants as he backed away.

The man's mouth twisted into a sardonic grimace. His eyes fixed Hooley so completely he feared being paralyzed. "You're dead, little man," he said. "But first, you're going to watch me take a red-haired scalp and skin that bitch alive." He swung the blade in a scything motion, as if tearing the air in front of him so he could step through it, one measured pace at a time, pushing Hooley farther back into the tented kitchen.

"Hooley, get away from that stinking animal! He might hurt you!" Margot brayed. "My house is on fire! Do something!"

The man took another step forward, and Hooley felt himself cornered between the kiln stove and the canvas wall of the tent. The knife swung again, and Hooley pressed backward, his fingers groping the seam of the canvas, trying to rip it open. There was no purchase on the hem of the fabric, and for the first time in his life, Hooley cursed the quality workmanship he had put into every stitch he had ever sewn. The seam would hold, no matter what. There was nowhere to run. The man was about to lay open his throat.

"Hey, Boss-man!" Metritous Jones' voice called, stopping the giant in his tracks. "This belong to you?" Beyond the big man's form, Hooley saw the old white-haired porter holding up a stained, bulging carpetbag. "Found this out in the snow." Jones' mouth turned down in a disapproving scowl. "Ain't no way to take care of a piece of luggage. Might get lost!"

The huge man spun around, let out an inarticulate bellow, and charged Jones, who skipped out of the tent and into the darkness beyond. Then the man stopped, looked momentarily bewildered, and turned again on Hooley, slashing the air as he came.

His hand still groping behind him, Hooley's fingers brushed against the hot coffeepot. The handle seared him, and he instantly jerked away. When the sharp blade whizzed by in a pass that was only inches from his throat, Hooley steeled himself, grabbed the pot, and smashed it hard against the giant's head. The blow collapsed the superheated metal, dousing the blond man's face with scalding black liquid. Hooley shoved past him, leaped over a table, and dashed outside.

"Run, Margot!" he yelled when his feet hit the boardwalk. Just then his bagging pants fell past his knees, tripping him and spilling him forward into the muddy snow, where he smashed his injured nose on something hard beneath the muck. His eyes were filled with sharp, brilliant flashes of pain, but he blinked hard and put his hands down to push himself up. Then he realized that what he had fallen onto was his old Winchester, the same rifle he had used once before to kill a man who threatened someone he had come to care for.

Grabbing the mud-and-ice-encrusted weapon, he rolled over just as the huge outlaw, one hand wiping furiously at his injured face, the other still brandishing the large blade, emerged, his mouth open and a incoherent scream of rage coming from his lungs.

"For goodness' sake, Hooley," Margot's voice came to his ears. She was on her knees, struggling to rise. "Hurry up! We have things to do." Hooley pulled the trigger, but the hammer fell with nothing but a click. The man smiled and started toward Hooley.

"Hey, Boss-man!" Jones' voice called. "Looky here. This here luggage is full of hair! You a barber?"

The outlaw's attention immediately fled to Jones. The white-haired porter stood on an upturned bucket in front of the blazing hotel tent, pulling wads of what appeared to be rotted knots of hair from the blackened carpetbag and throwing them into the fire, one by one. The giant stepped forward toward him, but Jones whooped in glee and flung the whole bag into the fire at once, then raced off into the night once more.

The big blond outlaw screamed into the snapping, popping noises from the fire. His fists clenched on the knife. He spun around toward Hooley, who had ratcheted the rifle's lever and again lifted the weapon as the huge man raised his knife and started for the tentmaker. Hooley pulled the trigger and shot the man in exactly the same place he had killed Craggy Phillips: directly through the eye. The outlaw dropped like a wall of bricks. The tentmaker gasped, then collapsed back into the mud. "Shit," he said.

"Hooley!" Margot was at last on her feet, but her arms were still bound. "Quit wasting time! Cut me loose this instant! We have to put out that fire." Hooley struggled to stand, the rifle still in one hand, the other pulling up his pants. He staggered over to Margot, then stood, confused as to which hand to use to help her. "I refuse to stand here all night while everything I've built burns to the ground. Do something, you idiot."

He dropped his pants again, found the knife with the naked-leg handle in his coat pocket, and began hacking at the knotted arms of the bearskin coat until she was free. "It took you long enough," she said, then shrugged off the coat's remnants and stalked away.

Heat from the fires blazing all around was melting the snow into a quagmire that sucked at Hooley's shoes when he hobbled after her. Flames flickered eagerly from wide rips in the sides of Hank's store. The whiskey shed was afire, and Mino's canvas-covered stack of milled lumber was flaming happily as well. Scraps of burning canvas were drifting to the café tent, and Hooley estimated that in a few moments it too would go up.

Margot reached a spot about twenty yards from the front door of the red tent, then put her hands on her hips, glaring at the burning structure, daring the fire to continue in spite of her anger. All at once, her hands flew to her throat. "Hooley!" she cried. "Somebody's in there!"

He peered through the flames and saw a figure seated in the middle of the parlor. The fire and smoke were too dense to tell who it might be, but the shape of a man sitting in the middle of the room was visible in the conflagration.

"Don't just stand there gawking," Margot ordered. "It might be someone we know."

"He's just sitting there," Hooley argued, instantly annoyed that his voice had a nasal pitch and that speaking brought more pain to his ruined face. "If he wants to come out, he'll come out."

"Are you going in there, Hooley, or do I have to do it myself?" She stepped toward the flame-framed opening. "You are the most useless man I've seen since I left Oklahoma Territory."

Hooley put his hand on her bare shoulder. She stopped. He had intended to reason with her, but somehow, touching her inspired him in a different direction. "I might die in there."

"Don't be stupid," she snapped. "Hurry before he burns up!"

Helpless as always to defy her, Hooley moved toward the blazing red tent. Heat and smoke stopped him at the doorway to Miss Margot's Place. Flames came from everywhere. The bar and hutch were engulfed, and hides hanging on the walls were fully engaged with individual blazes. His eyes instantly watered, and he was choking. He still couldn't make out the figure clearly. That the man was alive was obvious from the way he moved his head, as if casually looking around, awed by the blistering destruction. Hooley saw that resting in the man's lap was the familiar shape of Mino's squeezebox, and that it was smashed. It was the idiot carpenter.

Hooley jerked off his coat and wrapped it around his forearm to shield his face. He turned his head to gain a deep clean breath, then raced into the fire. Beyond the parlor, the internal canvas walls were shredded and utterly burning. The hickory-planked floor was awash in flame and broken glass. Here and there, individual blazes rose to lick the ceiling of the huge red building.

"Mino!" he yelled. The figure looked at Hooley, who stepped closer, then jumped over a yellow lake shimmering on the planked floor. Now he saw that the man's hands and feet were bound to the stool with canvas strips. "Mino, you stupid son of a bitch! What the hell have you done to yourself?"

The man looked up, but instead of the familiar naïve face of the carpenter, Hooley beheld a small man who resembled a large rat. His narrow, pointed mouth was wide in a toothy grin that accentuated scars that ran backward, resembling grotesque whiskers. "Ain't nothing prettier than a yellow flame," he yelled over the fire's roar. "Nothing in the whole wide world."

Before Hooley could react, he heard a ripping sound. The canvas roof, soused from melting snow and ice, was sagging dangerously. Weakened by the burning walls and flaming cross beams, the supports of the huge tent were giving way.

Holding up his trousers with one hand and mindful of the flames racing around his feet, Hooley fumbled for the knife and moved toward the man, but he felt himself held back by a firm grip on his shoulders. He turned and found himself looking into Mino's face. The carpenter's dark eyes slanted upward, then down at the man on the chair. Then he shook his head.

"No shit, Gil Hooley," Mino said, and unceremoniously threw Hooley across his back, knocking the breath out of him. Singing boisterously in his unintelligible language, he carried Hooley out of the red tent just as the roof collapsed behind them in a crash of smoke and steam.

5

"YOU PROBABLY SHOULDN'T have rushed in there that way," Margot said, kneeling down beside Gil Hooley, who lay in the mud where Mino had dumped him before galloping off into the darkness. She handed him the Winchester, and he used it as a crutch to push himself up onto his feet. "If Mino hadn't been handy, you might have been hurt."

Hooley shook his head, suddenly conscious that his trousers were pooled around his shoes. He stepped out of them and gave them as strong a kick as he could muster. He unwrapped his abused coat from his arm, threw the rifle aside, and put the seared garment back on against a chill he only dimly realized came from within.

Margot studied the red tent. Smoke and steam rose high over the ruin, and small flames danced around the edges. "I suppose that's a total loss," she said with a frown. "I wouldn't advise you to add fire fighting to your list of professions. You actually make a better lawman."

"Shut up, Margot," Hooley said, his voice a stuffy painful croak. "Just shut the hell up." He looked around. "Where did that son of a bitch go?" Hooley demanded.

"Who? Oh, Mino? I'm certain he went back to the girls. He's very conscientious, as you know. You may owe him your life."

"He's a damned fool," Hooley said. "An idiotic imbecile."

"He's a sweet man," she said. "I think you're jealous of him."

"Get away from me, Margot," he fumed. He was sorry he had come back. His stomach ached, and his smashed nose throbbed. He couldn't believe he was standing in the middle of a muddy street in his underwear dealing with her inane remarks once more.

Hank's store continued to burn brightly. Much of the inventory was flammable and fed the blaze. The roof, now sagging badly and occasionally spilling water into the flames, creating a steamy cloud and loud hissing that matched the snaps and pops from the other conflagrations, would soon collapse.

Hooley slopped away from Margot. He noted, ironically, that his own tent—the oldest structure in the settlement—was still intact and apparently not endangered by flames. The green-and-white awning material looked bright in the dancing firelight. The privies and the bathhouse were also unscathed, but the boardwalk was burning and the fire was inching toward them.

Hooley had never imagined being more defeated. That he was alive seemed small compensation for the utter uselessness of his life's only significant achievement. It had taken only a few minutes for everything to disappear into smoke and memory. He stepped off a few paces, then began aimlessly wandering around, clothed only in his mud-splotched coat and underwear, dried blood streaming down his unshaven face. In front of the café tent, he spied the bulky form of the giant outlaw, lumped onto the burning boardwalk. He spotted the other huge man, the rider with the saber, lying in the mud, impaled on his own sword.

"I don't think he's from Oklahoma Territory," Margot said, moving up behind Hooley and sharing his observation. "He was very polite. Civil, really. I think he was a gentleman."

"A *gentleman*? Margot, he was an outlaw!" Hooley shouted. "A killer! My God, Margot, the things you say!" Hooley spread his arms in frustration and turned, only to find himself confronted by a short, ugly bald man struggling to stay astraddle a shaggy mule. His mouth was full of black teeth framed by a long, scraggly beard, and his face was awash with sweat. His eyes bulged and glowed yellow in the fires' reflections. He held a long-barreled revolver Hooley vaguely recognized as having once belonged to Deputy United States Marshal Craggy Phillips.

"I want me that nigger," he gasped. "Trot him out, so I can I blow his nappy head off."

"You are apparently ailing," Margot said. "We've had our quota of sick people."

"I come here to kill me that nigger," the man wheezed. Hooley could hear the rattle of his lungs. The outlaw lifted his pistol. "I ain't no 'gentleman' like fat boy there," he said. He glanced toward the big blond outlaw's corpse. "But I ain't loco crazy like him or the other one you let burn up over yonder. That nigger shot me, and I aim to put a bullet in his brainpan." A fit of coughing seized him, and Hooley thought to try to grab the gun, but the man recovered and pointed it at him again, then shook his head. "Get that nigger out here," he gasped, weakly kicking the mule forward. "I can't hold my head up back in Arkansas with him walking around. Either get him or I'll start the killing"—He fixed his swollen, feverish eyes on Margot and pointed the pistol—"with her."

A blast instantly numbed Hooley's ears. The ugly man was lifted off his saddle as if jerked away by a rope. He flew off the shying, braying animal, his side split open and gore trailing after him, a red streak that seemed almost iridescent in the firelight. Hooley grabbed Margot and flung her down, throwing his body atop hers, expecting to be the next victim of whatever horrible firearm had created such damage.

Margot instantly began wiggling and pushing. "Get off me, you ox," she fussed. "You've utterly ruined this dress!" They pulled one another up. The ugly man lay in a ragged bloody pile. Standing over him was Metritous Jones, the odd, double-barreled weapon gripped in his hand. He looked up at Hooley and Margot, grinned, and touched a finger to the brim of an invisible cap.

"Evening, Boss-man, Boss-lady," he said. He casually cocked back the second hammer on the weapon, lowered the barrel close to the head of the body at his feet, and pulled the trigger. The outlaw's face disappeared in a bloody eruption. Jones then dropped the strange weapon on top of the ruined corpse and dusted off his hands. "Hate to leave a chore half-done," he said soberly. "Should of kilt him back in Kansas." He glanced at Tay, then over toward the other corpses. "I seen you done took care of the rest."

"You stole my horse, you son of a bitch," Hooley said, trying to understand what had happened.

Jones affected an expression of regret. "Was more of a swap, way I see it. Where *is* that mule, by the bye? I reckon we can swap back now, or I can just take this here animal. The owner sure won't be wanting him no more."

"You're a thief," Hooley said.

"Boss-man, it's plain as can be that it was a good thing I run up on you when I did."

"You could have shot *him*, too"—Hooley pointed to the lumped body of the blond giant—"instead of fooling around with that bag."

"Oh," Jones said, looking down at the weapon in his hand. "Might of done that, yessir. But I might of needed both barrels for this here rascal. Turned out I did." He looked down at the corpse. "Ridge-runners is sure hard to kill."

"I think we owe you our gratitude, Mr. Jones," Margot said sweetly.

Hooley turned and gaped at her, but she nodded toward the porter. "Tell him how much we're obliged, Hooley. He's been very useful. I told you colored people could be loyal."

"You beat everything, Margot, you know that?" Hooley yelled at her, and he stomped off through the mud while Jones mounted the mule and headed him around.

"Y'all get up to Missouri, give me a holler," Jones said cheerfully. He kicked the animal onward. "Oh," he called over his shoulder. "Merry Christmas to you all!"

Halfway across the compound, Hooley stopped, a thought colder than the atmosphere striking his heart. Turning toward the junction between the café tent and Mino's old quarters—which was no more than charred rubber now—he stared where the bell tripod had been. A smoldering mass of wood told him the huge beams of the frame had ignited from the tent fires and collapsed together, making a small natural hearth in the very place he had buried the moneybags in the snow.

He slogged over and plowed down into the slush. The blackened bell was in the middle of the charred remains of the tripod's heavy wooden beams, virtually buried in the ashy bog, but he shoved it aside. After groping beneath the greasy ground, his fingers found something hard and came up with a fistful of small coins—nickels, dimes, and two-bit pieces—and he realized that all that they had earned, all they had to show for three years' labor, all the paper money, the notes and credit receipts, were gone.

"For a while, I thought you took it all with you," Margot said, coming up behind him.

"No," Hooley said, still on his knees, the few coins he had found clenched in his filthy fists. Tears filled his eyes, and his heart was hollow. There was no anger, no passion, nothing but a deep sense of futility. If she had not thrown them at him, he never would have left them there. But how could he explain that? There was nothing he could say. He flung the coins at her feet, then rose and pushed past her. With nowhere else to go and no desire to discover any, he slogged through the deepening mud to his tent, where he could go to sleep and never wake up.

OVERTURES

1

GILBERT DARTMOUTH HOOLEY, tent-and-awning maker, opened his eyes and stared at the green-and-white striped ceiling of his tent. His face throbbed, and his nose was clogged with clotted blood. He had been breathing through his mouth, and his tongue and throat were more sore and dry than any hangover had ever left them. Gradually, he became aware that what had awakened him was someone—Margot, he realized—calling his name. It was broad daylight, and he was cold. Although his belly cramped for food and his body was numb with the unique fatigue brought on by a deep sleep, he was shocked to discover that apart from his smashed face, crusted with dried blood, he felt fine. He heard his name again, but in a curious, lilting tone, so unlike the redheaded harridan's usual commanding summons.

Memories of the previous night's horrors flooded over him, gave him a sense of dread, so he lay there a few moments, smacking his lips and trying to work up some spit, steeling himself against the pain of clearing his dammed sinuses and then of the harder prospect: facing her.

He was still in his filthy long underwear, streaked with mud and ash and blood, torn in several places, exposing the fish-belly whiteness of his skin beneath. Somehow, he had had the presence of mind to remove his shoes before tumbling onto his cot. He pulled them on, taking his time with the frayed and mud-encrusted laces. He had no other clothes but his soiled and tattered cord coat to wear over the pale red flannel underwear, so thus attired, he stepped out of the tent to meet his partner, a woman he still had no more idea of how to fathom than he had on the first day he had ever set eyes on her. When he emerged, blinking against the brilliance of the sunlight, he was immediately struck, as he had so often been, by her simple beauty and the inviting green of her eyes.

"Well, did you finally decide to rouse yourself?" she asked sharply. "You're developing a bad habit of sleeping the day away, you know. It shows a propensity for sloth, Hooley."

She stood on a patch of boardwalk that had somehow escaped the fire. And she had managed to locate a change of clothes. In welcome contrast to the frigid atmosphere that surrounded his head like an icy turban, she was outfitted in a bright yellow summer frock, with nothing more than a white veil of lace covering her shoulders. "Your face looks horrible," she said, but not with sympathy. Her hair was burnished from brushing and fell around her shoulders in a red cascade. When he broke his eyes free from her glare at last, the sight he beheld beyond her taxed his comprehension.

Apart from his own tent and one of the privies, all of the canvas structures were destroyed. Mounds of char stood in stark relief against distant white patches of unmelted snow. Hank's store was a huge pile of black rubble, with the large stove and the blackened frame of the couple's marriage bed sticking out of the sodden mess. Only the rock kiln remained of the café tent. Other buildings were mere piles of ash and half-burned lumber.

The remains of the red tent, Miss Margot's Place, was what struck him the hardest, though. The collapse of the snow-laden roof had prevented the structure's complete consumption, but there was no remaining hint of its former splendor.

The town and its buildings were all but gone. Even the boardwalk was visible only in places. As his eyes found the spot where Mino's bell had stood, he reminded himself that all the money was gone as well. Depression moved into his body like a wet norther, chilling him deeper than the winter day ever could.

"There's a man here to see you," Margot said, impatient with his continuing inspection of what had been Hoolian. "And I think he means business."

Hooley looked past her toward the middle of the ruined compound, now nothing more than a loblolly of ashy mud. There, an astonishing party was assembled. They watched him in silence, as if waiting for him to come forward.

"I'd tell you to watch your step," Margot said, urging him forward, "but if you were covered with mud, it might improve your appearance. Have you *no* clothes?"

"Shut up, Margot," he said. He was surprised and satisfied that she merely stepped aside, then wordlessly fell in beside him. Maybe he was learning how to deal with her, he told himself.

In the center of the group was a large, closed carriage that resembled a miniature omnibus drawn by a matched team of four black horses. Hinged walls, apparently designed to protect the occupants from the wind and rain, shielded the front and sides, leaving only the driver's box and platform exposed. Beside this curiosity stood a tall, heavy, thickly mustached man dressed in black serge with a bright plaid scarf wrapped around his neck. He had on a thick belt that carried two large revolvers worn butt out in the manner of gunfighters Hooley recalled from the illustrations in his dime novels. On his face was no less stern an expression than Hooley would have imagined belonging to the worst of the villains pictured in those same pulp stories. His eyes were like twin blue beams, scanning Hooley as he and Margot walked toward him.

Off to his right, Hooley saw, were the pards. Tidmore and Jake—his leg tightly bandaged—stood out in front, and Underwood, Plunk, and the rest were tightly gathered in front of their horses. Hank was near them, and Ina Moon and their baby sat atop Hank's piebald. They all looked as serious as the man who stood awaiting Hooley's approach. Anxiety arose inside Hooley: Rancher McPherson had come at last.

Oddly, though, Hooley was not afraid. As he padded toward the man with a deliberate stride, he adjusted the shredded lapels of his coat. He spotted the whores, wrapped in blankets and standing in the bed of Heinz's wagon. Nichols' acerbic form sat on the box, a retributive smile on his face. He was holding his animals' reins in hand, prepared for a quick dash if things went wrong again. Hooley almost smiled at the apprehension in the preacher's eyes. How could things ever go more wrong than they already had?

"You're the whoremonger and *pistolero*?" the man in black asked when Hooley came up to him. He had a thick Scottish burr, and his blue eyes were clear and well focused.

"I'm a tentmaker," Hooley said evenly. "Who the hell are you?"

"Angus McPherson." He made no offer of his hand. "This is my land you're fouling." Hooley glanced at the pards, all of whom suddenly found something interesting on their boot toes. "You've brought your criminal ways here," Rancher McPherson said flatly. "The lads have all testified to the fact—though not without persuasion." He reached up and stroked his thick mustache. Hooley noticed that his boots held a bright shine. "I'll have you gone before nightfall."

"You have no right—," Margot started.

"Silence, whore!" Rancher McPherson ordered, his eyes flaring a contemptuous look. "I do not deal with slatterns." Hooley stiffened in response, but Rancher McPherson continued. "I've been distracted with business, or I'd had you gone long before now." He swept a hand over the ashes and ruin. "Look what you've done. It's hell brought to earth. The wages of sin!" He stepped forward. "I'll have you and all your whores gone before nightfall."

"I don't—," Hooley started.

"By nightfall!" Rancher McPherson repeated, putting his hands on his pistols.

Hooley waited for the usual dyspeptic reaction that always accompanied personal stress. He sought the beginnings of fear, or at least outrage. There was nothing. Apart from the soreness of his face, he felt fine, almost giddy. He was hungry, a little thirsty—but for water. He had no desire for whiskey. "They're not leaving," he said calmly, "unless they want to."

Rancher McPherson's forehead wrinkled in surprise. "They certainly are," he said. "And you with them! I'll have you gone! You've corrupted my lads, you've stolen my stock, and you've murdered my best man and shot another in cold blood!"

"Go to hell," Hooley said politely, turning away.

"Lads," Rancher McPherson ordered, and Hooley heard squishing steps behind him as the pards moved forward as a body. When Hooley turned around, he saw that their faces were downcast, abashed.

"You boys can't do this," Hooley said, but without anger. He felt strangely calm, confident, even comfortable.

"Ain't nothing personal. Personal," Underwood said. "We got to do what he says. Says."

"It's his land," Hank confirmed, glancing nervously at Rancher McPherson. "Should of told you that."

"You *did*," Hooley replied, casting a steady gaze on the rancher. "I didn't give a damn."

"You'll give a damn when you're trussed up and hauled out of here on a goddamn rail," Rancher McPherson declared.

"We're sure sorry, Hooley," Jake said. "And I want you to know this don't have nothing to do with you making me shoot myself and all."

"I did not make you shoot yourself."

"We got to move you out anyway." Jake continued.

"You do not!" Margot exclaimed, positioning herself between Hooley and the cowboys. "You're pards! You're all pards!" she shouted. "Hooley's your pard! He's your friend!"

"Whoremongers don't have friends," Rancher McPherson said.

"He killed Chatsworth," Plunk argued weakly, glancing at the others for approval. They looked at one another.

"I may hang him myself," Rancher McPherson said.

"I don't reckon I'd do that." The assembly turned as a body to face the one-eyed figure of Texas Ranger Captain Brent Ellis, who emerged from behind the charred rubble of Hank's store on a handsome chestnut horse. "I object to foreigners coming into Texas and hanging our people." He guided his mount between Rancher McPherson and Hooley. "Even anarchists."

"I am not an anarchist," Hooley said flatly.

Ellis nodded toward Margot, touching the brim of his hat. Hooley now saw more of Ellis' company filing in to surround the impromptu gathering in the center of the old compound. The pards were instantly cowed. They backed away as the dozen men crowded their mounts into the compound's muddy expanse. "I dislike arriving after the crime has been committed," Ellis said, looking around at the ruined tents. "Makes for messy paperwork."

"I want this man arrested," Rancher McPherson demanded. "See to it. I have a shipment of cattle coming, and I need to be there to greet them."

"What you need to do is to shut your damn mouth," Ellis said in a quiet voice. "We'll soon shake this out." He looked at Hooley. "Now, what's all this about, and who burned this place?" He squinted at Hooley. "Somebody smacked you a good one," he observed.

Hooley tried to explain. He spoke of Cherokee Charlie, of Jones, of the large man whom he killed, and of the man on the mule, but he feared that what he was saying made little sense.

"Their leader was this capacious and odoriferous individual," Margot put in, and with a nasty look at Hooley, added, "*I* think he was a gentleman, but he was *not* from Oklahoma Territory. He introduced himself as Jefferson Tay."

"Jefferson Tay?" Ellis' eye widened. "Where's he at?"

"Up there," Margot said, pointing toward the flats, where some small lumps in the snow were barely visible. "We haven't gotten around to a funeral yet."

"You *killed* Ol' Jeff?" Ellis asked Hooley. "How?"

"He was defending me," Margot said, glaring at the pards. "He's the only real man in the whole state of Texas, from what I can see! Last night he saved my virtue and my life three or four times. I lost count."

Hooley gaped at her. Was this Margot?

"Whores have no virtue," Rancher McPherson declared.

Hooley's fists tightened, and his anger now stirred. "I won't tolerate that kind of talk."

"No shit, Gil Hooley." Mino came forward from behind Heinz's wagon, his fists doubled and a fierce expression covering his dark face. Hooley saw Margot suppress a smile.

"You heard the man, and it's good advice," Ellis said to Rancher McPherson. "I won't recommend that you pipe down again." He studied Hooley as he lit a small cigar and drew in the smoke deeply. "Ol' Jeff," he said. "That's one hell of a note. It shows you what happens when you let every goddamn idiot from every goddamn country in the world come here. They ruined where they were and are bound and determined to do the same damn thing here." He blew smoke out and studied the flats from his mounted perspective. "You *sure* that's Jeff Tay up yonder?"

"That's the name he gave," Margot said. "I rarely forget a name."

Ellis nodded. "Coltrain!" he barked. The lumpy Ranger kicked his mount to the front of the group. "Go up there and see if that's Ol' Jeff Tay." Coltrain grinned at Hooley and spurred his horse through the mud. "He's wanted all over the goddamn place," Ellis said to Hooley.

"I want this whoremonger off my land," Rancher McPherson said.

"I don't think you got a case, as a foreigner," Ellis said with a sigh. "So far as I can see, he ain't hurting nobody. And if he killed Jeff Tay, then he has consideration coming, even if he is a Yankee and an anarchist."

"I'm a tentmaker," Hooley said quietly.

"He's spreading sin and vice throughout my property, corrupting my lads," Rancher McPherson bellowed, stomping his foot and inadvertently splashing his trousers with mud. "I have cause to complain. He's running a whorehouse right here in the middle of my ranch!"

"Where?" Ellis asked, casting his good eye around the charred remains of the tent-buildings. "You got a whorehouse around here?"

"Not anymore," Hooley said.

"Any of you boys see a whorehouse?" Ellis asked the other Rangers. They all looked around and shook their heads sadly. "There you go then," he said to Rancher McPherson. "No whorehouse, no complaint."

"What about them?" Rancher McPherson railed, pointing at the girls. "If they're not whores, what are they?"

"Can't rightly say," Ellis replied, studying the women and touching the brim of his hat. They returned a chorus of giggles and bright smiles. "Might be schoolmarms, or they might be the women's auxiliary out for a picnic, so far as I can see."

"He's a horse thief and a murderer!" Rancher McPherson shouted.

Ellis' head snapped around. "That could be serious." He glared at Hooley. "You steal a horse?"

"Don't be stupid," Hooley shot back. "Do I look like a horse thief?"

"You look like an anarchist with a smart mouth," Ellis replied. "Be polite. I'm doing you some good here. What kind of horse?" he asked Rancher McPherson.

"A bay stallion. And he killed the man who worked it for me."

Ellis chewed on his cigar. "That'd be that boy Chatsworth?"

"That's right!"

"You can rest easy," Ellis went on. "He didn't steal the horse, didn't murder the man."

The pards' heads all snapped up at Ellis' words.

"Well, who did?" Rancher McPherson demanded.

"Crowder!" Ellis called.

The company parted to allow Crowder and another Ranger to approach. Between them, mounted on the famous bay stallion, was Cherokee Charlie. His hands were tied, his braids were gone, and his buckskin clothing was streaked with blood. It looked to Hooley like someone had tried to scalp him and made a bad job of it. Patches of bloody skin laced across his forehead, and his eyes were swollen shut.

Riding behind the trio was Heinz, on Margot's mare, and riding double behind him was Loretta, her perpetual gappy smile beaming. Bringing up the rear was a slight, well-dressed man who looked uncomfortable on a very large gray horse. He wore a homburg over thick glasses. All the riders were splotched with mud, and their horses were breathing hard, their breaths vaporizing in the chilly air.

"Ah, hell," Heinz whined, looking around with a pained expression. "You made a mess out of this, Hooley. Beats anything I ever seen in the name of the blue-eyed Jesus."

"There's your horse and your horse thief," Ellis said, nodding toward Cherokee Charlie. "From what I know there may have been a killing, but there wasn't no murder."

"What the hell happened to him?" Hooley asked.

"It was Loretta done it," Heinz said, dismounting and helping the Indian girl from the saddle with a straining grunt. He looked where the whiskey shed had stood, and a sorrowful expression clouded his bearded face. "Goddamn it, Hooley, you could have saved the whiskey!"

"Loretta?" Margot spoke up, moving toward the chubby, dark girl. "You did that?"

In reply, Loretta only grinned and linked her arm with Heinz's while he explained. "He hog-tied her and told her he was going to take her back to Chicago and make a proper whore of her, if that's what she wanted." Heinz said. "She got loose, though." He smiled proudly at the crowd. "She'd of took his scalp clean off if she'd had a sharp knife," Heinz concluded, looking at Loretta admiringly. She clutched him tightly.

"Where's Kitty?" Margot demanded. Cherokee Charlie only shook his bloody head and kept his eyes down. "I asked where's Kitty Cloud!" Margot repeated angrily.

"Drowned," Heinz said, shaking his head. "Son of a bitch drowned her in the river when he found out the bags she stole didn't have no money."

"Poor Kitty," Margot said quietly. "She always was such a fool."

"My hind leg!" Heinz snorted. "Whole thing was her idea. She was going to get Hooley in on it, but you took the rag off that bush when you caught her! Chatsworth was just handy. Anybody's worth a word of sorrow, it's that poor dandified son of a bitch." He nodded toward Cherokee Charlie. "When this one seen the horse was all he was going to get out of it, he done them both in. Stuck the boy, drowned the girl. Loretta told me!" Loretta gave a confirming nod. "Wanted to drown her, too," Heinz continued, "since she was the only one seen it all. But she swims good. Got away." Heinz squeezed her close. "Now she got even, sure as hell."

"When did you know all this?" Hooley asked. "Why didn't you tell us?"

Heinz spat and grinned. "Aw, hell, Hooley. It don't always do to tell everything you know. Things was going all right, wasn't they? Loretta and me needed a place, and here it was."

"That's one slippery woman," Ellis noted, "for a savage Indian."

Heinz grinned at the girl. "Don't matter now. My wife's done run off to San Antone to marry up with Jesus, so me and Loretta's getting hitched up," he said, "soon as Hooley can get around to it."

Hooley stepped back. "Don't be an idiot."

"Used to work for *you*, didn't he?" Ellis nodded toward Cherokee Charlie but directed his question to Rancher McPherson. "He another one of your 'lads'?"

"No," Rancher McPherson spat out. "He's a damn fool. I fired him for stealing."

"Then you won't mind if we hang him soon as we find a proper tree. You can have your horse back after that."

"I *still* want that man off my land," Rancher McPherson shouted, pointing at Hooley. "I want him gone. I'm in my rights!"

"He can't just make us leave Hoolian!" Margot declared. "It's our town!"

"What town?" Rancher McPherson railed. "If there's no whorehouse"—he shot a look at Ellis—"then there's no town, either!"

"Mr. Tarpwine?" Ellis spoke to the small man in the homburg, who was blinking his eyes rapidly behind his thick lenses. He awkwardly dismounted and scowled down at the deep mud, which smothered his shoes as he moved around to loosen a fat briefcase from the saddle.

"I told you we needed to put down some seashells," Margot whispered to Hooley.

"Which man among you would be Gilbert D. Hooley?" he asked, adjusting his spectacles and peering around the group. All eyes turned toward Hooley, who finally stepped forward, a sudden apprehension gripping him. Tarpwine looked at Hooley curiously, inspecting his dress and swollen facial features. "This is most irregular," he said.

"Get on with it, Tarpwine," Ellis said. "I didn't haul you out here to make casual conversation. I got a man to hang here."

The small man cleared his throat. "My name is Vincent Tarpwine. I'm from the office of the Attorney General of the State of Texas. In Austin," he stated. No one said a thing for a beat. "I'm looking for the mayor of a place called Hoolian."

"That'd be this man right here!" Heinz said, pushing a bewildered Hooley forward. "He ain't much to look at now, but he cleans up good."

Tarpwine began digging around in his briefcase, "I'm here to confer an official charter of township." His gaze swept the charred ruins. "Where would it be?"

"There's no town," Hooley said. "There never was."

"Hooley, shut up," Margot hissed.

"Oh, but surely you're mistaken," Tarpwine said. "We've official documentation. We've mailed all the paperwork, but it was never returned. It has to be signed and returned for filing. I was dispatched to come out here and take care of it in person." In spite of his small stature, the man drew himself up and suddenly took on an air of importance. "The Attorney General's Office requires papers to be signed by the mayor *ad hoc* and filed before an official charter can be recognized. Is there a notary public hereabouts?"

"There's no—"

"Well, of course there is, Hooley!" Margot said. She stepped up and flashed a brilliant smile on Tarpwine, who was instantly befuddled. "I'm a notary public," she said. "In Arkansas, at least." Taking the small man by the shoulder, she turned him toward Hooley's tent. "That's the mayor's office right over there, with the green-and-white covering. Snappy, don't you think? Better than anything you'll find in Oklahoma Territory. I know the attorney general there. Or I did."

"That's somewhat irregular," Tarpwine said uncertainly. Clearly flummoxed by Margot's charm, however, he added, "But if that's where official business is conducted—"

"What business?" Rancher McPherson yelled. "There's been no damned business conducted here but whoring."

"The hell there hasn't!" Heinz boomed out. He grabbed Tarpwine away from Margot's grip and spun him so quickly that the small man almost fell. "I do business here all the goddamn time! And there's been all kinds of officiousness. Hank, who hitched up you and Ina Moon?"

"Why, Hooley did," Hank said, surprised. Ina Moon nodded confirmation.

"You boys!" Heinz called out. "Put up your hands if you've gotten mail out of that tent!" Each of the cowboys raised a paw. "Well, there you go!" Heinz declared. "He's the mayor, the postmaster, main lawman, head business concern, and chief cook and bottle washer, if I know anything about it. There's your witnesses, and I'd say that puts the rag on the bush." He let go of Tarpwine, who had a dazzled look on his face. "Hooley," Heinz asked, "you sure you don't have at least *one* bottle of bug juice stashed away somewhere? I been riding for damn near two days, and I am in righteous need of a drink."

Hooley suddenly had the urge to run away, to flee back to his tent and hide.

Tarpwine swung back to Hooley. "I'm not certain," he said, "that one tent makes a town in the eyes of the Attorney General's Office. Without some official records . . ."

Hooley started to agree, but Nichols jumped down from the wagon and hurried over. Under his arm, Hooley saw, was his ledger. "I'm a schoolteacher and a minister of the Gospel," he said breathlessly. "I can testify that this man"—he pointed at Hooley—"has kept careful and Christian records of all births and deaths of this community since he came here. Including," he added with a downcast display of grief, "those of my own dear family." He grabbed Hooley's hand and shook it. "God bless you," he said. "You need to learn charity and stop blasphemy, and we shall have a word or two about fornication, but you are otherwise a very good man." He turned to Tarpwine. "Be assured, sir," he said, "that this righteous man is the proper mayor of this town."

Tarpwine looked at Ellis for confirmation, but the Ranger was watching Coltrain's return, so the befuddled official adjusted his spectacles and dug a large envelope out of his briefcase. "The town charter is in there," he said, thrusting it into Hooley's hands. "In triplicate. Sign two copies before a notary public and post them back to Austin, if you will, before the first of the month."

He turned back to the big gray horse. "If you would be so kind, Mr. Heinz," he said. Heinz bodily lifted the small man into the saddle. "Captain Ellis," Tarpwine said, "we should be going. I have four more sites to locate, and if we're going to be delayed by a hanging . . ." He looked at Cherokee Charlie, who seemed to shrink into himself, then shook his head.

Ellis, though, was in conference with Coltrain, who was grinning down at Hooley as they talked. Finally, Ellis turned his good eye on the tent-maker. "I guess I was wrong about you, anarchist," he said. "You might make a lawman yet." He reached inside his coat, removed a folded piece of paper, and handed it down to Hooley. "File this with the sheriff's office in Jack County."

Hooley unfolded the paper. It was a reward poster for Jefferson Tay, offering $5,000 for his capture, dead or alive. Margot moved up beside him and looked at the paper over his shoulder, and Hooley heard her express a low, almost soundless whistle.

"I didn't actually, uh, I mean, personally—," Hooley started.

"There's more where that came from," Ellis said. "He's wanted in five or six states and territories. Been chasing him for over three years." Coltrain coughed unnecessarily, and Ellis looked down and scowled. "All right," he said. Then to Hooley, he admitted, "That other rascal you got up there, the big yellow-haired galoot." He glanced at Coltrain, who nodded. "That's likely Billy Bob Blasingame. Runs through whorehouses like a fox through an arbor. Scalps people like a savage Indian. Women mostly. He's wanted in Louisiana and Missouri, and there's likely a consideration for him, too." Coltrain laughed. Ellis shook his head. "I ordinarily object to being shown up by an anarchist," he said, "but nobody can say I won't give the devil his due."

"I'm taking a whole new view of the Texas Rangers," Margot said, and winked at Ellis.

"I don't care what he says, or what he's done," Rancher McPherson shouted, striding forward until he reached Ellis' stirrup and looked up into the one-eyed Ranger captain's face. "A *tent* does not make a town." He described a full circle with his arm. "There is *no* town here."

"They got a graveyard and a privy," Ellis said, wearily. "That makes it more of a town than most." He shifted his weight in the saddle and looked down at Hooley.

"*There's no town!*" Rancher McPherson bellowed. "It takes *people* to make a town! There's no people here! Just whores and road bums!"

"Well, I forgot to say," Heinz spoke up. "Back in Jacksboro, there's a half-dozen wagons full of folks headed this way, just waiting for the weather to clear."

"What?" Hooley exclaimed. "Who?"

"Fellow name of Cooper is leading them, I hear." He winked. "Said he'd of come on sooner, but there was some worry about an uprising of savage Indians hereabouts. That was just a rumor, though."

"Wonder who'd start such a rumor as that," Ellis said, fixing his good eye on Hooley, who could only look down at the paper in his hand. After a beat, the Ranger stretched up in the saddle. "Well, that settles it. I'd stay and take a cup of coffee with you, but we need to be on the move."

"This is an outrage!" Rancher McPherson yelled. "I'll have you all up on charges!"

Ellis' face suddenly lost all amiability, and his jaw set. "I object to your tone of voice. You can complain to the attorney general or the governor. I don't give a good goddamn which."

Crowder nudged his horse and spoke to Margot. Hooley saw a glint in his eye that offset the grotesque hole in his cheek. "You take care of the anarchist, ma'am. He's growed on us. We'll be around if you need us." He glanced up at the girls, who extended giggles and finger waves toward him. He then gave Margot a wink and added, "Or even if you don't."

Ellis raised and dropped his hand in a military gesture, and the company spurred their horses, galloping off with the pitiful form of Cherokee Charlie in tow and the hapless Tarpwine bouncing in the saddle. As they rode out, they splattered everyone with mud.

2

HOOLEY STOOD TRANSFIXED in the middle of the compound, watching the Rangers depart as if he had been mesmerized. Margot gave his arm a quick, hard squeeze, and Hank started slapping Hooley on the back in congratulation.

"You need to put on some pants, Hooley," Heinz said. "It ain't decent for a mayor to be running around in dirty drawers. Some people might be offended by public nudity."

"You leave him alone," Margot snapped. "And don't just stand there. We've got to get those people up there buried. Go find a shovel!" She glared at the cowboys. "We've got a mess to clean up. Mr. Nichols?" she demanded. But Hooley spotted his form heading toward the flats. "You cannot depend on a preacher!" she yelled as she marched off through the mud. "Loretta, Gertie, Lulu! We're having another funeral, then we have to find something around here to eat." The women dropped down from the wagon bed and began scurrying after her.

She stopped and spun on Hooley. "I will *not* tolerate another Christmas turning out like this!" she said. "I shall hold you completely responsible if it does." Then she marched away, yelling, "Where's that filthy mule-skinner?" Heinz had disappeared. "We have orders to make," she announced. "I want him back in four days this time. There's work to be done!"

Hooley now stood alone with Rancher McPherson. The rancher watched, astonished, as his cowboy employees galloped up toward the flats, following Margot's commands. "This is not over," he said evenly. "You may have these people bamboozled, but I am a smarter man. I have lawyers, and I'm not afraid of the attorney general *or* the governor." He glared at the disappearing form of the Ranger company, "Or their hired hooligans."

He thumbed his belt one more time. "This is still my land, and I'll have you gone from it," he said with a nod, "or I'll have you underground where you belong."

"Angus, be quiet," a female voice came booming from the odd closed vehicle. A moment later it opened, and a tall, thin woman with a severe countenance and iron gray-hair stepped out. "You are becoming an embarrassment."

Hooley nearly swooned when he beheld the fabled Mrs. McPherson. His impulse was to run away and hide. Dressed in black silk, she had severe features that were honed to nearly preternatural sharpness, and she was much thinner than he recalled, but there was no question of the familiar piercing acrimony behind the eyes or the razor's edge of the thin lips and the almost pointed teeth they framed. He wanted to melt into the mud below, but he was unable to do anything but stand there, just as he always had when facing the indomitable presence and disapproving personal force of the scourge of his life, his mother, Bertha Hooley.

"How are you, Gilbert?" she asked as she found her balance on the muddy ground. "I have to say you do not look presentable, although you never were a sharp dresser. However, it does appear that you are somewhat more robust than I recall."

"You know this man?" Rancher McPherson asked, incredulous.

"Of course I know him. He's my son."

"Your son?" Rancher McPherson's voice rose, and he nearly laughed. "My dear, you told me your son was dead."

"I was premature in my assessment," Bertha said, holding her clear gaze on Hooley. Sweat ran down his back, and a strange vacuum opened in his chest. "He is yet very much alive, and standing right here before me."

"He's a whoremonger," Rancher McPherson said.

"He's the mayor of a town." She moved to Hooley. It was as if she were floating when she came up to him and looked into his eyes.

"There is *no* town!" Rancher McPherson insisted.

"Be quiet, Angus," she said stiffly. "You've said enough for one morning. There's no point in exposing your stupidity further. Go wait in the carriage."

He stood fuming until she glared at him, and then, slapping his thighs with his hands, he stomped to the vehicle, climbed aboard, put his elbows on his knees, and sulked.

"You needn't concern yourself with him," she said to Hooley. "I'm buying him enough cattle to keep him busy for a year."

"They'll die of Texas fever." Hooley didn't know what else to say.

"Of course they will," she said. "He's a bigger failure than your father was. He just doesn't know it yet."

Hooley put his head down. For some reason, he wanted to cry. She always made him feel that way. He swallowed hard. She was still staring at him, appraising him in her usual fashion. "How?" he asked at last. "I mean, you . . . here? It's not possible."

"Don't be silly, Gilbert," she said. "Anything's possible." She glanced away. "I had my legacy, as you recall. I needed adventure in my life. Angus came along with a dream of a cattle empire in Texas. It was silly, but better than remaining in Missouri and being reminded of my unfortunate first marriage to your father." She gave him an ironic smile, the closest thing to an affectionate gesture she had ever offered. "Angus is an utter fool," she continued. "Victimized by an uncommon devotion to moral values. Those have never been friends to profitable ventures." She glanced up to the flats, where everyone else was gathered. "Or to politics," she added.

"But you knew I was here?" he asked. "Knew who I was?"

"I am not unintelligent, Gilbert," she said. "I preferred to remain incognito. I disinherited you, remember?" He nodded. Her eyes flared, and he almost backed away. "It's so simple, even you can understand it." She looked back at the sulking rancher. "I kept him away from here as long as I could, waiting for you to make your usual mess of things and move on. But when that man Hank came in last night with his report of rape and robbery, and then the others arrived with that man you shot—well, it was out of my hands."

Hooley looked around. "I've made a mess of things anyway."

"Don't talk nonsense," she snapped. "From what I can see, you've prospered enough to become the mayor of a town." She cast her eyes left and right. "It's not *much* of a town, but you have shown some ambition. There's no disgrace in failure, Gilbert, not if you show ambition."

Hooley looked up toward the flats. Margot's yellow dress was clearly visible. "I had help."

"Of course you did," Bertha said with an affirming nod, noting the object of his gaze. "I can't say that a prostitute was the best choice, particularly given her taste in fashion for this time of year, but she obviously has uncommon good sense. That's something no Hooley I've ever known has ever enjoyed in commodity."

"She's not a prostitute," Hooley said, surprising himself with the defiance in his tone.

"Of course she's not," Bertha said, then gave him an incredible coy smile. "No more than any of us." Her expression instantly resumed its severity. "We won't return to molest you. Build your town as you will. Angus bought everything he owns with my money. If he raises trouble, I'll threaten to give it all to you."

"Would you do that for me?" Hooley asked.

"Don't be stupid, Gilbert," she snapped. With that she turned and, as if each step she took dried the mud beneath her shoes, strolled back to the carriage, then waited for a beat until Rancher McPherson abandoned his sulk, stepped down, helped her aboard, and seated her inside. He didn't look her in the eye. It was a familiar reaction, Hooley thought. He'd seen it in his father for years.

"Good-bye, Gilbert," she said. "I must say, you've turned out far better than I ever anticipated. If I ever see you again, I expect you to be fully dressed." She closed the carriage. Hooley stood mute while Rancher McPherson strapped his team into motion and they drew the odd vehicle out of Hoolian, carrying his mother out of his life, he hoped forever.

3

HOOLEY WAS STILL standing in the middle of the compound, forlorn and confused, but remarkably calm, when Heinz emerged from the cold cellar, a bottle under his arm. He slopped through the deepening mud, spat, and extended the bottle. "Loretta had this ol' partner hidden! Takes the rag off the bush, don't she? Told you she was a pistol."

Hooley's hands were laden with Tarpwine's envelope and the wanted poster. He accepted the bottle awkwardly, then he glanced up at the crowd on the hill. As he held the whiskey bottle in his hand, he realized he had no desire to drink from it. "Why did you do this to me, Heinz?" Hooley asked. "I was nearly out of this. Nearly gone."

"Hell, Hooley, we're partners," Heinz said. "Onliest friend I got is you. Freight office said they'd fire me if I didn't turn more profit, and you're the onliest profit there is around here. And"—he cast a glance at Loretta's large form, visible among the others on the flats—"there's that woman. She's a panther for love, I can tell you that!" He rubbed his mouth with the back of his hand. "You going to drink that or see if it'll start growing?"

Hooley looked at the bottle in his hand as if he had never seen one before. He shook his head and thrust it back to Heinz, who gave him a curious look, then uncorked the bottle.

"Loretta had this saved for a rainy day," the wagoneer said. "Guess today's as close to rain as we'll get. Plenty of mud, anyhow." He took a deep drink. "You know," he said, "if I was you, I'd put some clothes on. It's frosty out here."

Hooley turned back toward his tent in despair. He was now an official person, trapped in a position he didn't want in a town that didn't exist. And he had his mother's approval. He looked around. There was nothing left but a tent, a cemetery, a corral, and a privy. It was ludicrous. He stepped inside his tent and found Mino seated on his cot.

"What the hell do you want?" he demanded, instantly irked. "And if you say 'No shit, Gil Hooley' to me, I'll smash your face in."

Mino merely offered his patented grin. He lifted up two large burlap sacks. Hooley saw the outline of the smashed concertina in the bottom of one, and he understood: Mino was leaving. Hooley sat on the stool, emotionally spent. He buried his head in his hands. "I guess you won't tell me why."

"Take care with that rose, Gil Hooley. She has thorns." Hooley looked up, startled. But Mino was gone.

Hooley sat stunned for several moments, torn between frustration and astonishment. Was it possible that Mino had really said that? He couldn't be sure. Too much had happened at once. He stood to chase after the carpenter to face him to speak again, but before he could move, he heard singing, a hymn again, once more off-key. But there was no Mino to rescue the tune with his squeezebox. He then noticed a package on his bed. Inside it, he found a pair of heavy cord trousers, a flannel shirt, and some wool socks. Mino's.

Suddenly overcome with emotion, the tentmaker lay back on the cot, hugging the clothes to his chest. Tears ran down his cheeks, but he couldn't understand why or what they meant.

4

HE MUST HAVE fallen asleep. It was dark, and he was very cold, his teeth chattering and his fingers numb, when he became aware of a figure in the tent with him. Against the moonlight pouring in through the flap, he saw Margot, silhouetted against the silvery glow.

She put a finger to her lips and shushed him. "Be quiet. They're all sleeping in the wagons."

She pulled him to his feet, slowly unbuttoning his ragged, muddy underwear and allowing it to fall to the floor. "You're filthy, Hooley," she said. "I cannot abide a filthy man."

She brought in a bucket of warm water and a canvas cloth, with which she bathed him while he stood shuddering in the cold air. When he was clean, she pushed him gently down onto the cot and stood, then slowly removed her clothes until she was naked. Silently she slipped next to him on the cot, nestled her narrow feet between his, and pressed herself close. Her warmth passed through him with a comforting wave.

"Margot," he whispered once they were still. "What do we do now?"

"I shouldn't think you'd have to ask that question." She chuckled. "Not after all this time." For a moment they lay silently, listening to one another breathe. "You saved my life, Hooley." He lay silent. "I don't mean last night," she said. "You saved it long ago. When I first came here and you asked me to stay. To be your whore."

"You're not a whore."

"I know."

"You never were."

"I know."

"I lost the money," he said. "It's all gone."

She laughed softly, then pulled away from him, reached down beneath the cot, and brought up one bag, then two more, and put them on his chest. "You always underestimate me, Hooley," she said, snuggling next to him again as he ran his hands over the bags in amazement, feeling the bundles of notes inside and the heft of the large coins.

"One of them broke and we lost some coins, which wasn't very prudent of me." She laughed softly. "I got all the gold ones, though." A thrill of panicky fear shot through him. "I gave Mino his share, so we'll need every dime of it," she said, "*and* the reward money, but we'll have to share that with Mr. Jones, I suppose. We also have to hurry and rebuild. We're losing profits."

"Mino's gone," he said, and held his breath.

"There's other carpenters."

He soaked that in, started to say something, then thought better of it and pulled her closer.

"After we get things in order around here, I have plans," she said.

"Plans?"

"I've always wanted to see the sea. And I think you owe it to me, Hooley."

He took a deep, cleansing breath and pulled her close to him. "I love you, Margot."

"Well, it's about time you said so, Hooley. I was beginning to worry."

She kissed him then, long and deeply on the mouth, and in the distance, the twin cries of two coyotes sang across the snow-clad prairie, reminding Hooley that for the first time in his life, he was not alone. And he knew he never would be again.